Also by Holly Huntress

The Unbound Series:

Unbound
Disgraced

The Broken Angel Series:

Broken Angel
Condemned Angel
Forsaken Angel

Disgraced

∘Book Two∘

Holly Huntress

Copyright © 2022 by Holly Huntress
Published by Kindle Direct Publishing

All rights reserved. No part of this book may be reproduced or used in any manner without written permission of the copyright owner except for the use of quotations in a book review.

First edition: September 2022

Disgraced by Holly Huntress
Cover design and map art done by Holly Huntress

This is a work of fiction. Names, characters, places, and incidents either are the product of the author's imagination or are used fictitiously. Any resemblance to actual persons, living or dead, events, or locales is entirely coincidental.

This book is for you.

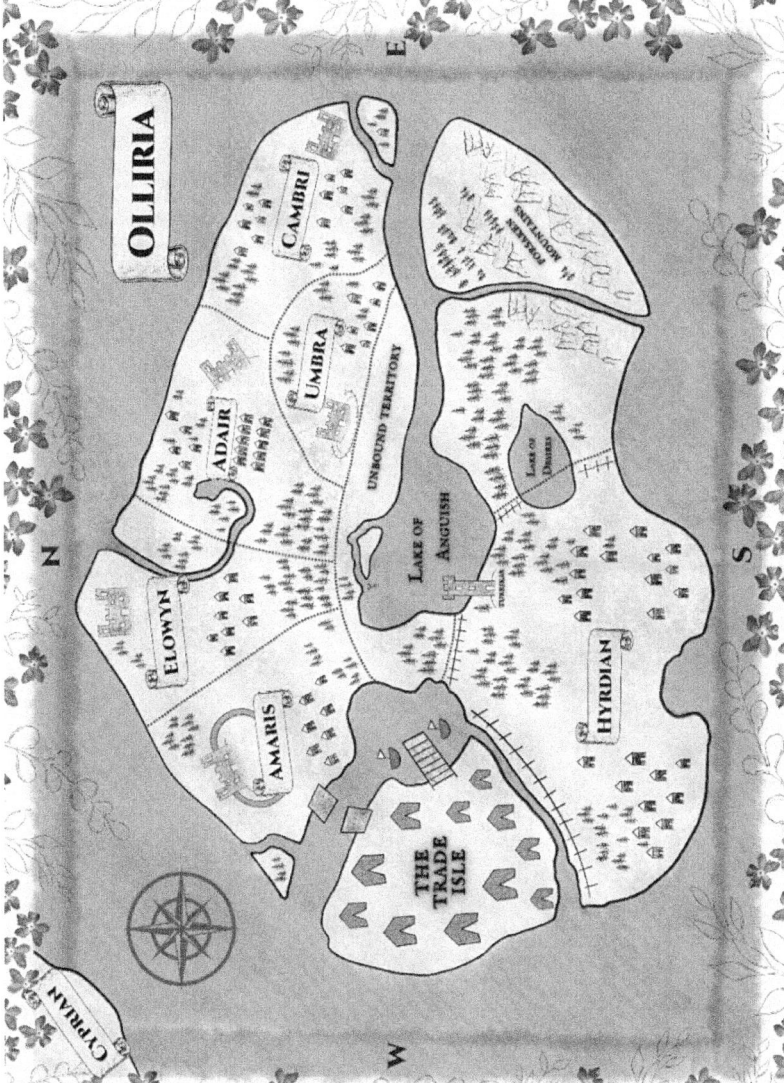

Pronunciation Guide

Characters

Mylah – My-luh
Emil – Eh-meel
Vita – Veet-uh
Castien – Cast-shien
Elias – Eh-lie-us
Edris – Ee-dris
Torin – Tore-in
Haldor – Hall-door
Lachlan – Lock-lan
Ailsa – Ail-sa
Keir – Care
Raelynn – Ray-lin

Places

Hyrdian – Her-i-dee-in
Adair – Uh-dare
Elowyn – Ell-oh-win
Cyprian – Sip-ree-an
Olliria – Oh-leer-ee-uh
Perynth - Pair-inth

Other

Shreeve – Sh-reeve
Hosath – Hose-ath

One

Once again, Mylah ran as if her life depended on it, but it wasn't her life that hung in the balance. Faster and faster, she pumped her arms, trying her best to outrun the arrows. Yet, every time, they found their mark. Garrick still wound-up dead. And then the nightmare would restart for her to try once more to stop the inevitable.

Mylah jolted up in bed.

Her head and her heart both pounded as she blinked the sleep from her eyes. A curtain of her brown hair obstructed her view before she brushed it aside, scanning the room and remembering where she was: the Elowyn castle. The same place she'd woken the past three weeks following their escape from Adair. Yet, every time it sent a hollow shock through her. *I can never go home.* The words echoed in her mind and brought with it the memory of her nightmare. It was always the same, yet she never once thought to stop trying to save Garrick. Sometimes her parents were the ones she was fighting to save, but no matter how hard she tried and how fast she moved, she had never been able to change their fate.

Mylah reached for her comforter before realizing that the blankets had been tossed onto the floor at some point in the night, along with most of her clothes. It all lay in a heap beside...

Right.

Torin's clothes mingled with her own. She turned her head to see a smooth, dark, tightly muscled back lying alongside her. His white hair was mussed from sleep. *Castien shouldn't have given me the room with the bigger bed.* She laughed to herself. It wasn't the first time she'd woken beside Torin in the past few weeks, though usually they wound up in his room. They never did anything other than sleep, but his presence had initially helped keep the nightmares at bay. Now, nothing helped with that problem, but she remained grateful for his efforts.

Mylah rolled out of bed, collecting Torin's clothes, and throwing them at him. He barely moved, still half-drunk from the night before. Mylah shook her head and grabbed her robe, heading to the bath. Thankfully, with her upgraded room, she now had her own private washroom.

Today was an important day, though Mylah had tried her hardest to forget it at every chance she got. It was the day they would be honoring Garrick's life.

She had avoided Elena and Crane as much as possible the past three weeks, but she still had to see them at meals. She skipped as many of those as she could, which had begun to show in her gaunt reflection in the mirror. A seemingly endless chasm had opened in her chest and filled with grief so deep it left her breathless every time she thought of Garrick.

Holly Huntress

It was her fault he was dead. She'd been stupid and careless, going back to her house which had been set alight as they fled.

It was her fault that a copy of the shreeve's Book of Creation was still in the hands of King Florian. There was nothing she could do that would make up for her mistakes, and in the time since, she'd been attempting to drown her emotions with alcohol.

She had no idea what Torin's excuse was, but he'd joined her most nights. If she had to guess, he held some of the guilt for failing their mission as well.

As for Elias, Mylah hadn't spoken with him since the night they'd fled Adair. She'd seen him in the halls, but whenever he saw her approaching, he turned or veered into a room, slamming the door in her face.

She didn't blame him. She wished she could be rid of herself as well. Unfortunately, there was no escaping her mind and the horrible things it tried to convince her of.

Bellingham was one of the only people Mylah talked to about anything, and only because he could see through her lies, but he spent most of his time outside of the castle now.

A fist banged on Mylah's bedroom door, forcing her awake again. She had dozed off in the tub.

"Mylah, get your ass out of bed," Crane yelled. The bedroom door slammed open, and he stomped into her room. "You can't avoid me anymore." Mylah rolled her eyes and climbed out of the tub, wrapping her robe back around herself. She strolled into her room, leaning casually against the door frame as she took in Crane's appearance. His eyes held a haunted look and stubble grazed his cheekbones and chin. He'd obviously been having trouble sleeping too, the bags under his eyes had worsened since the last time she'd seen him.

"This is ridiculous." Crane waved his hand towards Torin who had woken and was pulling on his pants. "You've been screwing around for three weeks now. You don't think I want to give up too? But I can't. I have to hold myself together for you, and mom, and Grey–" He stopped abruptly, his mouth pressing into a straight line as he recollected himself. Mylah's heart clenched at the sight of it, but she didn't say anything. "You don't think I want to drink myself half to death every night and fall into bed with the nearest willing person?"

Mylah pursed her lips for a moment, tempted to correct him, but instead decided to continue letting him believe she'd been sleeping with Torin. "You should try it, it might loosen you up a bit," Mylah grumbled, forcing a smirk. She hadn't truly smiled in weeks.

"Oh, shut it," Crane ground out. "You're coming with me to train today after the ceremony."

"No, I'm not." Mylah went about getting ready as she realized Crane wouldn't be leaving without a fight. "I'm perfectly happy with my life as it is."

"That's crap. You're so full of it. He was *my* father for Hosath's sake! I should be the one falling apart! Even mother is trying harder than you!" Crane threw his hands up in exasperation.

"Good for you and Elena." Mylah slipped out of her robe and pulled a soft green dress over her head, securing it around the middle with a gold braided rope belt. Crane had turned away, cheeks blushing. She realized Torin must have slipped out of the room while her back was turned because he was gone.

"I don't know you anymore." Crane turned back to her and the disappointment on his face was plain and mirrored the look Garrick gave Mylah every night in her nightmares.

"Good. That was the plan. Who I was sucked," Mylah retorted.

"This isn't funny, Mylah!"

"I can tell a better joke if you'd like," she said, running a brush through her hair. She twisted it up into a bun, pinning it in place. "Can we go now?"

"Fine. But this isn't over."

Broderick and Sabine met them outside Mylah's door. Castien had assigned them to guard her since he still hadn't learned who had tried to kill her before the mission to Adair. She hadn't found the will to tell him it had been an assassin sent by her own king. Mylah assumed Sabine and Broderick were the only ones who had been up for guarding her after everyone had learned she'd been lying to the entire kingdom since she'd arrived. Though, they were still cold towards her as well.

They walked in silence towards the gardens where the ceremony was being held. Mylah cringed as she saw Elena already waiting there, clutching her hands close to her heart.

"Don't be rude to mother or else," Crane whispered as they approached her.

"Or else what?" Mylah pressed into his side. "Nothing you could do to me wouldn't be something I haven't already wished upon myself."

Mylah left Crane and strode to Elena's side, putting her arm around Elena's shoulders. Elena leaned against her, and a shudder wracked Elena's body.

Disgraced

"You came," she breathed, her words so hoarse Mylah knew she'd been crying all morning.

"Of course I did. I wouldn't miss it for the world," Mylah lied. She would have done anything to get out of coming today. It didn't help that clouds had covered the sky, threatening to release a torrent on them at any moment, though it matched the mood perfectly.

Crane took his place on the other side of Elena and shot Mylah a glare. Ignoring it, Mylah scanned the garden. Guards stood in a line to her right, a few of them whispering to each other. Sprites hovered near the wall that encircled the castle, flitting around the bushes. A few had settled on top of the wall to watch the ceremony from above.

Castien arrived a few minutes later with Elias trailing closely behind him. Mylah tried to catch Elias' eye, but he never even glanced her way.

"Thank you for doing this," Elena said, grasping Castien's hand and squeezing it tightly as he neared her. She dissolved into a fit of sobs.

Mylah cringed and loosened her grip on Elena. Her own grief fighting to break free from her chest where it sat feeling heavier than ever.

"You're welcome, and if you need anything else, please let me know," Castien's voice distracted Mylah for a moment. She had never heard his voice so soothing and calm. It almost made her forget how coldly he had treated his own people in the past.

"We have gathered here today," Castien began, talking in a louder and more authoritative voice. Mylah turned her head and noticed a few more guards had joined the ceremony, probably to make it seem like there were more people for Elena's sake. Mylah felt a twinge of gratitude and smiled at them. They offered her nothing but cold stares in return. Guilt twisted her gut. She knew she deserved those stares. She had doomed them all if King Florian ever translated the Book of Creation.

"I will let Elena speak since she knew Garrick best," Castien said, stepping aside to allow Elena to take the spotlight. Mylah had missed whatever Castien had said prior, too focused on her surroundings. Elena left Mylah's embrace and began speaking in a soft, almost inaudible voice.

Without Elena beside her, helping to keep her standing, Mylah swayed on her feet. She was pretty sure the alcohol hadn't entirely left her system from the night before.

"Garrick was my everything." Elena choked back a sob. Tears welled in Mylah's eyes and brought a lump into her throat, nearly choking her. Her vision blurred and she squeezed her eyes shut to try to clear them. She gasped as she opened her eyes, and the tears broke loose. Crane shot her a look; mouthing, *pull it together*. Mylah knew this was for Elena and she didn't want to take away from what was being said, though she heard none of it over the ringing in her ears.

"Thank you to all who came today. I know most of you never even met Garrick, but it means..." Elena dissolved into sobs again, covering her face with her hands. Crane stepped up beside her, putting his arm around her shoulders and leading her back to her place beside Mylah who reached out and grabbed her hand.

"You've done much for those of us here since you arrived. In thanks, we wanted to honor your beloved," Castien said, and Mylah swore tears glistened in his eyes. She had no idea what he meant when he said Elena had done much for these people. She'd been so distracted the past few weeks; she'd barely registered anyone else besides Torin and herself.

"I'm so sorry, Elena," Mylah said, apologizing for so much more than Garrick's death. Elena said nothing in response but squeezed Mylah's hand a little tighter before dropping it.

"Come on, mother." Crane led her away as the rest of the assembled group began to disperse. Mylah went to follow them, but Castien cleared his throat, making her turn towards him.

"Not so fast," he said. "You're coming with me." Elias had begun to walk away but Castien reached out and grabbed his arm. "You too."

Two

Mylah followed Castien without argument, too exhausted to protest. Elias grumbled the entire walk to Castien's study. Torin waited for them there, appearing fresh as a daisy as he leaned against the windowsill on the back wall. Mylah shot him a sneer, jealous that he'd been able to recover from their night so easily. He smirked back.

"We've received a letter," Castien said by way of explanation and Mylah noticed a piece of parchment unfolded on the circular table in the center of the room. "Well, I should say *Mylah* received a letter." Mylah's eyes widened and her heart dropped.

"What?" She hurried forward, grabbing the parchment from the table, and immediately recognized Cassia's handwriting. "You opened my letter?"

"As *king* I think it is my duty and my privilege to open any correspondence that comes into these halls."

Elias stepped forward and leaned over Mylah's left shoulder. His nearness caused butterflies to erupt in her stomach and goosebumps to raise on her arms. She hated that he still had that effect on her after everything.

She read the letter, and the butterflies fled.

Mylah,

Bellingham has informed me that you made it back to Elowyn safely. I only had time to write this letter though before he had to leave again, it's too dangerous for him to linger. The king has eyes everywhere.

Things have changed since you left. The queen of Cyprian, Queen Aveda, has been spotted multiple times in the castle. No one is entirely sure what she's doing here. Only a few of the council members have been brought in by the king for the most recent meetings. I haven't seen Greyson in weeks, and I fear for him. I know there's not much you can do from where you are, but I wanted to write to you in case there was anything that could be done to help him.

I'm glad that you made it out with the rest of the Callisters. At least I know you all will stay safe.

Mylah's heart raced and sweat broke out across her brow. She wasn't sure if it was the effects of her hangover or the fact that she now had to worry about Cassia, Greyson, and the fact that King Florian seemingly hadn't told anyone that Garrick was dead, since Cassia thought *all* the Callisters had made it out safely. She continued reading.

There will be a meeting held in a few weeks for all the royals of the human kingdoms and some of the leaders from Hyrdian. If I hear anything else, I will do my best to get the information to you.

Give my best to Crane. I hope you all are well.

*Love,
Cassia*

"It was risky having Bellingham reenter Adair," Torin said, rolling his shoulders as he stepped away from the window.

"He went of his own accord," Castien responded without turning to face Torin.

Mylah remained speechless, unsure what it all meant. She stared down at the words in front of her, trying to imagine Cassia writing them, and her heart broke for the best friend she'd had to leave behind. One more thing for her to regret. It was only a matter of time before King Florian turned on Cassia for having been so close to Mylah.

"What are we supposed to do with this information?" Mylah asked, throwing the letter back onto the table and pacing towards the chairs against the left wall. "She knows I can't do anything to help her." Mylah's blood boiled thinking of King Florian possibly hurting Cassia because of her. "If he touches her..." she murmured more to herself.

"We will make sure he pays for all he has done," Torin's voice sounded right behind her, and his hand clamped onto her shoulder. She hadn't even heard him move across the floor. Sometimes she forgot they were for the most part inhuman, so used to their appearances and grace after all her time spent with them.

A knock on the door resonated in the too quiet room.

"Enter," Castien called out and the door swung inward. Killian and Korriane swept in, a breeze entering with them. Mylah shuddered.

Disgraced

"Castien," Killian said, and Mylah noticed his tight expression as he glanced around the room. "There is...unexpected news." His eyes flicked to Elias and then to the floor.

"Out with it then," Castien snapped. "We don't have all day."

"There is a mass of people at the gates, claiming that King Haldor was killed not by an Unbound, but by..." Killian gulped, most likely knowing what he was about to say would trigger the entire room. Mylah closed her eyes, awaiting the inevitable. The truth had been outed, most likely by King Florian or someone else from Adair, and it was her fault. If she'd only been honest with Greyson from the start, that she didn't love him like he loved her, he never would have been in the woods that day when Elias revealed his secret.

Tears burned hot behind Mylah's eyelids, but she refused to let them fall.

"By Elias." Korriane finished for her brother. "We know it can't be true."

Mylah opened her eyes and snuck a look at Castien whose nostrils flared as he whipped towards Elias.

"How –" Castien began, but Elias turned his head pointedly towards Mylah and Castien followed his gaze. "You." He rolled his eyes and groaned.

"What's going on?" Torin asked, confusion wrinkling his brow as he tried to decipher the truth.

"Shut the doors," Castien ordered, and Killian did as he was told. "I have some explaining to do I guess."

"I can tell them," Elias offered and Castien shook his head, his hair falling out of place for once and over his eye. He swept it aside and rubbed his forehead as Mylah assumed he considered how to tell his most trusted advisors that he had lied to them for over two years.

"So, it is true then?" Korriane gasped, her hand flying to her mouth. What interested Mylah most was that the gaze Korriane turned on Elias held nothing but sympathy. Mylah had expected anger or betrayal.

"We always suspected, but we never thought..." Korriane stopped and reached out to Elias, placing her hand on his forearm. He pulled away from her and stormed over to one of the chairs against the wall, slumping into it.

"I don't want your pity," he rasped out, his head falling into his hands. "I killed my father, and I lied to everyone about it."

"Only because I made you lie," Castien chimed in. "It was an accident, Elias. You are not to blame."

"Tell us what happened," Torin demanded. Out of everyone, Mylah was surprised he seemed the most upset. She thought that in his eyes, neither the prince nor the king could do wrong. But then again, she'd learned from her own betrayal that he was quick to anger, and almost as quick to forgive. After returning from Adair, it had taken an explanation from Castien and two nights of rumination before he forgave her for plotting to betray Elowyn. Mylah didn't think she deserved his forgiveness, or anyone's for that matter, but she'd accepted it.

Elias cleared his throat, bringing Mylah's thoughts back into the moment. "King Haldor and I were out hunting on the border of the Unbound territory. He told his guards to leave us, he wanted to speak with me privately," Elias began, his arms shaking as they supported his head in his hands.

Disgraced

"I can tell the story," Castien offered but Elias continued as if he hadn't heard him.

"I lost control of my magic and it... It killed him," Elias' voice dropped to a whisper. "There was nothing I could do. I tried everything to bring him back."

Mylah's heart stuttered. Though she'd heard Elias' story before, she hadn't thought about what had happened immediately after the king's death and how Elias must have dealt with those emotions.

"And you never thought we should know?" Torin's question was directed at Castien.

"Does it make any difference? What would the truth have changed?" Castien retorted.

"It would have explained why *you* became king instead of Elias," Torin waved his hand towards Elias. "Who was the rightful heir!"

"And, as I told the entire kingdom, Elias wasn't ready for that." Castien stepped towards Torin, and even though Torin was taller, Castien seemed to tower over him with his presence.

"Says who? Says *you*? Elias, why don't you weigh in on this?" Torin turned to Elias who still had his head in his hands.

"There was no way I could have become king. Not until my magic was under control again," Elias said. "Don't be mad at Castien, I asked him to take my place."

Torin said nothing and stormed out of the room. Mylah almost followed him, but Killian spoke again.

"There's something else," he said, and Mylah stopped in her tracks. "Not everyone is at the gates because of Elias." This time his eyes met Mylah's.

"Wonderful," Castien grumbled. "Just what we need in the midst of a war; a full-out rebellion."

"They're calling for her blood," Korriane said. "The only way we were able to get past them without being trampled was by promising we'd deliver her to them."

"What?" Mylah gasped, her eyes widening and her heart jumping into her throat.

"Don't worry, we'd never actually do that," Korriane said, winking at her. "For some reason, I actually like you enough to keep you from being torn apart."

"This is too much." Castien placed his hands on the table and leaned over it, bracing himself as he stared at the floor, shaking his head. "Queen Aveda... Elias... Mylah..."

"Just give them what they want," Elias said, and Mylah's head whipped towards him.

"You hate me so much you'd see me killed? After all I've lost for your kingdom?" Mylah took a step towards him as he raised his head and met her gaze. He held no emotion there, no rage, no sadness. Nothing.

"I deserve to be executed for my crimes. Killing a king... Killing my father..." He stared at the floor once more. "There is nothing I can do to change what happened, and there's no way to ensure it won't happen again."

"You can't kill King Haldor again," Korriane pointed out. "And I don't think many actually miss him, they're mostly upset that they've been lied to."

"That's not what I meant, and you know it. I've never been able to control my magic," Elias said.

"I've been thinking about that," Castien said, lifting his head, a grin playing at his lips. "And I have an idea." Clasping his hands, he pointed with them both to Elias and then to Mylah. "Elias and Mylah will go to Hyrdian."

"What will that solve?" Mylah asked at the same time Elias said, "I'm not going anywhere with her."

"Elias, you can find help there, someone who can teach you to control your magic. Maybe you can even find your real father." His eyes found Korriane's and Mylah watched as she betrayed no sign of surprise at that revelation. She wondered if Korriane had guessed it as so many others had. Out of the corner of her eye, Mylah noticed Killian's eyes widen before he reschooled his expression into indifference. She narrowed her eyes at him, but Castien continued talking and she returned her attention to him.

"If I let Elowyn know that this is our solution, it may help to appease them. And Mylah, we need to get you out of here until people start to forget what you've done. I'll let them know you were a spy for me, but that won't appease everyone. It will take time for them to accept you."

"I don't need them to accept me, I just need them to not want to kill me. I already have enough people waiting in line to do that." She flicked her eyes to Elias who stared at the ground, his jaw clenched. "But, fine. I'll go. In the meantime, I promised Crane I'd train with him today." Castien and Korriane exchanged surprised glances which irked Mylah, but Elias didn't react. He had already made it clear he couldn't care less what she did in her free time.

"Before you go, there is one more thing I would like to clear the air about," Castien said, rubbing the back of his neck as his gaze turned to the floor. Korriane groaned playfully, but her smile fell as Castien remained serious. Mylah had no idea what he was about to say, but her palms had begun to sweat with the anticipation.

"I've already informed Torin of this," Castien began again, lifting his head to face them all as he spoke. "It's important to me that you all know exactly why Mylah came here to betray us in the first place."

Mylah's jaw dropped and she hurried to say, "You don't need to tell them this."

Castien shook his head. "They deserve to know the whole truth."

Korriane, Killian, and Elias all wore confused expressions.

Mylah gritted her teeth as she stared down Castien. "Do. Not. Tell. Them. I don't want anyone's pity," she ground out.

"Fine, then leave. I'll tell them when you've gone," Castien said and Mylah turned on her heel, striding towards the door. "We'll be discussing plans regarding your trip to Hyrdian at dinner. I expect you to be there," Castien called after her.

Three

Elias watched Mylah storm out of the room, disbelief washing over him. He couldn't understand what was so bad that Mylah wouldn't want Castien to tell them, and how she dared walk out on a *king* like that. Then again, Castien had always seemed to have a soft spot for her. A flare of jealousy sparked in Elias' gut at that thought, followed by shame, and anger. He had no right to be jealous of anyone who may show interest in Mylah, she was no longer his to care for. In fact, she had hardly been his for a few hours before everything went to shit.

"Out with it then," Elias said as Castien continued to stare at the door Mylah had slammed shut.

Castien cleared his throat. "When King Haldor sent me to Adair all those years ago, to retrieve the Book of Creation, I didn't completely fail my mission."

"But you didn't retrieve the book," Elias reminded him, remembering the fear in Castien's eyes when he'd first returned from that mission. It had quickly been replaced by the guarded look he tended to wear more often than not now.

In all truth, Castien had changed after that mission. His cruelness towards others became less apparent, and he'd begun to draw into himself more, spending less time with Elias while he was home between missions.

"No, I didn't. But that wasn't the only order I had been given. King Haldor ordered me to kill the man who was attempting to translate the book. He wanted to ensure that if the book fell into the wrong hands again, at least they'd be disadvantaged without their translator." Castien clenched his hands into fists at his sides.

Elias cocked his head, trying to figure out what exactly Castien was getting at.

"That seems like a logical plan," Korriane voiced Elias' thoughts.

"It did to me too, at the time," Castien sighed. "I was unable to retrieve the book, but I killed the man and his wife, because I knew that he would have likely shared his knowledge with her."

"Again, logical assumption," Korriane said, shrugging her shoulders. "Why would you feel the need to hide this from us?" As Korriane spoke, Elias began putting the pieces together in his mind, and his face grew hot with the realization.

"After I killed them, I realized that they didn't have the book. They had given it to their daughter who fled out the window to a neighbor's house. To Garrick Callister's house, I know now." Castien turned his gaze to Elias who gritted his teeth so tightly that his jaw began to ache.

Disgraced

"A daughter..." Korriane's voice became a whisper. "Mylah is that daughter, isn't she?" She spoke the words that Elias couldn't bear to believe.

My brother killed Mylah's parents. Tears blurred his vision, and he wiped them away swiftly, though a bit too harshly.

"She came here to kill you, didn't she?" Elias said, the words clanging in his skull.

"Yes, along with what you all knew, which was to gain information about the Book of Creation," Castien confirmed.

Elias shot out of his chair and strode to the door.

"Where are you going?" Castien asked, appearing at Elias' side, and grabbing his arm.

"I don't know... I need some air," Elias said. The walls had begun to close in on him and he needed to get outside the castle walls to breathe and think.

My brother killed Mylah's parents. The words floated through his mind again, causing his gut to roil and a sweat broke out across his brow.

Castien released Elias' arm. "Just be sure to be at dinner tonight. We have to talk about your trip to Hyrdian."

Elias grunted in agreement before fleeing the room.

Four

Crane left Elena in her room to grieve. She'd been inconsolable since the ceremony, and he couldn't take much more of trying to stay strong for her. He needed to work out his frustration and grief in the training room.

Even though he had told Mylah she would be training with him after the ceremony, he had no reason to believe she'd actually show. Guilt nagged at him as he thought of her, on the verge of tears during the ceremony, and him telling her to 'pull it together.' It had been for Elena's sake, but Mylah needed to grieve too. He wasn't even sure she'd ever really grieved her parents' deaths. He remembered how she'd hounded Garrick to start training her in combat only days after they'd been murdered.

Crane reached the training room and pushed open the door with a sigh. Stopping in his tracks, he gaped towards the center of the room where Mylah stood, sweat seeping through her clothes and dripping from her. Her gaze flicked to his and she paused, lowering her sword. A mixture of surprise and relief passed through Crane at the sight of her there and he fought a smile.

"What?" she asked.

"I'm surprised you actually came," he said before he walked to the weapons wall and grabbed a sword for himself. "But I'm glad you did. It would be a burden to have to drag you down here myself."

Mylah stuck her tongue out at him. "Whatever."

"You smell awful, by the way." Crane wrinkled his nose as he approached her.

"I just washed this morning," Mylah said as she lifted her arm, trying to smell herself and scowled, making Crane laugh.

"But now you're sweating all that alcohol out from last night. I'd recommend another bath before dinner," he said, glad at the ease of the conversation after their rough start that morning.

"We'll see. Maybe I *want* to repulse people." Mylah placed her sword down as she tied her hair up into a ponytail.

"Show me what you've got," Crane said, swinging his sword up in front of him. Mylah smirked and raised her sword to meet his.

As they practiced, he noticed that she'd lost her edge when it came to fighting. She used to be able to beat him in a sparring match, but she could barely keep up now. He knew she hadn't done any training since they arrived in Elowyn, and it was showing. He was sure the amount of alcohol she'd been consuming didn't help either.

By the end of their training session, Mylah lay flat on her back, arms splayed out on either side of her, gasping as she tried to catch her breath. Crane laughed from the other side of the room. He had put his sword away after beating her for the fifth time that day. Mylah stared at the ceiling as Crane walked back over to her.

"Come on," he said as he stood above her. He held out his hand to her and she gripped it. Mylah tried to help pull herself to her feet, but Crane ended up doing most of the work. "Go take a hot bath and I'll have someone bring you some food."

"Why are you doing this?" Mylah rasped. Her gaze softening as her brows pulled together.

"What do you mean?" he asked as he helped her to the door. "I care about you." Since the day she'd moved into their home in Adair, Crane had seen Mylah as a sister and he'd always treated her as such, even though she kept trying to push him away the past few weeks.

"But why? I'm the reason Garrick is dead. I'm the reason you had to leave Greyson and Cassia." Tears glistened in Mylah's eyes. "You should hate me. You should scorn me, not be taking care of me." Crane stopped and stepped in front of Mylah, putting his hands on her shoulders. Anger built in his chest that Mylah thought he could ever hate her.

"I don't blame you for anything, Mylah. You need to stop beating yourself up over everything that happened. You couldn't control the fact that King Florian was able to make a copy of the Book of Creation. And my father chose to go back for you, that was *his* choice. Don't take that away from him." Crane stared deep into Mylah's eyes and tears began to stream down her face. He pulled her into his arms and held her tightly against him.

He wasn't sure how long they stood there like that, but Crane didn't rush her. He let her cry until she couldn't cry anymore and then he led her back to her room and prepared her bath for her.

"Th-thank you," she blubbered as she hugged him one last time.

"Don't thank me. I consider you my sister, Myles, and I'll always fight to pull you back from the edge." Crane's words brought fresh tears to Mylah's eyes, but she smiled through them.

"I promise to do the same for you."

"I know you will." Crane winked and left the room, relief filling him at the knowledge that he'd been able to have a breakthrough with Mylah. Whether she'd remain open with him, he couldn't be sure. But for the moment, he was grateful.

Five

Mylah attempted to undress but her hands shook so badly she could barely get out of her pants. Taking deep breaths to steady herself, she managed to undress.

Once she submerged herself in the bath, her aches and pains melted away for the moment. Mylah soaked until her fingers were pruned and the water had gone cold.

Mylah hadn't told Crane about Cassia's letter or that she'd be leaving. She hadn't been sure how to. Crane would want to return to Adair to help Cassia, as Mylah wished to, but there was no telling what King Florian had in store for them if they ever stepped foot across the border again.

Petra hadn't been around since Mylah had returned from Adair, so Mylah dressed herself. She didn't blame Petra for wanting to steer clear of the traitor.

Mylah left her room in search of Castien. Somehow, she'd avoided him quite successfully the past few weeks, besides when she'd briefed him on her failed mission and when they'd been in his study earler. But she figured they should talk now that she'd be leaving again.

Disgraced

She found him still in his study with Killian and Korriane. He waved her in as he continued talking with them. From what she could tell, they were determining whether they should cut down on border patrols and pull back some of their soldiers in case King Florian deciphered the Book of Creation and used it there first. Mylah felt Torin should be present for that kind of talk, him being the war general and all, but she assumed he had been MIA since their meeting that morning.

Mylah sat in a chair against the wall to wait as they finished talking. Castien dismissed the others and joined her in the chair beside hers.

"You seem...better, dare I say it," he commented, crossing his legs, and placing his arms on the arm rests of his chair.

Mylah had no response for that. She certainly didn't *feel* much better, but at least if she looked the part, people may stop pestering her about her self-destructive behavior.

Mylah noticed Castien wore rings on every finger, something he didn't usually adorn. He flexed his hand when he noticed her staring. Her eyes found the crown that sat atop the table in the center of the room. It hadn't been there earlier, and she'd never seen his crown before. It was a simple, thick, golden circlet with red gemstones set into each of the six points. The stones were the color of Mylah's ruby that she'd left in her room.

Castien noticed her staring. "I have a meeting with the war general from Amaris in an hour," he said, in way of an explanation for his gaudy jewelry.

"Will Torin join you?" Mylah asked, hoping that they had made up since that morning, though his absence was not promising.

"He is meant to, yes." Castien's lips formed a tight line as if he didn't exactly believe that Torin would show up.

"He'll come around," Mylah said, though she wasn't sure he would. The wound of betrayal could sink deeper than most, especially when coming from someone you loved. "That's not why I'm here. I wanted to talk to you."

"As you are," Castien pointed out. "But I gathered as much. Is this about Hyrdian? Because Elias already tried to talk me out of sending the both of you, but my mind is made up. It's the best and easiest solution."

"No." Mylah shook her head, a little stung, though not surprised, that Elias had tried to get out of traveling with her. "I'll go. This is about something I learned in Adair."

"Something you withheld from me?" Castien scowled and Mylah rolled her eyes. As if she'd continue keeping secrets after everything that had happened.

"I know who Sascha's mother was," she said, bringing up the old wound of the woman he loved whom King Haldor murdered. Unsurprisingly, grief flashed in his eyes as his eyebrows rose in surprise. "My grandmother on my mother's side, Jacinda. I never knew her, and my mother never talked about her."

"So that means..."

"Sascha would have been my aunt," Mylah finished for him.

"That explains why you've always reminded me of her. And that..." His jaw slackened and a haunted look overcame him. His head dropped into his hands and a groan escaped him.

"My mother," Mylah began.

"I killed Sascha's sister," Castien murmured, shaking his head as he gripped it. Mylah couldn't bring herself to comfort him. Her resentment towards him for her parents' deaths still ran deep, even though she'd chosen to forgive him. She traced the scar on her palm caused by the necklace gifted to her by her mother that she'd lost fleeing Adair. A reminder of who Castien had taken from her. Tears filled her eyes at the thought of her parents and grief threatened to overwhelm her as it always did when she dwelled too long on their memory.

Mylah cleared her throat. "We should discuss my departure." She needed to change the subject before she lost herself to her grief. "When do I leave?"

Castien pulled himself together and found her gaze. "Tomorrow. I've sent a letter ahead to Hyrdian's gatekeepers in hopes it will speed your entry into their land."

"Tomorrow. So soon." Mylah had been eager to escape Elowyn, but now that the prospect of it loomed so close, fear of the unknown gripped her.

"The sooner the better. We can't forget the threat building in Adair, especially since Queen Aveda is helping them now," Castien said. Mylah understood his urgency, but she wished she could spend a little more time with Crane and Elena before she left. Mylah didn't know much about the queen of Cyprian, but if Castien was wary of her, then Mylah should be too. So, she would follow his orders and leave the next day.

"I need to tell Crane about Cassia's letter. I can't keep that from him," Mylah said, not seeking permission but hoping Castien could help her.

"Fine, tell him." Castien waved his hand dismissively.

"You don't understand. He'll want to return to Adair to help her," Mylah clarified, though it didn't change Castien's countenance at all.

"He has the freedom to do as he pleases."

"He'll be killed!" Mylah burst out. "Or captured! I don't know which would be worse. Promise me you won't let him go. Cassia and I trained together; she can handle herself for a little while. There's nothing Crane can do for her right now. I will help him find a way to help her when I return." Mylah had no idea what they could do for Cassia, short of bringing her to Elowyn.

"I can't make that promise," Castien said.

"You are the king! You can do whatever you please! Promise me..."

He cut her off. "Fine, I promise, but that may mean throwing him in the dungeon if he refuses to heed my orders."

"Whatever it takes, so long as he's safe." Mylah reached over and took his hand in her hers, his rings scraping against her fingers. His eyebrows rose in surprise at the gesture, but he didn't pull away. "In return I promise to do everything in my power to keep Elias safe on our journey, even though he hates me now." Castien chuckled and Mylah released his hand. Before she could pull it away though, Castien captured it in his again, his eyes darkening as he stared at her hand.

"Where is your ring?" he asked. Mylah flexed her fingers, forcing him to release her.

"It's in my room," she said, unable to admit the reason for why she hadn't worn it the past few weeks. Though she couldn't get rid of the scar on her palm, she didn't have to wear her mother's ring as yet another reminder of all she had lost. Thinking of her parents led to thoughts of Garrick and then the guilt would roll in, tainting every piece of her.

"You need to wear it, always. Promise me you won't remove it again?" Castien's words were a command, his voice filled with urgency. Mylah leaned back, eyeing him warily.

"Why?" she asked, and a flash of irritation crossed Castien's face.

"Just...trust me," he said through gritted teeth.

"Fine. I promise I won't take it off again." Mylah didn't have any fight left in her at the moment. Castien stood from his chair, signaling the end of their conversation. Mylah followed his lead.

"I guess I'll go start packing." Mylah left the study and Castien behind, retreating to her room.

Before collapsing onto her bed, she stopped at her vanity and took her ring from the box. In bed, she closed her eyes trying to fall asleep. The weight of the ring on her finger kept bringing her back to thoughts of her parents, but there were a few dominating thoughts that kept pushing out the rest. *They'd be so disappointed in you*, followed shortly by, *Garrick would still be alive if it weren't for you.*

Mylah imagined how much easier it would all be if Garrick were there to help her. He'd be able to come up with a solution for everything. He'd know exactly what to do to help Greyson and Cassia, as he always knew how to solve all of Mylah's problems.

Sleep overwhelmed Mylah and when she woke, it was nearly dinner time. Jumping up from the bed, she hurried from her room with a new resolve. She needed to talk to Crane before dinner.

Mylah knew where Crane's room was, and she assumed he'd be there, but she hesitated before taking the turn towards it. She trusted Castien to keep Crane from returning to Adair, but she didn't want Crane to hate her for preventing him from doing so. She could take the easy way out and let the conversation at dinner reveal Cassia's information to Crane. That way there would be more people to talk him out of doing anything rash, but Mylah owed it to Crane to tell him herself.

Taking a deep breath, Mylah marched down the hallway towards Crane's room and knocked on his door before she could talk herself out of it again. To her surprise, Elena opened the door, tears glistening in her eyes.

"Mylah," Elena said, her voice hoarse from crying. "Come in." She stood aside to let Mylah in. Crane sat at the small table in the corner of the room. His room was about the same size as Mylah's, but the table made it seem like closer quarters. His bed was freshly made, and Mylah wondered if Crane had done that, or Elena. It had always been a calming practice for Elena when they'd lived in Adair. She'd smooth the blankets and tuck in the sheets, letting her hands mindlessly follow the pattern ingrained in her.

"I'm sorry to disturb you," Mylah said as Elena closed the door behind her. "It's just that, well, Cassia sent me a letter." Crane jumped up from his chair.

"What did she say?" he asked, his eyes rounding in worry. Elena took Mylah's arm and led her towards the table. They each took a seat and Crane returned to his, though his hands were restless, moving from his lap to the table and back again before he settled on crossing his arms.

Disgraced

"She mentioned that Queen Aveda has been frequenting the castle in Adair, but also that she hasn't seen Greyson in weeks. There's no telling what the King has him assigned to now." Mylah decided not to beat around the bush. It would help nothing, though from the despair on Elena's face, Mylah realized maybe she *should* have been more sensitive.

"And we can't expect the king not to take out his anger on Greyson," Elena said, her eyes darkening at the thought. Mylah's gut wrenched as the image of Greyson being tortured flickered in her mind.

"I don't know," she forced herself to say. "Greyson didn't exactly do anything wrong, but he was guarding Prince Elias in the tower when we escaped, so the king may place some of the blame on him," Mylah admitted. She prayed she was wrong, but she wouldn't put it beneath King Florian to take out his anger on Greyson.

Crane leaned forward. "Cassia shouldn't be sending any correspondence, if it gets intercepted–" Mylah cut him off.

"It will be seen as treason," she finished for him. "I know, and so does she."

"How could she be so reckless?" Crane ran his hands through his hair and stood again, pacing the room.

"Because she wants to help! Don't be so simple minded as to think that she can't handle herself and understand the weight of the actions she's taking." Mylah stood to face Crane as she spoke. "Do not underestimate her. Her mothers are both extremely intelligent women who have taught her everything they know about politics and life."

Crane turned on her. "You think I don't know that? You think I don't understand how amazing Cassia is? How smart and talented and all around wonderful she is?" Crane stopped, his eyes beginning to water. "I love her, and I never had the chance to tell her before we left." He deflated and dropped down onto his bed, sitting with his head in his hands.

Elena hurried to his side and sat, putting her arm around him. "We will help her, and your brother," she tried to reassure him.

"How?" Crane asked, desperation coloring his tone. "There's nothing we can do from here."

"That's not true," Elena said, but did not elaborate because they all knew that Crane was right.

"If I could figure out a way to get back into Adair–" Crane started but Mylah interrupted him.

"Absolutely not. I'm worried about Cassia too, but as I said, she can take care of herself for now. If I truly feared for her life, I'd storm in there myself and drag her out, kicking and screaming, if that's what it took." Mylah would, too. She'd do anything for her best friend.

The more time she spent away from Cassia, the more she feared that Cassia would replace Mylah with someone else. They'd joked about it before, but it was entirely possible that Cassia would want someone new to confide in. Someone who didn't live in another kingdom. Someone she wasn't technically at war with.

"I have to leave for Hyrdian tomorrow with Prince Elias," Mylah changed the subject.

"You're leaving?" Crane gaped at her. "Our brother and Cassia are potentially being tortured, or worse in Adair and you're leaving to go on a vacation to Hyrdian?" Crane shook his head.

"It's not a vacation!" Mylah slammed her hand on the table. "King Castien ordered that the prince and I go to Hyrdian to appease his people who want us dead. If you'd rather I stick around so you can see that come to fruition, I'll do it. I'll do whatever it takes to never hurt anyone I love again." Mylah couldn't stop the tears that flowed down her cheeks for the third time that day; the dam had broken.

"You know that's not what any of us want, stop trying to become a martyr," Crane said, his face reddening. As soon as he said it, though, regret flashed in his eyes and his face went slack. "I'm sorry, Myles, I didn't mean that."

"Crane," Elena chided before Mylah could respond. "We're all a little on edge. Let's take a break and talk again in the morning before you leave, Mylah."

"Fine." Mylah stormed out of the room and straight into Torin. "Oof."

"Watch it," he growled, clearly still upset from the big reveal earlier. His gaze landed on her as she righted herself. "Oh, it's you."

"Sorry to disappoint," Mylah said. "I was trying to get back to my room, if you don't mind..." She moved to the side trying to avoid him as he did the same. "Ah," she groaned.

"Wait..." He put his hands on her upper arms and turned so they were out of each other's way. Mylah started to walk away when he spoke again. "Do you want to go into town and get a drink with me?"

Mylah turned back to him. "Can't. The entire kingdom is out for my blood, remember?"

"Raid the wine cellar, then?" Mischief sparked in Torin's visible eye.

"Count me in," she said, letting Torin lead the way.

"How did the meeting go with the Amaris war general?" Mylah asked and Torin groaned. "That bad, huh?"

"Not exactly. Balmar is a decent guy, so he said he'd do his best to convince Sovereign Keir that this is a fight for us all, but he didn't seem too hopeful," Torin explained.

"Why wouldn't Sovereign Keir want to help?" Mylah couldn't imagine any being would be okay with their entire race being threatened.

"It's not that they don't want to help," Torin sighed. "It's that they don't exactly trust King Castien."

"Why not?" Mylah asked.

"Castien hasn't done much to foster that trust since becoming king, but he certainly did *a lot* to sabotage it when he was younger."

"Like what," Mylah's voice dropped. It was something she'd wondered about since arriving in Elowyn, yet she'd been too scared to ask anyone about it; why King Castien had been labeled as *cruel*.

"I don't want to go into it right now," Torin said.

"Please?"

"I'll say this, and then you're going to drop it. One of the reasons is Castien seduced both of the sovereign's daughters and broke their hearts during one of his visits with King Haldor. Let's just say, when we had our mandatory visit for when Castien became king, it turned quite awkward very quickly."

"Was that before or after Sascha?"

"Does it matter?" Torin gave her an incredulous look.

"Kind of," Mylah admitted.

"After. But that doesn't mean all the harm he inflicted was after Sascha. He did a lot of horrible things before she died, too." Torin clenched his jaw. "You should talk to him about this."

"I know," Mylah said, having no intention of doing that.

They stopped outside of a wooden door near the ballroom that Mylah had assumed was a closet until Torin showed her its secrets. Swinging open the door, Torin strolled in, the lights inside flickering to life above them. The lights had been magicked to ignite anytime someone entered the room.

Though Torin called the room 'the wine cellar,' but it held all sorts of alcohol and beverages. Mylah headed straight for the wall of whisky at the back of the square room. Each wall was lined with shelf upon shelf, filled with bottles.

Uncorking the bottle she held, Mylah took a swig from it and winced as it burned all the way down her throat and into her stomach. A cough escaped her, and she handed the bottle to Torin.

"You take this one," she said. "I like this kind better." She reached up for another bottle of whisky, this one with a blue label versus the green one she had handed to Torin.

"Why do you always do that?" Torin asked, laughing before taking a haul off the bottle.

"I like to try new things," Mylah said, shrugging. "But most of the time I don't end up liking the new things."

"Fair enough. Come on, let's go somewhere more comfortable." Leading the way once more, Torin left the room. They wound up in one of the many sitting rooms, this one closest to the entrance of the castle. It was also the smallest of the sitting rooms, with only enough room for the two couches on either side of the room and a low table in the middle. Torin and Mylah each took their own couch and lounged as they drank.

"That picture is creepy," Mylah said, pointing to the overly large portrait of King Haldor that hung over Torin's couch. He turned his head up to look at it and pointed with his bottle to the base of it.

"That one was done after his first wife died. I don't remember what he claimed did her in," he said, and Mylah winced. She hated to think about all the poor women who had died at the hand of King Haldor simply because they couldn't bear his children in a timely manner.

"Did you ever meet King Haldor?" Mylah asked.

Torin snorted. "Meet him? I *worked* for him. I wasn't the war general then, of course, but I was a captain of the border guard." Mylah's eyes widened. As much time as she spent with Torin, she realized she didn't know all that much about his past.

"Wait...how old are you?" she asked.

"Old enough," Torin answered, and Mylah rolled her eyes.

"Come on, tell me, pleeease?" Mylah drew out the last word and pushed her bottom lip out into a pout.

"I will say, I'm not as old as Sabine, or Broderick," he said, and Mylah gaped at him.

"Wait, how old are they?" Sometimes she forgot that shreeve had inherited their longevity from the fae. Though they didn't live as long, they still could live an excessively long life.

"Sabine just turned one hundred and ninety, I believe, but don't tell her I told you that. And Broderick is at least a few years older than her." Torin swirled the liquid around in his bottle before taking a swig. "Most of the guards here are much older and have been around since Elowyn became its own kingdom."

"That's insane…" Mylah trailed off thinking about what it would be like to live that long. To have lived through so much of history. "So, you're really not going to tell me how old you are?"

"One twenty-nine," Torin said, raising his bottle.

Mylah's jaw dropped and she raised her bottle towards his as they mocked a cheers.

"That's not too bad. Though, compared to Elias and Castien you're practically ancient," Mylah teased.

Torin wrinkled his nose at her. "Ha, ha. Very funny."

"Put me down!" A yell echoed down the hall towards them. The sound of a scuffle followed and a grunt before the yelling began again.

"This is ridiculous! Do you know who I am?"

Mylah's blood heated as she recognized the voice. Looking to Torin, she knew he had recognized it as well, as his eyes had darkened, and a scowl pulled at his lips. They both stood and hurried to the archway leading into the hall, peering around the corner to see Davina being dragged towards them.

Stepping into the hall, Mylah blocked the path of the guards and held up a hand.

"What's going on?" she asked, as if she had any right to know. The two guards holding Davina groaned and were about to go around Mylah when Torin stepped up beside her and they paused.

"General," they said in unison, dipping their heads to him.

"What is the meaning of this?" Torin asked.

"We found her banging on the gates and demanding to be let in. Thankfully the rest of the crowd had gone home for the night. She says she needs to speak with the King," the guard on the right said.

"Says that it's urgent," the other guard added.

"It is urgent," Davina said, lifting her head to look at Mylah and Torin. Even in distress, she looked as beautiful as ever; her honey blonde hair swept over her right shoulder, and her heart-shaped face flawless. Her eyes held Mylah in place. The blue appeared darker, and Mylah was reminded of the kind of desperation she'd seen in her own reflection often since returning to Elowyn. "Tell these two to unhand me," Davina said in a commanding tone. She was never one to back down.

"Why would I do that?" Torin asked, crossing his arms over his chest. "You have no right to be here. The king banned you from the castle."

"Should we take her to the king?" one of the guard's asked.

"No," Torin said. "Take her back to the gate. She isn't allowed inside the castle."

"No!" Davina cried out and Mylah truly saw the desperation then. Something tugged at her gut, and she realized it was sympathy. How she felt any sympathy for the woman who had tried to kill her on multiple occasions only a month earlier, Mylah had no idea. But it was there, and she couldn't ignore it.

As the guards began to turn with Davina between them, Mylah nudged Torin with her elbow.

"Let her speak with the king," Mylah said.

Torin turned an annoyed look on her. "You're drunk. You don't know what you're saying."

"I am not," Mylah countered. "Well, a little, but I still think there's more to this than we know."

"There is!" Davina said over her shoulder. "I can't go home, please." Her teeth clenched as she said the last word and Mylah could tell it hurt Davina's pride to be pleading with anyone.

Torin looked between Davina and Mylah before sighing and waving the guards back. "Put her in this room," he said, pointing to the sitting room. "I'll talk with her first and see if she has anything worthwhile to say to the king. Otherwise, I'll call you back and have you throw her back onto the streets where she belongs." He turned on his heel and strode back into the sitting room, grabbing his whiskey and taking a long swig. Mylah joined him on his couch and the guards sat Davina on the couch opposite them before stepping out of the room.

For a few minutes they stared at each other, until Torin finally broke the silence. "I can't help but wonder why you're *really* here." He pegged Davina with his gaze, a flame burning in his one visible eye. The patch covering the other had been swapped out, Mylah realized, from black to a deep navy color.

Davina steepled her hands in front of her as she leaned forward, a grin spreading across her face.

"Miss me?" she asked, winking at him.

There's the real Davina, Mylah thought.

Torin snarled and leaned away from her.

"Hardly," he said, snorting. "If you're planning on hurting Mylah again," he began but Davina waved her hand, scoffing as if his worry was absurd.

"That's water under the bridge," she said. "Right, Myles?" Mylah stiffened at the use of her nickname that only her best friends and family had used for her.

"What would make you think that?" Mylah asked, leaning forward to match Davina's position. "You tried to kill me, *twice*."

"Sorry about that," Davina said. "I didn't kill you, though."

Mylah gaped at her.

"I don't believe your apologies for one second," Torin said, leaning back and draping his arm along the back of the couch. "What is it you want? A way to worm yourself back into King Castien's favor?"

Davina laughed and Mylah marveled at the elegance of it. It came off so effortless, and a stab of jealousy hit Mylah's gut. "Is it so hard to believe I simply want to make amends and call a truce?" She widened her eyes innocently. "Though, you are right. That's not *all* I'm here for." Davina cast her eyes down to the table between them.

"I knew it. Here it comes." Torin waved his hands for her to continue before crossing them over his chest. "Go ahead."

Davina cleared her throat and her hands fluttered in her lap. Mylah could tell she was genuinely uncomfortable.

"It may come as a surprise, but I don't have many friends," she began, and Torin let out a snort. Davina shot daggers at him with her gaze. "And now, my family has thrown me out after realizing I'm no longer in the King's favor. I'm not worth anything to them without my sway with the king." A blush crept up Davina's neck and her cheeks reddened. Mylah watched her for any sign of deceit, but she seemed to be telling the truth. Mylah's heart panged with sympathy for Davina. It made sense that she had tried to eliminate Mylah as a threat if she needed her spot as the King's consort so desperately.

"As if I'd ever trust you again," Torin said, and Mylah knew that the heartache Davina had caused him was blinding him to the truth.

"Torin," Mylah murmured, placing her hand on his upper arm.

"I don't want your pity, or anything other than a chance to talk with King Castien." Davina clenched her hands in her lap. "If I had another choice... My parents won't let me back in the house unless I find favor with the king again. Otherwise, I have nowhere else to go." She cast her eyes away, but not before Mylah witnessed the tears there.

"I'll take you to King Castien," Mylah said, and Torin whipped his head to her. As much as it pained Mylah to show Davina any kindness, those pesky words her father had said to her years ago rang in her mind once more, *kindness is not weakness.* They'd caused a mess of her life before, but she wouldn't give up on making Emil, or Garrick for that matter, proud.

"No, you won't!" Torin cried out.

"Why, do you want to take her?" Mylah turned to him, and his lip curled. "Are you worried she'll be able to overpower you and hurt someone?" Mylah jabbed him in the side with her finger and he flinched.

"I've beaten him in a fight before. It's not out of the realm of possibility," Davina added.

Mylah groaned, "You're not helping your case."

Davina mimed zipping her lips with her fingers and sat back against the couch.

Footsteps echoed in the hallway coming towards them again. Both Mylah and Torin stiffened as they turned to the doorway.

"I've been informed that there's a traitor in my castle," Castien drawled as he came into view. He scowled at Davina and then turned an annoyed gaze to Mylah and Torin. "Does *mandatory dinner* mean nothing to either of you?"

"You never said the word *mandatory*," Mylah pointed out.

"It was implied," Castien said before turning back to Davina. "Now, why are you here?" Castien took another step into the room and clasped his hands behind his back.

"Her family kicked her out," Mylah spoke for Davina.

Castien turned his head to Mylah and cocked it to the side. "Was I talking to you?"

Mylah slumped back against the couch and waved to Davina to speak.

"As she said, my family kicked me out. I told them a few days ago that I was no longer in your favor. They started to be suspicious when I wasn't being invited to the castle anymore. Though, your scandal did help to explain why you may not be wishing for company for a few weeks," Davina paused and sat up straighter. "I came to request your leniency and to remove the blackmark from my name." She tried to force a smile, but it fell from her face and Mylah felt for her.

Disgraced

"And you believe you deserve my leniency?" Castien lifted one brow along with one side of his top lip.

"Probably not, but I'd much appreciate a chance to earn it. I wasn't made to live on the streets," Davina said, her lips pursing. "I'll do anything you ask of me."

"How do I know you're not trying to get close to Mylah in an attempt to harm her again?" Castien's eyes flicked to Mylah and the flash of worry there surprised her.

"Have the sprites question me," Davina said, lifting her chin and holding her head high. "I have nothing to hide."

"Very well. Guards!" Castien called out and almost immediately Nic and Alec rushed into the room. "Fetch me a sprite." The guards nodded and departed as quickly as they'd arrived.

"The sprites have names," Mylah couldn't help but point out.

"Yes, and if I bothered to learn them, they may mistake that for caring, which I don't." Castien picked a piece of lint off his sleeve and flicked it towards the wall. Mylah sometimes forgot the mask that Castien wore in the presence of others. It unnerved her and made her wonder what unspeakable things he had done in the name of creating and preserving that mask. Castien had a reputation for being cruel and wicked for a reason.

"Hosath forbid you show them an ounce of kindness," Mylah dared to say.

"You humans and your figure heads." Castien laughed heartily. "Hosath was not who your people make him out to be."

"Oh, I'm sorry, did you know him?" Mylah raised a brow and cocked her head to the side in mock question. Castien was only fourteen years older than her, so she knew he had never known Hosath, who had lived centuries before them.

"No, but I've met some who did, and they told me plenty of stories," Castien explained as Taz fluttered into the room and hovered over the table awaiting his orders.

"At your leisure, sir," Taz said.

"Yes, Davina- go ahead." Castien waved his hand towards her, and she licked her lips before beginning.

"I mean no harm to anyone in this castle, which includes King Castien and Mylah," Davina said.

"All true," Taz said after a moment. "Are you here for any reason other than what you've stated to the king?"

"No."

Taz narrowed his eyes before nodding to Castien. "Truth."

"I have no reason to hate Mylah anymore since I no longer have any interest in being your queen," Davina added.

"All true," Taz confirmed.

"So, what now?" Davina asked before Castien could speak again, attempting a smirk. The empathetic side of Mylah wanted to reach out to Davina and squeeze her hand to reassure her that everything would be alright, but the sensible side of her knew not to. Davina wouldn't want Mylah's sympathy and Mylah wasn't entirely sure what to make of this new side of her she was seeing.

"What do you think, Torin?" Castien turned to Torin who had remained silent the entire time Castien had been there.

Torin turned a blank stare on Castien. "You are the king, it's your decision to make."

Disgraced

Castien narrowed his eyes at Torin before turning back to Davina.

"You can stay in the dungeon," Castien said, surprising Mylah. She thought he'd be harder to convince, but then again, he was always surprising her. "And I'm putting you to work. Don't think your stay will be free."

Davina rolled her eyes dramatically.

Almost as an afterthought, Castien added, "And a sprite and a guard will accompany you anytime you are out and about in the castle until I think can be trusted."

Davina sighed, "Fair enough."

"I'll have the guards accompany you to your room," Castien said, smirking. The two guards, who must have remained right outside the room, entered, and approached Davina.

"Now, if you don't mind, I'd like to get to bed at a decent hour since Mylah and Elias will be departing for Hyrdian in the morning. Have a nice night." Castien strode out of the room.

"Just great..." Davina grumbled, placing her thumb and forefinger on either side of her head as she shook it.

"Be grateful he didn't throw you out on your ass," Torin grumbled before leaving the room, heading the opposite direction of Castien.

Mylah returned to her room and, with the help of the whiskey she still clutched, fell asleep with little issues. The alcohol did nothing to keep away the nightmares, but at least she'd be somewhat rested for her journey.

In the morning, Mylah was surprised to find an outfit laid out for her on the unoccupied side of her bed along with a note.

Holly Huntress

Be safe, and don't do anything stupid.

Petra

Mylah smiled at the scrawl written on the parchment and hugged it to her chest. *She doesn't hate me after all,* she thought. She wondered how she'd slept through Petra coming in and setting the outfit on the bed, but then her eyes found the half empty whiskey bottle on her nightstand.

Right. That'll do it. By some miracle, though, Mylah had no headache. Grogginess did fog her mind a little, but otherwise, she felt fine.

By the time she dressed and arrived at breakfast, everyone else had already eaten and vacated the dining room, besides Crane. He sat waiting for Mylah when she walked in.

"I wanted to make sure I saw you before you left," he said. Mylah thought back to their argument the day before and wondered if he was still upset with her.

"Sorry I kept you waiting." She sat beside him and began filling her plate.

"I'm sorry about yesterday," he started, but Mylah cut him off.

"Don't be. I'm worried about Cassia and Greyson, too. If there's anything we can do to help them, I promise I'll let you know right away."

Crane nodded. "I'll try to find a way to stay in contact with Cassia."

"Bellingham delivered the letter from her. Maybe he can become a courier, if he's up for it," Mylah suggested, thankful that Crane mentioned nothing of trying to go back to Adair and help them himself. He seemed to at least understand the danger in that. "I'll let Castien know."

"You two seem awfully close," Crane pointed out. "It's strange..."

"He spared my life when he could have killed me for treason. And he's helping me now when his people call for my head," Mylah tried to explain, but even she knew it was more than that. *He killed my parents, and I forgave him. He is seen as a monster by his own people, and I see him as a friend. We understand each other.* She kept all of that to herself.

"He's allowing us to stay here, so I guess I shouldn't complain or speak against him in any way. But there is something...off-putting about him." Crane pursed his lips as if considering that but said no more.

"You can trust him, if that's what you're worried about," Mylah said, lowering her voice as she reached over to take Crane's hand. "Don't be afraid to ask him for anything, he has promised me he'll keep you safe while I'm gone."

"He promised you? What does he owe you, Mylah?" Crane asked, and Mylah leaned back. She couldn't tell him Castien had killed her parents. There was no way that Crane would forgive him. Maybe someday... But not now.

"He doesn't owe me anything. Just don't be too demanding, he gets cranky," she joked, trying to lighten the mood.

"There is nothing truer than that." Castien's voice startled Mylah and she realized he was standing in the entryway to the dining room. "If you're ready, Mylah, it's time for you to leave." She didn't miss his gaze lingering on the ruby ring on her finger before he turned back to the hall and the relief that flashed in his eyes.

"Oh yes," Mylah said as she stuffed a biscuit into her mouth. She hugged Crane quickly and followed Castien from the room.

Castien escorted Mylah out through the servants' entrance. They weren't using the front gate since a small crowd of people had gathered there again, calling for her and Elias' punishments.

"They'll calm down by the time you return," Castien said, but doubt shadowed his gaze. When they exited the castle, everyone was waiting for them. Elias had already mounted his horse and continued to ignore Mylah's presence. Sabine and Broderick, who were accompanying them to the Hyrdian border, were waiting to mount their horses. Torin stood off to the side, avoiding Castien, Mylah assumed.

"Send word as soon as you arrive safely in Hyrdian. I have arranged for your lodgings already, and you should be taken there by one of the gate's guardsmen upon arrival," Castien said.

"I should be joining them," Torin huffed.

"I need you here," Castien reminded him. Mylah overheard Korriane mention they would be venturing to Amaris to seek aid there. "Good luck and try to return as swiftly as possible. We need all the help we can get."

"Of course," Elias said as his horse shifted from foot to foot, anxious to get moving.

Broderick and Sabine mounted their horses while Torin helped Mylah onto hers. He placed a bracer behind her to help keep her steady when the horse was moving at full speed.

"Don't miss me too much," Mylah said as Torin stepped away from her.

"Oh, I think I'll be hard pressed to find any reason to miss you," he smirked. "I'll be drinking less, so everything will be easier."

"And you'll be far less irritable," Castien added. Torin grimaced; they obviously still hadn't talked since the day before.

"And I'll be free to find myself a girl again," Torin said, ignoring Castien's comment. Mylah laughed.

"I doubt you'll have much trouble there. Sorry I claimed that space in your bed for so long. I shouldn't have been so selfish." Mylah could have sworn Elias stiffened, but he didn't say anything.

Castien cleared his throat. "Enough chatter, it's time to get going." He and Torin stood back as the horses began to move.

"Safe travels," Torin called out and Mylah turned back to wave before the horses took off at full speed and she had to grip the reins with both hands to stay on her horse.

Six

"Are you going to ignore me the entire time?" Mylah asked Elias as they made their way through the woods that would bring them into the Unbound territory. They had slowed so that the horses wouldn't trip over anything. No one had spoken to her since they'd left the castle and she was fed up with the silence. Sabine and Broderick were far enough ahead that she didn't worry about them overhearing her words for the prince.

"I was hoping to, yes," Elias said, and Mylah scoffed. "But it seems like that's going to be impossible." His hands tightened on his reins and Mylah noticed a few scars whitening across his knuckles as he did so.

"You know, your hatred of me is actually starting to sting a bit, oh wait," Mylah put her hand to her chest. "My tunic is chafing. False alarm."

"Hilarious," Elias murmured

"I know. It's all a part of my charm. Remember that charm you complimented me on the first time we met?"

Disgraced

Though Mylah had been on the brink of death, she remembered her first meeting with Elias vividly.

"I don't recall. I must have blocked that memory out." She could have sworn she saw a smirk on his lips, but it slipped away in a flash.

"Mm. Yes. I'll bet you blocked a lot of memories out then. Like the fact that despite having numerous chances to kill you or your brother while I remained loyal to King Florian, I never did. And when it came time to choose sides, I chose you. But like you said..."

"I blocked all that out," he finished for her. "Though, for that second part I was mostly unconscious due to a poison coursing through my veins that your king used to keep me from using my magic. Pain has a way of fogging up the memories, I guess. It may also be the reason I remember my secret being revealed to the entire world after years of keeping it safe only shortly after I told you." He pointed his finger accusingly at Mylah and she grimaced.

"The entire world is a bit of a stretch. Maybe the entire continent. But don't you feel so much freer for it? No longer living a lie and all that." Mylah tried to tease him, hoping to lighten the mood, but his jaw remained taut.

"Hmm let me think. Nope," he ground out.

"Fair enough. Though, technically you're the one who outed yourself. Greyson just happened to overhear it," Mylah pointed out, though she knew Elias wouldn't see it that way.

"Yes. The man who came to find *you*, but you were too busy betraying Elowyn to pay him any mind. Poor fool." The mention of Greyson had Mylah's mind racing. She couldn't help but remember Cassia's letter. *I haven't seen Greyson in weeks... I'm worried.*

"I should have told him the truth before I left," Mylah whispered, but Elias still heard her.

"Which was?" he prompted.

"I didn't love him like he loved me." She turned her gaze to her hands as she clenched her fists on the reins. Elias didn't respond and they returned to their uncomfortable silence. He rode ahead, while Broderick dropped back to ride beside Mylah. It took a few minutes, but Mylah schooled her features back to neutrality and evened her breathing.

"Sabine and I volunteered to be your escorts," were the first words Broderick said. Mylah turned her head to him and waited. "Plenty of other guards were happy to be Elias' escort, but not so many were as keen to take on the task of guarding you." Mylah closed her eyes. It had been that way since she'd returned to Elowyn, and she had come to expect it. It wasn't a surprise, but it still stung, nonetheless.

"Just like no one wanted to guard my room." Her voice wavered, and she cursed her emotions. "I'm sorry that you had to take on the burden."

"It's not a burden, Mylah," he paused and scrunched his nose. "It's still strange to say your real name."

Mylah laughed, but it came out short and harsh. They hadn't spoken much since her return, and he hadn't had a reason to say her name often.

"You don't need to lie to me, Broderick. I understand that what I did is unforgivable and that no one wants anything to do with me..."

"Stop talking, for like five seconds," Broderick said, flicking his gaze upward as a smile graced his lips, and Mylah couldn't help but smile back. "I'm trying to say that Sabine and I forgive you. Sabine's not one for sentiment, which is why she's hiding out up front with Elias, waiting until I give the speech and then she'll pretend nothing ever happened."

Mylah laughed again. Sabine reminded her of her mother sometimes. As Sabine didn't like confrontation, Vita had also been one to avoid them. It wasn't that Vita worried she wouldn't win in an argument, because she did every time, but she didn't care to take the time to deal with them.

"We understand why you lied," Broderick pressed on. "And we can appreciate the fact that you changed your loyalties to help our people. It's not lost on us that you did all that knowing you'd never be able to return home or see your family and friends again."

"Well, technically my family is either dead or now in Elowyn, so," Mylah pointed out.

"Let me finish," Broderick interrupted.

"Right, sorry." Mylah tightly pursed her lips.

"Sabine and I are here for you, and we still care about you. So, life goes on," Broderick said, clapping his hands together in finality before gripping his reins again.

"Thank you, that means more than you know," Mylah said, this time happy tears pricked her eyes. "I care about you both, too."

Sabine sensed, or maybe heard, that they had finished their conversation and had her horse drop back to trot beside Mylah's.

"You know this is right about where we picked you up the first time you came to Elowyn," Sabine said, skipping over any formalities, as Broderick said she would. A thought came to the surface for Mylah as she glanced around at the area. *Garrick's dagger is here somewhere.* She had buried it on her way into Elowyn.

"There's something I need to find," she said, and Sabine raised a brow. "I may have hidden a dagger here that day you found me," she admitted sheepishly. Sabine laughed, surprising Mylah.

"Of course you did."

"It was at the base of a tree," Mylah said as she turned her head to the side to see if she recognized any of her surroundings, but much of everything looked the same.

"I have a pretty good memory," Broderick said, coming up on Mylah's side. "If I'm remembering correctly, we found you right over there." He pointed to a grouping of trees that looked vaguely familiar to Mylah and she steered her horse in that direction, hopping down when she reached the spot she was sure she had buried the dagger.

Kneeling at the base of a tree, she brushed away some debris, revealing a glint of the metal handle half exposed to the air. Digging down, she revealed the rest of the dagger, pulling it out and clutching it tight to her chest.

I love you, Myles. Be careful and come home safe. Garrick's words, as he'd dropped the dagger into her cloak, rang in her ears and tears slipped down her cheeks.

"Does anyone think it's strange that we haven't come across *any* Unbound creatures yet?" Sabine asked, startling Mylah.

"What do you mean?" Mylah glanced around, not noticing anything, which *was* strange. Usually there was at least a pixie or a dryad lurking about. She got to her feet and stowed the dagger in her left boot, grateful it had a sheathe, before remounting her horse.

"It's too quiet," Sabine said, her own voice lowering. "Prince Elias," she called out, picking up her pace to be beside him once more.

"We should stick close together, come on," Broderick said as he motioned for Mylah to follow him and snapped the reins on his horse to catch up with the others. Mylah did the same and as soon as she did, a deafening roar filled the air around them, bringing them all to a screeching halt. *Troll*, Mylah thought.

"Quickly!" Sabine called to them and led the way through the trees as fast as the horses would allow, away from the source of the horrific sound.

Mylah kept glancing back to make sure they weren't being followed, but the troll never came into sight.

"There shouldn't be trolls this far North," Broderick hissed as they rode.

"Why don't you go tell that one then?" Sabine quipped. "I'm sure he'll understand and head back for the mountains." They broke free of the forest and galloped full speed towards the Lake of Anguish. Once they reached it, they slowed a little, but kept moving West towards Hyrdian.

"Genevieve mentioned that the trolls and orcs were coming out of the mountains more often lately," Mylah said once everyone had calmed down. They heard no more signs of the troll.

"Genevieve?" Sabine questioned, and Elias gave her a curt shake of his head. "Ah, right, siren."

Mylah always thought of Genevieve as a mermaid because she'd once believed mermaids and sirens to be two separate beings, as most humans did. Humans believed mermaids were good and sirens were evil. But now, Mylah knew better. Sirens and mermaids were one in the same and had the capability to be the monsters everyone feared, or to be a friend, as Genevieve was to Mylah.

"Genevieve told me that someone in Hyrdian may be able to tell us why the trolls are leaving the mountains. Maybe I can find someone while we're there who knows," Mylah suggested.

"That's not why we're going there," Elias said, but Mylah ignored him as he and Sabine ventured ahead, leading the way. There were no trees to conceal them anymore, but that meant no threats could be concealed either.

"So, you and Torin?" Broderick said.

Mylah burst out laughing. "That's what you want to talk about?" she sputtered.

"I mean...I've seen him coming in and out of your room the past few weeks. I assumed you were together, but then today..." He trailed off and smirked.

"Yeah, no. We're not together. Neither of us liked sleeping alone after...everything. We're friends."

Mylah had once thought about being more than friends with Torin, but after all they'd been through, and everything with Elias, they'd agreed on remaining friends. She half thought he may be interested in Ana for a while, but Ana hadn't been around since they'd returned from Adair. Mylah didn't blame her.

Shockingly, Ana hadn't been upset with Mylah when her treason had been revealed, but Ana's time in Adair's dungeons had impacted her much more than the rest of them. Korriane went to check on her periodically, but she only gave Mylah small updates. Guilt plucked at Mylah for not being the one to visit, but she hadn't been able to bring herself to go.

"I think that's smart. I don't think Torin ever got over Davina, to be honest," Broderick said.

Mylah gaped at him. "He *hates* her," she pointed out. From how he had reacted to her the night before, he was far from holding a candle for the woman who had left him for their king.

"The leap from love to hate is not as far as most people seem to think. Maybe I'm wrong, but I remember the way he used to talk about her. You don't get over that kind of love that quickly."

Broderick dropped the topic and let his gaze roam over their surroundings, checking for any potential dangers. Mylah considered what he'd said and wondered if maybe that was why Torin hadn't wanted Davina to return to the castle, because being close to her would make it that much harder to get over her. Then her eyes landed on Elias and a sense of longing hit her like a sucker punch in the gut.

"You might be right..." she muttered, but Broderick either didn't hear, or chose not to respond.

They picked up their pace again, making the horses go full speed, until they reached the edge of the forest that would lead them to the border with Hyrdian. The sun had begun to go down as they entered the tree line.

"Should we stop for the night?" Mylah asked.

"No, we should make it in a few hours. It's better to keep moving than linger too long out here. I'm sure you remember what happened the last time you spent the night in the forests of the Unbounds," Broderick said, as if Mylah needed the reminder. She still had the scar from the naga's fang running down her forearm.

"These horses make a big difference when it comes to traveling," Mylah said.

"Don't I know it. It would have taken us almost two days to get to the Hyrdian border if we'd used unenchanted horses. Never do I ever want to use a normal horse."

Broderick pulled up on his reins, motioning for Mylah to go ahead of him as they reached a narrower path through the trees. They stopped talking as they ventured further into the woods. Strange noises surrounded them, but nothing bothered them. Wings made small beats in the air by Mylah's ear, and she turned to see a pixie dancing beside her. When it noticed her attention, it flitted away into the branches of the nearest tree, giggling as it went.

Small, yellow, luminous orbs danced between the trees ahead of them but disappeared when they neared them. Mylah wondered which creature was responsible for those. They lit the path, which Mylah was grateful for, but once they winked out, everything appeared much darker than if her eyes could adjust to it before more lights popped up again.

"*Stray from the path...*" A whisper tickled Mylah's ear and she whipped her head around to find...nothing. She shuddered but continued on. "*Those who stray lose their way...*" The whisper sounded louder, but still, Mylah could see nothing near her.

"Do you hear that?" she asked Broderick who gave her a confused look and shook his head. "Right." *I'm going crazy*, she thought.

"*Leave them behind, come and play...*" The message changed. Mylah tried to block out the whisper which became more insistent. But her horse began veering off course, following the whispers.

"No," Mylah said, trying to steer her horse back towards the path. "A little help here!" she called out to the others, but none of them responded and she realized she could no longer see them. "The path was right there..." she muttered.

"Follow my voice, join the fray..."

"Someone help me!" Mylah's voice turned frantic as the horse continued on its own path, not caring about her trying to steer it back towards where she thought the path was.

Swinging her leg over the side of her horse, she jumped down, rolling into the underbrush, and scraping every part of her body that was exposed. "Oof."

She pushed herself up on her hands and knees and crawled until she could stand. Turning around in a circle, she saw nothing but trees and bushes. All the orbs of light had winked out and left her in utter darkness.

"Hello?" she called out into the forest, half hoping no one would answer.

"Hello," a deep, luring voice sounded directly behind her. She nearly tripped over herself in an effort to turn and see who it was while also keeping her distance from them.

"Wh-who..." she began as she took in the form that stood before her. A man with shocking white hair, bright blue eyes, and... "Greyson?" Her voice shook. It couldn't be him, but he wore her necklace which had been lost while fleeing Adair. She reached out towards him but snatched her hand back as her senses returned.

"You're not him," she ground out.

"Are you so sure?" The voice changed to Greyson's voice. "Mylah, I miss you..." The weight of grief in those words pressed on her, but she wouldn't let herself fall for any tricks.

"Stop." Mylah took a staggering step back. "You're not him." She forced out the words, wishing she could believe the lie.

"You're the reason my father is dead. You killed him, and now I'm going to die, too. It's all because of you." His voice turned venomous.

"No no no no no." Mylah closed her eyes and gripped her head. "You're not him! You're not him! *Leave me alone!*" She spun in a circle trying to block out flashes of the night Garrick was killed.

Greyson, or whatever creature imitated him, caught hold of her arm and wrenched her back, pulling her in close. The smell of death and decay struck her nose as she tilted her head up to stare into the eyes of her captor.

A horrified scream escaped her as she took in the sight that had now changed. Greyson was no longer his youthful, handsome self. His skin was gray and mottled, while his eyes had turned a milky whitish blue. Whatever beast held her was giving her a glimpse of Greyson's corpse.

"Are you already dead?" she couldn't help asking the fake Greyson. Smiling, the creature revealed yellowing and rotting teeth.

"Come with me and you shall see."

Mylah's eyes shuttered closed. Before she gave in, though, a soft voice whispered at the back of her mind, *Run*, and so she did.

Yanking her arm free of the creature's grip, Mylah turned and ran. Footsteps pounded behind her, and she didn't dare look back. A tree root sprung up out of nowhere, tripping her and sending her sprawling across the forest floor. *Damn dryads*, she thought.

Hands landed on Mylah's arms and pulled her up from the ground. *This is it. I'm done,* she thought, before strong, warm arms came around her and she leaned against the hard chest where a heart steadily beat. *Not him, not him,* the beats seemed to say.

"It's not real, Mylah." The body that held her had a familiar voice. "It's not real," he reassured her.

Mylah took a deep breath, inhaling the familiar scent of cedar mixed with a hint of leather. Recognition stirred inside her and stepped out of the arms, glancing up to see Elias staring back at her. Her breath caught in her throat and her blood heated as she realized *he* had been the one holding her.

"I think I'm okay now," she managed to say, and Elias gave her a curt nod, turning away before she could say anything else.

"Come on." Broderick approached on her left and led her back towards his horse. "We'll ride together." Mylah didn't ask what had happened to her horse. She didn't want to know what fate had almost befallen her.

"What was that?" she asked instead.

"That was a puca. They like to cast illusions to mess with unsuspecting travelers. They also tend to know all your secrets which is a bit of a nuisance." Broderick was clearly trying to sound lighthearted, but Mylah had been shaken and couldn't even feign a smile. "It's gone now."

He helped her up onto his horse, hopping up behind her and snapping the reins. Mylah's heart rate began to slow as they moved. Her breathing returned to normal, but she remained somber. The puca had reminded her why she'd drank so much every night back at the castle. She yearned for that oblivion now.

Seven

It hadn't even been twenty-four hours since Mylah and Elias left and yet everyone seemed to be going crazy. King Castien paced the halls, muttering to himself his speech for the kingdom about how he was handling the Mylah and Elias situations. Torin spent hours in the courtyard with the guards dueling, claiming he was brushing them up on their skills, but he appeared to be fighting some internal battle. Elena had spent hours helping the gardeners before someone had to practically carry her back to her room because she'd overworked herself and hadn't eaten or drank anything all day.

Crane sat beside her as she napped, keeping an eye on her. Petra had come in and given her an elixir to help rehydrate her and calm her nerves, because apparently her heart rate had been way too high. The first time Crane met Petra, he'd been surprised to see that Castien had a goblin working in the castle, because he'd never seen any goblins before. They more commonly lived on other continents, like

Cyprian. But he didn't question it since it was none of his business.

"I'll have to talk to Castien at dinner..." Crane muttered to himself as he tried to work out his to-do list in his mind. He wanted to talk with the king about sending Bellingham to Adair to try to get a message to Cassia.

"You should call him *King* Castien," Elena murmured, stretching her arms above her as she rolled towards him and smiled.

"He asked us to call him Castien inside the castle," Crane reminded her, though at first it had felt too familiar to call him Castien to his face. "What were you thinking?"

"What do you mean?" Elena sat up and rubbed her eyes. She looked so vulnerable, and it made Crane's heart clench. His mother had been through too much in the past few weeks alone. Crane had been so focused on making sure he held himself together for her, he forgot to make sure she didn't need help pulling herself together as well.

"You were severely dehydrated, and you didn't eat anything today," he reminded her, and her eyelids drooped down as if they were too heavy to keep open.

"You know, when your father used to go into the Unbound territory with Emil, he'd be gone for days. I never knew when he'd be back. They never packed enough food and water, but somehow, they were always fine," Elena rambled, and Crane sighed, but didn't interrupt. "He told me about Genevieve, though I didn't quite believe him at first. A siren who didn't want to eat him or Emil? Highly unlikely. But they kept coming back, and I had to believe him then, didn't I?" She forced her eyes open again to meet Crane's.

"I'd like to meet her," Elena declared. "She helped us during our escape, right? I want to meet her and thank her. I want to thank her for helping Garrick and Emil when they went on their adventures." Crane slouched in his chair, trying to keep himself from letting his emotions burst out of him. With everything that was going on, this was what Elena thought was important? Talking to some siren?

He took a deep breath, steadying himself before speaking. "I can ask Castien if he'll have someone escort us to the lake. But not now. There's too much else going on." Crane had promised Castien that he'd join a meeting in his study after dinner. Without Mylah around, Crane was the source of their intel on Adair and King Florian.

"I'll find a way," Elena said. She swept her hair back out of her face and pulled it into a low bun.

"No, Ma. Wait for me to talk with Castien." Some of Crane's frustration slipped out and his voice sounded more like a snarl. Elena was being unreasonable, but he couldn't blame her.

"I'm not useless, Crane. Let me do this." She turned her pleading eyes to him, and he caved.

"Fine, you can talk to him about it tonight at dinner, and I'm sure he'll be happy to let you go as soon as you'd like." Crane wasn't sure *happy* was the right word. He was pretty sure he'd never seen Castien actually *happy*. Content, maybe.

"We should get ready for dinner," Elena said, rising from her bed. "I'll be fine while you go change."

"I don't need to change," Crane objected. He looked down at himself, wondering if he truly looked so bad, but his clothing was unmarred and perfectly acceptable.

Disgraced

"Well, just leave me be." She waved her hands in front of her, shooing him from her room. Crane sighed but obliged her and left the room, bumping into Davina on his way out.

"Watch it," she snapped, straightening her dress that he had barely even touched. "Who are you again?"

Crane rolled his eyes. "No one," he countered, starting down the hallway.

She strode beside him, a sprite fluttering along behind her and a guard following her. "This place is becoming overrun with humans," Davina remarked, her voice laced with disgust. Crane wondered if humans had been that much of a burden to her, or if she had a learned hatred of them as he'd once had of the shreeve.

"Don't worry, I plan on getting out of here as soon as I can," Crane said. Davina didn't reply, but they'd reached the dining room and Torin was already seated at the table. His gaze flicked between Crane and Davina before a grimace settled on his face.

"Please, hold the applause," Davina quipped, dropping into the first empty chair.

"Torin," Crane greeted him as he sat beside Davina, trying to diffuse the tension. "Good training today?"

"The guards are certainly improving. We gave them too much time between training courses before. They've lost their touch, but I'll get them back into shape soon enough," Torin explained. He gripped the glass in front of him too tight, giving away his unease at Davina's presence.

Crane noted that the glass was filled with water and not whiskey, which had been his and Mylah's drink of choice the past few weeks. He wondered if Torin's sobriety would last. Torin held onto the betrayal of Elias' secret, and his guilt over the failed Adair mission, as Mylah clung to her guilt and shame. Crane understood why they had found comfort with each other in the previous weeks, though it hadn't exactly been healthy.

"That's good," Crane said, bringing his attention back to the conversation, sipping his own water that had been placed before him. "If you need an extra body out there, I'd be happy to step in."

"If you want to join us tomorrow, we'll be in the courtyard again," Torin offered.

Davina faked a cough. "Boring, ugh. Aren't there any revels or balls going on? I need a good time."

"There won't be any of those for a while," Castien said as he entered the room. "But you won't be invited anyway." He sat at the head of the table.

Elena strode into the room shortly after, taking the last remaining seat. Crane noticed that Mylah and Elias' chairs had been removed. The table was always perfectly set for the amount of people who would be eating.

"Why don't you join Torin and Crane in the morning?" Castien said, baiting Davina who sat tall and bared her teeth in a feral grin.

"I'd love to." Her eyes slid to Torin in a taunt, and he ignored it. Crane rubbed the back of his neck, trying to dispel the heat that had crept up from the discomfort of the interaction.

"Speaking of tomorrow," Elena broke in and Crane's head swiveled towards her. "I would like to travel into the Unbound territory to speak with the siren named Genevieve."

Crane turned to Castien to await his response.

"An interesting request," Castien said, tapping his fingers on the table in front of him. "But I don't see why that would be a problem." He snapped his fingers and servants carried food into the room. "I'll have Torin arrange it and select the guards who will accompany you. But now, let's eat."

After dinner, Crane followed Castien and Torin to Castien's study. He took a seat in one of the two chairs on the left wall as Castien and Torin stood by the table, side by side, but avoiding the others' gaze. Crane hadn't known them before the reveal of Elias and Castien's secret, but he could tell that this was not the norm for them.

"Is this it? Are we going to sit here in awkward silence the whole time?" Crane hazarded to ask. He didn't want to set either of them off, but it was time they hashed out their issues. They would get nowhere otherwise.

"We're waiting on Korriane and Killian," Castien said, and Torin huffed, crossing his arms over his chest. "What?" Castien turned to him, and Crane leaned back in his chair ready for the explosion.

"Nothing, everything's fine, as always." Torin ran his hand along the table as he circled it, flipping the documents over, and coming to a stop on Castien's other side. "We might as well talk about it. It's been two days."

"There's nothing to talk about, Torin," Castien said, the muscles in his neck visibly tightening. "Especially not in front of him." He flicked his hand in Crane's direction.

"What does it matter who hears? Are you trying to go back to keeping secrets from everyone? Secrets that could potentially destroy our kingdom? Invalidate your reign, eliminate Elias as an heir... I could go on." Torin's words hit their mark and Castien's shoulders jumped up as he ran his hands through his hair.

"I didn't know what else to do! My brother had just killed the king! How would you react in that situation? How would *you* respond? Is there some better way I could have handled this? Should I have told everyone that Elias had murdered their king? Sure, no one particularly *liked* Haldor, but he *was* our king." Castien paused to take a breath and then continued.

"Don't tell me that you wouldn't have done the same in my position. That you wouldn't have done everything in your power to ensure Elias' safety and credibility. I am *nothing* without him. I have nothing." Castien stopped, his chest heaving as he stared at Torin.

"You have me. You've *had* me," Torin said. "I would have done anything then to help you both, and I will continue to do everything I can to help make this situation better. You have to trust me and stop keeping secrets, because I can't be your war general, or your friend, if I don't have all the facts."

"You know everything now," Castien said, his gaze dropping to the floor.

Torin nodded, "Okay."

"Okay," Castien repeated.

Crane's mind reeled. Though he remained wary of Castien and his motives, he realized Mylah may have been right about trusting him to keep them safe. There was much more to him than what he presented to the rest of the world.

The doors creaked open and Korriane poked her head into the room. "Is it safe?" she asked, smirking.

Castien closed his eyes and shook his head slowly. "You heard everything, didn't you?" he asked.

Korriane pursed her lips as she shut the door behind her. "Yes. I did, and it was very sweet. I'm glad you two cleared the air." She took the seat beside Crane and patted the arm of his chair. "Good seeing you here," she said to him.

"I'm stepping in for Mylah while she's in Hyrdian," Crane explained. "Where's Killian?"

"I was about to ask the same question," Castien said.

"Running late. He had a few errands today and told me he'd meet me here." She flipped her hair over her shoulder and crossed her ankles out in front of her, lounging in the chair.

"Well, we'll get started without him." Castien sat on the edge of the table facing them all. "I've requested a meeting with Sovereign Keir in Amaris."

"We haven't been there since you were first crowned," Torin remarked.

"I've never been," Korriane added.

"I haven't heard back yet, so don't make any plans. But if Keir accepts my request, I'll be taking you all with me." Castien studied them all as he spoke.

"Me too?" Crane asked, unsure what use he would be in Amaris.

"Yes, you too. I'm hoping that by the time we receive a response, Mylah and Elias may be able to meet us there on their way home, but I have no idea. Keir could want us there next week, and we'd have to go. We can't miss out on this opportunity to make our appeal for reinforcements. I have a feeling they'll be willing to help, because the war affects them too, but I don't know. I've only met Keir the one time, and I don't recall much about them."

"From what I remember, they like to throw a great revel." Torin grinned at the memory.

Castien laughed. "I do remember having to carry you back to your room after you'd passed out on some poor woman's lap, and she couldn't shove you off."

Torin furrowed his brow before joining in with Castien's laughter. "That sounds accurate," he said. The door opened again, interrupting their reminiscing and Killian strode into the room.

"Sorry I'm late. What did I miss?" His eyes narrowed as he noticed the change that had come over Castien and Torin. "A rekindling of some sort," he said, answering his own question.

Korriane hopped up from her seat. "Yes, a very revealing and emotional rekindling, if I do say so myself," she said as she moved across the room to stand beside Killian. "But all you've missed otherwise is a possible invitation to Amaris to plead our case and beg them for help."

"We don't *beg*, Korriane," Torin groaned. "We negotiate, like real adults." He winked and stole her seat beside Crane.

"Fine. *Negotiate.* Can I bring a friend?" She grinned and from the anticipation on her face Crane realized she was only half joking.

Castien crossed his arms over his chest and scowled. "No, you can't bring a friend. We aren't taking a vacation – these are war negotiations," Castien answered.

"What if I tell you it's Ana? And I think she'd be useful," Korriane added, her tone becoming more serious. "She needs to get her mind off of what happened in Adair, and I think a more positive experience using her gift would help."

Crane had nearly forgotten about Ana who had helped them escape from the dungeons in Adair. She had been trapped in there with them for a majority of the time. He remembered hearing her screams when they 'questioned' her the last time before they were able to escape. At that point, there were no questions being asked, only guards taking out their hatred for shreeve on her and Torin.

Castien rolled his shoulders and pursed his lips, seemingly debating whether to give in to Korriane's request or not, so Crane spoke up.

"I think she should come. She deserves to be given the choice to be included in the efforts to save her people." All the eyes in the room fell on Crane, and Korriane gave him a grateful smile.

"I agree," Torin said at the same time as Killian.

"Very well, ask her if she'd like to go. But wait until I know if we're even going. I don't want word spreading about this until we know for sure," Castien said. He pushed off from the table and began pacing the room.

"Thank you," Korriane said.

"I have a request as well," Crane began, hoping that Castien wouldn't shoot him down immediately.

Castien paused in his pacing. "No one else is joining us," he said, putting his hand up to stop further discussion on it.

"This isn't about that. It's about Adair and Cassia." Crane stood from his chair and walked to the table where he found Cassia's letter laying among the maps and various other documents. He picked it up and traced her name scrawled across the bottom. "I want to reply to Cassia if Bellingham agrees to deliver a letter for me."

Castien glanced at Torin who raised one shoulder in response. "If Bellingham is seen or captured..." Castien began.

"I know. But if we can establish communication between us, then we can find out what's happening inside the castle. She and her mothers are a part of the council." Crane used war intel as an excuse, when all he wanted was to make sure she was okay. That her association with Mylah hadn't landed her in the dungeon, or worse.

"It's up to Bellingham," Castien conceded. "And I'll need to see the letters before they're sent." That surprised Crane, but only because he'd grown accustomed to being trusted. It made sense that Castien would want to oversee any mail that would be leaving the castle to ensure there was no sensitive information included.

"Of course." Crane placed Cassia's letter back onto the table and returned to his seat.

Crane went in search of Bellingham after leaving Castien and the others. Bellingham had been back and forth between the Elowyn castle and the Unbound territory since they'd arrived. He didn't want to stay in Elowyn, but he had promised to help in any way he could when it came to the war. He knew of Queen Aveda and feared her trying to take over the entire continent of Olliria. When Bellingham brought it up to Castien, Castien had told him, 'One problem at a time.' They would deal with the threat to the shreeve race first.

Crane headed to the courtyard where the other sprites could be found at any time of day. He didn't know where they slept, or if they even did, but he'd never *not* seen them out there. The sun had already descended below the horizon, making it hard to see in the gardens, but there were flickering lamps scattered about that helped.

"Bellingham?" Crane tried, hoping that he might at least catch someone's attention that would be able to help him find the sprite. A rustle sounded behind him followed by the sound of fluttering wings. He turned and came face to face with Briar, another sprite who had been helpful in their escape from Adair. Crane smiled at her.

"Bellingham isn't here," she told him. "But I can bring him a message." Her eyes were round with such purity that Crane almost felt bad asking her to do anything that may put her in harm's way. He figured there wouldn't be much danger for her in the Unbounds, though.

"Would you mind asking him if he will find me when he returns to the castle? I have a request for him."

"Can do! I'll go now!" Briar zipped off into the night before Crane could say anything else. There was nothing he could do but wait, so he headed back into the castle to get some sleep.

Eight

Greyson stood guard outside the council chambers, hand resting on the pommel of his sword. The guard beside him stared straight ahead, his expression blank.

Since the night of Mylah's escape, Greyson had been assigned to guard the council chambers more often than not, even on days when they were vacant. Queen Aveda of Cyprian was attending the meeting today, and the chamber was filled with the entire council. Greyson had no idea what they talked about in their meetings anymore. He didn't have the privilege of knowing that information. His family had a black mark on their name and though the king had allowed Greyson to stay on as a guard, he was no longer a member of the council.

Honestly, Greyson hadn't even expected that much. He had fully anticipated being thrown in the dungeon or worse, but the king had been lenient. After explaining to the king what had happened in the tower, leaving out the part about him letting Mylah leave, the king understood that there was nothing Greyson could have done to stop them. It was three against one, the odds were clearly not in his favor that night. No one knew the truth, that he'd let her go, unable to separate his own feelings from his task. If the king knew, he'd surely cast Greyson out as he'd done Mylah, and Greyson knew he deserved it. Thinking of her brought back too much heartache for Greyson, so he did his best to think of anything else, but it hardly ever worked.

"Greyson!" A familiar voice echoed down the hallway and quick footsteps followed.

Distracted from his thoughts, Greyson turned his head and smiled as he saw Cassia hurrying towards him. She threw her arms around him, but he did not reciprocate. He had been ordered not to fraternize with any of the council members while on guard.

"I can't talk now," he told Cassia and her brow furrowed in worry, but she nodded once in understanding.

She slipped a piece of parchment into his pocket. "I was going to leave that for you, but since you're here," she explained.

"I'll be sure to look at it later. You should get inside; the meeting is about to start."

Greyson opened the door for Cassia, and she waved to him before he closed the door again. This was the first meeting that had been opened to the entire council since before Mylah's escape. The meetings had been limited to a few select members, but the king had decided it was time to bring everyone in again.

"You used to be a part of the council, didn't you?" The guard beside Greyson broke their silence and it shocked him.

Normally no one spoke to Greyson while on duty. Greyson turned his head to look at him. He appeared only a few years older than Greyson, though his short brown hair and clean-shaven face made him appear more boyish when he smiled.

"Yes," Greyson answered, his tone thick with skepticism. He hadn't meant to sound that way, but he was wary of any of the other guards. Only a few had been outright rude to him since the night the shreeve escaped, but the rest weren't exactly welcoming either.

"Aren't you curious what they're talking about in there now?"

"I guess..." Greyson decided this might be a good chance to make a friend, or at least an ally among the guards. "I'm Greyson, by the way, I don't think we've met yet."

"Julian. I've heard a bit about you," Julian said, smirking. "You were dating that traitor, Mylah, right?"

Greyson's blood heated at the mention of her. An image of her back pressed against him and his sword at her throat flashed in his mind from the night of the escape.

Should I have killed her then?

The thought made bile rise in his throat. Gripping the pommel of his sword tighter, Greyson clenched his jaw and fought off the nausea roiling in his stomach. "I'd rather not talk about her," he managed to get out.

Julian put his hands up in surrender. "No worries. But I heard she set free a prisoner who'd been in the dungeons since before King Florian became king."

If it were true, it was the first Greyson was hearing of it. Though, no one would have told him anyway. The king may have let him remain among the guards, but that didn't mean the king, or anyone else for that matter, trusted him.

"What difference does it make?" Greyson grumbled.

Disgraced

"The prisoner was a fae and has been unaccounted for since escaping," Julian explained, curiosity sparking in his eyes.

Greyson couldn't help the uneasiness that prickled at his skin. The shreeve were dangerous enough, but a full blooded fae with a grudge against the king? That was something he wasn't prepared to deal with.

Greyson didn't respond to Julian and neither of them spoke for the remainder of their shift. When the meeting ended and the council members filed out of the doors, Greyson remained more alert than usual, wondering if the fae was among them. From the texts his father had made him read growing up, he knew that fae had the ability to glamour themselves to look like anyone.

A hand clamped onto Greyson's shoulder, and he turned to find Alessia, Cassia's mother, standing behind him. Her eyes were wide, and she wore a forced smile. She glanced around once before pulling him aside and leaning in to whisper in his ear.

"Don't trust any of them," she said, pulling back with that same smile plastered to her face. "It was nice to see you. Come visit when you can." She slipped back among the other council members before Greyson could even digest what she had told him.

Was it because she suspected one of them was the fae as well? Or was it for some other reason? Maybe Cassia's note would clarify some things for him.

That night, in the safety of the guards' bunkroom, Greyson pulled out his note from Cassia.

Greyson –

Holly Huntress

I'm worried about you. I hope this letter finds you, along with the others I have sent.

Greyson paused; he hadn't received any other letters from Cassia. His gut twisted but he kept reading.

When you get the chance, come to dinner. My parents and I have missed you. Let me know if you need anything. I'm sure you don't get a lot of free time, but I hope to see you soon.

Love,
Cassia

Greyson crumpled the letter and used the candle on his bedside to light it on fire before throwing it into his empty metal trash can. It was standard for the guards to burn any incoming mail they received, otherwise some of them were known to snoop and take any unattended property. That's the way it went when it was hard to come by anything within the walls of the castle. It didn't help that all the guards shared one large room. It was filled with bunk beds that were only slightly more comfortable than the floor. There were about a hundred guards, and enough bunks for them all, crammed into the space.

All the guards were given a day off per week and ordered to remain within the castle. The only exception was when they requested a day out.

Greyson penned his request for a day out, claiming it was to buy new pants rather than for dinner with Cassia's family. He had a feeling he shouldn't divulge that information. For a split second he forgot that he wouldn't be able to visit his own family, but he quickly remembered they had fled to Elowyn with Mylah. Sorrow filled him at the thought that his entire family was together without him.

"That from your friend earlier?" Julian commented, pointing to the dwindling flames in the trash can. Greyson nodded, unable to speak over the lump that had formed in his throat. "She was awfully pretty. Maybe a rebound from the traitor?"

Greyson whipped his head towards Julian. "Why do you keep bringing her up? I told you; I don't want to talk about her. And Cassia is a friend. Don't talk about her either," Greyson snapped.

"Right, sorry. What is a safe subject with you?" Julian sat on the end of Greyson's bed, much to his dismay.

"It's probably safer to not talk at all." Greyson stood and stormed out of the room, heading for the bathing room. He dropped off his request in the designated box along the way and prayed that when he returned, Julian would be gone. *So much for finding an ally among the guards,* he thought to himself.

"Greyson," Captain Andreas acknowledged Greyson as he passed him in the hall.

"Captain," Greyson said, inclining his head to his superior.

The captain at least hadn't treated Greyson any differently than any of his other wards. There were two captains among the guards, each in charge of one half of the lot of them. The other captain, Captain Mardoc, hadn't been as forgiving as Captain Andreas. Greyson would guess Captain Mardoc held Prince Elias' escape against him and assigned him to the worst duties, like cleaning the toilets, as often as he could. Thankfully Greyson answered to Captain Andreas for the most part.

Greyson approached the bathing room and paused as voices filtered out through the door to him.

"Did you hear about the meeting today? The king seems to be answering to Queen Aveda now," one of the guards said and Greyson heated.

Another guard scoffed. "He's gone soft."

Greyson recognized the voices, the first belonging to a guard named Kolt, and the second to Acton.

"I told you, it's only a matter of time before he hands over the kingdom to her," Acton said.

Greyson pushed open the door, letting it slam against the wall, creating a resounding bang. Both guards' heads whipped up and they blanched until they realized it was only Greyson. They stood at the sinks of the left wall, Acton fully dressed, while Kolt had his shirt slung across his shoulder. They were both only a few years older than Greyson and had been among the few who'd given him an exceptionally hard time.

"Oh, the traitor sympathizer," Acton sneered.

Kolt ran a hand through his thick, dirty blonde hair and gave Greyson a once over before pulling his shirt over his head. "Come for a show?" Kolt asked, rolling his shoulders, and causing the muscles to ripple there.

Greyson rolled his eyes and ignored them both, heading for the toilets which were sectioned off by stalls at the back of the room. The baths were separated into stalls as well, all along the right wall.

"In all honesty, I don't blame you. I'd have taken Mylah to bed too. Given the chance," Acton said.

Greyson stopped in his tracks, turning slowly to face them again. "*Don't* talk about her," he snarled, his fists clenching at his side.

Disgraced

Acton and Kolt shared a glance before advancing towards Greyson.

"Oh yeah? And what are you going to do about it?" Kolt asked, cocking his head to the side. "If she'd sleep with a shreeve, she'd sleep with anyone."

Greyson launched himself the rest of the distance between him and Kolt, his fist cracking against Kolt's jaw. Before Greyson could recover, Acton had tackled him to the ground, slamming Greyson's head against the stone floor. Stars swirled in Greyson's vision, and he gulped down air as he struggled to remove Acton from on top of him. Greyson's head whipped to the side as Acton's fist struck him. Kolt began kicking Greyson's side, and Acton hopped up, laughing as he did. Greyson rolled, trying to avoid Kolt, but his ribs screamed in agony. The pain caused blackness to creep in around Greyson's vision, slowly narrowing, until the blows stopped.

A new voice caught his attention, but barely conscious, he couldn't determine who it was. Before he blacked out entirely, he felt someone lifting him from the floor.

Greyson's eyes flickered open, and he shut them again immediately, putting his hand up to shield them, as a bright light shone directly into them. He blinked again, and realized the sun was shining in through a window onto him.

"You're alive!" Julian's voice caused Greyson to cringe as his head throbbed against the noise. He sat in a chair beside Greyson's cot.

"Where am I?" Greyson tried to take in the room around him.

Five cots lined the left wall where Greyson lay. A cart in the center of the room was filled with glass vials, bandages, and other medical supplies. Across the small room stood a man and woman chatting. The woman noticed Greyson was awake and made her way towards him.

"You're in the infirmary," Julian told him.

"How are you feeling?" the woman asked Greyson as she stopped at the foot of his cot.

"This is Mari," Julian introduced her. "She's my new best friend." Julian winked at her, and she rolled her eyes, but Greyson saw a hint of a smile.

"My head hurts, and my ribs." Greyson tried to move and sucked in a sharp breath as the pain radiated out from his side.

"That's to be expected. We have some potions that will speed your healing, but it will still take at least a week for your broken ribs to heal completely," Mari explained. "No training until then, and no more fighting."

Greyson blinked in surprise at the rate at which he'd heal, but then he remembered that the king had a witch or two employed in his castle. *Maybe Mari is one of them*, he thought.

"Don't worry, Mari, I'll take good care of him." Julian grinned and leaned back in his chair, placing his hands behind his head.

"I'm sure you will," she said before walking back to the other nurse.

"That's the other Julian over there," Julian stage whispered. "Obviously the less handsome one." The other Julian didn't react though he'd clearly heard. Greyson assumed the nurses were used to Julian's antics by now, though the other Julian probably wished he didn't share a name with this Julian after today.

"When can I leave here?" Greyson asked.

"Mari said I can take you back to the barracks as soon as you feel up to it." As Julian spoke, another guard hobbled in, and the nurses hurried to his side. A gash on his left side had blood spilling down onto the floor and his face was ashen.

"Training accident," the guard murmured before they lowered him onto the cot beside Greyson's. The metallic scent of the blood hit Greyson and brought on a wave of nausea.

"I think I'm ready to leave," he said.

Julian hopped up from his chair and Greyson let him help him to his feet. His first step left him nearly breathless as his head swam and each breath caused his ribs to ache. He closed his eyes and Julian waited for him to collect himself before they made their way out of the infirmary.

"Well that certainly made things a bit more exciting, eh?" Julian said.

Greyson groaned in pain. "You call this exciting? They're probably going to kick me out of the castle!" Greyson hated that he'd lost control of his emotions so easily, but where Mylah was concerned, he still felt as if he had to defend her for some reason.

"Nah. Guards get into fights all the time. It's not grounds for dismissal. Besides, they wouldn't kick you out, they'd probably exile you or worse. You know too much to be released back into the town." Julian said all this as if it was nothing to fear or worry about and Greyson gaped at him. His face blanched and he had to stop walking for a few moments to catch his breath, which had already been labored from his broken ribs.

"Joking," Julian said, holding an arm out towards Greyson but Greyson ignored it. They both knew he had spoken the truth.

"Did you...were you there?" Greyson's face heated at the thought of anyone walking in and seeing him being beaten to shit by Acton and Kolt.

"Yeah," Julian's voice lowered. "I don't know if they were planning on stopping." He cleared his throat and said in a much more playful and cheery voice, "A thank you would be nice."

"Right, ah, thank you," Greyson raised his hand to run it through his hair and stopped when a shooting pain went down his side with the motion. He grimaced.

Julian helped Greyson to his bunk in the barracks and thankfully, Kolt and Acton were nowhere to be seen. Captain Andreas stopped by and told Greyson he'd have the day off but not to expect any pity from him for the way he'd acted. *A king's guard should know better than to rise to the bait*, he'd said, and if it happened again, there would be consequences worse than a few broken ribs.

Nine

They reached the Hyrdian border and Mylah let out a sigh of relief. Thankfully they'd encountered no other creatures besides dryads and pixies. As they approached the border, a giant wall rose before them, topped with wooden spikes to deter any climbers, though Mylah couldn't imagine anyone being able to climb the monstrous wall. It stretched out of sight in either direction and a massive, solid, metal gate separated them from their destination.

"Stay here. I'll speak with the guards," Sabine announced before her horse trotted ahead and approached the gate.

Mylah couldn't see any guards until Sabine was closer and a section of the wall to the left of the gate opened to reveal an entrance. Sabine hopped off her horse and disappeared inside, the wall closing behind her. Mylah gasped, but no one else made any indication they were worried.

"Should we..." she started to say, but the gate began to groan and shift as it slowly opened inwardly. Sabine reappeared, remounting her horse, and joined them once more.

"This is where Broderick and I must leave you," she said. Mylah noticed a guard standing inside the opening in the wall. He wore heavy armor, held a staff, and appeared to be human. But Mylah assumed he must be a warlock of some sort to be guarding the gate.

"Send word when you will be returning and we will meet you back here," Sabine said.

Broderick hopped off the horse, helping Mylah down behind him. "You'll have to ride with Elias into town," he explained, helping her onto the back of Elias' horse.

Surprisingly, Elias didn't complain as she wrapped one arm around his waist. His warmth sent butterflies through her, but she inwardly cursed them, and they shortly ceased their fluttering. It was useless to pine after someone who would never see past her treachery, though she couldn't blame him.

"Thank you," Elias said to Sabine and Broderick. "We shall meet again shortly."

"Goodbye," Mylah waved to them as Elias led their horse through the gates. Once through, one of the guards from inside the wall came out and greeted them.

"Mylah, Elias," he began, bowing to Elias. "My name is Viktor. I shall be your escort into town," he introduced himself. A horse was brought out from a small stable Mylah hadn't noticed at first and Viktor took the reins.

Once mounted, he led them down a road that had been paved through the trees. Small orbs of white light hovered every couple of feet, similar to the ones they had seen in the Unbound territory. These ones were magic made, though, and didn't disappear when they approached them.

Mylah admired them as they passed by. But they were as they appeared – round spheres of pure light, a little hazy around the edges. It was hard to stare directly at them, so she turned her face forward to watch where they were going.

The trees that lined the road slowly decreased in size and density. Mylah wondered if they had been planted more recently or if that was another magic trick. Eventually the trees stopped, and buildings rose before them. To Mylah's surprise they weren't any different than the houses or shops in Adair. She had assumed they would be more...intricate. Instead, they were made of plain old wood and stone.

"Welcome to Perynth," Viktor said as they passed the first building.

They came to an inn that stood four stories high, which was taller than most buildings in Adair, besides the castle. She gazed up at it and the dim lighting from the lanterns that glowed in each window. Viktor left them without a word and returned to the border.

Mylah dismounted the horse first, wobbling as her legs threatened to give out. Elias jumped down beside her and led the horse around to the stables. Mylah had named their horse Smudge because of the black smudge-like markings across his white coat.

"Castien made arrangements for us so we should be all set with a room," Elias said when he came back to the front of the inn, strolling past Mylah without looking at her.

She trailed behind him into the inn, which turned out to be a tavern on the first floor. Occupied tables and chairs filled the space, along with a small stage off to the right where instruments were set up, but no one was playing.

Instead, the room was filled with the sounds of raucous laughter and chatter from the patrons.

The innkeeper stood behind the bar at the back of the room, serving the two men seated before her. Her gray hair was pulled up tight into a bun that did nothing for the wrinkles that caused her face to droop. Though that may make some people far more unappealing, she appeared more beautiful for it. Her wrinkles were laugh lines and were pulled up now in a beaming grin. She had no worry lines creasing her forehead as Mylah already had.

"Excuse me," Elias said as he approached her.

As the woman turned to him, she tossed the towel she'd been using to wipe down the bar over her shoulder. "Here for a drink, or a room?" she asked, the smile never leaving her face.

"My brother, King Castien, said he arranged for our stay while we're in Hyrdian."

The innkeeper's eyes widened, but she remained otherwise unfazed. "Yes, indeed. Just a moment." She turned to a shelf behind her and rummaged through a basket, pulling out a key with the number *213* engraved on the wide, flat, end of it. "Last room available," she said, handing him the key.

"Thank you," Elias said, dipping his head to her.

"Rooms are through there." She pointed to a door at the back of the tavern beside the end of the bar. "If you need anything, just ask. Name's Midge," she said, inclining her head in a sort of bow.

Elias returned the gesture and turned away from the bar. He said nothing to Mylah before he started towards the door leading to the bedrooms. Through it, a stairway led up to the second floor. After they climbed the first set of stairs, a long hall lined with black, wooden doors met them. Mylah was thankful they wouldn't have to go any higher. Her legs ached from riding all day.

"We should be right down here," Elias said, more to himself than Mylah. They passed a few doors, stopping towards the middle of the hall before Elias turned to his left and stuck the key into the door marked *213*. The lock clicked and the door swung open. Elias groaned as he took in the room and Mylah mimicked the sentiment when she saw that there was only one bed.

"This is Castien's idea of a joke..." he grumbled. "I'll go see if there's another room with two beds."

"She said this is the last room available," Mylah reminded him.

He huffed and dropped his bag beside the door. "I'm getting a drink."

He disappeared back down the hall and Mylah shut the door behind him. Alone in the room, she soaked in the utter *silence*. All day there had been whispers in the trees, leaves crunching, and other background noises. Now, there was nothing, and it was almost overwhelming.

Dropping her bag beside Elias', Mylah headed for the bathing room on the left side of the space, opposite that single bed only big enough for the two of them. She ran the water in the tub, which was mercifully steaming. The day hadn't been cold, but it hadn't been warm either. The weather hovered in a state of indecision as it turned from a warm fall towards a brisk winter. Thankfully, they never got much snow in Olliria, except in the mountains. To the north in Cyprian, more places received heavy snowfall. Though, Hyrdian was the furthest from home she'd ever been, so she'd rarely seen snow.

Mylah took a long bath before crawling into bed and falling asleep almost instantly. The long day of riding and her encounter with the puca had left her exhausted.

When Mylah woke to the sun streaming in through the one window in the morning, Elias had already gone. He must have come in late and left early if he'd returned to their room at all.

She dressed, making sure to pack Garrick's dagger in her satchel, and headed down to the tavern which was practically empty besides the few patrons who ate breakfast. Elias was seated at the bar chatting with Midge.

Mylah sat on the stool beside him, and Midge placed a bowl of porridge in front of her. "Eat up, dear. There's plenty more where that came from." Mylah eyed the bowl warily but took a spoonful into her mouth. Despite the appearance, the porridge had great flavor.

"So, what are we doing today?" Mylah asked Elias as she finished eating.

"Finding a man named Farren," he said.

"Is that..." Mylah began but wasn't sure if she should finish her thought.

Elias figured out what she'd been about to ask.

"No. He's not my father. But he would know where to find him if he's still around. Castien gave me Farren's name. He found it in some old parchments, but he couldn't find the name of the warlock who had actually helped my mother."

"Well, it shouldn't be too hard to find him, right?"

Mylah hoped they would find him swiftly so Elias could get the help he needed, and they could be back on their way to Elowyn. Cassia and Greyson needed her help, and she wouldn't let them down again. Greyson's words, or the puca's words technically, still haunted her.

"Midge informed me of a man named Farren she knows of in the next town over. We can head there first."

Mylah nodded. She wasn't sure what had prompted this tenuous alliance with Elias, but she would try her hardest not to remind him of why he hated her.

"Sounds good."

They rode to the next town, Korrindale, and stopped the first person they came across to ask for directions. Unfortunately, they had no knowledge of a man named Farren, but pointed them in the direction of a hairdresser, Illiana, who knew everyone in town.

Mylah and Elias entered the salon together, but Mylah approached Illiana while Elias chatted with the woman manning the front where a few others waited to have their hair done.

"Excuse me, miss," Mylah said. The tall, lithe woman with bright purple hair trailing down her back turned to face Mylah.

Illiana reminded Mylah a little of Genevieve with that hair color, but the similarities ended there. This woman was not nearly as striking, though she certainly had enough charm to woo anyone she pleased. Mylah had an overwhelming feeling like she wanted to spill all her secrets to the woman even though they had never met.

"You can make an appointment with Charlotte in the front," Illiana said to Mylah.

"I have a quick question, if you don't mind," Mylah said.

Letting out a long sigh, Illiana held up a finger in the mirror to the man in her chair saying, "Give me a moment."

He nodded and slowly, Illiana turned back to Mylah. "Very well," she drawled and waited as Mylah scrambled to gather her thoughts.

What is it about this woman... Mylah thought before blurting, "We're looking for Farren." Mylah blushed at her outburst, but Illiana smiled.

"I mean, do you know a man named Farren?" Mylah tried again, though her mind still pressed her to blurt more.

"Yes. The only Farren in town works over at the school for the magically inclined. Warlocks, witches, fae, that sort. I'd look there first. Follow this road to the end." Illiana turned away from Mylah, sensing that she was done.

"Thank you!" Mylah said before hurrying away. The further she got from Illiana, the less shaken she felt. Something was off about Illiana, but Mylah couldn't figure out what.

Elias leaned on Charlotte's desk as he spoke with her, and she fluttered her eyelashes as she giggled at something he'd said. Mylah rolled her eyes and grabbed his shoulder.

"Let's go," she said through gritted teeth and Elias thanked Charlotte before following Mylah out of the salon. Mylah filled him in on the location of Farren.

"Grab Smudge and we can go," Mylah said.

Elias gave her an odd look. "Smudge?"

"Your horse," she clarified.

"His name is Felix."

Mylah scoffed. "Smudge is better and more fitting."

Elias shook his head but didn't argue and untied Smudge's reins from the fence post outside the salon. "Come on." He helped Mylah into the saddle before hopping up behind her.

Disgraced

They followed the road to the end, as Illiana had instructed, and through wrought iron gates taller than two horses stacked atop each other. An ancient looking building with multiple tall spires and stained-glass windows rose up before them. The beauty was awe-inspiring, but also haunting. It appeared to be an old castle made into a school. They had added on a few sections, which weren't as dark and intricately designed as the original structure, but it was still impressive.

Elias and Mylah entered the building, both too distracted by the architecture to speak. Elias led the way, though Mylah was sure he knew as little as she did about where Farren's office would be.

Eventually, they came to the second floor and found a door with *Farren Aberon* carved into it. Elias paused outside the door, staring at it.

"Are you going to knock?" Mylah whispered, worried about disturbing the silence that had surrounded them their entire walk up there. It seemed there was no one else in the building that day.

Elias cleared his throat and raised his fist to knock, again hesitating, before he shook his head and knocked. It was quiet for a few seconds before shuffling feet could be heard inside. The door swung open and revealed a tall, middle-aged man with short blonde hair and light brown eyes. It still surprised Mylah after spending so long in Elowyn to see the whites around other people's eyes.

"Can I help you?" the man asked.

Elias remained silent, so Mylah stepped forward. "We're looking for Farren," Mylah said.

The man narrowed his eyes, "You've found him, now may I ask who *you* are?" He eyed them suspiciously, which

Mylah understood, seeing as Elias was still staring unblinking at the man.

"I'm Mylah and this is..."

"Prince Elias of Elowyn," Elias finished for her. He straightened, rolling his shoulders back as he remembered himself.

Farren's eyes widened only for a moment before he stood aside and waved them in. "Please, come in." Farren closed the door behind them as Mylah and Elias made their way into the room. "I suppose I know why you're here," Farren said, walking past them to take a seat in his oversized armchair that sat back-to a floor to ceiling window. The gold fabric that adorned the chair was well worn and fading from use. He waved to two matching chairs that sat opposite him on the other side of his desk.

"My brother told me you may know something about my father. My *real* father that is," Elias said, sitting beside Mylah.

Farren steepled his hands in front of him, resting his chin there. "If you've come looking for the man himself, you will find yourself disappointed. He hasn't been seen since...well since you were born." Farren's frown creased his forehead. Mylah studied him, wondering if he was a warlock, or merely human like her.

"Is he dead?" Elias asked, his voice coming out as a whisper. Mylah snuck a glance at him, but he showed no emotion on his face.

Farren's shoulders rose in a shrug but the sadness in his eyes pointed to yes. "I can only make assumptions, because his body was never found," Farren admitted. "Callum knew what he had done to help your mother was a great risk, but he was only trying to save her life."

"Callum." Elias tried out the name and Mylah realized this was the first time they had heard his name. He had always been known as 'the warlock who had helped Elias' mother.' "What was his last name?"

"Marlbec. Callum Marlbec. He was one of the greatest warlocks in Hyrdian at the time, and still would be. It's possible he fled knowing that the king would find out the truth and come for him."

"That Callum had sired me, and not the useless king who murdered all of his wives," Elias seethed, and Mylah thought she could see an edge of blue flickering around him. She gasped and it disappeared as Elias turned to her, confusion making his face go blank.

"I see you've inherited a little of his magic," Farren said, and Mylah realized he had seen the blue too.

"Yes, about that..." Elias started ringing his hands in his lap and then caught himself, laying them flat on the arms of his chair. "I was hoping that someone here would be able to help me learn how to control it."

"Hmm," Farren mused, pursing his lips. "It makes sense that your magic would be different than most shreeve since you are part warlock. I might be able to help you." He stood and strolled over to the bookcase that lined the entire wall to the right. Running his fingers across the spines as he walked the length of the bookcase, he paused and pulled out a book near the other end.

"Ah, here it is." He brought the book back to the desk and dropped it in front of Elias. Mylah leaned over to see what it was and read the title *A Beginner's Guide to Magic*. Mylah expected Elias to scoff, but he picked up the book and began flipping through it.

"Before we start any training, I want you to look this over. Try out a few of the techniques in there for how to safely call out your magic, in an open area with no one else around." His eyes flicked to Mylah. "Not even you."

"But –" Mylah began to protest, but he interrupted her.

"No one else," he added with a tight smile that had Mylah frowning. "I'd start your training right now, but I have a meeting in twenty minutes. Come back and see me tomorrow and I'll start teaching you what I know."

"Are you a warlock?" Mylah asked, wondering if it was rude to ask, but she figured they should know.

"Yes. Though, I'm not nearly as powerful as Callum was. I can only do a few small spells." He flicked his fingers towards the bookcase and a book floated off the shelf and flew into his hand. "Nothing fancy, but certainly useful."

"I would say so!" Mylah gaped at him.

She'd seen very little magic used in the past and it always left her in awe. The colors that swirled around the magicked item while the spell was in use was like nothing she had ever seen. Like a sunset with lightning striking through it.

He flicked his fingers again and the door to his office opened. "I'll see you in the morning," he said, dismissing them.

Ten

Crane met up with Torin and Davina in the courtyard the following morning. When he arrived, Davina was circling Torin almost catlike, her eyes slit and smirking, making her appear downright terrifying. Crane hoped he wouldn't have to go up against her today.

"Now," Torin said as Crane approached. "Never let yourself be distracted by the enemy." He was talking to the few guards who had been appointed to training that day. They couldn't leave the castle unguarded, especially with the unrest in the kingdom, so they separated the guards into groups.

Castien's planned speech for the Elowyn kingdom would be taking place that afternoon while Crane and Elena traveled into the Unbounds. Though Crane was curious to hear what Castien would say to explain away his people's worries, he had to go with his mother. He'd ask for a recap at dinner.

"Yes," Davina drawled, pausing in her circling. "Don't let a pretty face fool you into complacency." She gave Torin a pointed look and Crane couldn't help but wonder about their history.

Davina wore a long, gray dress with a slit that almost reached her hip. It had thin straps over her shoulders that held it in place, but the front V-necked down to her navel. It revealed much more than Crane was used to seeing of any woman outside of the bedroom. He blushed at the thought. He couldn't imagine fighting in a dress would be an easy feat, but Davina seemed perfectly at ease as she moved in it.

Torin made the first strike and Davina gracefully danced out of the way of his blade. He spun, anticipating her dodge, and met her on his other side, their blades clanging against each other. They continued moving as if in a choreographed dance, and Crane remained entranced by the whole thing. When it all ended with Davina pinning Torin against the ground, Crane had to blink and recall what exactly brought about that result. It had all happened so quickly.

"And that's how you bring down a war general," Davina said, holding her hand out to Torin.

He swatted her hand aside and stood on his own. "I won't go easy on you next time," Torin grumbled.

Davina laughed. "Believe what you want." She flipped her hair over her shoulder as she left the sparring circle that had been created by the guards. "Crane's turn," she called to Torin over her shoulder.

Crane startled, forgetting that he also had offered to spar with Torin. After watching the match between him and Davina, Crane feared he was far from capable of handling the war general.

"What are you waiting for?" Torin beckoned him into the circle.

Crane stumbled forward, his feet catching over the change in elevation between the grass and the gravel area that demarcated the training ring. A hand clamped onto his arm, steadying him. He glanced down to see perfectly manicured nails gripping his upper arm and his eyes flicked up to find Davina staring back at him, her blue irises shining bright and washing out the light gray color that surrounded them. He'd forgotten how quickly shreeve could move and hadn't even heard her approach.

"This one should be easy for you, Tor," she joked, one side of her mouth pulling up as she looked Crane up and down. "I'd like a go at him when you're finished."

Crane pulled out of her grip and held his head high as he marched into the center of the circle. He wouldn't let her get in his head.

"Here." Torin handed Crane a sword and took a few steps back. Crane adjusted his stance, considering the best way to go against a stronger and faster opponent. Though Mylah hadn't been in her best form before leaving for Hyrdian, she had held her own against shreeve in the past. If she could learn to fight them effectively, he could too.

"Ready," Crane said, gripping his sword tightly near the pommel with both hands and swinging it a few times to get a feel for the weight of it.

Torin waited a moment before advancing. Crane could tell that Torin was going easy on him, and he appreciated it. Normally, he would be annoyed, but he didn't know the shreeves' advantages and fighting styles well enough yet to go all out.

"You're not too bad, for a human," Torin commented, smirking at the last word.

He began to move faster, and Crane kept up smoothly. When Torin started to put more strength behind his blows, Crane faltered, but adjusted as well. Though Torin wore an eye patch over his right eye, he never faltered from attacks Crane attempted at that angle.

Stepping back as Torin made an upward swing with his sword, Crane noted that instead of the usual stance with the left foot ahead of the right foot, Torin stood the opposite way. *His right leg may be weaker...* Crane thought, trying to piece together a plan of attack.

After a moment of contemplation, Crane swung his sword up at a right angle to parry Torin's attack, exposing Torin's right side. Kicking out with his left foot, he struck Torin in the knee, buckling it. Torin swore as his knee hit the ground but was up again before Crane could take advantage of his blunder.

"You and Mylah are similar fighters," Torin commented, as they circled each other. "She pulled a similar move on me when we first fought."

Crane laughed. "I taught her everything she knows," he said. Though, Garrick had been the one who had trained them. Crane shook away the memory of his father and the sting it caused, trying to refocus on the fight.

They kept at it for a while longer, until Crane put up his hand to stop the match.

"I think I need a break," Crane admitted as his heart hammered in his chest. His breathing had become labored from the effort of keeping Torin at bay.

Torin stopped and put his arms out to his sides. "Anyone else want to take a turn while Crane recovers?" he asked, and no one stepped forward. "Come on, you're all going to have to go against me eventually."

Crane stepped out of the circle and found a bench in the garden nearby. He sat down, closing his eyes, and leaning his head back, letting the sun beat down on him and dry the sweat that poured from him.

"You held your own pretty well out there," Davina's voice found him along with the sound of her dress swishing as it moved across the grass.

"Not well enough," Crane grumbled, opening his eyes to find her standing before him.

He noticed she'd tied her hair back, a few strands framing her face. She wore a shawl over her dress now. The sun had chased away most of the chill in the air, but it was still a fall day. She sat beside him and draped her arm over the back of the bench as she angled herself towards him.

"Don't beat yourself up too much. Torin is a formidable opponent, even by shreeve standards," she said.

"That doesn't make me feel too much better but thank you." Crane leaned forward, placing his elbows on his knees and his head in his hands. "I need to be able to take on any opponent, no matter their skill level. If Queen Aveda is helping King Florian, we will be going up against fae, who are as strong, and fast as you all are."

"Some are stronger and faster," Davina pointed out. "But I get your point."

"I need to be able to protect the people I love. I need to be able to ensure that no one else gets hurt...or..." He shuddered and the weight of grief became crushing as he thought of his father.

Davina placed a hand on his shoulder and leaned in closer. "We've all lost someone, you're not alone. We all want to protect those we care about," she spoke quietly. Her brow creased, disrupting her flawless features, making her seem almost human. Crane wondered whom she had lost.

"We will be ready when the time comes."

"I heard the others talking about how you attacked Mylah before," Crane said.

Davina drew her hand back, a scowl marring her lips. "So what if I did? She was a *spy*. So, I was in the right to think she didn't belong here." She picked at her nails trying to seem unbothered, but Crane saw through it.

"Why did you really attack her? It couldn't have been because of some petty jealousy. You don't seem the type." Crane had only known Davina for a few days, but there was something about her that reminded him of Cassia. It could be the flair for the dramatic, or her ability to seem unbothered by everything.

Davina raised a brow at his comment. "Don't I?" She placed a hand over her heart. "Everyone else seems to think that's all I'm made up of. Jealousy, vanity, greed." She ticked them off on her fingers as she listed them. "It's the reason my family thought all I was good for was a potential connection to the throne." Her eyes darkened as she spoke and Crane leaned back, matching her casual posture, and angling himself towards her.

"I think that's what you *want* people to think," he said.

"And you know me so well, after having one conversation with me, do you?" Irritation brimmed in her voice and Crane knew he'd struck a nerve, so he backed down.

"You're right. I know nothing about you, except that you're an excellent fighter." Crane stood from the bench, knowing the conversation had ended now that Davina had closed herself off. "I hope you're still up for a match once

Torin's finished." He walked away before she could respond. He could see in her that she yearned to prove herself and he'd help her do that if he could.

He paused as he approached the circle of guards, struck with the realization that he was beginning to *care* for Davina, along with everyone else who inhabited the castle. The ease in which he had allowed his walls to come down here, he wondered if that was how it had happened for Mylah when she'd been there as a spy. Slowly, without much effort or thought, before it hit you like a wave.

Later that day, Bellingham found Crane as he was readying to leave with his mother for the Unbound territory.

"Briar told me you wanted to see me," Bellingham said, hovering before Crane outside his bedroom door. Crane shut the door behind him, and they began down the hallway.

"Yes, I wanted to ask a favor of you, but it's not something to take lightly," Crane warned.

"I'm intrigued. What is it?"

"I'm hoping to have someone who can deliver messages between myself and Cassia in Adair."

To Bellingham's credit he didn't react.

"Ah. I see..." Bellingham mused.

"I understand if this isn't a risk you want to take."

"That's not it. I don't mind taking the risk." Bellingham tapped his chin as if in deep thought.

Crane continued, "Well, I understand either way, if you choose not to help and return to the Unbounds."

Bellingham sighed, "I will not stand aside and let people die when I could have helped stop it. I will help you. Write your letter, give it to Briar and she will get it to me. I would remain in the castle myself, but I'm not exactly a fan of King Castien."

"He is...different. But I will do as you say. I'm on my way to the Unbounds now with my mother, if you would like to accompany us."

"I have some business to attend to in town, otherwise I would."

"Thank you for your help. I don't think you realize how much I appreciate this." Crane missed Cassia, more than he had when he'd been a guard on the Adair border. He'd known then he would be returning home and see her every so often. Now... He didn't know when he'd see her again.

Bellingham left Crane behind as Crane stopped outside Elena's room. Crane knocked once before she threw open the door. She wore a long, billowing, bright green gown, and a matching green overcoat. Her hair had been tied back into a tight knot and she smiled as her eyes found his.

"Ready?" she asked, her voice high and breathless.

"Yes," Crane replied as he tried to look over her shoulder to see what she had been up to before he'd knocked, but there was nothing out of the ordinary to be seen other than some fighting leathers strewn across her chair. He'd never seen his mother wear fighting leathers, but he supposed they'd all need them for the impending fight. Elena swept past him into the hall, slamming her door behind her. Crane followed her to the courtyard where two guards waited for them.

"Elena, Crane," one of the guards greeted them, inclining his head. Crane thought his name was Nic, but he couldn't be sure. There were so many guards to remember.

"This is Alec." Nic waved to the guard Crane hadn't yet met.

"Nice to make your acquaintance." Alec dipped his head to them as well. Elena beamed at Nic and Alec. Horses waited beyond them.

"There are only two horses," Crane pointed out. He'd rode their horses before without help, it was difficult to stay on when they moved at full speed, but it was manageable.

"Yes. These were the only two that could be spared," Nic explained.

"That will be fine. Shall we be going?" Elena asked as she fidgeted with her long sleeves, anxious to get moving.

Nic waved towards the horses and Elena walked up to one. He helped her up and climbed up behind her. Alec mounted his horse and Crane sighed, realizing he'd be on the back of the horse.

Once they were moving, Crane didn't mind riding with Alec. It gave him a chance to relax and take in his surroundings rather than worry about staying on course or staying on the horse. After passing the town, the horses broke into a full paced run which left Crane breathless, as it always did. If he were ever able to return to Adair, he certainly wouldn't miss the enchanted horses.

Tall pine trees rose in the distance and as they approached them, the horses slowed. They maneuvered through the trees easily enough but couldn't go at full speed or they'd be much more likely to trip or crash into something.

Trotting through the forest, Crane kept seeing glimpses of wings or little heads poking out. He assumed they were pixies, but they moved too fast for him to get a good look. None of them bothered the group moving through the forest, though. As soon as they cleared the forest, the horses broke into a full run again and they reached the lake within minutes.

After dismounting, Elena drifted towards the lake's edge, allowing the water to lap at the hem of her dress. Crane couldn't help thinking she looked ethereal out here, almost as if she belonged there, rather than cooped up in a castle.

"How do we call her?" Elena asked and Nic stepped forward, clearing his throat.

"Genevieve, Lady of the Lake," he called out over the water. At first, nothing happened, and they all stood in silence, anticipation filling the air around them. A ripple broke the smooth surface of the lake and a head of violet hair emerged. Matching violet eyes peered over the water before she lifted the rest of her head and grinned at them as the water rolled off her glistening brown skin.

"How daring," she purred. "How *bold*," she hissed and bared pointed teeth that had appeared normal only a few seconds earlier. Her eyes turned a deeper shade of purple, so dark they were almost black. Everyone but Elena took a step back.

"Genevieve," Elena breathed, and the siren's eyes met hers, her mouth closing slightly. "I came to say thank you."

Though Crane could not see his mother's face, he could hear the sorrow in her voice. He stepped up beside her and Genevieve cocked her head to the side. As her eyes roved over Crane, they widened and returned to their normal violet color.

"You are..." Genevieve began but tears filled her eyes. "Elena," she said, and Elena nodded. "I heard... I heard what happened to Garrick. Bellingham told me."

Crane put his arm around his mother as tears streamed down her cheeks. "We wanted to thank you for the role you played in our escape. We may not have made it out if not for you drawing away half of the royal guards." Crane finished for his mother since she could no longer speak through her grief.

"You're welcome." Genevieve dipped her head slightly and shoulders tensed, making Crane realize how powerful her arm muscles were. Strong enough to drag a few men to the depths of the lake, he presumed and shuddered at the thought.

"Would you mind telling me stories?" Elena choked out and Crane furrowed his brow as he flicked his eyes to her.

"Stories?" Genevieve asked and Elena bobbed her head.

"About him. About Garrick."

"Of course, dear. Come, sit." Genevieve waved her hand to a nearby rock and Elena took a seat, pulling her knees to her chest, appearing more childlike than Crane had ever seen her.

His heart broke looking at her. She had been so strong his entire life, and now, since losing Garrick, she seemed to be slowly unraveling. He wasn't sure how much longer she'd be able to hold herself together. Not having Greyson around didn't help. That would be his priority once he established contact with Cassia, he decided. He would find a way to speak with Greyson so that he could help his mother heal.

Genevieve and his mother were laughing as Crane walked back to stand with Nic and Alec. He had no interest in hearing stories about his father's adventures. It hurt enough thinking about him, he didn't need to be reminded of all he had lost.

Crane talked about mundane things with Nic and Alec while they waited. After Elena finished talking with Genevieve, Genevieve motioned for Crane to come closer. The others all returned to their horses.

"What is it?" he asked, trying to avoid stepping into the water.

"I don't trust the others, they're shreeve after all, and I didn't want to worry your mother," Genevieve paused as she glanced towards Elena, concern creasing her brows. "I have one of my girls scouting around Snake Head Lake every few days to see if she can catch any word from Adair. This last time she was lucky, and a few soldiers were passing by on their way out to the border. She caught some of their conversation." The grimace that Genevieve now wore had Crane's pulse quickening at the thought of more trouble in Adair. He couldn't help but worry about Cassia and the fact that if the king realized she was corresponding with Crane, she'd be punished for treason.

"They were talking about Queen Aveda and feared that she holds the power in Adair over King Florian right now. Apparently, she's been the one leading all the council meetings and they were wary of her intentions."

"We could have guessed as much," Crane said, his heart rate slowing at the realization that the news wouldn't affect Cassia too much. "She is a powerful woman."

"She is more than that, she is also a vengeful woman. And those two traits combined create a lethal woman. Do not underestimate her and do not let her gain any leverage over you. She is one who likes to play on your worst fears and use them against you," Genevieve warned. "As someone who has known her since she was young, I know not to trust a single word out of her mouth." Though Crane wanted to ask her more on that topic, he knew better than to pry.

"Thank you for the warning, I shall pass it on to King Castien." Crane dipped his head to her, and she waved her hand through the air.

"King Castien can do as he pleases. It's not him I worry for. Garrick held a special place in my heart, and I will always look out for his family."

"And we will return the favor," Crane promised.

Genevieve smirked. "I can take care of myself. Stay safe, Crane." She drifted backward before slipping beneath the surface of the lake. The ripples slowly spread thin, and Genevieve did not resurface. Crane sighed and turned his back on the lake, rejoining the others near the horses.

That night at dinner, Elena wore a smile for the first time in a while. No one at the table mentioned her brighter disposition, but Crane caught them all smiling in her direction once or twice. All except Castien, of course. Crane worked up the nerve to ask how the speech had gone and he received an indecipherable grumbling from Castien.

"The people have not been appeased," Davina provided instead. Crane turned his gaze to her and waited as she continued. "They accepted Elias' position more readily, but Mylah... Not so much. As you may have noticed on your way back from the Unbounds, there were still quite a few people outside the gate demanding justice." Crane hadn't noticed, but they hadn't been brought past the front gate. They'd gone to the side gate which led to the servants' entrance, which now he understood was so they could avoid being exposed to those people.

"They will come around, I'm sure," Crane said, trying to sound hopeful. He couldn't blame the people of Elowyn for being wary of someone who had set out to betray their entire kingdom.

"How was your venture into the Unbounds?" Castien asked, changing the subject.

"Uneventful. Though, Genevieve did have a warning," Crane began. His eyes flicked to his mother as he decided whether she could handle the truth or not. *She deserved to know what is happening in Adair*, he thought. "Apparently some of the Adairian soldiers are afraid that Queen Aveda is the one in control of Adair now."

"If they are *afraid* of her, then maybe they would turn on her," Davina pointed out. "It could work in our favor."

"That is simple minded," Torin retorted, and Davina visibly flinched, but she shrugged as if she didn't care. "King Florian is who they are loyal to, and they will side with whomever he sides with. Besides, fear is a tactic often used to force loyalty. The soldiers will not turn against her for fear that she will punish their loved ones."

"Not everyone has loved ones to worry about," Davina mumbled, stabbing her fork into a piece of meat on her plate. Crane wanted to reach across the table and take her hand to comfort her, but he guessed that would only upset her further. From what he had learned of her in the short time they'd spent together, she was not one to want help from anyone else.

"Genevieve also said that she has known Queen Aveda since the Queen was young, so maybe she has more information we could use against her," Crane said, taking the attention away from Davina.

Disgraced

"Noted," Castien said, though his eyes remained on his plate. "Crane, after dinner, meet me in my study."

Before Crane could ask why, Castien stood from the table and strode out of the dining room. Everyone else seemed to settle back into their own thoughts for the remainder of dinner.

Crane did as Castien had asked and met him in his study once he'd finished eating. It was time to write his first letter to Cassia.

He wrote about ten different letters before deciding on the right words. Castien had watched over his shoulder as he'd written them, ensuring that Crane wasn't giving away any vital information. His bad mood had soured the air and brought tension upon Crane, making him irritable. But they'd finished the task.

Cassia,

I miss you. I'm sorry I couldn't see you before we left, there was no time. Bellingham has agreed to be a courier for us, so we can communicate. I wish I could come to you myself, but there is no way I wouldn't get caught.

If you have any news about King Florian's plans, I hope you will share them with me. We've been lied to all our lives. He's not the man we thought he was. He plans on wiping out the entire shreeve race and needs to be stopped.

If you have any information about Greyson, too, my mother is suffering and in need of something to lift her spirits.

Again, I'm sorry. I will see you again, I promise. There is nothing that can keep me from you. If you have any sense that the king will turn on your family, you can find refuge here. I will ensure it.

Castien raised an eyebrow at that line but said nothing to the contrary.

Trust no one.

Love,
Crane

He had wanted to write so much more. More on how he pictured her every night in his dreams, how she filled his waking thoughts and how he heard her voice sometimes when he was alone. But those words would have to wait until they could be together again.

Finding Briar in the garden was easy. She took the letter away into the night, on a mission to find Bellingham. Crane watched her go and thought about what he may do to repay her and Bellingham. Without them, he would have gone to Adair himself to speak with Cassia again, and he couldn't do that to his mother. Turning, he trudged back into the castle to find himself a drink.

Eleven

Mylah and Elias rode to Korrindale the next morning, and again, Elias said nothing about Mylah having to ride with him. His lack of complaint or a disgruntled comment had her suspicious. So, unable to ignore his change of disposition, she decided to pry.

"Should we stop somewhere to see if we can get another horse?" she asked, once they had slowed and a conversation could be held without screaming over the wind.

"It seems unnecessary," he said, but he stiffened under her hold. She loosened her grip on him and leaned away slightly, though her front still rested against his back. There was no way to avoid that on the horse.

"I guess," Mylah said, wondering if she should pry any further, but her curiosity would always get the better of her. "I thought maybe you might like your own...space." He shuddered and from behind, Mylah couldn't tell if it was from laughter or anger.

"If you'd like to take the time to find another horse, be my guest. I, on the other hand, have too much else to worry about and too little time to deal with it all."

Ah. So that was all it was – a matter of convenience, not acceptance.

"No, you're right. I'm sorry I asked. I just thought…" she trailed off.

Elias finished for her, "You thought maybe I'd forgiven you? Maybe because I'm forced to be here with you, that everything you did would fade into the past?" His words cut straight to her heart and left an aching wound there. Despite the risk of falling, she dropped her arms to her sides, gripping the saddle instead of Elias.

The tall, brick clock tower of Korrindale came into view, followed by the vast expanse of buildings, stalls, and streets.

"Let me off here, I'll go find myself a horse while you meet with Farren," she said, steam practically coming out of her ears as her blood boiled at the thought of spending another second with Elias. He stopped the horse and Mylah jumped down, sending a jolt up her legs.

"You don't have any money," he pointed out.

"That seems like my problem. You worry about yourself," she spat before stomping towards the nearest shop. It looked like a bakery, and she pushed her way through the crowd that had gathered beside it. At the front, she realized that everyone had stopped to stare at a young woman who played her fiddle beside the door. Mylah stopped to watch as well.

The woman, who didn't appear to be much older than twenty-five, had long, thick, curly hair that was wound up into a pile atop her head. The curls were much more intense and tighter than Mylah's wavelike curls. Sweat gleamed on the woman's light brown skin and her eyes were closed as she swayed to the music streaming from her instrument.

The music, that sounded like a lilting lullaby from a time long past, had captivated the crowd and they all swayed along with the woman, some of them dropping coins into the fiddle case that laid open at the woman's feet. Mylah had the fleeting thought that she could grab some of the coins while everyone was distracted, but guilt gnawed at her just thinking about it. She'd find another way to afford a horse. She continued into the bakery and the delicious scent of cinnamon and pastries hit her like a wave, making her salivate.

"How can I help you?" The man behind the counter grinned up at her.

He had to be at least a foot shorter than Mylah, which after spending so much time with the shreeve who tended to be taller, both shocked and relieved her. In Elowyn, almost everyone was taller than her, even though in Adair she'd been of average height. She pasted a smile on and stepped up to the glass case that displayed all the delicious and decadent treats available.

"Hmmm...everything looks so amazing," Mylah murmured. She knew she had a few coins somewhere in her crossbody satchel, and what little she had wouldn't be much help in buying a horse anyway.

"Today's special is this chocolate croissant," the man said, waving his hand over the platter of croissants beside him.

"I would love one!" Mylah said, and the man put one onto a napkin before handing it to her.

"Is this your first time in town?" the man asked, looking her up and down.

"Yes," she nodded as she reached into her satchel to find her coins.

"Well, this one is on the house," he said, putting his hand out to stop Mylah from dropping her coins onto the counter. "Just be sure to tell all your family and friends about us." He winked and turned back to the counter behind him where he continued preparing more goodies.

"Thank you," Mylah said before ducking out the front door.

The crowd had dispersed and the woman who played the fiddle was bent down over her fiddle case, collecting the coins she'd been given.

"You're very good," Mylah commented, though she figured the woman heard that all the time.

The woman's face turned up towards her. Mylah was surprised to see the lilac color that surrounded her deeper purple iris. She hadn't been expecting a shreeve.

"That's why I tend to close my eyes when I play out here," the woman said, chuckling and Mylah realized her shock had shown plainly on her face. She reddened.

"Sorry. I didn't see any markings, and I've been in Elowyn for so long now ~" Mylah started, but the woman cut her off.

"You're from Elowyn?"

"Well, no, I'm from Adair, but I live in Elowyn now. It's a long story. I'm Mylah." Mylah stuck her hand out, trying to erase the awkwardness from before.

The woman gave her a once over but stood upright with her fiddle case and shook her hand. "Raelynn. It's not often I meet anyone from Elowyn around here. I haven't been back there since...well since King Castien took the throne." Raelynn's lip curled as she mentioned the name.

"You don't like him, I assume?" Mylah had yet to learn all the reasons people had for disliking Castien, but she figured not many of them could top her own, and she'd been able to forgive him for that.

"Not after he killed my brother, no. I don't care for him," Raelynn said.

I guess that does equate to my own experience, Mylah thought. "I'm so sorry for your loss," she said. "If you don't mind me asking, what exactly happened?"

"I do mind, actually. I'd rather not talk about it." Raelynn stepped back and flattened her hand against her side, pressing down the wrinkles in her gown, which was the same lilac color as her eyes. It grazed her ankles and Mylah realized she had bare feet.

"I'm sorry. I'll leave you alone, I just... I forget myself sometimes." Mylah inclined her head to Raelynn and took a step away from her.

It had been so long since she'd talked to someone who didn't want to answer her questions, even after becoming a traitor. Castien, Torin, or Crane had always been ready to talk or listen and now she had none of them. Elias barely tolerated her and only strangers surrounded her now.

Raelynn turned away from Mylah and gave her a slight wave before disappearing around the bend in the road. Mylah tore into her croissant, trying to drown the emotions churning in her, but to no avail. Once the croissant was gone, Mylah went in search of a tavern or bar. She knew there had to be one somewhere, and she found one on the second street she checked. People streamed past her as she fumbled with the door, realizing there was no handle and she only had to push it to open it. Her cheeks blazed from embarrassment, but no one said anything to help or jest at the poor girl who entered the tavern before noon to drown her sorrows.

"I think you have the wrong place," a low, gruff voice sounded right beside Mylah making her jump.

The man chuckled and pointed back out the door. In the dimly lit room, his face remained mostly hidden in shadows, and he stood beside the door with his arms crossed over his wide chest. Mylah assumed he must be a guard of some sort.

"No, this is where I'm meant to be," she said, standing a little taller and straightening her shoulders to appear older.

"Take a seat then, my apologies," he said.

He didn't appear sorry, only slightly annoyed, but he waved to all the empty tables. The only seats occupied in the place were along the bar itself which took up the whole left side of the tavern. Only the sorriest of men and women frequented the taverns during the day, and Mylah could officially count herself among them.

Mylah made her way to the bar, taking one of the seats separated from any other patrons. The bartender took his time getting to her and she didn't mind. As he took orders for the others, it stole their attention from Mylah, and eventually they all ignored her presence, just as she wished it. She fiddled with the ruby ring on her finger while she waited and wondered what Castien and the others were up to.

"What can I get for ya?" the bartender asked when he finally stood in front of her. She gazed up at him and noticed pointed ears poking out from his coarse, gray hair. He had no wrinkles or signs of age, but he wasn't quite as explicitly *handsome* as the fae and shreeve she'd seen in the past.

"Hello?" He snapped his fingers at her.

"Sorry. Whiskey, please?"

A few hours later, all thoughts of buying a horse forgotten, Mylah stumbled out of the tavern. The sun had begun to descend in the sky, but it still shone brightly, lighting her way. Though, she had no idea where she was going. Mylah tripped over the cobblestones that made up the streets and found herself caught between two strong, but lithe arms.

"Woah," the familiar voice said, and pushed Mylah back into a standing position. Raelynn wrinkled her nose and wiped her hands on the front of her dress as if tainted. She still held her fiddle case in one hand, and Mylah assumed she'd just finished playing somewhere else.

"Sorry," Mylah managed to say. "Thank you." She went to move past Raelynn, but the woman caught her arm and pulled her back.

"You shouldn't be out here in your state." She glanced around and sighed, "Come with me."

Raelynn draped one of Mylah's arms over her shoulders and helped her down a street lined with residential buildings. There hadn't been homes like those in Adair or Elowyn. Everyone had their own homes, or no home in some cases. But these residential buildings were made up of multiple families, all living in the same house, similar to the inn.

Raelynn reached into the pocket of her dress and pulled out a key, sliding it into one of the doors along the front of the building. Inside, she dropped the key onto a table by the door. Mylah gaped at her surroundings. It was like any other house she'd been into, with a kitchen to the right, and a sitting room to the left. But attached to other homes.

"Strange..." Mylah said as Raelynn removed Mylah's arm from her shoulders.

"The houses? No other place in Olliria has anything like them. It makes it so we can fit more people in a smaller area, so we don't need to disturb too much of the surrounding woodland areas. Too many creatures would be displaced." Raelynn waved towards the sitting room before veering towards the kitchen. "Go have a seat. I'll get you some water and something to eat."

Mylah dropped onto a thick, plush couch that melded to her body shape. It felt like a warm hug and her eyes drifted closed as she sank into it.

"Here," Raelynn said.

Mylah's eyes popped open to find Raelynn holding out a glass of water and a plate of muffins towards her.

"Thank you." Mylah drank the water greedily while Raelynn set the plate onto the small table in front of Mylah.

"Eat up and rest, I'll check on you in a while. I have an errand to run."

Raelynn left the room and Mylah splayed out on the couch. A blanket was draped over the arm of the couch and Mylah grabbed it, pulling it over herself, and fell asleep shortly after.

Twelve

Elias yearned to turn back and make Mylah come with him, but he forced himself to stay on route to the school. *She wanted to go,* he reminded himself. *Only because I made her feel unwanted.* The second thought brought with it the rush of guilt that had overwhelmed him the second those words had left his mouth. 'You thought maybe I'd forgiven you?'

He wasn't sure why he'd said it. Things had been fine, not great, but fine, up until that point, and he'd had to go and ruin it.

After learning that Castien had murdered Mylah's parents, Elias had wanted to go straight to her. He wanted to forgive her for everything, and apologize for not realizing sooner she'd only been trying to avenge her parents and save the ones who'd taken her in.

But he hadn't gone to her.

Instead, he hid in his room, packing for Hyrdian, and trying to figure out why he couldn't bring himself to go to her. Something held him back, and he wasn't ready to forgive her yet.

When he saw her the next day as they were preparing to leave, he realized what it was: Torin. Mylah had been spending her nights with one of his best friends, someone like a brother to him. As much as he wished he could be happy for them, jealousy and regret stung too keenly to let it go so easily.

The school of magic rose up before Elias, bringing him back to his senses and reminding him why he was there. A few students roamed the grounds, but it was still fairly empty.

Farren waited in his office, surrounded by stacks of parchments. He set a stack aside as Elias entered and removed his glasses as he pinched the brim of his nose.

"These kids are going to be the death of me," Farren mumbled. "You'd think, after eighteen or more years in school, they'd have some idea of how to write a basic essay?"

"Sorry?" Elias asked, unsure what Farren wanted him to say. Farren waved a hand through the air and motioned for Elias to sit in one of the chairs before his desk.

"Never mind all that. Let's talk about your magic." Steepling his hands before him, Farren narrowed his eyes on Elias. "Shreeve warlocks are not unheard of, but they are more common in other parts of the world. Here in Olliria, we're all so separated that shreeve and witches or warlocks don't mingle often."

"So, what does that mean for me?" Elias tensed as Farren frowned at his question.

"It means we don't have a whole lot of knowledge to understand the kind of magic you may possess," Farren admitted. Elias was about to respond when Farren clapped his hands together and grinned, which confused him. "So that means we get to do some research!"

"You seem all too happy about that," Elias said, leaning away from the man who clearly got too excited when it came to academia.

"Nonsense! Research is fun!" Farren stood and strolled over to his bookcase. "At least, that's what I keep trying to tell my students."

"I assume most of them don't agree with you?" Elias laughed to himself when Farren didn't respond.

Grabbing a book off the shelf, Farren returned with it to his desk. A purple, glowing hand on the cover caught Elias' attention. The words *'Mysterio Magical'* curved around the hand.

Farren flipped the book open and began scanning the table of contents. Stopping near the bottom, he nodded his head and turned to the page he'd chosen.

"A spell to test your level of magic," Farren explained before reaching out across the desk and placing his hand down, palm up.

"Do you want me to…" Elias trailed off as Farren nodded. Placing his hand palm down in Farren's, Elias felt an itching sensation spreading from his palm up his arm. "What's happening?" Elias whispered, worried he'd break Farren's concentration and ruin whatever spell he was performing.

"Not all spells need to be spoken aloud to be used," Farren said, which didn't exactly answer Elias' question. "I'm sensing what level of magic you possess, which if I'm correct, is quite powerful."

Farren closed his eyes and Elias remained silent as he waited for Farren to finish. After about a minute, Farren opened his eyes and removed his hand from Elias'.

"Your magic is at the same level, if not slightly higher, than your father's." There was a note of surprise in Farren's voice.

"You said my father was one of the greatest warlocks in Hyrdian," Elias pointed out, shaken by this revelation.

"Yes. I did, and he was. I didn't say he was the most powerful, though." Farren lifted a finger and pointed to a picture on the wall beside his desk. "That honor belongs to those three." Elias studied the picture and noticed a plaque underneath with '*Governing Council*' engraved on it.

"They are Hyrdian's council?" Elias asked, even though he knew the answer.

"Yes. Your father should have been among them, but he chose to continue working here instead. That is what set him apart from the others, making him the greatest; his selflessness and quest for knowledge."

Elias couldn't help but scoff at that, making Farren raise his brows.

"You think he should have given up his position here, teaching the future witches and warlocks of our society, to join the council?"

"I think that on the council he would have been able to do more for the people here," Elias said.

Farren shook his head. "There is much you need to learn about Hyrdian's politics before you speak on that topic, *Prince*."

Elias' cheeks heated as he realized that Farren was right, he knew little to nothing about the politics of Hyrdian and what the council actually had authority over. He always assumed they were akin to a king or sovereign, with all the power to do as they pleased.

"I would much appreciate if you taught me more about it while I'm here," Elias said, bowing his head to Farren.

"Let's focus on your magic first." Farren turned to the next page in the book sitting before him and scanned it quickly. "We now know how powerful you have the potential to be, but we need to figure out how to harness all that power."

Elias leaned forward, trying to catch a glimpse of the words on the page, but upside down, he couldn't make it out easy enough.

"Did you do as I told you to when you left here yesterday?" Farren asked.

Elias pulled the book Farren had given him from his satchel and placed it on the desk. "I did as you said and had the most success when I used my emotions to help call out my magic."

"That is common for most witches and warlocks, but it is not the most reliable way to go about it. It is a good place to start, though, so show me what you practiced." Farren leaned back in his chair and waited as Elias tried to call out his magic.

Focusing on the happiest memory he had, a time he and Castien had been out playing in the Unbounds, he was able to manifest a blue orb of magic in his palm.

"Well, that's something," Farren said, seeming unimpressed. "What emotion are you using to manipulate that?"

"Happiness," Elias said.

Farren pursed his lips. "Not strong enough." He walked to his bookshelf once more and grabbed another book, bringing it back and placing it in Elias' lap.

"Look in there and tell me what you see," he said before returning to his seat on the other side of the desk.

Elias sighed but opened the book as he was told. Flipping through the pages, he realized it was a picture book made up of images of witches and warlocks using their magic. Their magic manifested in all different colors, shapes, and magnitudes.

"What is this?" he asked, finding Farren's gaze once more.

"Those were all taken during a research study on the different types of magic. Notice not everyone has a visible magic source coming from them." Farren leaned over and pointed to one of the pictures on the page. It was of a woman who stood, her hands at her sides and a smirk on her lips, but with no seeming magic emanating from her.

"What kind of magic did she wield?" Elias asked.

"The same kind as Illiana, the hairdresser who sent you to me," Farren said.

Elias opened his mouth to ask how Farren knew they had been to see her, but he continued talking before Elias could cut in.

"She is a good friend of my wife's and informed us that someone had asked about me," Farren explained. "But her magic is one that cannot be seen, only felt. Illiana is able to manipulate people's emotions, even without trying. If you get close to her, you will notice your mood start to change, or maybe feel as if you want to spill all your secrets to her."

"I wouldn't know, Mylah is the one who talked with her," Elias said. Mylah hadn't mentioned anything about it to him, but then again, they weren't speaking much about anything when they were together. Guilt gnawed at him again. He'd be sure to apologize to her about his blunder earlier.

"Well, those with this kind of magic are often recruited for guards or armies. Since Hyrdian hasn't had need of armies for hundreds of years, witches like Illiana are able to choose their own paths."

"I know a shreeve who has a similar power," Elias said, thinking of Ana. "She is able to manipulate emotions as well."

"All magic, be it born of witches, warlocks, fae or shreeve, comes from the same place: the land. Witches and warlocks have an easier time harnessing all the types of magic, while fae and shreeve are often limited to being able to harness only fractions or pieces of the magic. And, as you know, a shreeve's magic is more potent during the day, which is the universe's way of keeping some balance."

"You are a warlock, yet you can only perform basic spells?" Elias asked, hoping it didn't come off as insulting.

"I may be able to do a variety of different types of magic, but my own source within is fairly small and so I can only manage basic magic before my source is empty," Farren explained.

"So, in essence, my source is much larger than most?" Elias asked.

Farren nodded. "Which is why we have to be careful when we start testing your limits." Standing, Farren came around the desk and waved to Elias to stand as well. "We have a magic proofed gym in the basement of the school that we can practice in today. Come on."

After hours of practice, Elias had barely learned anything about the depth of his magic. Farren kept telling him that he was letting fear hold him back, but he'd been unable to overcome that hurdle. They decided to call it a day and pick up again in the morning.

Farren invited Elias to dinner with him and his wife at their house, and though Elias worried about where Mylah had wound up, he agreed. She could take care of herself.

"I want you to work on some of the other methods of calling out your magic in your downtime," Farren said as they entered his home.

"I'll try, but as I said, the only one that made any kind of difference was when I –" Elias paused as a young woman appeared on their right in the entryway to what looked like the kitchen.

"Hush," she said, putting her finger to her lips and pointing into the room across the way where someone slept on a couch.

"What– Oh!" Farren said, lowering his voice. "We have another guest?"

The other guest sat up slowly on the couch, putting a hand to their head and grabbing a glass of water from the table before them.

"Raelynn?" the person called out, their voice cracking, and Elias realized he recognized the voice.

Raelynn walked across the hall to the living room.

"Oh good, you're awake. Dinner is almost ready, if you'd like to join us," Raelynn offered, turning on a light in the hallway. It streamed into the room and Elias' suspicion was confirmed as he saw Mylah sitting there, squinting against the light.

Elias could tell she'd been drinking, and his heart dropped into his stomach. *I was too hard on her this morning*, he thought, but then backtracked. *She made her own choice to drink.*

"Sorry," Raelynn said, though she smiled.

"I should be going..." Mylah rose from the couch and shuffled towards the hall. She clearly hadn't seen Elias yet.

"Rae, shall I finish the potatoes?" Farren asked, stepping into Mylah's line of sight. He grinned at her, and her eyes widened in surprise.

"This is Mylah, dear." Raelynn held her hand out towards her.

"We've met," he said, tipping his head to her and Mylah groaned inwardly.

"Sorry about Mylah, she has a bit of a drinking problem as of late." Elias walked forward to join them and Mylah closed her eyes. A whole host of emotions washed over Elias. Regret, embarrassment, guilt...but he ignored them all and kept a straight face.

"We all have our share of demons to drown," Farren said, winking at Mylah. "Let's hope yours have been fully sated for a while."

"Yes," Elias said, grinding his teeth to hold back his frustration.

Farren and Raelynn turned back into the kitchen and Elias followed, though he considered leaving right then and there.

"How did today go?" Mylah asked as she walked up behind him.

"Well. Farren has high hopes that I'll be able to learn to control my magic quickly once I overcome a certain... Obstacle." Elias didn't want to admit to his fear. "He doesn't think it will take much more than a month." Elias stared down at the table as he took a seat rather than look at Mylah.

"A month?" Mylah balked and Elias narrowed his eyes at her.

"You used to tell me I should learn to control my magic, rather than suppress it. Now that I'm doing that, you think I should give up because it will take too long for you?" Irritation bloomed in him, and he didn't lift his head, but his eyes found hers.

"That's not what I meant. I just..." She stopped, leaving her sentence unfinished. "A month is fine. I can find someone who knows about what's going on in the mountains while you train. That way, once you're done, we can leave."

"Eager to leave us behind so quickly?" Farren joked as he set down two plates of potatoes on the table. Raelynn sidled up beside him and placed a plate of meat between the other plates. "It will only take a month for him to learn to control his magic, but it will take much longer for him to learn how to use it properly."

"As much as I'd love to stay and take in the sights," Mylah said, leaning back in her chair. "We're needed back in Elowyn."

"Ah, yes. The war Elias mentioned."

"You mean you didn't know about it before?" Mylah's brows rose and she frowned.

Elias had been surprised as well, when he'd mentioned the war to Farren, and he had been unaware that there was anything going on.

"Well, it hasn't been so much of a war as a border skirmish up until now, hasn't it?" Raelynn pointed out.

"I guess...but it would affect you too," Mylah said. Elias cleared his throat to stop Mylah from giving away too many details and her head jerked towards him.

"This is delicious," he said, changing the subject. Mylah pursed her lips but said nothing. Elias hadn't told her that Elowyn had kept the fact that they had lost the Book of Creation a secret from the rest of the continent. Though, they would need to reveal that information to the council to ensure they knew how dire the situation was when it came to finding aide for the war.

"You wouldn't happen to know how we could get in contact with the Hyrdian council, would you?" Elias asked, and Farren nodded.

"I actually have a friend on the council, and I could set up a meeting for you, if you'd like," Farren offered.

"That would be much appreciated."

For the rest of the meal, Elias and Farren talked about more mundane news from each kingdom. Mylah picked at her food, but Elias noticed she didn't eat much of it.

"Thank you for dinner, we should be going," Elias said, pushing his chair back from the table. Mylah followed suit.

"Will you both be back tomorrow?" Raelynn asked. "I could show you around town, Mylah. If you'd like."

"That would be nice," Mylah responded, though Elias heard the tightness in her voice and knew she probably didn't care either way.

"Perfect. We shall see you in the morning, then," Raelynn said, leading them to the front door.

Outside, Elias led the way down the street to where a stable held their horse.

"I assume you didn't find another horse today, since you spent the day and what little coin you had at the tavern?" he asked and the derision in his voice caused him to wince as Mylah stiffened. He hadn't meant for it to come out so harsh, but she *had* wasted both her time and money by choosing to spend the day at the bar instead of doing something more useful, like finding another horse.

"You'd be correct," Mylah said, pursing her lips. Elias said nothing and they rode the whole way back to the inn in Perynth in silence. The tension between them felt like a barbed wire waiting to snap.

When they returned to their room, Mylah climbed into bed while Elias washed up. Reentering the room, he knew she was pretending to be asleep when he climbed into bed next to her, careful not to touch her. Her breathing was unsteady and her body too still.

Her body heat reached him quickly and his skin prickled from the sensation of it. It took every ounce of restraint in him not to turn to her. Sleep evaded him as he longed to feel her in his arms again, and he knew she'd probably never forgive him for all he'd said to her that day.

Thirteen

In the morning, Mylah and Elias ate breakfast at the inn before heading back to Korrindale. Standing outside of Farren and Raelynn's house, Elias finally broke their silence.

"Try to be a bit less...indulgent today," he said before opening the front door and leaving her behind.

Mylah seethed but said nothing as she followed him inside. He didn't need to know the effect he still had on her. The way that being so near to him, without being allowed to touch him, hurt so badly it made her sick, unless she was drinking. Her drinking habits had started as a way to drown out her guilt over Garrick's death, but a lucky side effect had also been forgetting Elias for a few blissful moments. Not to mention that Greyson and Cassia needed her help, and she'd be able to do nothing for them in Hyrdian. She had enough guilt weighing her down without letting them down too.

Raelynn met her in the entryway. "Ready for a walk?" she asked, and Mylah nodded reluctantly. She noted that Raelynn wore shoes today and wondered if she'd only been barefoot for her performance.

They walked down the cobblestone street that led to the center of town where the bakery and tavern were.

"Do you perform on these streets often?" Mylah asked, trying to break the strange tension that had formed between them since leaving the house.

"No, yesterday was a rare occurrence," she smirked. "We don't need the money, but sometimes I like to play for someone other than Farren."

"Well, you play beautifully."

"Thank you." A silence settled around them again, broken only as they passed by other pairs walking the streets. Mylah decided to try another question.

"I have to ask, yesterday you mentioned your dislike of King Castien..."

"And you're wondering if my disdain extends to your prince?" Raelynn finished for her. "No. Prince Elias has done nothing to earn that sentiment. As far as I know, he is generally beloved by his people." As Raelynn said this, Mylah silently added *'Until now.'* The news of Elias' secret must not have spread this far yet.

"Now, let me ask you a question," Raelynn interrupted Mylah's thoughts.

"Hmm?"

"What has you so messed up that you're spending your time getting drunk at the bars?" The sympathy in Raelynn's voice made Mylah's jaw clench. Everyone loved to pity her lately, and she hated it. Everything that had caused her to spiral was her own fault and she was sick of people trying to tell her it wasn't.

"As you told me yesterday, *'I'd rather not talk about it.'* And I won't be answering that." Mylah didn't want to receive any more lectures.

"Ah, well played. Fine then. If I give you my answer, will you give me yours?" Raelynn's story had piqued Mylah's curiosity the day before, and she couldn't help but be interested now.

"If it means so much to you," Mylah said, trying to mask her anticipation.

"It doesn't, but I'm curious anyway. My family used to live in Elowyn. We weren't very well off, but we managed. I would play my fiddle in the streets and make decent money with that, while my parents worked at the meat market." Raelynn began her story and Mylah listened intently, waiting to figure out where Castien came into play.

"My brother, Darius, decided he wanted to join the king's royal guard." Raelynn paused and cleared her throat. "He wound up being delegated to the border patrol and we only saw him once every few weeks."

"Well, at least there wasn't much going on along the border then, right?" Mylah asked, hopeful, even though she knew how the story ended.

"For a while, yes. Before long, though, Elowyns who strayed too far over the border began showing up dead, even though there was no war or rule that we couldn't cross the border at the time." Mylah blinked in surprise, realizing Raelynn was older than she'd first suspected. Then again, she should be used to that, seeing as all shreeve and fae appeared to be much younger than they were.

"But my brother was not one of the ones who was killed, if that's what you're thinking. He did, however, demand from King Haldor that something be done about the murders." Raelynn stopped walking and gestured to a bench. "Let's sit."

After they sat, Mylah cut into the story.

"Did your brother know General Ansel?" Mylah thought back to the journal she had read and the similar story he'd told of the shreeve showing up dead on the border. It seemed like months ago rather than a few weeks that she'd read it.

"Yes, that's who he went to the king with to demand justice, but the king brushed them off."

"I found out recently that King Florian and my grandfather..." Mylah stopped, her words catching in her throat. She pressed on, having no reason to protect either of the men who had committed the atrocities. "They were responsible for the murders. The king at the time was only seventeen or eighteen, but my grandfather was older. He should have known better." Raelynn placed her hand over Mylah's, which she had clenched in her lap.

"They *both* should have known better, but Florian was the one making the commands, I'm sure. As the future king, he would have had far more power than he deserved."

"He was a war general. His father obviously thought him capable of such power at such a young age. He was wrong." Mylah's face burned with rage at King Florian.

"There is nothing we can do to change what happened." Raelynn's voice had dropped to a low and calming tone. Mylah realized she had taken them away from Raelynn's story.

"So, what happened to your brother?" she said, bringing them back to the main reason they had begun going down memory lane.

"He went back to the border. For years, he went back and forth from the border to the castle, slowly working his way up, and was occasionally used as a royal guard member within the castle for special events. We watched as King

Haldor cycled through his wives, all of them meeting an untimely death, while no one spoke up to help them. Of course, that's a perk of being king; if anyone speaks against you, you can pin treason on them and have them killed. So, that helped to quiet the whispers of his murders. King Haldor made executions public events, and we always went to ensure it was no one we knew. We witnessed many wrongful deaths, including one of a young woman."

"Sascha," Mylah let slip.

"I guess, I never knew her name. I only remember King Castien in the crowd. My brother was one of the guards with him, and I stood on Darius' other side. When the girl, Sascha, was lit on fire by King Haldor, something happened. Something I still can't explain, but I *know* was King Castien."

Mylah cocked her head to the side and frowned. "What happened?" She hadn't heard this part of the story from Castien.

"King Castien screamed, but it seemed like no one heard him, besides me. No one reacted anyway. Then there was this... ripple of power, and my brother dropped dead beside me, along with a few other guards who had surrounded King Castien. He ran from the room and was never held accountable. Darius' death was ruled a freak accident and that was the end of it."

Raelynn dropped her head and let out a long sigh. Mylah's head was reeling with thoughts about Castien and the possibility that he had been hiding his magic all this time. She thought back to when she had asked Petra about it, and she had told Mylah never to bring it up again.

"King Castien has magic," Mylah said more to herself, but Raelynn responded.

"Yes. But no one believed me. My own family barely believed me. But they agreed when I said we should leave Elowyn. We packed up, moved here, and never looked back. I don't want to be anywhere near King Castien when he finally explodes or decides he's done hiding his powers." Mylah decided she would try to ask Elias about that later, though she imagined he would either ignore her or brush her off, as usual.

"I am so sorry for your loss, I know what it's like to lose family," Mylah said, clenching her fists in her lap.

"I've come to terms with it, though I miss him every day." Raelynn placed her hand over Mylah's fist and squeezed it.

"I guess it's my turn, then," Mylah said, and it came out as a whisper. She tried to tear her mind from the overwhelming thought of Castien being far more powerful than she had realized. "Well, I might as well start with my parents being murdered when I was fourteen. Then, jump ahead a few years to the man who had become a father figure to me also being murdered right in front of me. And now, there is a very real possibility that my two best friends back in Adair are about to, or may have already, met the same fate." Mylah paused to let out a rattling breath and realized tears streamed down her cheeks. She tried to brush them away, but they continued to flow.

"That is a heavy burden for someone so young. But believe me when I say, alcohol is almost never the answer," Raelynn said the exact comment Mylah had known would follow her story, and she deflated, realizing she had hoped for something *more*.

"*Almost* never?" Mylah asked, clinging to the one piece that had been different from everyone else's critiques of Mylah's coping mechanism.

"I don't pretend to be all knowing, but in this case, I would say, in order for you to be of any use to Elowyn or Adair, whomever you so choose, cutting back on the drinking would be a great first step. If that's what you want to do."

Mylah scoffed, "As if it's so easy. You're not the first person who's told me that."

"And I won't be the last," Raelynn said, shrugging. "Hopefully, somewhere along the line, it will stick."

"Doubtful," Mylah grumbled.

"Just take it one day at a time. I was once where you are, in that empty, seemingly bottomless, pit of despair. Farren helped to pull me out of it." A pensive smile pulled at Raelynn's lips, and a far-off look entered her eyes.

"I don't need a man to help me, if that's what you're suggesting," Mylah disputed. She hated to think that Raelynn thought her so weak that she'd need *anyone* to help her.

"Not at all. Farren may have helped me by staying by my side and lighting the path, but I had to choose to follow that path and stay on it. I did all the hard work. And some days I think about going back to that place, but he helps to remind me of why I don't. Because I hated that version of me."

"Everyone thinks I want to drink..." Mylah whispered. "But it's the only thing that drives away my guilt...and fear."

Raelynn took her hand and held it tightly. "Find something else. For me, it was my fiddle and Farren. Find *your* reason to stay out of that darkness, out of that void. And don't be afraid to ask for help. Needing help does not make you any weaker."

"I'll try..." Mylah couldn't make any promises. At the moment it seemed possible, but it was when her thoughts strayed to Greyson, or Garrick, or her parents... That was when it would be the hardest.

"Come on. Let's go get some pastries. We need to brighten this day up a bit," Raelynn said, taking Mylah by the arm and leading her towards the bakery. Mylah leaned into her warmth and strength, soaking up all the positivity she could to carry with her in her darkest moments.

Raelynn made dinner for them again that night. Farren and Elias were outside practicing how to sense magic. From what Mylah had overheard before they went out, it appeared like a sort of aura that could be seen by magic users if they focused hard enough.

"Do you need any help?" Mylah asked Raelynn as she stirred the pot of soup on the stove.

"Do you mind setting the table? All the dishes are there." She pointed to a cabinet above the sink. "And the silverware is in the furthest drawer to the right."

Mylah set the table with bowls, spoons, and little plates for their bread. Sitting at the table, she could see out the kitchen window to where Farren and Elias stood. They were talking animatedly about something, and Elias looked happy. It tugged on Mylah's heart because it wasn't something she'd seen since before their mission in Adair. Since before she'd betrayed him.

"Easy on the eyes, huh?" Raelynn remarked as she placed the pot of soup onto the table with a ladle. Her tone was playful, and the light danced in her eyes as she looked out the window towards her husband.

"Which one?" Mylah joked. "I know who *you're* ogling."

"Sometimes it's hard to fathom that he's mine. That he chose *me*." Raelynn sat beside Mylah and placed her chin in her hand as she rested her elbow on the table.

"I don't know why he wouldn't. You two seem perfect for one another." Mylah couldn't help but be reminded of her parents and how she'd envied their relationship. Her heart clenched at the thought.

"Remember what I said earlier? Sometimes it's nice to have a friend in the dark." Raelynn placed a hand on Mylah's shoulder and squeezed. Mylah ignored her but continued watching Elias out the window.

Elias and Farren came inside shortly after and joined them at the table. It was quiet at first while everyone enjoyed their food.

"So," Farren broke the silence. "Elias mentioned you were hoping to gain some information on something that may be occurring in the Forsaken Mountains." Mylah perked up at that. "I sent a message to a friend on Hyrdian's governing council, and she said they've heard nothing."

Mylah deflated, letting out a huff. "How would I go about finding out what's happening then?" she asked.

"The only way would be to go out there yourself, which could be dangerous if there *is* something going on. Not to mention there are trolls, orcs, veela, sirens, and other vengeful creatures out there," Farren explained, shuddering. Mylah wondered if he had gone into the Unbounds as her father and Garrick had when they were young.

"Where would I find someone to take me out there?" Mylah asked.

"You're not going out there," Elias snapped, and Mylah stiffened.

"I didn't ask you," she snapped back.

"I could take you," Farren offered, despite his previous reaction to the creatures they may encounter.

"No. We won't ask you to put yourself at risk in that way," Elias said before Mylah could respond.

"I've been out there a few times, it's not a problem." As Farren spoke, Mylah noticed Raelynn reach out and cover his hand with hers in a show of support. "If there is something going on in the Forsaken Mountains, we should know about it. They are closer to us than any other kingdom."

"What about Elias' training?" Raelynn asked, though Mylah could tell she was only asking because Elias seemed too bothered to ask himself.

"We shall train daily for the next two weeks, and then we will leave for the mountains. It won't take more than a week to do a little investigating and return here. We can train while we're traveling, too. It will give Elias a chance to use his powers in the real world without too many people around."

"Thank you so much, Farren. You don't know how much I appreciate you offering to help with this. I'll owe you." Mylah would hug him if they were standing. This was the one thing that she could help with, finding out this information for Genevieve. Otherwise, she'd felt useless for weeks.

Elias remained quiet, not saying anything else on the topic. The conversation changed to preparations that would need to be made and finding someone to take over Farren's classes for him while he was gone.

On the ride home, Elias didn't say anything to Mylah, and she went over and over in her mind how she would go about apologizing to him. Raelynn had been right, and Mylah wanted to try to make amends with Elias, but she wasn't sure exactly how to go about doing that. Not that he didn't also owe her some sort of apology, but she figured she could at least begin the reparations.

Back at the inn, they took their turns bathing and readying for bed and all the while, Mylah played out different conversations she could have with Elias in her head. Each one ended in an argument of some kind. As she was about to climb into bed, she finally worked up the courage to say something.

"We should talk," she started, and Elias sat up in the bed, turning to her. The blanket fell to his waist, revealing his bare chest which had Mylah blushing. Trying to gather her thoughts again, she paused before continuing. "About…" he cut her off.

"Your decision to go on a mission endangering us and Farren?" he suggested, his fists clenching at his sides, bunching up the blanket.

"No," Mylah said through her gritted teeth. "Though I feel like *you* want to talk about that. Which is interesting because you've said nothing to me since dinner." Elias turned away from her, throwing his legs off the bed and standing, revealing his rippling back muscles and scrambling Mylah's thoughts once more. *Damn it, pull it together,* she cursed herself. He faced her once more and Mylah struggled to maintain a straight face as her entire body heated.

"I didn't want to fight, so I decided to say nothing," Elias said as he began to pace the room. "We have to live together for the next month, so I'm trying. I'm trying…" He ran a hand through his hair.

"Is it so hard? To try to be nice to me?" Mylah gulped passed the lump that was forming in her throat.

Elias paused his pacing. "Things are weird, Mylah. Just saying that, saying your name, is weird." He bit his lip and rolled his head back. "I don't *want* to fight with you anymore. I don't *want* things to be weird. But they are."

Mylah dropped her head down and stared at the wooden floorboards beneath her bare feet.

"I'm sorry. For everything. Have I said that yet?" she asked. She couldn't remember much from the past few weeks.

"I'm sorry, too. I said so many horrible things," Elias sighed. "I wanted to talk to you sooner, but Torin was always there," he paused, his jaw clenching.

Mylah closed her eyes.

"Torin and I…" she started, trailing off before taking a deep breath and continuing. "He helped me get through the aftermath of Garrick's death. We never…"

"You don't need to say anything. I understand, Mylah, and you don't need to apologize," Elias said, his hand reaching out towards her for a moment before he let it drop back to his side. "Castien told me what he did. He told me about your parents."

"Don't. I don't want to talk about that. I asked him not to tell you." Mylah's voice shook. "I don't want your pity, and if that's the only reason you're forgiving me, then I don't accept your forgiveness." Turning on her heel, she stalked to the window, gripping it with her palms.

"You're making this more difficult than it needs to be," Elias said softly, approaching her.

Mylah watched in the reflection in the window as Elias stepped up behind her and held his hand out to her.

"Please, accept my forgiveness," he said, his voice cracking.

Mylah leaned her forehead against the window, taking deep breaths as she considered his words. There was no pity in his eyes, only longing.

"Can we start over?" Mylah asked, holding Elias' gaze in the reflection. Elias didn't speak for what felt like too long and Mylah began to worry he would never respond when he let out a long sigh.

"That's all I want," he said, dropping his outstretched hand back to his side. He lingered behind her for a moment, seeming to consider something, and Mylah wondered what would happen if she turned towards him. They'd be nearly chest to chest. Her entire body heated at that thought and as she began to turn, Elias stepped away from her, grabbing his shirt, and heading towards the door.

"Don't wait up, I'm going for a walk," he said before slamming the door behind him. Mylah furrowed her brow, thinking maybe she'd heard him wrong, but he had definitely agreed to start over, which was the best she could hope for at the moment.

That night, Mylah's nightmares returned for the first time since reaching Hyrdian. Once again, she tried to outrace time and save her parents before she was planted back in the moment Garrick died. Every time, she was too late. Every time she lost them all over again. Every time the heartache grew to the point where it woke her and left her in agony. Elias didn't return to the room that night, and Mylah was free to cry uninterrupted until she felt hollowed out.

In the morning, Elias told Mylah a second room had opened up, so he'd be staying there. He promised it wasn't because of her, that he only needed his own space, but she couldn't help thinking he couldn't stand to sleep in the same bed as her, despite their agreeing to start over. She accepted the change with a smile but feigned a headache so she could remain at the inn that day. As it turned out, the whiskey in Perynth was not as good as the whiskey in Korrindale, but it was just as strong.

Fourteen

Crane wandered the castle grounds. He'd spent the morning training with Torin and Davina again. They tried to get to the courtyard to train every morning, but some days there was other business to attend to. Yesterday Castien had called them all to his study to inform them that Sovereign Keir had accepted their request, but they needed time to prepare so it would be about a month before Castien and the others would depart.

Elena had been spending most of her days in the castle gardens. She'd either sit on the bench staring into space for hours, or she'd help the gardeners water and deadhead the flowers. Crane sat with her sometimes, trying to talk to her. Though she answered his questions, she often looked to be far away, her eyes glazed over and never fixed on him. Today was one of those days and he'd left her on the bench after giving up trying to have a real conversation with her.

"Fancy a trip into town?" Davina's voice startled him from staring at the ground.

He turned to her and watched as she strode towards him, her dress billowing behind her, and her jacket buttoned up to her chin. It was an exceptionally cold day, not that it had deterred Elena from remaining in the gardens. Crane had brought her a blanket and wrapped it around her before leaving.

"What's the occasion?" Crane asked, allowing Davina to snake her arm around his and begin pulling him back in the direction she had come from. A sprite followed her as always, though her usual guards were missing. She'd also been moved out of the dungeon into a real room now that Castien trusted her a bit more.

"Who needs an occasion to leave the castle? We've been cooped up here for days. It's about time we escape for a few hours."

A few wisps of her hair had escaped her braided bun and tickled the side of Crane's face. He inhaled deeply, letting the cool air quell the heat that rose in him. It happened anytime Davina was nearby. He certainly was attracted to her, but he had Cassia to think of. Friendship with Davina was all he would allow, though sometimes he wondered if she wanted more. From all her sidelong looks at Torin during training, he doubted it.

"Will Torin be joining us?" Crane asked and Davina wrinkled her nose. "I'll take that as a no," he chuckled.

"Torin and I don't play well together. Fighting is about all we do," she explained.

"Crane," a voice squeaked behind them, and Crane turned his head to see Briar flitting at his shoulder. "Bellingham delivered this message this morning." She held out a letter towards him.

Disgraced

"Thank you, Briar," he said, releasing Davina's arm and taking the letter. He ripped it open without a second thought and his body relaxed at the sight of Cassia's looping letters scrawled on the parchment.

Crane,

I miss you too. Please don't worry about me. I'll be fine. I haven't been able to talk with Greyson much, but let your parents know he is doing well. I saw him standing guard outside one of the council meetings the other day and mother invited him to dinner. I'll let you know what comes of it.

The king has been keeping a lot of secrets from most of the council. He has a select few that he brings in for every meeting while the rest of us are only allowed to attend some of the meetings. Queen Aveda has been present at all of them. She doesn't say much, but I fear she is pulling the strings.

Queen Aurelia on the other hand has been absent from the meetings. I don't know what that means, if anything. King Florian may be keeping her out of this whole mess, I can't be sure.

I will let you know if I have any other useful information. Give Mylah my best.

Love,
Cassia

Crane's hands were shaking as he lowered the letter. 'Let your parents know...' Cassia didn't know that Garrick was dead. Which meant the king had not told the council. Rage boiled inside Crane, and he wanted to scream. Davina's hand landed on his arm, and he recoiled at the touch.

"Is everything alright?" she asked, her voice softer than he had ever heard it.

"No," Crane spat, and Davina pulled her hand back, her face hardening. Crane blinked, realizing the effort it took for Davina to show her true self, to care about someone else, and regret replaced his rage. "I'm sorry," he muttered.

"Don't be," she said curtly. "I'll find someone else to drag into town with me." She strode away from him towards the castle entrance and didn't look back. Crane hung his head in shame. He'd taken out his anger on Davina who was already troubled enough, though she would never admit to that.

"How did it come to this," Crane groaned. Briar, who he hadn't realized was still with him, flew in front of him and stared him down.

"If you need to send another message," she began, and Crane put his hand up to stop her.

"Not now. But thank you. I will find you when I'm ready to respond." Briar nodded and flew towards the rest of the sprites who hovered back towards the gardens. Crane could see his mother's head poking out over a rose bush. He sighed and trudged over to her.

Crane had thought that telling his mother Greyson was doing well would help lift her spirits, but she hadn't reacted much at all when he'd told her. He couldn't help but become frustrated and storm out of the gardens into the castle, leaving behind the heady floral scented, fresh air he'd grown to hate. He found himself in the library where rows of books stretched away from him, leading to what looked like a sitting area at the other end.

Disgraced

He had never been one for reading, though Garrick had loaded war and political strategy books onto him and Greyson from the time they were old enough to attend council meetings. Elena had been hesitant for them to enter that world, but Crane had been excited. There was nothing he wanted more than to be a part of the council meetings where he could learn all the goings on in the kingdom and be of service. Of course, he hadn't actually been able to speak at the meetings until he'd turned eighteen, and even then, his parents had warned him to keep quiet unless spoken to.

His fingers trailed over the covers on the shelves, but he couldn't bring himself to choose one. Someone cleared their throat in the sitting area which drew Crane down to the end of the aisle. Castien sat in one of two armchairs that were placed on either side of an unused fireplace.

"Briar informed me she delivered you a letter," Castien said when he saw Crane. Crane produced the letter from his pocket, handing it over. Castien scanned it and handed it back with a curt nod.

"The king is withholding information from his people, from his council. He didn't even tell them about my father being killed." Crane ground the last words out, his fists clenching at his sides.

"It would cast a harsh light on himself to admit that one of his own council members was killed by his men. He probably would rather withhold the information that Garrick was killed after turning against his king. It might make him into a martyr, stirring the idea of rebellion in people's minds."

"I guess..." Crane muttered, his anger still festering under his skin.

"That doesn't mean I think he's right," Castien clarified. "I've kept information from my people in the past, but no good has ever come of it." Castien's eyes clouded over, as if lost in a memory for a moment until Crane spoke and brought him back.

"You are a better man than King Florian. I'm sorry it took so long for me to realize it." Crane hated to admit that Castien had grown on him, but there was no denying the fact that the shreeve had proven themselves to be far from the monsters he'd grown up believing they were.

"Don't speak so highly of me just yet," Castien warned, a slight smirk on his lips. "You've yet to hear the tales of my past misdeeds. Though, I'm sure Mylah told you the worst of it."

Crane furrowed his brow trying to recall whether Mylah had told him any stories of Castien.

"Mylah told me nothing, other than that I should trust you," Crane said, shaking his head.

Castien's eyes widened in surprise. "Well," he pursed his lips. "I'll let her be the bearer of that news." Castien shut the book that had laid open in his lap and placed it on the table beside him. "In the meantime, feel free to ask Davina or Torin for some stories. I'm sure they have no shortage of them." Castien rose from his seat.

"Why are you so determined to have everyone hate you?" Crane questioned, doubting his decision to trust Castien.

"You'll understand someday," Castien said, remaining cryptic. Striding to the door, Castien paused at the threshold and turned his head back towards Crane. "Mylah was right though – you can trust me," he added before leaving Crane alone to ponder his words.

Disgraced

On his way out of the library, Crane bumped into Torin.

"Sorry," Torin said, moving to pass Crane. Before he could go, though, Crane caught hold of his arm as he noticed fear in Torin's one visible eye.

"What's going on?" Crane asked.

"Trouble on the border," he said and pulled out of Crane's grip.

"Can I help?"

"No –" Torin started but then cocked his head to the side. "Actually, you're human. You might be of use if they're trying to use the Book of Creation spell, since you can't be affected by it."

"Okay, take me with you," Crane said, spreading his arms out, offering himself up.

Torin nodded and turned on his heel, waving to Crane to follow. Horses already waited for them at the front gate of the castle, along with a few other men. Castien appeared from inside the castle, his face red and a look of pure rage transforming his features to someone Crane would be terrified to meet on a battlefield.

"Alec informed me of the body," Castien ground out. "Don't do anything reckless." His eyes landed on Crane and widened. As Castien opened his mouth to speak, Torin started talking.

"Crane is human and if they found a way to use the spell, he won't be affected by it. I need him," Torin explained.

Castien narrowed his eyes at them but kept his mouth shut, giving Torin a curt nod before turning to head back into the castle.

Before Crane and Torin could make it out of the gates on their horses, Davina came running out of the castle. She wore fighting leathers that clung to her every curve, and Crane didn't miss the lingering stare Torin gave her before turning his eyes back to the gate.

"I'm coming with you!" she yelled, stopping beside Crane's horse. "I want to help." Torin said nothing, so Crane held a hand out to Davina, helping her up onto the horse behind him. She wrapped her arms around his waist, and they resumed their trot out of the gates, pushing the horses to their maximum speed once they cleared them.

As they reached the forest between them and the border, they slowed the horses again to a trot. "What exactly are we expecting to find when we reach the border?" Crane asked Torin.

"I'm not sure. All I know is that the body of one of our men was found dead inside our border on the eastern most edge that touches Adair. He'd been missing for a few days before they found him," Torin paused, swiveling his head to look at Crane. "There were no markings on the body to indicate what happened, so we're going to investigate the scene it was found at and return it to Madame Edris so she can discover what truly happened."

"Horrifying," Davina commented.

Crane arched his neck to look at her. "Really? You seem too unbothered by this," he said.

Davina lifted a shoulder and sighed, "I've heard it all before. My brother is a guard on the border, and he used to tell me horror stories about all the creatures they'd come across and the men who'd turn up dead. It doesn't affect me anymore."

Disgraced

Crane turned forward, watching as Torin and the other guards disappeared into the underbrush ahead of them.

"I spent four years guarding Adair's borders," he started. His breath caught as a vivid memory from his time on the border resurfaced.

A moonless night's darkness surrounded him, and screams ripped through the forest followed by a garbled cry for help. Crane stiffened, not daring to move or draw attention his way.

I should help them, he thought. I should do something, *anything rather than stand here. But he couldn't move his legs. They trembled and soon, the screams stopped.*

Shame washed over Crane at the memory. In the morning they had found the body of one of the royal guard's men torn to shreds. Not much was left, most of the body having been consumed by whatever had killed him. Crane was sure there was nothing he could have done to save the man, but it still haunted him.

"You don't know what it's like out there. Stories don't do it justice," Crane said.

Davina's grip on him tightened. "You're right," she said, her breath brushing past his ear and making him shiver.

Their horse pushed through the underbrush bringing Torin and the other guards back into view.

"The body was found over here," Torin announced, turning his horse to the right and leading them away from the main path. "They had to move it so it wouldn't attract any creatures from the Unbounds, but we'll see it after we check out the area they found it."

It... Crane couldn't help but notice how Torin kept referring to the body as 'it.' Maybe it helped him to separate his feelings from the situation, but to Crane, it seemed disrespectful. He said nothing, though, and they soon came to the spot where the body had been found.

"You can see where it was drug across the border," Torin said, hopping off his horse and striding to the clearing. There were obvious drag marks in the leaves. Whomever had dumped the body there hadn't worried about covering their tracks.

"They just wanted rid of them," Crane said. Crouching down near one of the bushes that had been displaced by the body being drug past it, he noticed small smears of blood in the dirt. "The body had no visible wounds you said?"

"Other than the scratches from being dragged out here, none," Torin answered, crouching down beside him. "He would have been bleeding enough from those minor wounds to have left these marks."

"I don't think we'll find much here," Torin said, standing up once more. "Whoever dropped the body here may not have cared if it was found, but any evidence there might have been will have been wiped away by the elements."

It had rained the day before, Crane realized. That would have wiped away any traces that might have pointed them in the right direction as to who murdered the man.

"We can assume that Adair is at fault, but we won't rule out an Unbound creature until Madame Edris runs her tests." Torin circled the area one last time before remounting his horse and signaling for the others to do the same. "Let's go get the body."

The body was being kept cold by the magic of a shreeve who looked like he'd seen better days. Crane could only imagine how gruesome a task it was to have to remain by the side of a dead body for a whole day in order to preserve the remains.

"We're here to relieve you of your duties, Trip," Torin said, patting the man who sat beside the body on the back. "Go get some rest."

"Yes, sir." Trip hopped up and practically ran out of the tent.

"Nic, why don't you and Crane take a walk. See if you can sense any non-shreeve in the area, and if you do, find them, and bring them to me," Torin commanded.

Davina stepped forward, crossing her arms over her chest. "Why aren't I going with them?" she asked.

"You're staying with me," Torin barked, and Crane could have sworn fear flashed in Torin's visible eye.

Davina huffed but didn't argue as Crane and Nic left the tent.

After they did a few passes on the closest section of the border and found nothing, they returned to the tent to find that Torin had the body loaded onto a cart and ready to haul back to the castle.

"Nothing, sir," Nic reported. "Not even another border patrol."

"They're playing it safe. They know we'll be on high alert," Torin mused, running his hand through his short, white hair. "There's nothing more we can do here."

As the last word left his mouth, a thunderous boom shook the entire border camp. A few shrieks followed, but an immediate silence descended on them, as if the entire forest held its breath as they all waited for whatever came next.

"What was that?" Davina whispered, breaking the silence. Before anyone could answer, another boom shook the world around them.

"That's the sound we heard before we realized that Jayce was missing," one of the border guards said, pointing to the body on the cart.

"And no one thought to mention it before now?" Torin bit out a curse as he grabbed Davina's arm and practically dragged her to the nearest horse.

"Ow!" she cried out. "What are you doing?" Yanking her arm free from his grip, she stepped back towards Crane.

"We need to get you out of here. I should have never let you come." Torin's eye widened and a grimace pulled at his mouth.

Davina placed a hand over her heart. "Why, Torin, are you worried about me?" For a moment she seemed to be flirting with him, but then she dropped the pretense and scowled at him. "I can take care of myself."

"Sir!" Trip sprinted towards them and skidded as he came to a stop before Torin. "We figured out the source of the explosion."

"Explosion?" Torin's eye narrowed.

"It's a distraction. Another of our patrol is missing."

"If you know that, then go find them!" Torin bellowed and Trip cowered before him.

"S-sir, we would, but whoever took them must have used magic. There's no path or indication of where they went. We think they were transported with magic," he finished, keeping his head bowed to Torin.

"There's more than one missing," another guard walked up to them. "I received word from the other patrol camp that they had a few men and women go missing a day ago."

Torin's eye closed slowly, and Crane could almost see steam coming off his head as his body trembled. Taking a step forward, Crane took Davina's hand and pulled her back, away from Torin's range. It wasn't that he didn't trust Torin, but he knew what could happen if you were too close to someone who was about to explode. He'd seen it on occasion with the captains of the Adairian guard.

"Someone get me a headcount of both patrol camps. *Now.*" He kept his tone neutral, but Crane could hear the threat in his words. "I want each and every person accounted for. No one sets foot outside this camp without at least two other guards with them, and everyone will check in and out before so much as taking a piss in the woods."

"Yes, sir," all the guards around them spoke in unison.

"Nic, take Davina and the body – Jayce," he corrected, and Crane gained a bit of respect for him. "Back to the castle. You're with me, Crane." Torin strode towards the source of the boom and Crane could do nothing else but follow.

Fifteen

Mylah sat in an armchair in Farren's office reading a book on magic while Elias trained. She'd been attending training with him the past few days since it helped keep her mind off everything else.

While a shreeve is reenergized by the sun, they channel their power from the elements, as the fae and witches do. Air, earth, fire, and water.

Though they are not bound by the sun, fae have a limit on their magic stores and they can usually only harness one of the elements. So, a fae who draws power from air, can only use air-related magic. Though, all fae can cast basic healing and glamours. The more powerful they are, the more in-depth magic they will be able to perform.

As Mylah read, her fingers skimmed the page, keeping her place as Elias kept distracting her. He used his magic to throw a book across the room and swore as it collided with one of Farren's vases.

Disgraced

"Don't worry about that," Farren said, waving it off. "Keep going."

Elias tried lifting the book again. The goal was to have it hover in front of him without flying off. Elias needed to learn control before he could think about any kind of fancy tricks. Mylah returned her focus to the book in front of her.

As for a witch or warlock, they can almost never fully deplete their magic stores. However, if they were to use an immense amount of magic at one time, it would take a while, depending on their strength, to recover that magic completely.

Mylah barely flinched as a book whizzed by her head for the second time that session. She lifted her gaze from her book, though, and pinned her stare on Elias.

"I'm starting to think you may be aiming for me," she commented, her lips pulling up in a smirk. "Maybe something a bit more...higher stakes would be helpful in keeping him focused, Farren." She turned her head to Farren who appeared thoughtful at her suggestion, tapping a finger against his lips.

"Hmm..." He strode to his desk and opened the top drawer. Peering inside, his eyes flicked from Mylah to Elias and back. "Let's start with something that won't end with you being impaled." He grabbed something and closed the drawer.

Walking back towards Elias, he held his hand out to him and revealed an orb of some sort. Mylah squinted at it.

Elias took it, his eyes widening. "This may not impale anyone, but it could do some serious damage," he said.

Farren shrugged. "I think Mylah is right. You need some external motivation to help keep you focused."

"I'm focusing as much as I can!" Elias protested.

"You're not. You haven't made any progress this week, and we don't have time for that. You said yourself you need to be back in Elowyn as soon as possible, so we need to help you make some serious strides."

"I'm good at dodging," Mylah joked, though her muscles were clenched from her nerves. She knew it was important to give Elias something more to think about than hitting someone with a book, but she wasn't entirely convinced he would want to protect her from being hit with the orb.

Elias huffed but no longer argued. He held the orb out in front of himself and began focusing on it. Lowering his hand, the orb remained aloft. It bobbed a little, but otherwise, it didn't move.

"Good. Better," Farren murmured and as he did the orb launched straight at Mylah. Sinking down into her chair, Mylah's heart raced as the orb stopped mere inches from where her head had been. Elias' arm had shot out and he'd caught the orb with his magic in the nick of time.

"Sorry about that," he said, slightly breathless.

"But that's the first time you've been able to regain control," Farren pointed out. "Impressive."

Elias pulled the orb back towards himself and grabbed it out of the air as it hovered before him again. "I guess you were right about the external motivation. Sorry I doubted you."

"I think I need a break," Mylah gasped out, pushing herself up from the chair and hurrying out of the room before either of them could say anything.

As soon as she'd shut the door behind her, Mylah broke out into a run as she fled from Farren's office. Down the halls, down the stairs, out through the front doors and into the whirlwind of students. Mylah turned in a circle, her breath catching as she realized she was surrounded. People milled around her, entering and exiting the building. Her mind whirled as she registered that she'd passed people in the halls and how they must have thought she was insane.

"Are you alright?" someone asked, and Mylah nodded before jogging away from the crowd. She found a large tree that mostly concealed her from everyone, and she slumped against it to catch her breath.

Fear had gripped her in the moments before Elias had caught the orb. A large part of her thought he wouldn't be able to stop it. Not because he wasn't strong enough, but because he wasn't motivated enough to save her from harm. Her hands shook as she clenched them against her thighs and tears pressed against the backs of her eyes.

A memory surfaced as she sat beneath the tree, and though she would rather not think about her parents right then, the memory refused to leave her alone.

A six-year-old Mylah knocked softly on her parents' door.

"Come in," Vita's voice filtered through the door. Mylah could tell from the deep tone that her mother was still half asleep, but she pushed the door open and crept inside. The pitch darkness made her pause, but then a match struck, and a flame came into view as Emil lit the candle beside the bed.

"What is it, Bun?" he whispered though everyone was now awake.

"I had a nightmare," Mylah said, her voice quavering. Emil patted the center of the bed and without hesitation Mylah

climbed onto the foot of the bed and crawled to lay between her parents. Her nightmares were a common occurrence.

"One of these days you're going to have to learn to face your fears," Vita said, a yawn punctuating her statement. Vita's arms curled around Mylah as she pulled her close and hugged her tightly. "But not tonight."

"Not tonight," Mylah affirmed, her eyes already drifting closed as sleep found her.

Mylah snapped back into reality as a bird squawked in the tree above her. The tears she had been holding back flowed freely now, and she wiped them away. That had not been the last night she'd spent in her parents' bed, and she wasn't sure why it stood out to her now. It may have been the fact that it was usually Emil who had done the comforting. But that night, Vita had taken that role. Mylah hadn't found it unusual at the time, but now she cherished the memory and clung to it.

The fear that had been holding Mylah hostage moments before had dissipated, leaving warmth in its wake. Though she wasn't sure if she believed in an afterlife, Mylah was sure that if there was one, her mother had sent her that memory to help her.

Recollecting herself, Mylah lifted her head high and headed back inside. If she was going to be of any help to Elias, she would have to face her fears and learn to trust him. Trust him...as she'd done before...before *she'd* betrayed *him*. It was the least she could do.

Mylah steeled herself as she strolled back into Farren's office. Elias seemed to be doing well keeping the orb aloft in front of him and he didn't falter when she entered. Pulling Garrick's dagger from its sheath at her side she held it out, hilt first towards Elias. He narrowed his eyes in confusion.

"Take it. I trust you," she said, her voice unwavering. Her mind screamed at her to take the dagger back, protect herself, don't let anyone in. But she stood tall and stayed strong.

Elias began to protest but Mylah shook her head and pressed the hilt of the dagger into his hand. He let the orb drop to the ground with a *thud*.

"I don't think that's the best idea," Farren said from his desk.

"You said he needs more external motivation," Mylah reminded him.

He sighed, "Yes, but there are other, *safer* ways to go about doing this."

"Do you want Elias to learn to control his magic or not? If you're willing to let him do this, then so am I." Mylah crossed her arms over her chest and straightened her spine.

"Very well. I can stop the knife if I stand beside you."

"No," Mylah said, and it came out much harsher than intended. "I mean, you have more to lose."

"Is that what this is about?" Farren's eyes widened but he did not seem surprised. "Elias, give me a second alone with Mylah please."

Elias left the room, closing the door behind him and Mylah groaned as she turned to Farren.

"Your wife already gave me the talk, you know. The one about trying to find something to help *pull me out of the darkness*, as she put it."

"Good. That's not what I want to talk to you about." He sat on the edge of his desk, hitching one leg up and interlacing his fingers over his knee to hold it there. "Elias cares about you."

Mylah jolted, that was not what she had expected.

"As a friend, sure," Mylah said, though she had doubts about that.

"No. He cares deeply about you. Enough so that I believe you're right in that he wouldn't lose control of the dagger if it meant harming you."

"So, then why wouldn't you let him do it without you there to help?"

"Because he's not perfect. We all make mistakes, especially when we're learning. If something went wrong, and I wasn't there to step in, what do you think that would do to *him*?" Farren's eyebrow rose in question and Mylah rolled her neck as she considered his words.

"I didn't think about it like that," she admitted.

"Right. You went as far to think that *you* were okay with it if he hurt you. That you aren't worth worrying about. Which is ridiculous, even Raelynn and I who have only known you for a week would be affected if anything happened to you. We care about you, Mylah. A lot of people do."

"I get it," Mylah muttered.

"Whatever is going on right now, that will pass. I don't know when, but it will. I want to make sure you don't do anything to jeopardize that future for yourself, because you deserve to find happiness."

"Now you're starting to sound like Raelynn," Mylah pointed out. "You said you weren't going to be giving that talk."

"Fair enough." Farren inclined his head to her. "Think about what I said. Don't come back tomorrow if you're not ready to truly help Elias."

Mylah nodded. Farren called Elias back into the room and returned to his chair behind his desk. Elias glanced between the two of them, and Mylah kept her eyes trained on the floor.

"Head back to Perynth and practice for the rest of the day, *alone*, with the dagger. Tomorrow we will try the dagger when I have more safeties in place." Farren gave Mylah a pointed look and she scrunched her nose. "Oh, and before I forget, I received a response from the council – they can meet with you in three days."

"Perfect! Thank you." Elias grinned.

Mylah's heart leapt that they were getting their chance to request help for Elowyn. It felt like they were standing still, waiting for the war to truly begin. Talking with the council would mean steps forward.

"Someone will show up at your door and escort you to the meeting at noon, so be sure to be ready on time," Farren warned. Elias and Mylah both nodded before Farren sent them on their way.

Back at the inn, Elias did as Farren instructed while Mylah went inside and soaked in the bath. It was her new coping mechanism instead of automatically running to the bar, which was difficult with there being one only a floor down from her. But she'd taken what Raelynn had said to heart and begun trying to find other things to fill her darkness.

Writing in the bath helped. She'd started with writing letters to her parents, to Garrick, to Greyson, and to Cassia, even though she could never send any of them.

After, she progressed to writing her own stories. She'd recreate the tales her father used to tell her of his adventures in the Unbounds and write herself into them. It kept her busy for hours, until the water in the bath had gone cold and she'd curl up in bed and write some more.

That night, she fell asleep with a pen in her hand, sleeping through dinner. Nightmares found her yet again and drove her from her bed, sweating and shaken. On instinct, she walked into the hall and crossed to Elias' room, raising her hand to knock. Before she did, though, she caught herself, realizing he would probably think she was crazy for waking him so late at night over a nightmare. Lowering her hand to her side, she turned back to her room, glancing back at Elias' door in longing.

"Don't be stupid…" she muttered to herself before striding back to her own room. Before she could open the door though, a creak sounded behind her and she turned to find Elias standing at his own door, bare chested and his hair a mess. A smile pulled at Mylah's lips and any residual fear from her nightmare dissolved.

"Is everything alright?" Elias asked, scratching the back of his head, and squinting into the dim light of the hall.

"Fine…it was just…" Mylah debated telling him the truth, but then figured he couldn't think any less of her anyway. "I had a nightmare, but I'll be fine."

His eyes widened slightly before he opened his door wider and stepped to the side. "If you don't want to be alone," he said, leaving the statement open ended. Mylah thought about it for a moment before crossing the hall again and entering Elias' room.

"Thank you," she said as she walked past him. Though her fear was gone, she knew that the nightmare would only return if she went to bed alone again. She could hear her mother's voice chastising her, *'One of these days you're going to have to learn to face your fears...'* Mylah laughed to herself and thought, *Not tonight.*

Mylah stood with her back to the wall in the training room Farren had taken them to in the basement of the school. A dagger hovered in front of her chest. Though every instinct screamed at her to move, she remained rooted to her spot, determined to see this through.

"Good," Farren said as Elias concentrated on pulling the dagger back towards him. It hadn't flown towards Mylah as the orb had the previous day, but it had dropped to the floor a few times. A much better way for it to go. Mylah wore a chest plate, so even if it *had* struck her, she would have been fine. A little bruised maybe, but fine. Farren had asked a colleague to join them. Another professor named Locke had placed an invisible barrier around Mylah's head and neck to protect her from harm there.

Locke could have shielded her whole body but figured the motivation for Elias to control the dagger would lessen because he would have no pressure on him not to hurt Mylah. They promised she couldn't be hurt anyway, but there was always a chance Elias' magic would be faster than Locke's or Farren's.

Elias had been moving the dagger all around, concentrating on not letting it drop or fly out of his control. So far, he'd done well. He seemed to have much more control than the day before, which relieved Mylah.

The next couple of days were much the same. Elias attempted to control his magic, and every day, he improved. Farren began teaching Elias other tricks, like opening and closing the door, pulling specific books off the shelf, and creating energy balls, which manifested as blue flames for Elias.

On the day of the meeting with the council, Elias and Mylah didn't go to Korrindale. They spent the morning in Elias' room preparing what they would say to convince the councilors to help Elowyn. It kept coming back to the possibility that Queen Aveda would want more land if she took over Elowyn. But they had no proof of that.

A knock sounded on the door precisely at noon. Elias answered it and revealed a short, bald, bulky man wearing a loose fitted tunic and tight pants.

"Prince Elias of Elowyn?" the man asked.

"Yes," Elias said.

"Good. I am Leanardi, here to pick you up for your meeting with the council." He bowed slightly and waved his arm out to indicate Elias should step into the hall. Mylah followed as well, and she shut the door behind her. "If you would each take an arm." Leanardi stuck out his elbows on either side for Elias and Mylah to link their own arms through.

Mylah glanced at Elias, their gazes meeting, and cocked an eyebrow at him. He shrugged and stuck his arm through Leanardi's. Mylah did the same and in the blink of an eye, the inn disappeared, and they were in a whole new room. Mylah staggered as Leanardi released them. Nausea washed over her and Leanardi placed a bucket in her hands as if expecting her reaction. The nausea passed though, and Mylah handed the bucket back to him. Elias' face gave away no signs of distress, and he had no need for the bucket either.

Taking in the room around them, Mylah realized there were two men sitting in high backed, velvet lined chairs at the front of the room. There was an empty chair there as well. Behind them, a stained-glass window with the image of a woman with flowing white hair and a white gown depicted on it. A long, marble topped table had been placed in front of them and they each had stacks of parchment they were sifting through. The rest of the room seemed ordinary to Mylah. The walls were made of stone and the floors were some kind of dark brown wood.

"Welcome," one of the men greeted them. "Thank you, Leanardi. You may go."

Leanardi bowed to the men before leaving through a glass door at the back of the room.

One of the councilors was tall and lanky while the other was a more average build, sitting almost a whole head shorter than the other man. They both wore black tunics and pants that seemed to match. What threw Mylah off was that they both had dark red eyes, though they shared no other features.

"I am Councilor Eryx Aspertine," the lanky man introduced himself. "And this is Councilor Rogue." Mylah wanted to ask why Councilor Rogue had no last name, but she bit her tongue. "Councilor Nala Bergine was unfortunately unable to be here today." A wave of annoyance passed over Mylah at that. For some reason, to her, it seemed like they weren't taking this as seriously as they should. If the council truly wanted to hear them out, they would have all bothered to show up.

Elias spoke first, as they'd planned. "Thank you for seeing us on such short notice," he said, bowing his head to them.

"We assume you are here to talk about the war that has been declared between Elowyn and Adair?" Councilman Rogue asked, his face remaining impassive.

"Yes, sir. Certain circumstances have arisen that have left us in need of assistance. We hoped to discuss a possible alliance with Hyrdian, or at the very least gain some backing from you." Elias recited the carefully thought-out speech they had planned, and Mylah nodded along beside him reciting it in her mind as well.

"And why should we offer you any assistance?" Councilman Aspertine asked flatly. Mylah's cheeks heated and her mouth tightened into a thin line as she fought to keep it shut.

"Queen Aveda of Cyprian is now working directly with King Florian of Adair. They have access to the Book of Creation and are planning on using it against Elowyn, and possibly all shreeve," Elias said. Mylah was surprised at the complete calm he emanated despite the councilmen seeming to be uninterested in helping Elowyn.

Both councilors raised their eyebrows, but otherwise appeared unphased by the news.

"If they were planning on starting a war with Hyrdian at some point, why would they have invited us to a meeting in Adair to discuss aligning with *them*?" Councilor Aspertine asked as he tapped his fingers on the table before him.

"King Florian invited you to Adair?" Mylah let slip and Elias glanced back at her but said nothing.

"Yes. I will be attending in a few weeks," Councilor Aspertine answered.

"What if we were to get more proof that Queen Aveda is planning on attacking more than Elowyn?" Mylah asked, catching Elias' eye again. "Would you agree to assist us then?"

Councilor Aspertine pursed his lips and leaned forward to steeple his hands on his desk. "If you were to have that proof, then it would certainly cause us to more seriously consider aligning our army with Elowyn's."

"Well for now, we have no more information regarding Queen Aveda's plans," Elias said, drawing the councilors' attention back to himself. "King Castien will send a formal offer and all we can do is hope that you decide to align yourselves with us," Elias said.

Mylah wanted to scream at them all that they were being ridiculous, but she had no idea how all this political stuff worked.

"And we will be sure to deliberate fully after meeting with King Florian and discussing with Councilor Bergine. Thank you for coming." As soon as Councilor Aspertine finished speaking, Leanardi reentered the room as if he'd been listening in. He offered his arms to Mylah and Elias and in a flash, they were back outside Elias' room at the inn.

"Thank you," Mylah said to Leanardi before he was gone again. Elias said nothing, but he opened the door and let it slam against the wall as he stormed into his room. Mylah hesitated before following him and shutting the door behind her.

"That was a waste of time. They're not going to help us," Elias spat out.

"They might..."

Elias cut off Mylah, "They're going to Adair! Queen Aveda will sway them to join her side."

As much as Mylah wanted to reassure him that the Hyrdian council would side with Elowyn, she had no faith in them after that brief meeting. Elias dropped down onto the end of his bed, placing his head in his hands.

"We will figure this out. We don't need them," Mylah said instead, though she wasn't sure she entirely believed that either. She stepped towards Elias, thinking to put her hand on his shoulder or arm, but she stopped herself, unsure whether he'd want that.

"Without their help, Elowyn may fall to Adair if they figure out how to use the Book of Creation." Elias lifted his head and the helplessness revealed there had Mylah's heart breaking for him. She knelt before him and placed her hand over his hand on his knee.

"Don't give up hope," she said, unsure where her own sense of hope was coming from. In the past few weeks, she'd given up on any sense that anything good would be coming her way, but something about seeing Elias so low had her fighting for the hope she'd once clung to before losing Garrick.

Elias said nothing as he looked into Mylah's eyes, but the hopelessness seemed to lift, and his eyes lightened. For a moment, Mylah wondered what was going through his head as he looked at her, but then he turned away.

"I should train," he said before standing and striding out of the room, leaving Mylah alone on the floor.

Sixteen

It took a week, but Greyson received permission from Captain Andreas to spend his next day off in town. When the day finally came, he nearly sprinted from the castle first thing in the morning. He planned to spend most of the day in town, buying the pants he'd claimed he needed, and then meeting up with Cassia for lunch before they headed back to her house.

Greyson took one of the royal guard's horses, and trotted into town at a meandering pace, allowing himself to take in all the sights he'd missed so much. It was his first time leaving the castle in weeks and he took full advantage. The shops were bustling, and townsfolk littered the streets. Greyson recognized a few of them, though he didn't know many of them personally. Growing up as a son of a council member, most of his time had been spent among other council members' families.

He continued past the village to a house set further back in the woods that surrounded the village. The familiarity of it struck Greyson harder than he'd thought it would, causing his chest to clench and his breathing to hitch. Tying the horse to a nearby tree, Greyson approached his home.

The name *Callister* that was engraved above the door had been scratched out. Greyson tore his eyes from his family name and put his hand out to push on the door. It swung open too easily. It should have been locked to keep out any unwanted visitors. As he stepped inside, though, he realized that he needn't worry about that, the place had already been ransacked. The emblem of Adair had been burned into the center of the entryway's floor, a sign that the house was now property of the king. Greyson was honestly surprised they hadn't burned the house to the ground along with Mylah's.

He held his breath as he walked down the hall to his old room and opened the door. It remained untouched. He released his breath and closed his eyes. For whatever reason, the king's men hadn't torn apart his room as they'd done the others, though it was still a mess. Perhaps it was because he'd remained loyal to Adair and its king, but he could only guess. His eyes strayed back down the hall to where Mylah's room had once been, and he found himself drawn towards it.

He made his way to the opposite end of the hall and braced his hand on her doorknob, before turning it. The moment he entered; anger welled in him. It rose through his gut into his chest and balled up in his throat. Of course, there was nothing left in that room. Everything had been removed and searched after her betrayal.

He snarled and turned on his heel, marching out of the house that was no longer his home. His family had turned their backs on Adair, on *him*. They deserved the fate that had befallen them and their home.

Disgraced

He began trudging back towards the village. The horse whinnied in protest of being left behind, but Greyson planned on returning for him after dinner. On his way back through the woods, he ran into Cassia.

"Greyson!" she squealed as she ran into his arms. "I've missed you so much." Cassia's words came out muffled against his shoulder. Greyson waited until she pulled away before removing his arms from around her, not wanting to let her go.

"I missed you too," he told her as she stepped back and smoothed out the front of her tunic. "We should get some food," he said as his eyes flicked to their surroundings. The trees were a great place to hide and there was no telling if the captain had him followed. He wouldn't put it past him.

They went into town for lunch but didn't talk much, wary of any prying ears. They commented on the weather and village gossip while they ate and left as soon as they finished.

Needing a more private space to talk, they headed towards Snake Head Lake. There, Cassia finally opened up.

"I've missed you so much," she said, looping her arm around Greyson's. "You and Mylah both."

Greyson whipped his head around. "Don't talk about her. Here or *anywhere*. If the king finds out..." Greyson trailed off. He had no idea what the king would do, but he knew that any talk of Mylah would bring suspicion upon Cassia, and she didn't need that kind of attention. Greyson had already lost too many people.

Cassia stopped and turned to Greyson. "I will talk about her if I want to. If the king sees me missing a friend as a punishable offense, then I will happily expose him for being irrational and overdramatic." Greyson couldn't help but laugh. Cassia smiled and continued walking.

"What is it like, being part of the royal guard?" she asked, and Greyson was thankful she'd changed the subject.

"Different from being a guard on the border. There is less fear of being attacked obviously..." As he said it, he realized that wasn't exactly true anymore, though he had started the fight with Acton and Kolt. "The bunks are a bit more comfortable, and since it's getting colder, it's nice to be inside."

"Do you hear anything exciting? Like secrets or war plans," Cassia paused, her eyes darting around the expanse of lakeside ahead of them. Greyson could tell she was on edge too.

"No. I overhear rumors sometimes, but only the captains know what's really going on," Greyson said.

"If I asked you to try to learn more, would you do it?" Cassia's voice lowered and she leaned closer to Greyson as they walked. Greyson understood what she wanted; intel to pass on to Mylah, but he wouldn't make her say it. Otherwise, he'd have an obligation to tell the king.

"Don't say anymore, and don't ask me again," he warned her, and she reeled back. "I can't."

"But you realize none of what is happening is right, don't you?" Cassia's eyes widened, pleading with him. Greyson closed his eyes and let his head drop as he sighed.

"It's more complicated than that. It doesn't matter what I think anymore. I'm bound to him...King Florian."

"Bound? With magic?" The disgust in Cassia's voice was enough to tell Greyson what she thought about his devotion to their king.

"As I said, I can't help you."

They walked back to her house in silence. It was the first of the council houses on the outskirts of town. Alessia and Caroline were cooking dinner inside when they entered.

"We're here!" Cassia yelled as they walked in the door.

"Thank you for the invitation," Greyson said as he made eye contact with Alessia. She smiled genuinely and it made him smile back.

"You're safe," she said in relief, which had Greyson furrowing his brow in question.

"Of course," he responded, turning to Cassia as if she'd explain.

"Come sit, dear." Alessia motioned to the table and Greyson waited for Cassia to sit first before following her lead. "A lot has been going on that you don't know about." Her eyes flicked to Caroline's and then to Cassia's. "You too, Cass."

"You've been keeping things from me?" Cassia asked, her voice rising in disbelief.

"The king is the one who has been keeping things from you, from everyone," Alessia clarified.

"I'm sure he has good reason to. He is the king after all," Greyson countered, but as he said it uneasiness stirred inside him.

"Greyson, there's something you need to know," Alessia started, but her eyes filled with tears, and she had to pause to take a deep breath. "Your father," she stopped again, wiping tears from her eyes.

"He ran away with the other traitors, I know," Greyson retorted, and Alessia shook her head.

"The others got away, but your father didn't."

"He was captured? Why haven't I seen him in the dungeons?" Greyson's heart raced with the thought that his own father had been so close all this time.

"Not captured, dear. Killed. The king's men killed him," Alessia finally finished. "I'm so sorry."

Greyson's vision narrowed and the room began to spin around him. "That's not possible," he murmured. "He's in Elowyn, with Crane and my mother." His breaths became short and shallow as he started to hyperventilate.

Cassia put her hand on his back and began making slow circles. "Breathe, Greyson." Her voice sounded as if it was under water. "Why wouldn't they have told us at the meeting?" Cassia asked her mother.

Greyson still swayed in his seat, barely holding on as his thoughts swirled with memories of his father.

"I hoped the king would announce it at the last meeting, but when he didn't, I realized he was hiding it. He didn't want to make Garrick into a martyr. He wants him to remain a traitor."

Greyson snapped back to reality at that. He forced himself to sit straight and breathe deeply. "My father *was* a traitor," he growled. "Just like Mylah." Contrary to the rage he felt towards his father for the part he'd played in betraying Adair, the pain that now resided in his chest from learning the truth hurt so much worse. Tears welled in his eyes, but he wiped them away and rose from the table. "I'm sorry, but I have to return to the castle."

"No, please. Stay for dinner," Cassia pleaded.

"Let him go. He needs to process." Alessia placed her hand over her daughter's.

Disgraced

"I won't say anything to the king, I'll keep the secret," Greyson promised. "Enjoy your dinner." He strode out of the house and back towards his horse.

Greyson's ride back to the castle was a blur. He couldn't remember exactly how he'd gotten back inside and into his bed, but there he lay, wide awake as the room spun around him. Noises sounded ten times louder, while being distant at the same time. His whole world seemed to be shifting, morphing into something else, and he could do nothing to stop it or slow it. The movement of it all made him nauseous. Yet he was lying completely still.

My father is dead, he thought. Dead. Killed by the king's men. Killed by someone most likely in the very room Greyson laid in now. How had he not known? How had he not felt...different? As if a piece were missing. He certainly felt it now. A hole had opened in his chest, and he couldn't fill it. No matter how much rage, grief, pain, or other emotion he tried to fill the gaping wound with, it remained hollow.

Greyson had signed his life over to a man who lied and manipulated him... And he couldn't undo it. He had made an oath to the king to never betray him or Adair. The oath had been bound with magic so if Greyson broke it, he would die. At the time it had seemed logical; of course, he would never betray his king or his kingdom. But now...

He shook his head. His father's death changed nothing. He would remain loyal to his king as he'd sworn.

"You look like you could use a drink." Julian stood beside Greyson's bed holding a glass filled with an amber liquid out towards him.

"No thanks," Greyson said, pushing the drink away. "I don't drink." He had never drunk, and he wasn't planning to start now, not when he needed his wits about him.

"Mind if I ask what's eating you?" Julian asked, sitting on the end of Greyson's bed. Greyson pulled his knees to his chest.

"Nothing. I'm fine."

"I've seen fine. You're not fine. But..." He shrugged. "Keep your secrets."

"You seem to know enough about me as it is," Greyson muttered.

Julian laughed, "That's only because everyone couldn't stop talking about you the first week you were here. There's not often scandals in this town, so you can't blame people for latching onto every detail thrown their way."

"People shouldn't be so absorbed in other people's problems." Greyson wished that everyone would go back to ignoring him, but since Julian had befriended him a few weeks back, everyone thought Greyson was willing to talk. The other guards didn't always ask him about Mylah, but she came up more times than he cared to count.

"I heard a rumor that Mylah is in Hyrdian," Julian said, and Greyson perked up. He hated being asked about Mylah, but that didn't mean he didn't still care about her wellbeing, as much as he wished he didn't. "I thought that might interest you."

Greyson groaned, he needed to be better about masking his emotions. "What did you hear?" he caved and asked. Greyson figured he may as well accept that he and Julian were friends.

"Queen Aveda has an inside man in Elowyn who said the prince of Elowyn and Mylah were sent by King

Castien to Hyrdian. The Queen doesn't have much interest in them, so she didn't ask for more information." Julian played with the edges of the fraying blanket that covered Greyson's bed. "The king was much more interested though, seeing as she's a wanted traitor."

"Is he going to send someone after her?" Greyson's heart began to race at the thought of Mylah being in danger.

"Doubtful. He's under Queen Aveda's thumb and to send someone into Hyrdian could stir up some unwanted attention," Julian said, and Greyson let out a breath of relief. "Interesting that she's there with the prince, though."

"You're prying," Greyson pointed out and Julian smirked.

"Only a little. I can't help it."

"Tell me something," Greyson started, realizing that though Julian knew way too much about him, Greyson knew nothing about Julian. "How long have you been here, in the castle?"

Julian leaned back on his elbows and looked as if he were considering his answer.

"Well, I came here not long after you. There was no better place for me in town. Becoming a guard wasn't as hard as I thought it would be." Julian took a sip of his drink. "My sister has always been the stronger one, so my family was a little surprised when I wound up here."

"You seem pretty capable to me," Greyson said. He hadn't seen Julian during any training sessions or anything, but he had some solid muscle mass and always seemed alert while on watch.

"Hmm." Julian stood from the bed and saluted before walking away. Greyson narrowed his eyes and waited for him to say a goodbye, or end the conversation, but he kept walking.

The next afternoon, Greyson and Julian stood outside the council chambers, neither of them speaking as they waited for the meeting to adjourn. The doors had been shut when Greyson arrived, taking over for another guard. Apparently, the meeting had been going on for hours with no end in sight. He couldn't imagine what they were discussing.

After another hour of standing so still Greyson thought he might fall asleep, the doors finally creaked and opened outward. Two guards pushed the doors towards Greyson, who stepped out of the way, and people Greyson didn't recognize began filing out of the council chambers. They all wore long, red robes that looked brand new. They had their heads bowed as they exited.

"Hosath be with you," one of them murmured to Greyson as she passed, and Greyson realized with a start that these were Hosath's worshippers.

He tried to meet Julian's eyes, but the other guard remained staring straight ahead. Greyson could have sworn a smile tugged at Julian's lips. There were at least fifty people who streamed out of the chambers, all wearing those robes. Once they had all exited, the doors closed behind them, but not before Greyson peered in and saw King Florian and Queen Aveda standing on the platform at the front of the room, both wearing smug expressions. Queen Aurelia was absent, which was odd to Greyson, but he assumed she may be with her children.

Greyson and Julian followed the group of worshippers out of the castle where they were all ushered into carriages and whisked away, back to the Hall of Hosath, Greyson assumed.

"That was strange," Greyson commented as he and Julian turned back inside.

"Was it?" Julian cocked an eyebrow in amusement.

"I mean...yeah. What could the king possibly want from them? They're all half out of their minds." He stopped when he noticed Julian's growing smile.

"The best kind of people to recruit for a cause. They're moldable and disposable."

Greyson reared back, struck by the flippancy of Julian's explanation.

"That's horrible! They may have differing ideals, but they're still citizens of Adair. For the king to use them like that..." Greyson trailed off, thinking back to the conversation he'd had with Alessia the night before. *The king is capable of much more trickery than we'd ever known*, he thought.

"What are you going to do about it?" Julian asked, his eyebrow arching.

Greyson deflated. There was nothing he could do about it without going against the king, and if he did that... Well, he'd be dead. Then he'd be of no help to anyone.

"Nothing. I serve the king, and there's nothing that can change that."

"Hm," Julian huffed, his smile faltering. "I need a nap."

"I have another shift in the garden. I'll see you later." Greyson veered away from Julian towards the castle's gardens.

Since Mylah had left, he'd found it hard to be in the gardens, not that he had a choice. He could picture her walking through the paths, admiring the flowers, picking the blue dahlias, and putting her finger to her lips, making Greyson promise to keep her theft a secret. He knew the king wouldn't mind her picking a flower or two, but he had loved being the one that Mylah pulled into her confidence on all matters, even those as trivial as flower thievery.

"Callister!" A harsh voice barked at him from down the hall. He glanced up to see Captain Andreas hurrying towards him. "You've been reassigned. Come with me."

Greyson followed Captain Andreas in the opposite direction of the gardens, towards the king's tower. Greyson had never been trusted with the task of guarding the king himself, which he attributed to Mylah's escape. He wondered if that was finally coming to an end.

Captain Andreas led him to the foot of the king's tower. If they took the stairs up, they'd enter the king and queen's chambers. The children's rooms were also up there. The tower itself was quite large and spanned almost half of the castle in width. Greyson had never been beyond the door that stood before him now.

"Stay here. The king will be with you soon." The captain left him alone at the base of the tower.

Greyson's heart began to race at all the possible reasons that the king wanted him. What if he had finally decided that Greyson couldn't be trusted and would dispose of him? Would the king *kill* him for allowing Mylah to escape with the prince of Elowyn?

No, Greyson forced his mind to stop. It had been weeks since that occurrence and the king wouldn't have waited this long to punish him.

Footsteps came from behind the closed door and Greyson stiffened. After a few moments, the door inched open until the king stood before him, towering over him, with a fire in his eyes. A grin spread over his face as his eyes met Greyson's.

"Greyson Callister, I have a task for you."

Seventeen

Two weeks had passed by much faster than Mylah anticipated, and it was time to prepare for their journey into the mountains. Elias requested the innkeeper keep their rooms vacant even while they were gone, paying her double what she would have made if she'd filled the rooms. She gave them a pack full of non-perishable food and canteens of water in thanks.

Farren arrived early in the morning at the tavern to begin their journey. Mylah rode with Elias, and Farren led the way. They were headed to the Lake of Desires where they could board a ship to travel to the other side. There was no other way to leave Hyrdian on that border. Thankfully, as Farren had told them, the ship was large enough for the horses, so they'd be able to continue riding to the mountains after they made it across the lake.

Farren warned that the Lake of Desires was not to be taken lightly. His exact words were, '*Many seasoned sailors have lost their minds traveling across the lake.*'

Even traveling at full speed on the horses, it took them the whole day to reach the Lake of Desires with breaks for the horses and pit stops to eat and go to the bathroom.

On each break, Farren had Elias practice sensing if there were any other people around. He would send out a wave of his own magic that could tell if there were any other magic users in the vicinity. Humans and witches gave off different auras and he could sense the differences in them through that wave. Mylah was always amazed when she watched him, even though he was still learning, his power was immense.

As the moon rose high in the sky, they approached the dock and Mylah noticed a few heads peeking out from under it, their eyes glowing a deep red color.

"Naiads," Farren said, answering Mylah's unasked question. "Don't worry too much about them. It's the lake itself you have to watch out for."

Mylah furrowed her brow. She wasn't entirely sure how a *lake* could be a danger, other than if she couldn't swim, but she knew not to question it. Elias had remained quiet most of their journey. Mylah's gaze found his and held it for a moment before looking away.

"Come on," Farren beckoned them forward, leading the way down to the dock.

A single man stood at the end of the dock next to the ship tied there. Mylah figured that the ship would be able to hold maybe twenty people maximum. It wasn't nearly as large as she'd expected, but at least it appeared Farren was right, and the horses would fit. Mylah supposed a larger ship would be a little superfluous on the Lake of Desires, since it wasn't nearly as large as the Lake of Anguish.

"Good evening," the man grumbled as they neared him.

"We are looking for passage into the Unbounds. We are headed for the mountains." Farren spoke for them, which Mylah was grateful for.

"That'll be ten silvers each." The man smirked as if the price might deter them.

Elias stepped forward, dropping the amount the man had requested into his outstretched hand. The man's eyes widened for a moment before he waved them forward onto the ramp up to the ship's deck. Another man took their horses on board and brought them into a covered stable-like area.

"That seems like a lot of money," Mylah pointed out.

"They don't have a lot of traffic through here, and there is a lot of risk traveling across this lake," Farren explained.

There were fifteen people manning the ship. One stood at the helm, another sat in the crow's nest. The rest prepared the sails and pulled up the anchor.

Once they'd made their way out onto the water, Mylah stood at the railing, her elbows resting on it as she peered down into the lake. The water was fairly clear, and she could see the shadows of fish swimming beneath them. A breeze brought fresh scents of the nearby grass and flowers, which thankfully helped to mask the smell of must and unwashed sailors that had become stagnant as they'd prepared to set sail.

As she stared down below the surface, ripples marred the perfectly round reflection of the moon, and her own face materialized in the water, staring back at her. Startled, she stepped away from the rail, but curiosity brought her back and she peered down to see herself still gazing up at her.

You should join me... A voice floated through her mind. *It wouldn't hurt, it would be like falling asleep...* The voice was her own and it didn't scare her. Instead, she found herself considering the words, deciphering them, and leaning further over the railing. Her reflection smiled at her, starlike twinkles in her eyes and Mylah smiled in return. *You're right, they wouldn't miss you. But I would. Join me...*

Mylah leaned further over the railing until she lost her balance and began falling. Hands grasped her waist, hauling her back onto the deck.

"Woah there, miss. Watch yourself," a gruff voice said behind her.

"Sorry, I slipped," she lied, turning to see a goblin standing there.

His raised eyebrow and curled lip told her he didn't believe her, but he didn't care enough to ask any more questions. He left her and returned to mopping the deck. Once he was far enough away that he couldn't bother her again, Mylah leaned back over the railing to find herself, but this time, Garrick stared back at her. She cocked her head to the side in confusion.

"Garrick?" she whispered to the wind and his voice came back to her.

"Mylah," he spoke softly for only her to hear. "Mylah, don't you want to be with me again? Don't you want to see me again?"

"Of course, but I can't," she closed her eyes. "You're gone," she said.

His laugh rolled across the water. "You can," he said, and Mylah opened her eyes to see his reflection reaching for her. "Come with me," he beckoned. Mylah wanted to follow his voice, follow him into the depths of the lake, but something nagged at her.

"No," she said forcefully, pushing herself away from the railing as the reflection shifted and brought her to a halt. Her mother stared up at her. "Ma?" Tears sprang to her eyes.

"Mylah..." Vita's voice carried to her on the wind. "What a disappointment you've become." The reflection of her mother twisted, and her face became vicious and cruel, a way Mylah had never seen her in life. "Your father and I died for nothing because of you..."

"Mylah!" Elias' voice brought Mylah back to awareness and she whipped around to face him as he hurried towards her. "What are you doing? Stay away from the railings!"

"What do you care?" she muttered as she wiped the tears from her eyes.

He stopped before he reached her, and his hands flexed at his sides.

"I care," he growled before stalking away to go below deck. Farren strolled over, passing Elias as he approached Mylah.

"What's got him in a mood?" Farren asked, smirking.

Mylah shrugged. "Couldn't tell you." She had no idea what went through Elias' head these days. She couldn't figure him out.

"Do you hear them too?" Farren asked suddenly and Mylah shook her head before a faint hum reached her ears.

"Wait..." She listened intently, and the hum grew louder. "Is that...singing?" Farren appeared horrified and Mylah didn't know why.

"We need to get below deck," he said, putting his arm around her shoulders and steering her towards the stairs.

"Are they sirens?" she asked.

"No. Not sirens," he said, but didn't elaborate.

Mylah let him lead her below deck where they found Elias sitting on a barrel next to three other men. It was cramped down there, which Mylah had expected from the size of the ship. There were a few cots towards the hull, but no one occupied them. Mylah and Farren sat on a box next to Elias. They could still hear the strange humming down there, but it was more muted.

"The veela…" one of the men commented, shuddering. "Last time we had a newbie with us, and he didn't know better than to accept one of their bargains. He'd been pulled under before any of us could get to him."

Mylah turned her head to him. "What are veela?" she asked.

"Accursed creatures," he hissed. "They can appear as human, shreeve, fae – whatever you fancy. Then they offer you something you can't refuse, but what they don't tell you is the price is your life."

"Are they what make the reflections in the lake? The ones that look like people you've lost?" Mylah realized her mistake as everyone turned to stare at her.

The man who'd been speaking chuckled. "You've fallen victim to the Lake of Desires. So, tell us, what does a woman like you desire, hm?" His mouth curled into a sneer, and it sent shivers down Mylah's spine as his gaze raked her up and down. She wrapped her arms around herself, pressing closer to Farren.

"As if any woman would even think twice about you," Elias bit back. Mylah blushed and clenched her jaw. The men dispersed, leaving her alone with Elias and Farren.

"It was myself," she whispered. "Then Garrick, and then my mother," she admitted. She didn't want to hold it inside.

"I've seen my family in these waters. It's best to ignore them. They only tell you what you're already thinking, but it's always your darkest desires," Farren said.

"They wanted me to join them," she gulped. "In the water. Except for my mother, she told me..." Mylah took a deep breath. "She told me that she and my father died for nothing because of me."

"I see." Farren took her hand, but the tightness of his posture told Mylah he was uncomfortable with comforting her. "Sometimes, we may not understand why the lake shows us what it does, but it's best if you stay down here the rest of the journey. It won't be too much longer now." Mylah wasn't sure what response she'd been hoping for, but that wasn't it. Though, she did appreciate his attempt as he squeezed her hand before leaving her and Elias alone.

"I heard voices too," Elias spoke, startling Mylah. "My mother's and my father, or King Haldor." He cleared his throat as if something stuck in it and continued. "They told me the same thing." He didn't say anymore, but Mylah scooted a little closer to him, taking his hand, and he let her, without shying away. They sat like that in silence for the rest of the journey.

Eighteen

Mylah stretched her limbs as they debarked from the ship. The horses shook their manes and stamped their hooves in the grass, happy to be back on solid ground. Mylah couldn't help but share the sentiment. She could see why people liked to sail, but after dealing with the accursed waters and hearing horror stories about the veela, she would pass on any future excursions that led onto the Lake of Desires.

"We should find a place to make camp for the night," Farren said as they led the horses away from the ship. The trek across the lake had only taken them a couple hours and the moon was still high overhead.

"Let's at least make it to the trees where we'll have more coverage," Elias suggested.

Mounting their horses, they traveled at a normal horse's pace, letting them grow accustomed to being on land once more, until they reached the edge of the trees. The horses halted at the line of trees that demarcated the start of the forest, wary to move forward. Smudge pawed at the ground with his hooves as he resisted Elias' urging to continue.

"That's not a good sign..." Mylah murmured and Farren grunted in agreement.

"We'll stop here, then. Maybe once the sun rises whatever is spooking them will have gone." Farren hopped off his horse, who Mylah had dubbed Boots because of his dark brown coloring on his legs against his lighter brown body that made it look like he wore boots.

They set up their bedrolls a little ways into the forest to help protect them from being seen by any creatures that may be passing by in the night. For the same reason, they decided against a fire. It was cold, but not so cold that a fire was necessary. They had all worn long, lined jackets knowing it would be colder in the mountains.

"We should make a plan." Farren unfolded a map in front of him and held up a ball of light he'd created so they could see it. "Here." He pointed to a line he'd drawn on the map. "It's a straight shot to the heart of the mountains from here, but we have to be careful. If what you said is true, there could be trolls and orcs roaming the woods that separate us from the narrow pass leading up through the mountains. And once we enter the mountains, it's very likely we'll encounter a few."

"We can't take the horses into the mountains; they'll be too visible. We have to be able to stay hidden in case there is anything going on up there," Elias pointed out.

"That's why I'm going to stay behind at the base of this mountain." Farren pointed to the first one they'd come to. "I'll set up a camp here. I know of a cave I can keep the horses in. It's protected from the elements, and we should be able to stay concealed from any threat."

"So, Mylah and I will venture into the mountains alone," Elias said, and Mylah thought she heard a hint of apprehension in his tone.

"Yes, if you think you can handle it. It's not too hard to navigate. You should be able to get to this peak." He pointed to one of the central mountains. "Easily enough, and from there, you'll be able to see the next mountain. Hopefully, that will be enough to find out if anything is suspicious or out of the ordinary."

"I think we can handle it," Mylah said, and Elias nodded in agreement.

"We don't have the time or resources to be out here longer than a week, so keep that in mind. The trek up the mountain should take about two days if all goes well."

"That will leave you alone for at least four days then," Mylah said, a stone dropping in her stomach as she thought about Farren facing a troll alone, or something worse.

"As I said, the cave will keep me concealed." He patted Mylah's shoulder. "Don't worry about me. I've been alone out here longer before." Mylah nodded reluctantly. She thought they would be sticking together the entire time. "Now, get some sleep. I'll wake you when the sun comes up." Farren folded up the map and placed it in a pocket inside his jacket.

Mylah woke with an ache in her side from sleeping on the ground. A small rock had dug into her most of the night, and she hadn't realized it until it was too late. Elias chatted with Farren by the horses, already packed and ready to leave. Mylah stretched her arms over her head, twisting to try to ease the muscles that had knotted in her back, but it didn't do much.

After Mylah packed up her bedroll and relieved herself, they ate a quick breakfast and continued through the forest. The horses were less reluctant to move forward than the night before, but they still acted wary which put everyone on edge. Every snap of a twig or crunch of a leaf had them all jumping and swiveling to catch a glimpse of the culprit.

Moving at a slower pace than normal to avoid drawing attention, it took them four hours to make it to the edge of the forest where they could see the mountains again. The mountains loomed over them, seeming to warn them away. Mylah shuddered as a breeze swept around them, bringing cooler air and the scent of snow. Farren had said there wouldn't be any real snow built up except on the highest peaks, but that they should expect a flurry or two while climbing.

They continued onward towards a pass that would take them between the first two mountains, which were the smallest of the range.

"Stay alert," Farren warned, as if they hadn't been on high alert all morning. "There's a reason these are named the *Forsaken Mountains*. Nothing here is anything you'll want to remember later." A roar echoed down the pass as if in answer. Mylah and Elias stiffened but Farren remained unbothered.

"Should we..." Elias started but Farren cut him off.

"Don't pay that any mind. It could have been miles away for all we know. This pass is like a funnel, amplifying all the sounds coming from the mountains on the other side." Mylah glanced back at Elias who appeared as wary as her, but their horse continued to follow Farren's.

The only sounds that reached them as they continued were rocks falling. It seemed ominous to Mylah, but she said nothing. All she could smell as they walked was a faint scent of pine, overwhelmed by the dust in her nose.

Another hour passed before they reached the end of the pass, putting them at the base of the mountain Mylah and Elias were to hike. It was far from the tallest of the mountains in the range, but it still appeared menacing.

"The cave is over here," Farren said before steering his horse to the left.

Smudge followed without much direction from Elias. Before they reached the cave, Farren dismounted from Boots and indicated that Elias and Mylah should do the same. They led the horses forward on foot until they came to the cave.

"Here it is," Farren said, leading Boots towards the entrance. Boots pulled back on the reins for a moment but then allowed Farren to take him inside. Smudge did the same, but after they were inside, the horses calmed down. There was plenty of light in the cave coming from the entrance so it was easy to see the large, open cavern that Farren would be camping in. Mylah noticed drawings on the cave walls and wondered if Farren had done some of them on his past adventures. Otherwise, the cave was empty.

"I'll set up camp here." Farren reached into his inner jacket pocket and pulled out the map. "You should take this. Follow this path, it will lead you to the mountain peak."

"We can help you set up camp," Elias offered.

"No, you should go now. The sooner you leave, the sooner we can get out of this place," Farren scowled, showing the first sign of discomfort since arriving in the mountains. Farren had already separated the provisions into packs for Mylah and Elias to take while they'd slept that morning.

"If we're not back in a week…" Elias said but trailed off. Farren knew what he meant and jerked his head in a curt nod.

"And if I'm not here when you return…" Farren said, and Elias reciprocated with the same nod.

"Glad we have those plans in place," Mylah said, trying to lighten the morose mood. "In the meantime, let's try *not* to die."

Elias led the way out of the cave and towards the path that would lead them to the mountain peak.

Mylah and Elias' first day trekking up the mountain ended without incident. They found a small area surrounded by large boulders to make camp for the night. All they had seen that day was boulders. There wasn't much life on the mountain, besides some patches of grass here and there. It made Mylah more confident that they wouldn't run into much trouble since there was no reason for anything or anyone to be on that mountain, but it also made her doubt they'd find any useful information there.

Elias laid out his bedroll and sat down, pulling his jacket tighter around himself before grabbing a loaf of bread from his bag. He pulled his knees up towards him and rested his elbows there as he picked at the bread. They hadn't eaten since breakfast – trying to ration their food in case something went wrong, and they ended up in the mountains longer than they'd planned.

"Should I...?" Mylah motioned to the ground beside Elias. Even though they'd decided to start over and be friends, things had still been awkward. She wasn't sure if he would want her lying beside him, even though the extra warmth would be vital, at least for Mylah.

Elias glanced beside him and then his eyes widened for a moment as he realized what she was asking. He cleared his throat and ducked his head before grunting in acceptance and shoving a piece of bread into his mouth. Mylah tried to hide her smile as she laid out her bedroll beside his.

Sitting down, Mylah pulled her knees to her chest, and wrapped her arms around them. Her feet were sore from walking in boots, and she was certain she had a few blisters, but the warmth the boots provided was more important than comfort while walking.

Elias handed Mylah some bread and she nibbled on it while contemplating what they may encounter the next day.

"What's on your mind?" Elias asked, breaking their silence.

Mylah put the bread down. "I'm worried that the lack of life on this mountain means we're on the wrong one," she said, and Elias opened his mouth to say something, but she continued. "I know it's a gamble we'll find out anything, and we chose this mountain because it's towards the center and it would be the easiest to climb, but..."

"You think we're wasting our time," Elias finished for her, and Mylah dropped her head to her chest. "Don't lose hope yet. If we don't find anything out, I'll make sure Castien sends a scout out when we return to Elowyn."

"You would have him do that?" Mylah peeked at him and noticed his hands fidgeting with his remaining bread as he stared at the ground.

"I know I was hesitant to come out here before, but it truly does seem important enough to investigate. If...if you and Genevieve are worried about it." He pursed his lips and his jaw clenched.

"Thank you."

Mylah finished her bread and drank from her canteen. They had enough water for a few days, but if it snowed, then they'd be able to hydrate with that as well. Mylah smirked as she remembered when she and Cassia used to dream of eating real snow on the hottest days of summer. They'd put chunks of ice into bowls and smash it up until it was little chips. Half of the ice had usually melted by the time they ate it, but they didn't care. They'd had small flurries in Adair, but never full-on snowstorms like they had on other continents.

"We can take turns keeping watch. I'll take the first half of the night," Elias said, standing and heading towards the path.

There was a smaller boulder he sat on beside the larger boulder that blocked them from view. *So much for sharing body heat,* Mylah thought as she stared at his back. Settling into her bedroll, she tried to fall asleep. The cold crept in, but her jacket and boots helped keep it at bay and allowed her to get some sleep.

Nothing bothered them in the night. Mylah couldn't help thinking as she kept watch that she could have been sleeping instead of watching a barren mountain.

During the day, the only other living beings they encountered were bugs. Mylah swatted at them as they walked through a whole swarm of tiny flies.

"Blech," she coughed as one of the flies went down her throat. "Disgusting," she groaned. Elias chuckled and then coughed as a fly went into his own mouth. Mylah smirked and stuck her tongue out at him.

"That's what you get for laughing at me," she said, prodding him in the side as they both laughed. Mylah paused as she noticed something past a grouping of rocks off to the left. "Hold on," she said, veering from their path and maneuvering her way towards what looked like a wooden stake. As she neared it, she realized that the mountain dropped off into a cliff and there were two stakes with a bridge made of planks and rope attached to them. The bridge swayed in the wind and the stakes creaked with the weight of it.

The bridge led to another mountain that had trees sprouting along the edge. Mylah couldn't help but wonder if there was more life on the other side of the bridge.

"What is it?" Elias asked as he approached Mylah and stopped beside her taking in the sight. "There's no chance I'm going across that thing," he said, guessing what Mylah wanted to do. Instead of talking about it, Mylah ventured forward, placing a foot on the bridge, testing it.

"Come on. Where's your sense of adventure?" she asked as she put her whole weight onto the first plank, and it dipped beneath her weight but held her up. "There's clearly nothing on this mountain. Maybe we'll get lucky over there."

Elias placed a hand on the rope railing of the bridge and groaned. "I don't really have a choice, do I?" he said.

Mylah grinned. "I knew there was a reason I kept you around." She patted his hand before taking the next step. The bridge swayed and she clutched the railings as her heart dropped into her stomach.

"Change your mind?" Elias asked, sounding hopeful.

Mylah shook her head and took another step. "Never," she breathed. She kept moving, trying not to look down as she reached the halfway point on the bridge. Elias stayed close behind her, his hands nearly on top of hers on the railings.

"Almost there," he murmured, and she jumped at his nearness. Her boot slipped off the board beneath her and the sensation of falling hit her as her stomach dropped and a scream ripped out of her. An arm wrapped around her middle and a hand clamped over her mouth, stifling her scream, as Elias caught her.

"Sorry," Mylah muttered once he'd removed his hand from her mouth. He breathed heavily behind her, still holding her against him.

"We need to get across this bridge before someone comes to investigate that scream," he huffed.

Mylah started moving again, though her whole body shook, and she could barely keep herself steady enough to balance on the bridge.

Elias had one hand on the railing and the other fluttering back and forth from Mylah's waist to his side, giving away his nerves. They reached the other side of the bridge as voices and footsteps began, headed their way.

Trees rose around Mylah and Elias as they ran into the thick of them, trying to find a place to hide. The voices grew louder, and Elias grabbed Mylah's arm, pulling her towards a slope and they slid down the side of it until they were beneath the edge and out of sight.

"I heard someone. I swear," a man's voice grumbled.

"It was probably a bird or something," another man responded, sounding annoyed as if this was a common occurrence for them.

"I guess..." the first man didn't sound confident. "Let's take a look around, just in case." The other man didn't argue, and the footsteps faded, but then returned shortly after.

Mylah began slipping further down the slope as they clung to the small rocks jutting out. She couldn't find purchase with her clunky boots. Elias' arm was around her as he attempted to hold her up, but he began sliding too. They were making too much noise.

"We have to let go," Elias whispered.

He let go first, catching himself every few feet. Thankfully it wasn't so steep that they couldn't hold themselves in a spot for a few seconds. Mylah slid down beside him, and they were able to reach the bottom of the slope without much more than a few scratches. Glancing back up, Mylah realized the slope had seemed much bigger when they were sliding down it. It only had brought them down about a hundred feet from where they'd been.

"Come on," Elias said, taking Mylah's hand and leading her away from the ravine they'd landed in. "We need to get out of sight in case they look over the edge. We can make our way back up once we're under cover."

Once they were under the cover of trees, they paused to take a break.

"At least we know we're on the right mountain now," Mylah pointed out.

Elias said nothing as he sipped water from his canteen.

They found a path that led upwards and began picking their way up it. Mylah's muscles were sore from sleeping on the ground the past two nights, but she was able to climb over the rocks and keep up with Elias for a while.

Had she kept up with training for the past few weeks, she'd have been in much better shape, but she couldn't think about that now.

They kept walking once their path flattened out and Elias paused every few minutes to see if he could sense anyone nearby. After an hour or so of nothing, he finally sensed people nearby. Fae specifically.

"If you can sense them, won't that mean they can sense you?" Mylah asked.

"Not necessarily. My ability to sense other magic users comes from my warlock side. If they *are* strong enough to sense us, there are a lot more of them than there are of us. I know to feel for anyone other than myself and you. If they were to sense us, they'd assume we are part of their group and hopefully not dig any deeper."

"How many are there?"

"I can't tell... but a lot. More than two hundred I'd guess."

Mylah gulped. They moved forward, crouching as they neared the end of the grouping of trees they were concealed by. A whole host of tents, fire pits, tables, and other gear were set up in a large clearing before them, but most of their view was obscured by the back of a tent.

"Don't eat that," a woman nearby said, hurrying after a man. The man paused, and she grabbed whatever it was he'd been about to put in his mouth, throwing it into the woods. "Freida is the cook today."

The man scowled at that. "I'll be sure to skip dinner then, too," he said. They both laughed and continued out of sight.

"We're not going to learn anything of use from here," Mylah said, craning her neck to try to see around the side of the tent. Elias moved to the left and Mylah followed until they had a better view of the camp.

A group of fae sat at a table, playing cards. Mylah prayed to Hosath or whoever watched over them that the fae wouldn't see them crouching in the underbrush. She was sure that if they were visible, Elias would have moved them back, but fae had exceptional sight and hearing.

"Pass," one of the men at the table grumbled.

"Pass," the next man said, followed by a woman who laid her cards out and grinned wickedly at them both.

"Pay up," she drawled. The men groaned and dug into their pockets, each dropping a coin onto the table. The other two women playing laid their cards out as well, neither paying anything. Mylah wondered what game they played. She'd only played cards a few times before, but she'd watched her parents play often when she was little.

"Much more of this and we'll have to sail home to Cyprian on a raft," one of the men joked.

"It's a good thing Queen Aveda takes your service as payment for your passage," the woman who'd won responded as she scooped up the coins on the table.

"I think I'll find myself a nice castle to settle into once we take over."

"You act as if there are castles just scattered about. There are exactly two you can choose from once we're done here. Maybe three. But the Queen has already claimed one for herself, and I'm sure she's not saving any for *you*."

Mylah blanched. She couldn't help but wonder if the castle Queen Aveda planned on claiming was the Adairian castle. Which would mean she planned on turning on King Florian after using him to start her war.

"A man can dream."

"Another hand?" The woman began shuffling the cards and all talk of the Queen dropped so Mylah and Elias crept away. They stopped as they heard the clanging of swords and headed towards the sound.

"Ha! You're going to have to do better than that if you want to take on the shreeve!" someone said. Mylah and Elias stopped as they saw two men sword fighting in a small clearing.

"We've got an army of four hundred men, I don't think we need to worry about whatever pitiful resistance Elowyn is going to put together," the other man said.

"Don't get too cocky. Queen Aveda told us to plan for the chance that Hyrdian will lend them aid. If that happens, we'll be up against witches and warlocks as well."

Elias tugged Mylah's sleeve and they began backing away from the fae.

As they made their way back to safety, Mylah lost sight of Elias. Pausing to get her bearings, she realized she had no idea if she was even headed in the right direction.

A branch broke to Mylah's left and she whipped her head that direction. As she did, a hand clamped onto her arm and yanked her from her cover.

"What a surprise," a woman's voice hissed in her ear. "We don't get many visitors up here."

Shaking, Mylah turned her head to face the woman and recognized her as the one who had been playing cards.

"I-I-I'm not a spy," Mylah sputtered, cursing herself inwardly for how pathetic she sounded. "I was hiking and got lost."

"No one hikes these mountains," the woman hissed. "I don't like liars." The woman began half dragging Mylah into the camp as Mylah stumbled along beside her. She ripped the pack from Mylah's back and tossed it to the side.

"What do you got, Irene?" a tall, red-haired man asked as Irene flung Mylah forward.

Mylah wrapped her arms around herself and turned in a circle, trying to come up with a plan of escape. These were fae, though, and to escape them would be nearly impossible. She'd have to wait until no one was watching her.

"I found her spying in the bushes," Irene said, stepping forward so she could stare down her nose at Mylah more effectively.

"What's a human doing all the way out here, all alone?" the man asked, stepping forward to study her. As he looked her up and down, his lip curled, and his brows pulled together.

"She's nothing special, just dispose of her."

"You know I can't do that, Kal. I have to wait for the captain to return, or he'll have my ass sent back to Cyprian for some stupid infraction." Irene backed away from Mylah and began pacing. "He's been waiting for me to slip up."

"Whatever," Kal murmured, walking past Mylah, and slamming his shoulder into hers. "I'm going to get some food. Want anything?"

"Grab me a bowl of whatever there is," Irene said. "I'm going to tie this one up to the post."

Mylah blanched. *The post?* she thought. *They have a specific place for tying people up? This can't be good.* A sharp pain began in her chest as her heart started beating faster and fear had her muscles twitching to run.

Irene grabbed her arm again and pulled her further into the camp. They passed more fae as they went, most of them intrigued by the intruder. Mylah noticed a few non-fae among the rest, and wondered if they were human, witch, or other.

When they reached the post, which literally was a post sticking up out of the ground in the center of the camp, Irene tied a rope around Mylah, securing her to the round, wooden fixture.

"Please," Mylah gasped out as Irene tied the final knot. "I won't tell anyone what I saw out here," she tried, but Irene laughed in her face.

"You think I'd trust you?"

"But your queen has allied with the humans, and *I'm* human! I'm from Adair, the very kingdom your queen is staying in right now!" Mylah said. A crowd had begun to gather around them. "King Florian sent me to," Mylah paused trying to come up with something that she could have been sent to tell them. Something that wouldn't seem too farfetched. Before she could come up with anything though, the whole crowd that had gathered laughed.

"King Florian?" Irene said through her laughter. "Darling, King Florian doesn't even know we're here."

Mylah leaned her head back against the post in defeat. She'd revealed herself a liar after all and now they would never trust her.

Irene leaned in closer. "We're not here to help King Florian," she whispered. "We're here to end his reign and claim his land."

Mylah's eyes widened and a spark of hope lit in her chest. "So, there isn't going to be a true war against Elowyn? The Book of Creation won't be used against the shreeve?"

Irene covered her mouth to hold back more laughter and Mylah furrowed her brow in confusion.

"Oh, you're so naïve. It's adorable, really." Irene's smile turned to a scowl, and she slammed a hand against the pole above Mylah's head. "Shreeve shouldn't even exist in this world," she growled.

"I brought you a bowl of...whatever this is," Kal interrupted, drawing Irene away from Mylah. Irene took the bowl and stalked into the crowd, throwing one last withering glare back at Mylah.

Eventually, the rest of the crowd dispersed, no longer holding any interest in Mylah. When all eyes were off her, she began trying to wriggle out of the ropes, but Irene had secured them too well.

Ugh. Where is Elias? Mylah wondered, hoping that he was planning a rescue rather than considering her a lost cause.

As the day wore on, and there was no sign of Elias, Mylah began to worry he may not come. She hadn't thought he would leave her behind, but if she were in his shoes, she couldn't say she'd choose to save her either.

The sun dipped below the horizon and darkness overwhelmed the camp for a moment before orbs of light, like those Mylah had seen in Hyrdian, popped up all over the camp. Shadows were cast along the tents that blocked most of Mylah's view of the rest of the camp. Every time a shadow moved, Mylah's entire body stiffened in anticipation, but no one came her way.

As her eyes grew heavy, and the chill of the night settled in around her, a voice drew Mylah back to full consciousness.

"I tied her up on the post, as we were instructed to do with any intruders," Irene said as a pair of footsteps approached Mylah from behind. "She's a human, and she says she's from Adair, but she's a liar, so I don't know if that's true."

"Stop. Talking," a deep, angered voice followed. "Your presence in not needed."

Mylah heard an exasperated sigh before one set of footsteps began to retreat while the other continued towards her. Mylah may not like Irene, but she wanted to punch the man, whom she assumed was the captain, for how he spoke to her.

Finally, the captain came around the post and Mylah could take in the massive bulk of him. She had to crane her neck up to see his eyes which were a bright, icy, gray color. His matching gray hair had been tied back into a top knot of braids on his head, and rage poured off him in waves.

"What brought you to the mountains?" he asked, his voice deep and demanding.

Mylah wanted to curl in on herself, but the ropes held her in place. Everything about the captain was intimidating. From his size to the leather gear he wore, to the giant sword strapped at his hip. It could easily slice Mylah in two before she could scream.

Gazing down at his boots, the least intimidating part about him, though they could also do some serious damage, Mylah found the courage to speak. "Hiking," she stuck with her lie. After all she'd seen and heard, she was dead no matter what she told these people.

He placed his index finger under her chin and raised her face to his. "Do. Not. Lie. To me," he said the words with deliberation, but they were quiet, for only her to hear.

"I-I'm not." She tried to turn her face away, but he gripped her jaw now with his thumb and forefinger. As Mylah stared at the man before her, a strange thing happened. One second, he was the fearsome captain, and for a single instance, a small fae woman stood in his place before they were the hulking man again. If she had blinked, she would have missed it.

"What the –" she started, and the man released his grip on her, stepping back.

"My magic is depleted and my glamour slipping," a woman's voice came out and shattered the intimidating aura that had exuded from the man a moment earlier.

Mylah blinked rapidly, trying to comprehend what was happening.

"So, you're not the captain?" Mylah asked.

"Oh, no. I'm the captain. I just don't look like this," he said, using the deeper voice again. He set about untying Mylah before gripping her wrists together in one hand and pulling her away from the post.

"What are you going to do to me?" Mylah gasped out, pain flaring in her shoulders from being dragged around so much that day.

"Question you away from prying eyes. Only a select few know of my true form," as the captain spoke, Mylah noticed that there were two women standing guard, but no one else in the immediate vicinity.

They must be some of the few who know, Mylah thought.

"Where is everyone?" she asked.

"There is some kind of bug going around the camp. Let's just say, I'm glad I wasn't here for any meals today," the captain joked.

Mylah couldn't believe the complete one eighty in the captain's demeanor from a minute before. Though, Mylah was still on edge and wary of what was to come.

The captain led Mylah to a tent on the edge of the camp and the two women who stood guard before, stayed outside to watch the entrance. Dropping her glamour, the captain revealed her true form.

A woman shorter and slighter than Mylah replaced the hulking form from before. Her eyes and hair were that same icy gray, and her skin was paler than anyone Mylah had ever met.

"Do not make the mistake of believing I am any less powerful in this form," she snarled as she released Mylah from her grip.

"I would never," Mylah said, meaning it.

"My glamour started out as a joke between myself and Queen Aveda, but I found I liked how it fit me." She studied her hand, wiggling her fingers as she spoke.

"Now," she started, but before she could continue a wail sounded from outside the tent. Groaning in frustration, she poked her head out the front entrance to speak to the guards. "Can you quiet them down?"

Mylah frantically scanned the area, searching for a weapon of some sort. She'd left her dagger from Garrick in her pack this time instead of strapping it to her thigh as usual, which she deeply regretted now.

"What? Why can't they..." the captain still spoke with the guards.

A cot had been placed against the right wall of the tent, and a desk had been tucked into the opposite corner. Otherwise, the tent was open. Mylah had the thought that she could slip out underneath the side of the tent, but the captain turned back towards her.

"Where were we?" she mused as she tapped her chin.

A scuffle could be heard outside the tent, followed by a thud and an '*oof.*'

"For the love of... What now?" the captain turned to the entrance once more. A blazing ball of blue flames flew through the tent flaps and slammed into her chest, throwing her across the space.

A short scream escaped Mylah before Elias ran into the tent, his frantic gaze finding hers and softening as he beckoned to her to follow him.

The captain was already righting herself, rising from a crouched position behind them. Mylah hurried to Elias' side, and they fled the tent with the captain on their heels. A ball of deep red flames flew past Mylah, so close it singed the ends of her hair.

"You cannot escape me," the captain, having glamoured herself once more, yelled in her deeper voice.

As they ran, a twinge in Mylah's lower back made her cry out in pain.

"What's wrong? Are you hurt?" Elias asked as they continued running, unable to stop or else be caught by the captain.

"No, I'm fine. My back's been bothering me since the first night we slept on the ground." It was true, though it hadn't bothered her all day until now.

"I think she stopped following," Elias said, letting out a huff as he paused to listen intently. "Almost everyone else is sick, which made it much easier to sneak in unnoticed."

"She probably doesn't want to come after us with such little manpower," Mylah suggested. It nagged at her though, that the captain would give up so easily.

Once they were a safe distance from the camp, and were sure no one was following them, they stopped to catch their breath. Elias found his pack which he'd stowed away while he'd gone to rescue Mylah.

"Thanks for coming back for me," Mylah said once she could breathe properly again.

Elias stood from the rock he'd been perched on. "I would never leave you behind."

Mylah stood as well, watching Elias closely as he stepped towards her, his gaze darkening.

"I thought they were going to hurt you. I wasn't sure what I'd find when I found you." His breath hitched and he reached out, brushing his hand against hers before taking it.

Mylah squeezed his hand and turned her face up to meet his. His grayish blue eyes, slightly darker than her own, widened as he gazed down at her. The green surrounding the gray iris was muted in the dark, as if reflecting the fact that without the sun, his magic would also be slightly less powerful. But it hadn't seemed that way when he'd attacked the captain of the fae camp mere minutes ago.

"You were able to control your magic," Mylah said, breaking the tension of the moment.

Elias cleared his throat and stepped back but Mylah kept hold of his hand. "Yes. Farren's training has been working. We should get moving so we can get back to him." Elias turned away and Mylah released his hand reluctantly.

As they made their way back to the bridge, Mylah filled Elias in on all she had learned in the fae camp.

"So, we still don't know if Queen Aveda plans on taking over all of Olliria, or only Adair," he pointed out.

Mylah sighed, "I know. But maybe there is some way we can tell King Florian her plans and he won't want to help her anymore," she suggested, but even she knew how unlikely that was to happen.

"He'd never believe you. He'll have to find out the hard way, if he doesn't already suspect it." He held his hand out for Mylah to help her down from a large rock they'd climbed over.

"Queen Aveda wouldn't be stupid enough to launch a war against the witches and warlocks... Would she?" Mylah had no idea who would win that fight. Fae were powerful, but were they more powerful than an army of witches?

"She has the manpower, it seems. Especially if the other human kingdoms join her side," Elias pointed out.

"We have to warn the Hyrdian council, even if we don't have solid proof. Maybe they'll join Elowyn."

"Maybe," he didn't sound very hopeful.

The trek back over the bridge was much less eventful, but by the time they reached the other side, it was well after midnight. They found a sheltered spot to set up their one remaining bedroll, but it did nothing to shield Mylah from the cold. It had to have dropped another twenty degrees from the night before.

Elias offered to keep watch first again, but Mylah couldn't fall asleep because she was so cold. Her teeth chattered and her entire body was wracked with tremors as she lay on the ground. Puffs of air blew out from between her teeth as she breathed.

"I can hear your teeth chattering from over here," Elias commented.

"T-thanks f-for p-pointing that out," Mylah managed to get out. "C-can we s-start a f-fire?" she asked.

"Not now that we know there's a whole camp filled with fae across that bridge. They'd probably smell the fire and come to investigate."

"S-so d-death by f-fae or death by f-freezing?" Mylah tried to laugh but her muscles were too sore from clenching against the cold. "How are y-you not f-freezing?"

"I'm cold, but I have a higher tolerance for the cold than you."

Mylah often forgot about the shreeve's different abilities thanks to their fae side.

"M-must be n-nice," Mylah ground out. "Mind lending m-me s-some of that b-body heat?" Mylah figured she had no shame in asking Elias to cuddle her if it meant she'd survive the night.

"I suppose it's the least I could do. If you say, please." Elias stood from where he'd settled against a rock and Mylah could see his smirk in the moonlight.

"P-p-please warm me up?" Mylah's body began heating at the thought of Elias being so close to her. He moved around her and lifted the bedroll blanket, letting in a rush of cold air, making Mylah shudder. Elias laid down behind her, pressing his chest against her back and replaced the blanket over the both of them. He draped his arm over Mylah and his breath stirred her hair, tickling her ear.

"Better?" he murmured.

Mylah's toes curled in her boots. "Mhmm," she managed to get out.

Her heart raced and she could no longer tell if her goosebumps were from the cold or Elias' touch. His warmth leached into Mylah and calmed her tremors. Eventually, her teeth stopped chattering and she was able to close her eyes and relax.

Mylah hadn't even realized she'd fallen asleep, but Elias woke her as the sun rose. They packed up their bedroll, ate what little breakfast they had left, and set out down the mountain.

They didn't talk as they walked, and Mylah assumed Elias was as lost in his own thoughts as she was.

At lunchtime, they ate the remainder of their food.

"At least we didn't run into any trolls," Mylah said, as they rested.

"Don't jinx us, we haven't made it back safe yet," Elias said, glancing around as if a troll might jump out at them.

"True." Mylah chewed her last bit of bread slowly. "I don't have Garrick's dagger anymore to defend myself," she said. An ache in her chest swelled as she realized she'd lost the one thing that had connected her with Garrick. Tears pricked her eyes. First her necklace, now the dagger...

"I'm sorry about that," Elias sighed. "I tried to find your pack on my way, but I was more focused on getting you out."

"It's okay. I can get a new one in Hyrdian." Mylah hated the sound of that, but she would do it. She needed some sort of protection. Even if it would be practically useless against most opponents, it brought her comfort.

"Come on, we need to keep moving." Elias held his hand out to her and helped her to her feet.

As night fell, they found Farren's cave, announcing themselves so as not to startle him. Farren greeted them jovially, embracing Mylah. She flinched, and he frowned in worry.

"I think I pulled a muscle in my back," Mylah explained as she bent over into a stretch, her arms hanging down. It had been bothering her all day, but she figured it would be fine once she had a good night's sleep in a real bed.

"Are you well enough to keep moving? We shouldn't remain here any longer than we need to," Farren said.

"Yeah, I'm fine. It's more of a nuisance than anything." She flexed her shoulders and shook them out. "We can get going."

Farren nodded quickly before busying himself packing up his stuff. Elias placed his pack back on the saddle and readied the horses.

Once they were riding away from the mountains, relief washed over Mylah. They had done it; they had made it out of the mountains safely.

Nineteen

Crane remained with Torin on the border for a couple days, but they were unable to figure out a way to help the missing shreeve without venturing into Adair, and that wasn't possible at the moment. So, Crane and Torin returned to the castle.

On their ride, they stopped for a drink in town. Everyone knew Torin, which made Crane a little jealous. It had been that way for Crane whenever he went anywhere in Adair, before he'd been exiled.

They sat at the bar, sipping their whiskeys, when Crane realized this was the first time he'd seen Torin drink since Mylah left.

"Not to pry, but I thought you'd quit drinking?" Crane asked.

Torin laughed. "You don't know me well enough if you'd think I'd ever give up whiskey." He raised his glass to Crane before taking another sip. "Sometimes I take breaks."

"Understood," Crane said, smirking. "I can understand why you'd need a drink every now and then, with what you see as Elowyn's war general."

Torin's face pinched and he set his glass down. "That and I love whiskey."

"Right, sorry to assume," Crane muttered, his cheeks getting hot. "It's just that Mylah found an escape in alcohol, and I thought you may have been doing the same."

"No, you're right," Torin sighed. "I shouldn't have gone down that road with Mylah, but it made things easier. Coming back to Elowyn, I mean, knowing that we'd failed. The whiskey helped me to forget my failings."

"Again, I'm sorry. I didn't mean to pry," Crane said, unsure how to comfort Torin. With Mylah it was different because she was like his sister, but he'd only known Torin a few weeks and wasn't sure what would help cheer him up.

"I've been through it so many times, it's easier for me to bring myself back from that place of darkness. I forgot that it wouldn't be so easy for Mylah. I should have helped her rather than encouraged her drinking." The guilt was written on Torin's face.

"You *were* helping her," Crane retorted. "It may not have been in the healthiest of ways, but by being there for her in that dark place, at least she wasn't alone. Who knows what would have happened if she were."

"Yeah, well, I won't let it happen again. After Castien told me what he did to her parents, I realized how much worse Garrick's death must have impacted her," Torin said, but Crane's mind snagged on *'what he did to her parents.'*

"What do you mean?" Crane turned his head slowly to face Torin. "Castien is the one who killed them? He *murdered* Mylah's parents?" If rage could become a physical thing, it would have leapt out of Crane's body in that moment. He'd never known such an all-consuming rage before that moment. Blood-boiling, heart pounding, mind centered on one thought: *Castien murdered Emil and Vita Orson.*

Whirling in his stool, Crane slammed his feet to the ground and stood. "I'll kill him," he growled.

Torin's hand grabbed Crane's arm before he could move any further. "Woah, woah, woah." He pulled Crane back towards the bar. "I didn't realize she hadn't told you."

"Wait, Mylah knows this?" Crane's mind whirled as he tried to think of some explanation for how Mylah could ever forgive the man who had murdered her parents.

"She's known since she arrived in Elowyn the first time. Before she betrayed Adair, even," Torin said.

The rage still simmered in Crane's gut, but it had lessened enough for him to sit back down.

"That makes no sense." He took a sip of his whiskey, reveling in the burn as it trailed down his throat, helping to ground him once more.

"Castien was acting on King Haldor's orders at the time," Torin said, hand clenching around his glass as he spoke. "King Haldor created a monster with Castien, it's a miracle he turned himself around."

"That's not an excuse for what he did," Crane hissed, cracking his knuckles. "If someone orders you to murder someone –"

"If your *king* orders you to do anything, you do it. Or else face their wrath." Torin waved to the bartender. "Another round," he said, and the bartender nodded. "Did you ever deny a command given by King Florian?"

"No, but that's different," Crane started, but Torin shook his head. Crane deflated. "Alright, I get it. But I'm not forgiving Castien so easily."

"Fair enough," Torin assented.

Crane's anger didn't entirely dissipate, but he certainly had a lot to think about. He made a plan to talk with Castien about it the next time he found him alone.

As Crane settled back down, someone bumped into him from behind, making him slosh his drink over the bar. "Oof," Crane grunted.

"Watch yourself," a gruff voice said from behind him. Already on edge, Crane whipped around to find a tall, pale, shreeve man scowling down at him.

"You're the one who bumped into *me*," Crane reminded him, and the man's frown deepened.

"Human filth," the man spat, before turning and stumbling away.

"What was that about?" Crane asked, facing Torin once more.

"Not everyone here takes kindly to outsiders," Torin said. "I'm sure they're especially wary after everything that happened with Mylah, though they weren't happy with her even before they found out she was a traitor."

"But she's not a traitor. She risked her life to try and help save this kingdom." Crane readjusted on his stool, discomfort seeping into him. He felt as if all eyes in the bar were on him now.

"That's apparently not the story they were told. Someone, either from Adair or here, let slip the entire sordid tale of our failed mission and put emphasis on Mylah's betrayal," Torin explained, sipping from his drink as he finished.

"An inside man? Or... What?" Crane couldn't imagine anyone from Adair caring enough to risk their life to spill Mylah's secrets, true or not, to the Elowyns. In his mind, it had to have been someone within the Elowyn castle who had overheard the story. There were so many guards though that could have been listening outside Castien's study anytime it was brought up.

"I doubt it, but it's possible." Torin seemed unbothered by the idea, so Crane decided it wasn't worth his time to worry about it either.

A few days after Torin and Crane returned from the border, Castien summoned Crane to his study. Crane entered to find that Korriane, Torin, and Ana were all there. Killian and Davina were absent, but that was not unusual. What was unusual was Ana's presence. As far as Crane knew, she hadn't been to the castle since they'd returned from Adair. Torin leaned against the back wall as Castien searched one of his bookshelves for something. Korriane sat in one of the armchairs to the left while Ana sat on the floor, her back pressed against Korriane's legs.

"What..." before Crane could finish, Castien whirled.

"Here it is," he said, a smile actually lighting his face. Crane couldn't remember if he'd ever seen Castien smile. When Castien noticed Crane, his smile faltered, and he straightened his shoulders. "Thank you for coming. Bellingham mentioned he delivered another letter."

"Yes, I received a letter from Cassia." Crane handed the letter to Castien as he tucked whatever book he held under his arm. Crane had already read the letter and knew what it held.

Crane –

The king announced to the council that they've deciphered the shreeve book and figured out the ingredients needed to perform the spell that will, as the king put it, 'put an end to our troubles with Elowyn.' He's also saying that the spell will save shreeve by returning them to either a fae or human state, not kill them. I don't know if they have what they need yet, but I can only hope the ingredients aren't easy to come by. Though, with Queen Aveda here, I'm worried it won't be a challenge for them to put this information to use soon.

Greyson came over for dinner, and he seems well, though, my mothers told us about Garrick... I am so sorry. Greyson was also unaware, and he didn't take it well, as expected. The king concealed the information, letting the council believe that Garrick left with your family. I don't know what this means for the rest of us, but it can't be good.

I'll let you know if I talk with Greyson again.
Stay safe.

Love,
Cassia

"Well, this certainly puts a strain on things..." Castien dropped the letter onto the table.

Torin picked it up next and his eyes darkened as he scanned the lines. "So, they've done it. I wonder if this has to do with the shreeve who've been going missing on the border."

"If they have the ingredients, I'm sure they want to test the spell before using it on a large scale," Crane added.

Korriane held her hand out and Torin brought the letter to her before she passed it to Ana.

"What do we do?" Ana asked, her voice small and broken. Crane remembered Korriane mentioning that Ana had been having a hard time since returning from Adair. He hadn't known Ana before, but he could tell that she was most definitely still suffering.

"We can't pull our men from the border," Torin said, his jaw tensing.

"No," Castien said in agreement, though pain clouded his eyes. "But we can reposition them. Give them a fighting chance."

"I'll start refiguring their positions. I'll go back there tonight." Torin grabbed one of the maps from the table and left the room.

A heavy silence remained in his wake as Castien considered the book that he still gripped in his hand. He replaced it on the shelf with a sigh.

"We'll have to walk down memory lane another day," he said to Korriane who gave him a weak smile.

"Elias will be home soon," she said, and Crane realized whatever the book had been that Castien had sought out had something to do with him missing Elias.

"We can't worry about that right now." Castien straightened his tunic and grabbed his robe from a table at the back of the room, draping it over his shoulders. Crane had never noticed him wear a robe before. Every day he was enacting small changes within the castle and with his own self that made him seem much more king-like. "I need to keep my people safe. Elias can take care of himself."

Castien swept out of the room, leaving Crane, Ana, and Korriane to themselves.

"Do you miss Cassia terribly?" Ana asked, and Crane turned to her. She played with the ends of her hair, not meeting his eye.

"Yes," he answered her honestly. "More and more every day."

"I'm sorry she can't be here with you. I'm sorry she has to remain in that foul place." Ana's eyes welled with tears, but they didn't fall.

"It wasn't always so bad," Crane said, striding over and sitting beside Ana on the rug. "Growing up there was quite nice, actually."

"Everything is quite nice when you're living in ignorance," Ana said and Korriane reached down to put her hand on Ana's shoulder.

"Ana," she warned.

"We were all ignorant as children," Ana clarified. "Me much longer than the two of you, I assume. I know now what's at stake."

"As do I. Which is why I'm here and not with Cassia." Crane clenched his fists in his lap. "I'm sorry for what you endured. I was there, I heard you." Ana flinched but nodded in understanding.

"I heard you, too," she murmured. "And Torin. He was the strongest of the three of us." She surprised Crane by smiling. "I hope to be at least half as strong as him someday."

"You already are," Korriane said.

"If you don't mind me asking, why didn't you use your power to escape the dungeons sooner?" Crane hazarded to ask.

"I can only use my power on one or two people at a time, if I'd made it out of the cell, I would have been caught trying to flee," Ana explained. "Besides, Castien warned me we may be caught and if so, to wait until Mylah's cue to do anything."

"So, you endured the torture on Castien's word that Mylah would come?" Crane tilted his head slightly, considering that.

"No. I endured the torture on *Mylah's* word that she would come," Ana corrected.

Korriane interrupted them, standing as she said, "Come on, we should get you home."

Ana sighed but stood and left with Korriane. Crane sat on the floor a while longer, considering what Ana had said. He *had* lived in ignorance for far too long. Their entire kingdom had, and because of that, King Florian now threatened an entire race because of his own prejudices and fears. Because of their ignorance, a war was about to tear their world apart.

Torin returned to the border for the next few days, so Crane trained with Davina in the training room. No matter how hard he tried, he couldn't best her in a match, and she wasn't the kind of person to let him win, which he was grateful for.

"Do you think she'll wait for you?" Davina asked on their third day without Torin. It was the first day she'd been unaccompanied by a sprite, Castien having deemed her trustworthy enough. They were hanging up their weapons for the day and Crane wiped sweat from his face.

"Hmm?" It came out muffled as he moved the towel over his chin and mouth.

"Your girl back home. Cassia, right?" Somehow, Davina didn't appear to be sweating at all. She stood casually, leaning against the weapons wall as she picked at her nails. For once, she wore training leathers rather than her usual dresses and gowns, which she still fought in effortlessly.

"Yes – Cassia. I have no reason to believe she won't, though I wouldn't hold it against her if she didn't. We never...I never..." He cleared his throat, throwing his towel over his shoulder. They'd never made their relationship official in any capacity and he regretted that every day. "Either way, I'll wait for her."

Davina pursed her lips, but Crane could see the smile beneath. "She's lucky to have you."

"What about you? Do you have anyone special you're waiting on?" Crane had seen her cast glances Torin's way when she thought no one was looking, but he wouldn't assume anything. Davina was nothing if not an enigma.

"Maybe. Though I don't think he'll ever come around." She pushed away from the wall and they both headed for the door. "I royally messed that up." She laughed a little and Crane hid his chuckle with a cough.

"Give him time. Show him your true feelings, and I'm sure he'll come around," Crane said what he would want to hear, but he wasn't entirely sure it was true. He didn't know Torin well enough to puzzle out whether he was the forgiving type. Though, he had forgiven Castien for lying to him, but that was different. Davina had broken his heart and that wasn't something that Crane had enough experience in to speak on. He'd had flings growing up, but nothing serious enough to leave a mark. Until Cassia. If she *didn't* end up waiting for him...He didn't even want to think about it.

"Pretty, pretty," a hoarse, piercing voice called out to them. Davina and Crane both turned to see a hobbled old woman standing in the doorway of a room Crane had passed several times and never truly noticed before.

"Madame Edris," Davina greeted the woman, her jaw clenching.

Crane realized this was the witch who had almost killed Mylah with belladonna. He scowled at her.

"Be a dear, would you, and fetch me the king. I'd go myself, but my knees don't do well on the stairs." The smile Madame Edris offered them had goosebumps rising on Crane's arms. He couldn't understand why Castien would want this witch in his home. But then again, King Florian also had a witch in his castle who had proved useful time and again.

"And what do I get for my trouble?" Davina asked, her voice rising as she sneered and took a step forward. From the way Davina was acting, Crane wondered if he wasn't so wrong in thinking there was something off about Madame Edris.

"Your trouble?" Madame Edris cackled. "Greedy little things the lot of you."

Davina lifted a shoulder as if she couldn't care less what the woman gave her so long as she didn't walk away with nothing. But Crane had been wanting to talk with Castien alone all week, so he stepped forward.

"I'll fetch him for you," Crane offered.

"Oh, why thank you," Madame Edris turned her eyes on him as if noticing him for the first time. "Quite the human specimen. Won't you let me run some tests on you?" Her lips turned up in a sneer and Crane grimaced.

"Leave him be," Davina said, putting her arm in front of Crane and moving him back towards her. "Come on, then. Let's go find the king."

Crane stood awkwardly for a moment, Madame Edris surveying him, before he turned and scrambled after Davina, anxious to get away from the witch.

"Does she stay in that room all day, every day?" he asked as soon as they were out of earshot of Madame Edris.

"I've no idea. For all I know, she has a secret portal in there and travels between realms every night."

"Realms?" Crane reeled back at the thought of that.

"As I said, I've no idea. All I know is that she's bound to this castle and can't leave freely because of King Haldor's father, King Bastien. I don't know the story, but trust me when I say, you do not want to get on Madame Edris' bad side."

Davina veered to the right as they made it to the top of the stairs. "We can check his study first," she suggested.

Castien intercepted them along the way.

"Crane, just the person I was looking for," he said, clasping his hands behind his back. "Come with me."

"Actually, we were looking for you," Crane said and Castien pursed his lips.

"Madame Edris wants you," Davina announced.

"Probably concerning the body from the border," Castien mused. "That can wait. First, I'd like to speak with Crane." He gave Davina a pointed look and she took the hint, leaving them alone in the hall.

Crane couldn't help but feel a little nervous, like a child who was about to get in trouble with their parents. Castien didn't seem upset, but he also didn't seem particularly enthused either.

Castien led Crane to his study, closing the door behind them.

"Elias sent me a letter," Castien waved his hand to the table in the center of the room where a new letter sat atop the pile of maps. It was where most of the important documents were kept, Crane had come to realize.

"And Mylah?" he asked as he stepped up to the table. Castien said nothing, so Crane decided to read the letter.

Castien –

We made it safely to Perynth. Don't worry, I was able to get a second room. Well played, brother.

I found Farren in Korrindale and he's been teaching me how to control my magic. Mylah has been a great help with that as well.

We met with the council and all I can hope for is that you do a better job convincing them to help us because they gave me little to no indication that they will be willing to.

We're about to leave for the Forsaken Mountains to find out what has the Unbound creatures so backward these days. It shouldn't take us more than a week, according to Farren. He's escorting us. As soon as we return, I'll send word.

I hope you're not missing me too much.

Elias

"They're going into the Forsaken Mountains?" Crane asked, his heart pounding as he set the letter back on the table.

"Apparently. I assume this was Mylah's idea. She mentioned something about owing a debt to Genevieve regarding the unusual troll activity in the Unbounds." Castien's lip curled as he spoke.

"You can't blame this entirely on Mylah. Elias must have some interest in going too, or else he'd refuse," Crane rebuked.

"No, he wouldn't. His interest is solely in making Mylah happy," Castien said.

"Good. She deserves to be happy." Crane folded his arms over his chest, trying to show Castien he wasn't going to accept being chastised for Mylah and Elias' decisions.

"At the cost of their lives? Do you know what lives in the Forsaken Mountains?"

Crane bit his lip, not wanting to reveal he had no idea. "I've heard stories," he said.

Castien scoffed, "Stories... You better hope they come back unharmed. If Mylah gets my brother killed, you and your mother will be on your own. This isn't a wayward house for lost souls."

"Don't take out your fear on me," Crane said, pointing his finger at Castien. "I never asked for any of this, and I can't control what Mylah does. If I could go home to Adair right now without being executed, I would." Crane's chest heaved as he finished, only a few inches from Castien.

Castien's eyes blazed for a moment before the fire in them died out and he took a step away from Crane, shaking his head.

"You're right. I'm sorry. I don't know what came over me..." Castien mumbled the last few words and stalked towards the chairs against the wall, dropping into one. "Elias is going to be the death of me, I swear it."

Crane followed Castien's lead and sat in the chair beside him, picking at a loose thread on the seat cushion.

"They'll come back safe. I don't know your brother all that well, but I do know Mylah and she won't go down without a fight." Crane smiled as he said it, knowing it was true. No matter how she had been acting in the few weeks before she left, when push came to shove, she'd be the person he'd want beside him in a crisis.

"I know," Castien said, leaning his head back against the wall. "She's proven herself time and again."

"Will you tell me why you trusted her enough to send her on a mission to Adair even after you found out she was a traitor?" Crane asked. He'd tried to get the answer out of Mylah a few times, but she'd never been straight forward with him, either dodging the question or diverting the conversation.

"Her father and my father were once friends," Castien answered.

With that one sentence, all the anger Crane felt towards Castien came rushing back. He'd almost forgotten the whole reason he wanted to talk to Castien alone.

"And yet you still killed Emil?" Crane spoke the words slowly, deliberately.

Castien's lips parted, and he closed his eyes for a moment. "Who told you?"

"Does it matter?" Crane ground his teeth.

"I guess not." Castien stood and turned away from Crane, clasping his hands behind his back as he stepped away. "Then I'm sure you also know that it was King Haldor who ordered me to do it."

"Yes." Crane crossed his arms over his chest and tilted his head as he watched Castien pace. "How did Mylah forgive you?"

"Maybe she hasn't," Castien retorted, but there wasn't much conviction in his words.

"We both know that's a lie. She told me I could trust you, that *she* trusts you. How is that possible after what you did?" Tears pricked at Crane's eyes as he thought of the pain Mylah had been put through, and the pain of losing his own father.

"I don't know," Castien said.

"That, I believe." In the short time Crane had known Castien, he'd seen how self-deprecating he could be. He believed himself a villain, though he was far from it.

"Let me know if you hear from Elias again," Crane said, standing and turning for the door. There was nothing more Castien could say that would change the past. Crane would take a page from Mylah's book and learn to forgive in his own way.

Twenty

Once Mylah, Elias, and Farren reached the docks, Farren used his magic to light the massive torch at the end of the dock, signaling that they needed a ride back to Hyrdian. Mylah realized it made sense that the ship wouldn't wait around for them to return, though she wished that it had. She wanted to be out of the Unbounds.

They made a camp in the shelter of some trees to wait, since it would take a few hours for the ship to arrive. The horses were acting strange again, as they had on their way into the forest when they'd first arrived in the Unbounds.

"Now that we have a moment to talk, did you run into any trouble in the mountains?" Farren asked.

"Well..." Elias started, sharing a sheepish look with Mylah before filling Farren in on their excursion.

"So, you used your magic against a fae?" Farren asked as Elias told the story.

"Yes, and he blew her away! Literally!" Mylah exclaimed. "You would have been proud."

Elias rubbed the back of his neck as Mylah and Farren both sang his praises. "It's not that big of a deal," he muttered.

"It's a huge deal! You've proven you can control your magic, at least well enough to fight off an attacker momentarily. This will be of great use to you!" Farren said. "Which tactic did you use to call it out?"

"I stuck with the usual," Elias said, his eyes flicking to Mylah, and she tilted her head in confusion.

"Ah, heightened emotions are the most obvious way to go about it. But when we're back in the training room, we'll work on calling forth your power without that piece." Farren kept talking, but Mylah's mind stuck on the fact that Elias had cared so much about saving her that he'd been able to take down a fae with his magic, long enough for them to escape.

A warming sensation grew inside her as she thought about that, until a shriek derailed her train of thought. Mylah jumped to her feet. Elias and Farren already had their weapons drawn, ready for a fight and Mylah itched to reach for hers as well, a stark reminder of its absence.

"What was that?" Mylah asked.

"Banshee," Farren hissed.

"But that means…" Mylah gulped.

"Death is near," Farren finished for her. "We need to get out of here."

"But the ship hasn't arrived yet," Mylah said. "Where are we supposed to go?"

Another ear-piercing shriek split through the air. Mylah slapped her hands over her ears and cursed. The horses pulled hard against their reins that had been tied to a tree. Farren struggled to free them, holding tight to the reins as he handed one of them to Elias.

"Don't look back. If we're separated, we'll meet at the docks. The ship should be here in an hour. Hopefully we last that long," Farren said, patting Elias on the shoulder before mounting his horse and taking off.

Elias beckoned to Mylah and helped her onto their horse, hopping up behind her and following Farren. The shrieking continued, coming closer even as they rode.

"Will it follow us?" Mylah asked.

"I don't know. The death that will occur may not be ours, but..."

"We're the only ones around," Mylah finished for him. He said nothing but she could feel his breath on her neck as his chest pressed against her back.

"If we outrun the banshee, does that mean we outrun death?" Mylah could hope that she'd once again be able to escape a death sentence.

"I guess we'll find out." Elias had barely gotten the words out when a white cloaked figure crossed their path and Smudge reared up, sending both Mylah and Elias flying from his back. Elias landed half on top of Mylah, knocking the air from her lungs, and leaving her gasping. He readjusted so he was no longer on top of her, but neither of them stood.

The figure turned to them, and Mylah screamed as she saw the horror beneath the tattered hood. Sunken eye sockets devoid of flesh, an elongated jaw, and a mouth stretched wide revealing decaying teeth. A shriek pierced her ears once more, coming from the figure, and Mylah knew immediately that this was the banshee. It hovered above the ground as it floated towards them.

Elias' arms wrapped around Mylah, pulling her back against him. They had no time to rise from the ground before the banshee was before them.

"*Death comes for you...*" The voice was like nails grinding against stone and Mylah cringed, turning her face into Elias' shoulder. Tears streamed down her face, unbidden. Never in her life had Mylah been filled with such fear or sadness, not even when her parents had died. But as soon as it had overwhelmed her, it was gone. Turning her head away from Elias, she realized the banshee had also gone.

"Are you alright?" Elias murmured, his hands rubbing up and down her arms. Mylah pushed away from him and stood, brushing herself off.

"Fine," she murmured. Discomfort had replaced her fear and all she wanted was to be back in her bed at the inn. "We should find Farren."

Elias' face pinched in confusion at her sudden change in disposition but he said nothing before he went in search of Smudge. Mylah trudged behind him, hoping that by the time they reached the docks, the ship would be waiting for them.

On the ship, Mylah remained below deck so she wouldn't have a repeat of the previous trip. She'd learned her lesson about staring into the depths of the Lake of Desires. After their run in with the banshee, she wasn't about to tempt fate. She overheard Farren talking with one of the crewmen who told him that a banshee's warning was not always predictive of an immediate death, but that it usually did not precede a death by more than a week. Because the banshee hadn't specified who the warning had been for, they had no idea whether it would be her or Elias who faced death in the next week.

I've faced death before and overcome it, Mylah thought, though it didn't comfort her too much.

Her mind flickered to the veela who they had heard on their voyage to the Unbounds and Mylah kept thinking she heard their phantom song.

As soon as they made it back to Perynth and the inn, Mylah crawled into bed and pulled out her journal. She wrote down everything that had happened on their journey and everything they had learned.

She spent two days cooped up in her room, writing and catching up on sleep, while Elias continued his training with Farren. They were all content to pretend that their run in with the banshee never happened in hopes that its prediction had been wrong. The fall from the horse though, had only worsened Mylah's back pain and it twinged every time she moved.

When Mylah finally left her room for dinner on the second day, Elias was nowhere to be found. She assumed he was still in Korrindale either training or eating with Farren and Raelynn.

As Mylah ate her soup alone at the bar, a man sat on the stool beside her.

"Where's your friend?" he asked, and Mylah paused in her slurping to look at him. He was tall and a little bulkier than Elias, though not quite as handsome, but his smile was contagious and had Mylah smiling back. His blonde hair was pulled back into a bun and his ears were pointed, but he had no markings as a shreeve would.

Fae, she thought.

"He's out," Mylah said. "Should be back soon, I assume, if you're interested in chatting with him."

"It's not him that I'm interested in." He smirked and Mylah couldn't hold back her laugh.

"You shouldn't be interested in me. Trust me." Mylah finished off her soup and dropped her spoon into the bowl.

"So, if I ask you to get a drink with me, you'll say no?" he teased.

"I don't even know your name…"

"Mikhail." A glint sparked in his eyes.

"Okay, Mikhail. I'm Mylah. If I agree to get a drink with you, can we go somewhere other than *here*?" She waved her hand around the room. "I've been cooped up here for a few days and need to get out."

"If you agree to get a drink with me, we can go anywhere you want. Shit, I'd take you all the way to Korrindale if you wanted to go." Mylah leaned back on her stool, her laughter making Mikhail smile even more.

"How about down the road?" she compromised.

"Perfect. Shall we?" He stood and held his arm out to her.

Mylah considered it for a moment, realizing how stupid she was being, trusting this stranger, but after everything she'd been through the past few months, and the run in with the banshee, she figured; what did she have to lose? It did also cross her mind that this could be the decision that brought about her death, but it was coming either way if all the stories about banshees were to be believed. There was no outrunning death once a banshee presented itself to you.

Mikhail brought Mylah to a bar a few streets over from the inn where everyone knew his name. Mylah figured that was a good sign, at least. He led her to an empty table and then left to get them drinks. When he handed Mylah her drink, she took it but didn't take a sip. She'd been doing her best to avoid alcohol and didn't plan on ruining her streak tonight. Anytime Mikhail wasn't paying attention, she'd spill some of her drink onto the floor or into a nearby plant. It wasn't the best plan, but it worked. He was too preoccupied with talking about himself to worry too much about her.

Her eyes roved the room as Mikhail spoke and her eyes stopped as she took in Elias sitting at the bar. She had to do a double take to make sure her eyes weren't playing tricks on her. But there he was, sitting beside the pretty girl from the front desk at the salon whom he'd been flirting with on their first day in Korrindale.

Mikhail waved his hand in front of Mylah, trying to get her attention. He turned his head to see what she was looking at.

"Isn't that your friend?" he asked.

"Yes," Mylah said through gritted teeth.

"Should we say hi?"

"No!" Mylah said too quickly. She cleared her throat and spoke again. "I mean, he seems busy."

As she watched Elias, the girl he was with laughed as he touched her arm and Mylah felt a white-hot rage simmering beneath her skin. She closed her eyes, trying to force the anger back down, knowing she had no right to feel that way. Elias was free to see other women. She was on a date with another man after all.

"Are you okay? You look a little pale…" Mikhail said.

Mylah opened her eyes, forcing a smile. "I'm fine. I'm going to grab another drink." Leaving her half full glass on the table, she walked to the bar. Elias still hadn't noticed her.

Leaning against the bar, Mylah waved down the bartender.

"I'd like two more ales please," she said, and as soon as she spoke, Elias whipped towards her. His eyes met hers and confusion lit in them. Mylah acted surprised, widening her eyes as she leaned back.

"What are you doing here?" Elias asked, his eyes roving over her as if looking for anything out of place or wrong.

"Same as you – getting drinks with a friend," Mylah said, gesturing to Mikhail who waved from their table as she made eye contact with him.

Elias' eyes narrowed. "Charlotte invited me for a drink because she lives down the road from here. We bumped into each other on our way back from Korrindale."

"I didn't ask for an explanation. You can get drinks with whomever you want," Mylah said, tapping her fingers on the bar in irritation.

"Right," Elias said, but he pursed his lips. The bartender placed Mylah's drinks in front of her.

"Well, enjoy yourselves," Mylah said, leaning over Elias so she could include Charlotte, who smiled prettily back. Grabbing her drinks, Mylah strode back to her table.

"Thanks," Mikhail said, taking his drink from Mylah and gulping it down.

"You can have this one, too," Mylah said, sliding the other drink to him. "I still have a bit left of my first one." Mikhail took it without questioning why she got it in the first place, clearly too focused on himself still to notice anything amiss.

Mylah couldn't help staring at Elias and Charlotte. But, before long, Charlotte stood from her stool, kissing Elias' cheek as she left the bar. Mylah waited to see if she'd come back, but she didn't. Curious, Mylah decided to get Mikhail a few more drinks.

Approaching the bar on Elias' left again, Mylah ordered her drinks and waited for Elias to say something. He watched her and she picked at her nails idly.

"Why are you drinking?" he finally said. "You were doing better."

"Who said I'm drinking?" Mylah asked, not looking up from her nails.

"You said," Elias pointed out and Mylah met his gaze.

"These are for Mikhail. I haven't had a drop all night." *Despite desperately wanting to*, she added internally.

"That's good."

Mylah scoffed, "I'm not doing it for you."

"Good," Elias said.

"Good," Mylah repeated before pursing her lips as she bit the inside of her cheek, trying not to snap at him again.

"You deserve better," Elias said, jerking his head towards Mikhail.

"Better..." Mylah mused. "That's funny coming from you."

"Mylah, I..." He was interrupted by the bartender sliding Mylah her drinks.

"I'll leave you alone. I know when I'm not wanted." Mylah turned but before she could walk away, Elias gripped her upper arm, pulling her in close and putting his lips beside her ear.

"If we weren't in a room full of people right now, I'd show you how wrong you are." His words sent a thrill through her, and her toes curled in her boots. She pulled away slightly so she could meet his gaze.

She quirked her lips up and raised her brow. "Is that a promise?" she said, flicking her eyes to his lips which parted slightly.

He released her arm and turned back to the bar, cracking the tension that had built around them. Mylah let out a huff of air, disappointed. Her gaze found Mikhail's from across the room. He beckoned to her, and she forced a smile for him.

A thud made her turn back to the bar as she realized Elias had finished his drink and stood from his stool. He loomed over her, a question in his gaze as he held out his hand towards her. Without a second thought, she placed the drinks back on the bar and slipped her hand into his, letting him lead her into the night, and giving Mikhail a quick wave. They didn't make it far before tucking into an alley and crashing against each other.

Mylah's hands roved over Elias' back and through his hair. He gripped her waist as he backed her against a wall. Their lips met with a need that caused Mylah's chest to ache, and she couldn't get enough of him. She brought her hand to his chest and dropped it lower, lower, until he groaned and hardened against her. Mylah paused, searching for his gaze. His eyes opened slowly, and he grinned when their eyes met.

"We should probably take this somewhere a little less..." he started.

"Gross?" Mylah finished for him, realizing that the alley they had chosen stunk of days old fish.

"Yeah. Come on." He took her hand again and led her back out into the open. Thankfully, the cover of night kept them partially concealed. Mylah leaned against Elias as they walked, soaking in his warmth. She hadn't noticed how cold it was before.

As they walked, Mylah itched to feel Elias against her again, but she had to settle for holding his hand until they reached the inn. A large part of her wanted to shove him into the next alcove she saw so she could kiss him again. His eyes kept flicking to hers and she wondered if he was thinking the same thing.

"I'm not going to be able to wait to get back to the inn if you keep looking at me like that," he said.

Mylah's eyes widened as she laughed.

"I'll try not to look at you," she said, turning her head away from him.

His hand came up under her chin, surprising her, and he turned her head back towards him. They stopped in the middle of the road.

"I never want to lose sight of these eyes again," his voice came out low and rough as he leaned down and kissed her. Mylah melted against him, but he pulled away before she could put her arms around him. He took her hand again but picked up the pace. The inn came into view and they both sighed in relief.

They waved to the innkeeper at the bar before slipping up the stairs.

"Your room or mine?" Mylah asked, smirking as Elias watched her hungrily.

"Yours..." he said as they reached her door. He pressed her against it and kissed his way up her neck. Mylah couldn't help laughing as she struggled to unlock the door with her back to it.

As soon as they were inside and the door shut behind them, Mylah practically threw herself at Elias. He chuckled, catching her, and backed them towards the bed as he kissed her shoulder, her neck, her lips.

Mylah grabbed at Elias' jacket, pushing it off his shoulders and flinging it to the side. The back of his legs hit the bed and he stopped kissing her long enough to pull his shirt over his head, revealing all the blue and green markings Mylah had only seen the edges of before when they peeked out above his collar. She traced one of them that led down to the hem of his pants. He shuddered under her touch and took her hand in his, kissing it.

Mylah shrugged out of her own jacket and let it drop to the floor. The rest of their clothes followed suit and Elias leaned back onto the bed, pulling Mylah down with him. Her skin electrified in all the places it touched his.

Time seemed to be passing by way too fast for Mylah and she prayed for it to slow down. Each touch sent a new shock through her while every kiss soothed her, chasing away all her hurt and worries.

The next morning, Mylah woke in Elias' arms with his bare chest pressed against hers, and their legs tangled together in the sheets. Turning her head, she felt an ache in her neck from sleeping at a slight angle. She breathed in the scent of him, a mixture of cedar and freshly washed linen. Closing her eyes again, she nuzzled closer to him. His arm tightened around her, and she smiled. She wanted to remain there forever, however, she had to go to the bathroom.

Inching away from him, she tried to lift his arm without waking him, but as she sat up, he stirred, and his eyes fluttered open.

"Good morning," Mylah said, leaning back and kissing him.

"Good morning, indeed," he said, his voice still rough and heavy from sleep.

"I'll be right back," she promised before disappearing into the washroom.

After going to the bathroom, she grabbed her monthly contraceptive tonic from her bag and choked it down. It wasn't as bad as the one they'd had available in Adair, but it still made her cringe.

When she returned to the bedroom, Elias still lay sprawled on the bed, eyes closed again. She smiled and made her way towards him once more, trailing her fingers down his back before sitting on the edge of the bed, her back to him. He turned over to face her, smiling as he took in the sight of her. His smile faltered though as his eyes roved down her back. Mylah strained to see what he looked at, but she wasn't flexible enough for that. His fingers grazed her lower back, and a sense of dread came over her.

"What is it?" she asked.

"Does this hurt?" He sat up, putting more pressure on her back. Mylah shook her head. She hadn't felt any back pain since the previous day. "Stay still," he said. The pull from his magic created a strange suction like feeling in her back.

"No..." the words escaped Elias' lips and Mylah whipped her head towards him again.

"Tell me what it is," she demanded, but the sight of the viscous, grayish black liquid that dripped between Elias fingers answered her question. *Poison.* Mylah couldn't help but groan.

"Again? I swear the universe has it out for me. Can you get it out like last time?" Mylah found his gaze and the helplessness that shone there stopped her blood cold. "I'm guessing that's a no," she whispered.

"It's too far along. It would kill me, or you, or both of us..." Elias climbed out of bed. "Get dressed."

"I don't want to. If I'm going to die, I want to do it here. With you," Mylah tried to keep her voice steady and strong, but it betrayed her and wavered.

"I've said it before, and I'll say it again, *I am not going to let you die.*" He grabbed his clothes and started dressing while Mylah remained sitting, staring at the floor. She blinked slowly, trying to process how she'd been poisoned, *again.*

"It happened in the mountains," she realized. "I felt a twinge right here," she pointed to the spot on her back even though Elias was doing everything but looking at her. "I thought it was muscle pain or something from sleeping on the ground. But it was the captain of the fae camp. That's why she stopped pursuing us."

"Come on," Elias said, throwing her shirt to her. "We're going to see Farren. He'll know what to do."

"I'm lucky to still be alive, but I won't be for much longer. There's nothing that can be done." Heart racing, vision narrowing, Mylah let her head drop into her hands. "The banshee sealed my fate."

"I won't accept that. *Let's go,*" Elias growled.

Disgraced

Mylah decided to stop arguing and stood, but when she tried to dress herself, the pain in her back returned with a vengeance, Elias' prodding most likely having aggravated it. Tears sprung to her eyes as she tried and failed to pull her tunic over her head. Elias stepped forward to help her, his touch sending shivers through Mylah.

"Do that again," she murmured, gripping his bicep as he went to turn away. At her words though, he paused and lifted his hand to her cheek, brushing his thumb over her lips before kissing them.

Mylah sighed, leaning into his touch, and pulling him closer. The way he made her feel made the pain almost bearable.

"We don't have time for this," he said, pulling away from her once more. "Put these on." He held her pants out to her and she reluctantly stepped into them.

Once they'd made it outside, Elias helped Mylah onto Smudge. She protested that she wasn't dead yet and could do it herself, even though she hadn't even been able to dress herself. He didn't find her joke very funny. They rode to Farren's office, assuming he'd already be there, waiting for them for Elias' usual training session.

Elias pounded on the door, his nerves clearly agitating him. Mylah held his other hand in hers and squeezed it tightly.

"I'm still here," she said, and Elias glanced at her, his brow furrowed. "No need to be upset. Farren's door did nothing to deserve your beating," she smirked, and Elias sighed, his shoulders slumping as hurried footsteps sounded behind the door.

"Yes?" Farren said as he opened the door, and he visibly relaxed when he saw them. "Oh, I figured it had to be an angry student or something from all that banging."

"Sorry about that," Mylah said. "Elias is a bit on edge." She kept her voice perfectly calm and level. Outwardly, Mylah knew she appeared unbothered by her fate. Inside, her stomach twisted itself in knots, nausea roiling like a cauldron.

"It's urgent," Elias said, dropping Mylah's hand as he entered Farren's office.

The gesture meant nothing, but his hand in hers had been a lifeline she'd clung to in hopes to stay standing. She gulped past the lump in her throat and shuffled into the room, leaning against the wall inside. She did her best to appear casual though her world crumbled around her.

"What's going on?" Farren looked between the two of them.

"We figured out who the banshee was there to warn," Mylah said, grinning despite the fear gripping her.

Farren opened his mouth to ask another question, but Elias interrupted him.

"Mylah was poisoned in the mountains," Elias burst out. "Show him," he said, waving his hand towards her. Mylah wrapped her arms around herself, trying to shrink against the wall.

"Poisoned?" Farren approached Mylah. "May I?" he asked, before reaching towards her. Mylah nodded, turning her back to him and slowly lifting her shirt to reveal the wound that had caused all the turmoil. Farren and Elias both gasped at the sight.

"It's already gotten worse," Elias said and Mylah's calm façade nearly shattered.

She held on by staring at the wall in front of her and focusing all her thoughts on the knots and whorls in the wood. Fingers traced a shape on her back and pain lanced through her. Arching her back against the agony, she gritted her teeth and placed her forehead against the wall, closing her eyes and allowing a single tear to trail down her cheek.

"This is too far along, there's nothing we can do. The poison has spread throughout her entire body. To try to remove it..." Farren didn't bother finishing that thought. They all knew what would happen; it would kill either her or the person attempting to remove the poison.

"I told you, Elias," Mylah whispered. It was all she could do to form the words as she fought back her growing panic.

"And I told you I won't accept that," he countered. "There has to be some way – someone who can help," he pleaded with Farren.

"There is no way," Farren said. After a few moments he inhaled sharply. "Well, there may be one person who would know," he stopped, and Mylah let her shirt fall back down as she turned to face him.

"Who?" Elias asked, his eyes widening with hope and Mylah couldn't help but let herself feel a spark of hope as well.

"It's crazy, I shouldn't even have brought her up..." Farren muttered to himself.

Elias stepped forward and put a hand on Farren's shoulder. "But you did, now tell me who she is." Elias utilized his princely voice once again. It was the different, more commanding voice he used when he spoke as Prince of Elowyn, versus as just Elias.

"Very well. I'm sure you've heard of the witch Ailsa?" Farren asked, wringing his hands in front of him.

Elias and Mylah both said, "Yes."

"She created the shreeve, but she's been dead for a long time, hasn't she?" Elias asked.

Farren shook his head. "I'm fairly certain she's still alive, and she may be the only one who can help you."

"Where can we find her?" Elias demanded.

"That's the thing, she's easy to find, but not so easy to get to." Farren ran his hand through his hair, concern wrinkling his forehead.

"What do you mean?" Elias asked, his eyes narrowing.

"She's in Turrikar," Farren said, making Elias groan and Mylah furrow her brow.

"What's Turrikar?" she asked.

"An impenetrable prison on the bank of the Lake of Anguish," Farren answered.

"So, we can go see her, right?" Mylah asked.

"It doesn't work that way. Anyone in Turrikar is there for a reason, and they are never allowed any visitors. Otherwise, it would increase the risk of escape, making it penetrable," Farren said, his mouth quirking up at his little joke.

"Ah, got it." Mylah nodded.

"I can put in a request with the council and see if they'll allow it, but that could take weeks." Farren's eyes flicked to Mylah, and he grimaced. After their first meeting with the council, Mylah had very little faith in them helping her.

"Mylah doesn't have weeks; we don't even know if she has days…" Elias muttered.

"Thank you for your vote of confidence in me," Mylah teased, though her hope was slowly burning out.

"We'll have to go and hope that the guards at Turrikar are feeling generous today." The lack of conviction in Elias' voice didn't help Mylah's outlook.

"Let me send a message to my friend on the council." Farren hurried to his desk, pulling out a pen and parchment and scribbled something on it. He muttered a few words, and it disappeared in a wisp of smoke.

Mylah blinked in surprise.

"We can send messages like that, yet we've been sending them with messengers all this time?" she asked, slightly annoyed.

"Not exactly. Most places have protection charms that don't allow any outside magic sources in, so letters wouldn't be able to reach them. Also, a lot of shreeve don't have the magical capabilities for the long-distance magic needed to send letters," Farren explained. "The council allows my letters to be sent this way since I'm an instructor here."

Mylah realized that made sense or else people could transport anything into a place in the same way, be it harmful or not.

"Now we wait?" Elias asked, breaking Mylah's train of thought.

"Now we wait. It shouldn't be long." Farren sat in his chair and leaned back. "Have a seat."

Elias sat but Mylah was too antsy, she couldn't sit down for fear of not being able to get back up. Who knows how far the poison had spread? What if she dropped dead any second?

"Mylah," Farren's voice reached her through her consuming thoughts. Elias had crossed the room and stood a few feet from her; she hadn't even noticed him get up.

"I'm fine," she said, but it came out strangled.

"Let me help you," Elias said, and Mylah jolted back, hitting the wall. "Tell me how to help. Right here, right now."

"I can't. Just, don't... Don't leave me alone," Mylah gasped out. The thought of dying alone...

Elias pulled her into his arms, and she let out a sob against his chest.

"I will never leave you," he murmured, tilting her head up with his forefinger so he could look into her eyes. "Stop trying so hard to be fine. It's okay to not be fine."

Another sob escaped Mylah. A small staticky sound came from behind them at Farren's desk.

"I've got a response," Farren said, and Elias turned back, keeping one arm around Mylah. "She wants to meet with you."

They all jumped as someone knocked on the door. Farren rose to answer it and adjusted his jacket before opening the door wide.

"I heard it was urgent," a woman's voice said from the hall.

Farren stepped aside revealing a lithe, blonde woman with blazing red eyes. It shocked Mylah for a moment, but she quickly recovered, realizing that they only blazed when the light hit them. It must be magic of some kind. The woman, who stood half a head shorter than Mylah, stepped into the room and grinned, her smile revealing sharp, elongated canines that grazed her bottom lip.

Disgraced

This must be the other council member – Nala Bergine, Mylah thought. The other councilors had the same red eyes, though theirs hadn't been nearly as piercing.

"Lovely, darling," Nala said as she gazed at Mylah. "You must be the one who needs Ailsa's help."

"Y-yes," Mylah glanced at Farren who seemed unfazed. If he trusted Nala, then so would Mylah.

"And why should I let you see her? You know, she's been alone down there for over five hundred years. She may have gone crazy by now."

"I have no other choice, I'm dying." Mylah's stomach flipped as she stated the fact out loud.

"As many others are, every day. What makes you so special?" Nala's gaze narrowed on Mylah as she analyzed her.

"She is a guest of King Castien, that should count for something," Elias snapped.

"I wasn't asking you, *Prince*," she spat the last word like a curse and turned her gaze back to Mylah. "Tell me dear, why should you be spared?"

"I don't..." Mylah pressed closer to Elias. "I'm not..." she tried again and failed at finding the words. "I shouldn't. I'm not worth saving." Elias jerked beside her.

"Don't say that! That's not true," he countered.

But Mylah knew if she found his gaze, she'd see her grief reflected there.

"Interesting..." Nala tapped her finger against her chin. "You're not making a very compelling case for yourself."

"The girl is still healing, Nala." Farren said, stepping forward and placing his hand on the woman's arm.

"Healing from what? You said she couldn't be healed," Nala said, peering over her shoulder at Farren.

"Unprocessed traumas and a guilty conscience. Give her the chance to finish her healing and right her wrongs by helping us to see Ailsa," Farren pleaded.

"Unprocessed traumas? Don't we all have those?" Nala turned her head back towards Mylah. "Tell me about them. I want to know that you are worthy of Ailsa's help."

"I-I can't," Mylah hadn't been planning on reliving her past that day, and she had no idea what it would change.

"Can't, or won't? Out with it," Nala demanded.

"M-my parents died, er...well they were murdered when I was fourteen."

Mylah gave her list of traumas, as she had done for Raelynn only a few weeks earlier. But she added her near deaths from the naga poison and the belladonna this time. Before, she hadn't considered them traumas, but now, as she relived that feeling of helplessness and facing down her mortality again, she saw them for what they were.

"I understand," Nala's voice changed. It held a hint of anger, which surprised Mylah. "Your fate has been decided, and you're trying to outrun it. You've succeeded up until now, and it's my turn to help you escape fate once more."

"I don't believe in fate," Mylah countered.

A grin slowly spread on Nala's face. "Good, neither do I. I shall grant you passage into Turrikar." She turned on her heel. "I'll send what you need as soon as I get back to my office. Good luck and tell Ailsa I said 'Hi.'" Nala strode out of the room and disappeared in a flash.

Farren clapped his hands together and he laughed.

"We did it! *You* did it!" he exclaimed. "I knew she'd be willing to help."

"Really? Because I'm pretty sure she was set on *not* helping for most of that conversation," Mylah said, a bit breathless from the interaction.

Farren waved his hand and scoffed, "That's all for show. She loves the drama." Farren hurried to his desk and as he reached it, a *poof* revealed the documents that Nala had promised. "Perfect! She's done it." He lifted the documents and scanned them.

"Why would you say that?" Elias said from beside Mylah, and she finally looked up at him. "Why would you tell her you don't deserve to be saved?" His brow was furrowed and his shoulders tense.

Mylah stepped away from him. "Did you want me to lie to her?"

"You deserve to be saved," Elias ground out, anger flashing in his eyes.

"More than any other person who is dying at this moment?" Mylah shook her head. "We don't have time for this. Poisoned, remember?" She stalked away from him to the door. "Are you coming or not?"

Farren followed her and after a moment, Elias did as well.

"This conversation isn't over," he said before passing her on the way out the door.

Farren closed the door behind them and led the way.

Twenty One

Greyson paced beside his cot, fidgeting with the buttons on his coat. It had been two days since the king had approached Greyson and the day had come for him to follow through with the king's request.

"Chin up, soldier." Julian walked up from behind him.

"I'm no soldier," Greyson muttered. *Far from it...he* thought. When signing up to be a part of the king's guard he'd thought there would be a lot more combat training, border skirmishes, and other more exciting tasks, but he had been sorely disappointed. Though, he guessed that wasn't a bad thing. He'd kept up with his own physical training on his off days to ensure he didn't lose any of his combat skills.

"Sounded good to me," Julian shrugged, flopping down onto Greyson's cot. "What's eating at you?" he asked, popping a candy into his mouth.

"The king wants me to accompany Queen Aveda into town today." Greyson paused his pacing to face Julian.

"There will be other guards with her...but I don't know why the king chose me to go with them."

"You're one of the better trained men here. It makes sense to me," Julian pointed out.

Though Greyson was inclined to agree with Julian, it still didn't make sense.

"But I failed him the last time he had me guard royalty. The Prince of Elowyn escaped under my watch. Why trust me with this task?"

"You're not keeping the queen from escaping back to Cyprian, you're going shopping with her, or whatever it is she's planning on doing in town."

"Well, that's just it, I'm not going to be watching her shop. He wants me to go with Kolt and Acton somewhere," Greyson admitted. "What if," he paused, gulping past the lump in his throat. "What if he wants them to get rid of me?"

Julian sat up, concern pinching his features for a second before they smoothed out again and he smirked.

"Don't sweat it. You'll be fine," Julian said, hopping off the cot and striding away. He turned, skipping backward as he gave Greyson a wave and turned on his heel once more.

Shaking his head at the strange interaction, Greyson finished readying himself before meeting up with the other guards for Queen Aveda in front of the castle. A carriage waited for the queen, and horses were waiting for the guards. Among the guards were Kolt and Acton. Greyson groaned inwardly. Going off alone with them in town would only bring about something horrible, he knew it. But he'd follow his orders.

Queen Aveda strode out of the castle and Greyson got his first good view of her. He'd only seen glimpses in the past. Her dark brown hair had been twisted up into an intricate braid and the edges caught the sunlight, making it appear golden in places. Her eyes matched her hair in luminance and color, and not a single wrinkle marred her face. Pointed ears poked out of her hair and when she turned towards Greyson, a radiant smile sent butterflies drifting through his stomach.

"You must be one of my new guards," she said, her voice delicate and songlike in its breathy but melodic sound. Greyson had never seen anyone as beautiful as her.

"Greyson Callister," he managed to say, though his brain had seemed to stop functioning in her presence. If she asked anything else of him, he'd surely flounder and lose any respect he had remaining for himself.

"Lovely to meet you." Her eyes fluttered and she turned, continuing towards her carriage. The train of the spring green dress she wore moved like water behind her as it trailed over the dirt and rocks. Greyson couldn't help wanting to hold the train for her so it wouldn't tear or become muddied, but he remained in place.

Once she was secured in the carriage, all the guards mounted their horses and surrounded it. As a unit, they began moving towards the village. Greyson remained on high alert for the short trip. He would not screw up this assignment.

"You seem a bit tense, Callister," Kolt jeered from behind Greyson. "Still a little stiff maybe?" Greyson did his best to ignore Kolt's comments. The queen could probably hear them from inside the carriage and he wouldn't say anything to incriminate himself with her or the king.

Disgraced

Thankfully, Kolt didn't say anything else to Greyson as they rode. Their cavalry came to a stop outside a dress shop in the village. Greyson waited, thinking some of them would move to clear the road enough for villagers to get by, but they continued to block the street. Everyone remained mounted on their horses except for Captain Andreas, who had walked into the store, assumingly to warn the shop owners of who was about to enter their shop. The queen had two guards whom she'd brought with her from Cyprian on either side of the stairs leading down from the carriage. One of them opened the door and the other held his arm out for Queen Aveda to steady herself as she descended.

Making her way into the shop, she paused to glance to either side of her, noticing the villagers who had stopped to gawk. She gave them a smile and disappeared inside.

Greyson watched some of the guards shoo away some of the gawkers, ensuring people couldn't gather and cause a scene. There were a few groups gathered to Greyson's right as well and he overheard some of their whispers.

"I heard she's the one in charge now..." a woman's voice reached Greyson. "The council is a farce, and no one has any say. The king might as well hand over Adair to Queen Aveda."

"Get out of here!" A guard yelled at the woman who puffed up her chest and stalked away with the rest of her friends.

Greyson watched her curiously and wondered whether she was the only one who was thinking that Queen Aveda had taken control. He couldn't exactly dispute that fact since he no longer had access to the council meetings.

Shuffling started behind him, and he turned in his saddle to see Kolt and Acton backing their horses away from the other guards and veering down a side street. Greyson groaned inwardly as he remembered he needed to go with them.

Leaving his place among the rest of the guards, Greyson followed Kolt and Acton towards the one bar in town. They hopped off their horses and headed inside, but not before slapping a large sheet of parchment on the door and nailing it in place.

Greyson caught up to them, but Acton let the door slam in his face. Reading the parchment they'd stuck there, Greyson's gut clenched.

By royal decree, this establishment is hereby closed until further notice.

Inside, Acton and Kolt were yelling to the patrons to exit in a timely manner as Greyson entered. A few people left without a fuss, but more lingered and nursed their drinks.

"What authority do you have to close down my bar?" A short and stout man went toe to toe with Kolt, though Kolt towered over him.

"We are the royal guard, sent by King Florian himself," Kolt said, sneering at the man. "If you want to take it up with him, be my guest, but you'll have to go through me first." Kolt's eyes danced with anticipation and Greyson could tell he wanted the man to fight him.

"Everyone, out," the man hollered to the room of people who all groaned in response. "As this *royal guard* said, feel free to take it out on him on your way out."

A few chuckles broke up the annoyed groans and shuffling of feet as more people began to leave. Acton gripped a man by the collar of his shirt and shoved him towards the door. Greyson recognized some of the people in the bar and couldn't help but shy away from their stares as they stalked past him.

When all but the owner and two patrons had left, Kolt spoke again.

"Greyson, Acton, get them out," he commanded. Acton moved immediately towards one of the patrons, grabbing both of their arms and hauling them towards the door as they kicked out and flailed as much as possible.

"Greyson," Kolt said again. "Get. Them. Out."

Greyson clenched his fists as he approached the other patron, a woman who had been friends with his mother.

"Please, leave," Greyson said under his breath so only she would hear. She turned and spit at his feet.

"Make me," she taunted, her eyes narrowing on him.

Taking a deep breath, Greyson grabbed the woman's arm and pulled her roughly from her chair. Every fiber of his being screamed at him to stop, but he had to follow Kolt's orders. This was a test from the king, he knew it.

As he tried to grab her other arm, the woman swung her fist at Greyson, and he let it hit him square in the jaw. He teeth clacked together, and the pain radiated down his neck. He deserved it, but that didn't mean he could let her stay in the bar. Avoiding her next hit, he got hold of her other arm and wrenched it behind her back as he led her out of the bar before him.

Kolt and Acton watched, grinning as they followed him out of the bar. Nausea rose in Greyson as he released the woman outside and she let out a frustrated cry.

"The king can't do this! He'll find out soon enough what happens when he starts taking away his people's freedoms," she said before stomping away from them.

"Well done, Callister. I didn't think you had it in you," Kolt said in a mocking tone. "Time to get back to dress shopping."

Back in the castle, Greyson returned to the bunkroom to find Julian lounging on his bunk. He sat up as Greyson approached and swung some kind of chain around his finger.

"How'd it go?" Julian asked.

"Fine. The queen needed to buy a dress." Greyson knew it sounded ridiculous and Julian's laugh confirmed he agreed.

"Of course she did," he said, shaking his head. "Though, giving the village her business will only help her gain their favor." Julian appeared thoughtful for a moment, and then he laughed again.

"I guess." Greyson glanced around and then sat beside Julian. "The king closed the bar in town. I'm not sure what the purpose was, but I had to help Kolt and Acton clear it out."

Julian tapped his finger against his chin as he brought his knee up to his chest and rested his elbow there.

"The bar is a good place for ideas to spread, especially traitorous ideas," Julian said, his eyes flashing with intrigue.

"I guess," Greyson sighed.

Julian fiddled with the chain he'd been swinging earlier. Greyson reached out to grab it and Julian pulled it back, clucking his tongue. "Finders, keepers," he chided.

"What is that?" Greyson asked, the silver chain looked like a necklace, but Julian held the charm in his palm.

"How badly do you want to know?" Julian raised a brow and smirked. "I'm in need of some information on Queen Aveda, and now that you're a part of her guard..."

"What kind of information could you want on her?" Greyson scowled. Julian had been strange since they'd met, but this was a new kind of random for him.

"Anything I can get. What are her plans? Why hasn't she made any serious moves yet? What is she waiting for?" Julian's eyes blazed and Greyson realized that he may be in over his head.

"Why do you want to know all that? Are you..." Greyson glanced around again but no one was within earshot of them. Most of the guards were still performing their duties.

"Am I, what? A *spy*?" Julian whispered the last word dramatically before throwing his head back laughing. "Aren't you curious about these things too?"

Greyson shrugged and Julian leaned forward, placing the hand that held the necklace flat on the bed. Greyson leaned away but felt a charge like static between them as Julian held his gaze and licked his bottom lip.

"There is more to life than kingdoms and wars," Julian said, his gaze dropping to Greyson's mouth for a moment before he cleared his throat and leaned back against Greyson's pillow. "Don't be so serious all the time." He rolled off the bunk and strode away, turning back to give his usual wave before leaving the bunkroom.

Greyson took a minute to regain control of his senses. His breathing had quickened without him realizing. As he returned to normal, he looked down at his bed and realized

Julian had left the necklace there. A silver chain with a diamond heart and a sapphire stone in the middle. His heart stuttered. Grabbing the necklace, he shoved it into his pocket before anyone could see, not that anyone else would know what it was, or *whose* it was.

Closing his eyes and taking deep breaths to calm himself, Mylah's image rose in Greyson's mind. Her smile, her blue-gray eyes, and the necklace, resting in the hollow of her throat. He'd dreamed of kissing her there and everywhere, but now... Now he would probably never see her again. Besides, he knew who she truly pined after, and it wasn't him.

The way he'd felt every time he looked at Mylah before she'd left was the same way Julian had made him feel moments ago. He frowned and opened his eyes to see Kolt and Acton entering the room. All thoughts of Mylah and Julian shoved to the back of his mind.

Kolt aimed directly for Greyson and Greyson sighed, knowing he was in for some kind of harassment. Acton trailed behind Kolt, seeming distracted.

Greyson stood to face them. "Can I help you?" Greyson asked, folding his arms over his chest, and rolling his shoulders back.

"I'm surprised," Kolt said, a grin spreading across his face.

"Why?" Greyson decided to play along. The sooner the interaction was over, the better.

"That your guard dog isn't here." Kolt made a show of checking under the bed and laughed as he straightened.

"Unfortunately, he had other duties to attend to," Greyson remained unfazed. He'd let Kolt get to him before, he wouldn't make that mistake again. "I have a good whistle, if you want me to call him." Kolt sneered and matched Greyson's stance.

"I don't know why he bothers with you. The king will find a reason to discharge you soon enough," Kolt sneered. Acton's head whipped up at that and he narrowed his eyes at Kolt.

"Let's go, Kolt," Acton grumbled.

"Go on." Greyson flung his arm out and smiled. "Nothing's keeping you here."

"I'd never have let that prince escape. I'd have gutted him and that bitch before allowing them to leave that tower," Kolt hissed as he passed Greyson.

Greyson sucked in a breath and clenched his teeth.

"I was going to let it go..." Greyson said before turning and grabbing the back of Kolt's jacket, yanking him backward. Taking him by surprise, Kolt slipped, losing his footing, and landed hard on the floor. Greyson pressed his boot against Kolt's throat and spit to the side of his face.

"Mention Mylah again and I'll be sure her name is the last word to leave your lips," Greyson hissed, heat searing its way through his veins.

Kolt coughed and gripped Greyson's boot, lifting it enough so he could talk.

"You're a traitor, just like her. I'll be sure the king learns of this," Kolt warned. Greyson removed his boot from Kolt's neck and stepped back. Acton held his hand out to Kolt and helped him off the floor.

"Be sure to tell him how you were criticizing him and how you think he's gone soft while you're at it," Greyson said casually. Kolt may be able to damage Greyson's reputation, but Greyson would be sure to take Kolt down with him.

Kolt spit at Greyson before turning and following Acton towards their own bunks. Greyson fled the room before he decided to follow through on his threat to Kolt. He had kept a calm demeanor through the interaction, but his blood boiled, and his hands were now shaking.

Pacing the halls, Greyson bumped into Queen Aurelia. Thankfully he hadn't actually collided with her, or else he was sure that would be grounds for dismissal. It was strange to see her out and about. She'd been mostly absent since Queen Aveda had arrived.

"Greyson Callister," she said, her lips turning up into a smile. The dim lighting of the hallway deepened the tone of her dark brown skin and made it almost glow. The gold accents that had been placed throughout her plaited black hair glinted as she moved.

Greyson's eyes widened, surprised she'd remembered his name. He wasn't sure they had ever formally met, but she'd been at every event the king had hosted for the council members which he'd also attended, prior to becoming a part of the royal guard.

"Your majesty," he said, bowing low before her.

"You may rise."

Greyson did as he was told and straightened himself but kept his eyes on the floor. "I'm sorry to have interrupted your walk," he said.

"Sometimes I enjoy an interruption. My days have become quite monotonous since Queen Aveda arrived." A flash of annoyance crossed her face.

"Really?" Greyson asked before thinking better of it. He had no grounds to be asking the queen any questions. "I'm s–" he began to apologize, but she cut him off.

"King Florian spends most of his time plotting and planning these days, and when he's not doing that, he is entertaining Queen Aveda. In the meantime, I have been spending more time in the gardens and keeping the peace with the children." She smiled and Greyson did as well. He saw an opportunity to possibly answer some of the questions Julian had asked of him.

"But Queen Aveda is here to help the king at least," he commented.

"So she says," she sighed, and Greyson could tell from her pinched look that she was wary of Queen Aveda. "I'm probably boring you."

"Oh no!" Greyson shook his head. "Not at all."

"Well, things will be changing around here for a few days at least," she said, and Greyson cocked his head to the side in question. "When the other royals arrive, along with the Hyrdian council representative, there will be a gala to welcome them. I'm sure you will be attending, as a guard or a guest."

"This is the first I'm hearing of it," Greyson murmured.

"It is a strange thing to be out of the loop, isn't it?" She seemed to ponder that for a moment, her eyes glazing over. "I guess that comes from no longer attending council meetings." He wasn't sure whether she was talking about him or herself, but he nodded anyway.

"I should be getting on. I'm sure you have somewhere you need to be," she said and smiled once more.

Greyson bowed to her again and only rose once she'd passed him.

As he walked, he thought about the gala. He'd known the other royals were coming to Adair, but he hadn't realized there'd be any kind of celebration. If there was a gala, that meant the council would all be invited, which meant Cassia would be there. It would give him a chance to talk to her again. The royals wouldn't be arriving for another week, though, so he had plenty of time to think about all the things he wanted to talk about with her.

Greyson returned to the bunkroom after walking the rest of the castle, avoiding Kolt for as long as possible, though he missed dinner in the process.

When he entered the bunkroom, he half expected to see Julian back on his bunk, waiting for him, but he was nowhere to be seen. Disappointment pricked at Greyson, and he tried to ignore it.

Striding towards his bunk, Greyson kept his head high and avoided glancing around the room, not wanting to make eye contact with any of the other guards. As he sat down on his bunk, Julian entered the room with a plate of food. He made his way towards Greyson, careful not to trip over any of the various items strewn in the pathways.

"I noticed you were missing at dinner, so I brought you something." Julian held the plate out towards Greyson who stared at it blankly for a moment. Julian moved the plate back and forth. "You want it, or no?"

"Oh. Yes," Greyson said, taking the plate from him.

As Greyson ate, Julian sat on the end of his bunk and watched the room.

"I heard some interesting information at dinner tonight," Julian began, and Greyson nodded for him to go on as he ate. "Kolt and Acton have been assigned by the king to some task having to do with Hosath's worshippers."

"That's strange," Greyson mumbled through a mouthful of food. He swallowed and set his plate down.

"First meeting with them here, and now this? What does the king want with the Hosath worshippers?"

"I've no idea, but who are we to question the king's motives?" The way Julian looked at Greyson made it seem as if he was testing him and Greyson wasn't sure how to respond.

"Right," Greyson decided to play it safe, no matter how much he trusted Julian. "I guess the answer doesn't really matter."

"Hmm..." Julian pursed his lips and frowned slightly.

"I did find out a little information too," Greyson said, and Julian perked up again. "From Queen Aurelia." Julian's eyes widened.

"When did you talk with the queen?" Julian asked.

Greyson smirked. "I ran into her while walking the halls. She had a lot on her mind, I think, but she did imply that she doesn't quite trust Queen Aveda."

"How?" Julian leaned forward, intrigue sparking in his gaze.

"I mentioned how Queen Aveda is here to help the king, and Queen Aurelia didn't seem so confident that is the case, but she didn't elaborate." Greyson kept his voice low so as not to be overheard, though he wasn't sure anyone else in the room fully trusted Queen Aveda either anyway.

Julian leaned back again. "Old news. Queen Aveda is always on her own team."

"She didn't seem so bad when I met her earlier today," Greyson pointed out. Queen Aveda had been kind and warm to everyone she'd interacted with.

Julian waved his hand. "That's all an act."

"How do you know?" Greyson realized Julian talked about Queen Aveda as if he knew her, yet he'd tasked Greyson with finding out more about her.

"I don't," Julian shrugged. "But I'd be willing to bet on it. Someone doesn't remain queen for five centuries by being *nice*. She has some play she's trying to make, and I want to get ahead of it."

"Again, why do you care so much about her?" Greyson wondered if Julian did just care so much about Adair that he didn't want her to betray them.

"I don't really." Julian shrugged. "But what else is there to do around here? Other than guarding council rooms, that is."

"I guess you're right," Greyson admitted, though curiosity still pricked at the back of his mind.

A few days passed without much ado, before the Captains, Andreas and Mardoc, made the official announcement about the gala, though word about it had already been spreading like wildfire through the castle. Every guard would be on duty, either inside the ballroom, roaming the halls, or on the perimeter of the castle.

Assignments would be announced two days before the gala, and everyone assigned to the ballroom would be required to wear formal attire so they would blend in with the crowd. Of course, they'd still have their weapons on them, which would be difficult to conceal, so Greyson thought trying to blend in was pointless, but he didn't argue. He hoped to be assigned to the ballroom so he might get a chance to speak with Cassia.

Disgraced

"Excited for the big event?" Julian appeared at Greyson's side at breakfast, making him jump. He had the ability to sneak up on Greyson no matter where they were.

"We don't get to actually enjoy ourselves," Greyson pointed out. "We'll be on duty."

"Who says we can't still enjoy ourselves?" Julian raised a brow and smirked. "There is little chance we'll even be needed for any sort of disturbances. Adair is fairly docile as far as villages and towns go." It always threw Greyson off when Julian talked as if he'd already seen the world, though he'd never mentioned leaving Adair.

"You're probably right, but that doesn't mean the king won't expect us to be on high alert the entire night anyway." Greyson even more so because of his past blunder.

"He's going to be so distracted by the fancy guests, he won't have time to worry about what a few of the guards may be doing."

"For your sake, I hope you're right, and I hope you *do* enjoy yourself. I, on the other hand, will be vigilantly manning whatever station they place me at and not ruining my chances at remaining among the royal guard," Greyson said, and Julian scrunched his brow.

"Is being a guard so important to you?"

"It's all I have left." Greyson cleared his throat and picked at the bread on his plate, trying to distract himself from the grief welling up inside him.

"Well, I think we need to change that," Julian said, and Greyson glanced up at him. "Starting with the gala."

"Whatever you say," Greyson decided not to argue with Julian anymore. He'd just avoid him at the gala. There was a chance they wouldn't even be assigned to the same area that night, which would make it all that much easier.

Twenty Two

Turrikar was visible from miles away. It loomed over the surrounding trees and lake beyond. There were no houses or towns near Turrikar, and it took them three hours on horseback to reach it from Korrindale. Mylah was grateful for the wind drowning out any sound as they rode, because she didn't want to finish her conversation with Elias. He didn't understand her self-loathing, and that was fine by her, but she wasn't in any mood to try to explain it to him.

The horses slowed and eventually came to a dead stop, refusing to go any further, once they were half a mile from Turrikar.

"It's a magic defense system. We have to go on foot from here," Farren said.

They dismounted their horses and tied them to a nearby tree. The forest there was sparse, and the creatures were few.

"This is eerie," Mylah commented.

"That's the point. Anything to deter people from approaching Turrikar." Farren walked ahead.

Elias held his hand out to Mylah, and she took it, gripping it tightly as they strode towards her fate. She had lied to Nala when she said she didn't believe in fate. After nearly dying from poison twice before, and now for a third time, she was finding it hard to overlook her seeming destiny.

As they walked, fatigue pressed in on Mylah. It was the first symptom besides pain she'd had from the poison, and she feared that it would kill her before they reached Turrikar. Her breathing became slower and more deliberate, but she pushed onward, keeping pace with Elias.

"State your name and business," a harsh voice grumbled.

Mylah whipped her head around trying to find where it came from.

Farren pulled out their documents.

"Councilwoman Nala has given us permission to enter Turrikar in order to talk with the witch Ailsa," Farren spoke loud and clear, his head swiveling as he also tried to determine where the voice had come from.

"You may approach," the voice surrounded them as if it were being amplified.

They continued walking and reached the end of the trees. Turrikar rose before them and Mylah leaned her head back to take it in, her mouth agape.

It stretched towards the sky, taller than any house or building she'd seen, taller than even the Adair or Elowyn castles. It sat on the lake shore, but only took up as much space as her home in Adair. The only way that such a small base could hold up such a sheer mass of stone would be magic. There were no windows and only one door at the base of the tower. A single guard stood outside the door. He held a staff in one hand and a flail in the other.

"State your names," the guard demanded as they approached him. His had been the voice they'd heard in the forest.

"Farren Aberon of Korrindale, Prince Elias of Elowyn, and Mylah Orson of Elowyn," Farren spoke for them all.

"Documents," the guard held his hand out and Farren placed the small stack of parchment there.

The guard rifled through them and muttered a few words under his breath that sounded like some kind of spell or incantation. He stuffed the documents into his pocket.

"Rules," he growled. "No talking to *any* other prisoners. No magic can be used within Turrikar's walls. You will have one hour inside, no more. You will be under surveillance the entire time. If we suspect any kind of suspicious behavior, you will be removed. Understood?"

"Understood," Farren confirmed.

The guard's eyes found Mylah's, waiting for her to speak.

"Understood," she echoed, followed by Elias.

The guard lifted a key to the lock and turned it full circle before the door clicked and swung inward. He stepped aside, allowing them to pass, before shutting the door behind them and locking them inside.

For a moment, they were in complete darkness and Mylah gasped. Torches began lighting along the hall that stretched out before them. Doors lined the hallway and a guard stood outside every other door. They stopped at the first guard.

"We are looking for the witch Ailsa," Farren said.

The guard grunted, "Bottom floor."

They continued down the hallway to the stairs. There was a set that led up and a set that led down. Mylah glanced back at the hall behind them. None of the other guards had spoken or so much as moved as they'd passed them.

"Let's go," she said, turning back to the stairs.

Farren had already begun to descend them. Elias let Mylah walk ahead of him, but never let go of her hand.

The stairs turned in a spiral, leading them down into an impossibly darker pit of despair. The only lights Mylah could see were the dull, yellow orbs marking each floor of cells. As they passed floor after floor, any hope seemed to be sucked out of Mylah until tears pressed against her eyes and grief clogged her throat. Breathing became even harder and she had to pause a few times before continuing.

Screams and laughter echoed through the stairwell from the prison cells. Sometimes she could make out distinct voices muttering to themselves, but she tried to block them all out.

"How far down does this go?" she asked, keeping her voice quiet in hopes that none of the prisoners would hear her.

A screech split the air around them and she knew she'd been heard.

"Help me!" a horrific, squawking voice sounded behind her on the level they'd just passed. "Come back!"

Elias pressed against Mylah's back, and she realized she'd stopped walking.

"We're almost there," Farren said, and Mylah wondered if he had any clue or if he was only trying to reassure her. But they reached the bottom of the stairs after two more floors.

There weren't as many guards on this floor. Only two that Mylah could see. Farren repeated their quest to the first guard who led them to the last cell on the left and unlocked the door for them.

"Ailsa, you have guests," the guard said in a mocking tone.

"Don't be cruel, Gerald," the witch crooned from inside her cell.

"See for yourself." Gerald stepped aside, allowing Farren, Mylah, and Elias to be seen.

Mylah peered into the cell that was only lit from the torchlight in the hall. Shadows filled most of the cell, but the torchlight cast a glow over a figure hunched in the back corner on a bed of straw. The figure unfurled from the wall and crawled towards them. Mylah wanted to cower behind Elias, but she stood her ground and watched as the witch revealed herself.

Though she'd been in the prison for hundreds of years, according to Nala, Mylah thought by her body that she looked to be in her late fifties or early sixties in human years. Her long silver hair had been wound up into a loose bun on top of her head and her eyes had Mylah taking a step back. They shone in the torchlight, all white and without pupils.

"Don't worry deary, I can still see you," Ailsa said, staring directly at Mylah. "Gerald, leave us be. My guests will behave." She winked at the guard and Mylah shuddered.

Gerald returned to his post and Mylah stepped into the doorway. Ailsa sat down cross legged in the center of the cell grinning at the three of them.

Disgraced

"I need your help," Mylah stated, figuring she may as well get to the point. They only had an hour and it had taken them a good fifteen minutes to find her cell.

"Obviously," Ailsa snorted. "Tell me something I don't know. Like why the Prince of Elowyn would deign to visit me." Though her eyes didn't move, Mylah could somehow tell they had found Elias standing behind her and were now solely on him.

"Mylah has been poisoned and we need your help to heal her," Elias said.

Mylah was surprised he didn't use his princely voice against the intimidating woman. Ailsa chuckled, revealing perfectly white and straight teeth, and rolled her hips side to side.

"All of this I know. I can smell the poison pumping through your veins." She inhaled deeply through her nose as if making a point. "You are closer to death than you think."

Elias stiffened beside Mylah, and she took his hand once more.

"Can you help me?" Mylah asked.

"Of course I can help you. But that's not the right question, is it?" Ailsa leaned back until she laid on the floor and cackled.

Chills skittered through Mylah, leaving goosebumps in their wake.

"*Will* you help me?" Mylah revised her question.

Ailsa sat up, pointing to Mylah. "That's the question!" she cried out. "Will I help the poor, human orphan whose heart has been torn in two? Grief, heartbreak, and guilt are all dangerous poisons. Would you like me to root those out as well?"

"No, just the poison that's killing me," Mylah clarified, though she knew the witch was only toying with her.

"Hmmm...interesting. Prince, *prince*," she seemed to be tasting the title as she repeated it over and over. "King? Do you want me to tell you a secret?"

"No," Elias snapped. "Just help Mylah," and as an afterthought he added, "Please?"

Another cackle wracked the witch's body.

"Hold on there, *Prince*. I haven't had visitors in, well, *ever*. I want to chat." Her eyes widened with feigned innocence.

"About what?" Elias asked, his tone wary. Mylah squeezed his hand in reassurance.

Ailsa took a deep breath and rolled her shoulders back. "Tell me..." She pointed to Elias. "Tell me why you let your brother take the throne from you."

"If you've been down here for five hundred years, how do you know so much about what's going on now?" Elias narrowed his eyes, and Mylah knew he was avoiding the question.

"No, no, no, no. I ask the questions here. You don't get to know *my* secrets." Ailsa placed her hand over her breast dramatically. "If you want my help, answer my question."

Elias huffed but answered her, "My brother took the throne because I wasn't ready."

"I want the *real* answer," Ailsa whined and pouted.

Mylah leaned back, offput by the witch.

"I don't know what you mean, that is the real answer," Elias argued, his brows pulling together in confusion.

Disgraced

"I see all," Ailsa whispered, leaning forward, and widening her sightless eyes. "You were ready, my prince. Your brother knew it too..."

"Fine!" Elias said, cursing under his breath, though Mylah caught it. "I was scared, and I'd killed my own father! How was I supposed to rule a kingdom?"

Ailsa cackled. "A scared little prince and an orphan fighting fate... Two disgraced runaways," Ailsa cooed, grinning widely.

"We didn't run away," Mylah cut in.

Ailsa waved her hand towards her.

"Didn't you?" Ailsa put her arms out to indicate their surroundings. "You're certainly not facing your problems in Elowyn alongside King Castien."

"We don't have time for this – the guard gave us one hour and we've already wasted half of it!" Elias groaned.

"Very well. We've yet to discuss my payment." Ailsa flicked her hand up before her, wiggling her fingers and surveying her nails as she did so.

"Payment?" Mylah asked. "What do you want?"

"As you well know, I'm not going anywhere anytime soon." Ailsa waved her arms about her and then laid them at her sides. "So, I need something to keep me entertained."

"Like what?" Mylah narrowed her eyes; unsure she would be willing to give whatever it was Ailsa asked for.

"A story," Ailsa smirked.

"You want me to tell you a story?" Mylah shook her head in confusion. It couldn't be that simple.

"No!" Ailsa crowed. "No, no, no. Let me *see* your story." Ailsa reached her hand out towards Mylah.

Elias gripped Mylah's hand tighter, pulling her closer. Ailsa waved her hand at him either sensing or seeing the movement. Mylah still wasn't sure if the witch could actually see or not.

"I won't bite," Ailsa said, beckoning Mylah forward. "Come sit." She patted the floor in front of her and Mylah stepped towards her, prying Elias' hand from hers.

"This is the only way," Mylah reassured him. He let out a sigh and released her hand. She sat cross legged on the ground in front of Ailsa and placed her hand in the witch's grasp.

"Ahh, good." Ailsa closed her eyes.

After a second, Mylah's hand started to tingle, and then her entire body. Her instincts were screaming at her to pull away, to run and never look back, but she remained rooted to her spot. Ailsa's grip tightened on Mylah's, and she laughed, a lilting and girlish laugh that surprised Mylah after the cackles she'd heard.

Ailsa tilted her head back and a smile transformed her face. "What a beautiful day," she murmured.

Mylah realized she was experiencing Mylah's life in her mind. Feeling what she felt, and basking in the sunlight that Ailsa hadn't seen in over five hundred years. They sat like that for a while longer until Ailsa opened her eyes and released her grip on Mylah's hand.

"So, will you help me now?" Mylah asked, hoping the witch hadn't tricked her into sharing her memories for nothing.

Ailsa placed her hand on Mylah's knee and leaned her head closer to Mylah's.

"Before I can help you, I need to know; how attached are you to dying?" Ailsa's words caused Mylah to balk, unsure what the witch meant by them.

"I-I don't want to die," Mylah sputtered. "That's why I'm here."

Ailsa leaned in closer and lowered her voice, "In order to help you," she said, her eyes seeming to flick to Elias behind her. "You need to become one of them." Ailsa leaned back and waved Elias closer.

"What do you mean?" Mylah asked as Elias stepped up beside her and crouched down, so he was level with the witch.

Ailsa reached out and gripped Elias' wrist, he jerked back slightly, but then relaxed.

"I mean exactly what I say. You can either be consumed by the poison and die or become something that this specific poison does not affect, and it will be destroyed by your new and improved body."

"You mean, you want to make Mylah a shreeve?" Elias clarified; his voice strained.

"Yes. It is the only way to help her. Even if I were able to remove the poison from her human body without killing her, fate would only try to take her again. As a shreeve, she will be much more...durable." Ailsa smirked.

"What do you mean *fate*?" Mylah scrunched her nose. Though she'd discussed it with Nala briefly, she couldn't believe that the witch also believed in fate.

"Fate, dear. It may be unavoidable for most, but you seem to keep outrunning its course for you." She made a running movement with her fingers through the air. "I sense you've angered the divine."

"The divine?" Mylah asked.

"Fate, destiny, the divine – whatever you want to call it. It has a way of catching up to you. But..." Ailsa's eyes twinkled as she scrunched her nose with a smile. "You keep avoiding it. So interesting. I saw the banshee in your memories... Even she foresaw your fate. Yet now I have the power to change your fate yet again." Excitement sparked in Ailsa's eyes.

"Can you see the future?" Mylah asked, unnerved.

"Not exactly. I can see your past, because you shared that with me, and I can see which path you are currently on and where that leads. But that doesn't mean you won't change course along the way. Most people do. The future is never set in stone."

"So, there's a chance I could still live as a human?" Mylah doubted it, but she had to ask.

Ailsa scoffed, "No. But, you can live a long, happy, poison free life as a shreeve, if you want."

"Can she think about it?" Farren's voice jolted Mylah from her thoughts. She'd forgotten Farren was with them.

"We don't have time," Mylah reminded him. She turned to Elias who was still crouched beside her with his wrist trapped in Ailsa's grip. "What do you think?" Mylah asked him and he closed his eyes.

"You know my answer," he said, his jaw clenching. "Whatever it takes."

Ailsa giggled and used her free hand to cover her mouth. "Oh, speaking of poisons! Young love, how potent a poison," Ailsa said, cocking her head to the side as she studied Elias. "It poisons the brain, making you do things you would have never done, and your heart... How fragile." Her eyes flicked to Elias' chest.

"The pain," Ailsa murmured, and Elias jerked forward, clenching his fists as he gasped.

"What are you doing?!" Mylah cried out, her hands fluttering over Elias' arm, but she had no idea how to help him. He relaxed, but his breathing had become shallow.

"I'm fine," he gasped out. "What was that, Witch?"

Ailsa giggled again, "An experiment," she shrugged. "I wanted to see what your heartbreak would feel like for you if it were more...physical."

"Why?" Elias asked.

"I'm bored, that's why." Ailsa reared back slightly as if offended by the question. "Are we doing this or not? I don't have all day," she smirked. They all knew she would be going nowhere for a very long time.

"Yes. Let's do it," Mylah said, knowing it was her only option.

Ailsa's grin widened and she reached out to Mylah. "We don't have a fae, so Elias' blood will hopefully be strong enough to suffice."

"Hopefully?" Elias snapped. "You mean you don't even know if this will work?"

"Have some faith, *Prince*. I've only done this a thousand and one times." She flourished her free hand before them dramatically.

Before either of them could protest anymore, she sliced open Elias' wrist with a nail faster than they could realize it was happening. The cut wasn't deep, but blood welled to the surface and dripped down from his wrist to the floor.

"Thanks for the warning," Elias mumbled, and then Ailsa did the same to Mylah.

Mylah cried out in surprise, though she should have expected it after Elias. Ailsa began muttering unintelligibly while still gripping Elias and Mylah's wrists. Mylah assumed she was speaking the old language of the shreeve that the Book of Creation had been written in. The drops of blood on the floor began to quiver and inch towards each other, forming one perfectly round circle.

"How is this possible? I thought magic couldn't be used inside Turrikar," Farren said from behind them.

Ailsa ignored him and continued her muttering. A dim glow began from Mylah's ring which she'd worn every day since Castien told her to.

"Interesting..." Ailsa muttered, her eyes fixing on the ring. "I look forward to finding out what that's about."

Mylah shivered as a wave of magic passed through her.

After another few minutes, Ailsa stopped muttering. "It is finished," she stated, dropping Mylah and Elias' wrists.

"I don't feel any different," Mylah looked down at herself and noticed no changes.

Ailsa scoffed, "You heard your friend; magic does not work inside of Turrikar. This is a magic older than Turrikar itself, so the spell works, but you will not be affected by it until you are well away from Turrikar. Pity, really. I'd like to see my handiwork, but alas."

"I don't understand," Farren said. He had moved into the cell and stood beside Mylah.

Ailsa groaned and turned her eyes to him. "Do you think that they can ward this place against every single type of magic there is? It would be impossible. I am the only witch or warlock in existence that still knows how to use the old magic. So, why bother trying to ward Turrikar against it when I'm already inside?"

"Couldn't you escape?" Farren asked.

"Who says I haven't?" She cocked an eyebrow and then rolled back, cackling. "Foolish man!" Returning to her sitting position she fixed her stare on him again. "In order to escape Turrikar I'd need much more than a few old spells. Though magic may not be used here, magical wards are in place to prevent me from leaving."

"Thank you," Mylah said before Farren could ask any more questions.

"Don't thank me yet. You're about to endure the worst pain you've ever experienced and will probably ever experience in your extended life. Send word if you survive it, will you?" Ailsa's grin unsettled Mylah but she forced herself to nod. Her nerves had returned, and a prickling began in her back. Rolling her shoulders, she tried to ignore the sensation.

"You best be going, lest the poison kill you before you make your transition." Ailsa waggled her fingers at Mylah.

"Just, one more thing. If we used the reversal spell in the Book of Creation, would I return to being human?" Mylah asked.

Ailsa's face went slack before she snarled, "*Never use the Book of Creation.* That accursed book is why I'm in here. I should have never written it."

"Unfortunately, it wound up in the wrong hands and will be used if he can figure out the translation," Mylah admitted, guilt bubbling up in her. She was the reason King Florian still had the book.

"Then you best stay as far away from that man as possible," Ailsa warned.

"But wasn't it meant to return those who were transformed into shreeve to their original fae or human state?" Elias asked.

"A shreeve is neither human nor fae any longer. In the beginning they were a perfect blend of both. I thought that if they were still in that base form, not further muddled by breeding between humans, fae, and shreeve, that they could be returned to their initial state of being, human or fae. So, I created the Book of Creation with the spell to do that, in an attempt to help a man who had decided he wanted to return to his fae form."

"I used the spell on him, and at first, it seemed to work. He reverted to a full fae male and went on his merry way. Come to find out, the spell *continued* to work, tearing apart his genes and in the end killing him. When a shreeve who used to be human came to me, requesting I try to revert him back to *his* former state, I warned him what had happened to the fae. He thought maybe it would be different since he was human. So, we tried again. And the same result occurred." Ailsa took a deep breath as she finished talking.

"So, the Book of Creation..." Mylah began before Ailsa cut her off.

"Is useless. Unless your goal is to murder shreeve. Then it is very effective in doing that."

Mylah nodded. This they knew, since it was the whole reason that Castien had been fighting to get the book back in the first place.

"And the spell in the book works on multiple shreeve at a time," Mylah pointed out.

"Another fatal flaw. After creating the shreeve for the purpose of garnering peace between races, I realized the role they were then going to be forced into. Peacekeepers, and basically slaves to the fae. Humans couldn't overpower shreeve, so they were less likely to mistreat them, but it wasn't uncommon. I created the first spell for the fae, and when we thought it had worked, I adjusted the spell so it could be used on a larger mass of people, so we could help everyone." Ailsa rolled her eyes at the memory. "Both spells are in the book, along with a few others I created, just for fun." A smile tugged at her lips, and she wiggled in place.

Mylah tucked that piece of information away for later.

"Why not destroy the book once you realized what happened to those you tried to help?"

"Someone stole the book from me before I could destroy it. It's funny what you'll do to cover up for your mistakes." Ailsa grinned which made Mylah uncomfortable. "*That's* how I wound up here. Don't pity me, I know what I've done."

"I don't pity you," Mylah countered, but Ailsa saw through her lies.

"You think I was put here unfairly? Then ask *him* what stories are told of me around campfires to scare the little ones." She jerked her head to Farren. Mylah glanced at him and when she turned back to Ailsa, the witch had slunk back into the shadows of the cell.

"Is there anything else we should know about Mylah's transition, or the book?" Elias asked as he stood. Mylah remained on the floor, but he held his hand out to her and helped her up. Exhaustion hit her like a wave. They needed to get out of Turrikar as soon as possible.

"If that book is used, any shreeve within a five-mile radius will be torn apart from the inside. The spell must be wielded by a witch or warlock, and there are certain ingredients, or totems that they must be holding when they use it. That may slow them down," Ailsa said. "And it takes a week or so to take full effect. A long, agonizing death." The spark that lit in her eyes at that had Mylah drawing back.

"So, is it possible to save them – reverse the reversal?" Mylah asked, hope sparking in her, but Ailsa shrugged.

"I suppose it may be possible... I never got that far though."

"Times up," a gruff voice sounded outside the cell.

"Thank you," Elias said as he bowed to Ailsa.

"Enjoy my memories," Mylah said. "They aren't very pleasant."

"All the better to keep me entertained, my dear. We are connected now, and I look forward to seeing where you go from here."

Though Mylah could no longer see the witch's eyes, she felt them on her. It unnerved Mylah to think that the witch could see inside her head.

"Does that mean you can see everything I see?" Mylah asked.

"Not exactly, but you'll sense when I'm there," Ailsa said.

"That's not what she agreed to," Elias argued.

"Would you rather she be dead?" Ailsa retorted.

"No."

Mylah watched as Elias' jaw twitched and he turned to the exit.

"Let's go," Farren said, waving to them from the hall. "We have little time left."

Mylah and Elias followed him out of the cell and the guard moved to lock it behind them. Before he could Mylah remembered one last thing she needed to tell the witch.

Poking her head back into the cell, Mylah said, "Nala says 'hello.'"

Ailsa screeched in delight and hurried forward once more. "The queen of fate herself! If you see her again, let her know I'm watching her." The ominous words were punctuated by the guard slamming the cell door shut, muffling the sounds of Ailsa's near maniacal laughter.

None of them spoke as they ascended the stairs, again passing floor after floor.

"Help me!" The same screeching voice met them as they passed one of the floors and Mylah cringed but kept moving.

At the ground level, they exited the stairway and passed by the guards, the torch lights flickering to life once more. Mylah thought it odd that the guards were normally in pitch darkness, but she kept her thoughts to herself.

At the exit, the final guard waited for them outside.

"Thank you," Farren said as they passed him by.

He said nothing and stood stoic beside the door until they all exited, and he closed the door behind them, locking it.

Farren led the way back to their horses and none of them dared speak. Once they'd mounted their horses and were on their way back through the forest, Elias finally broke the silence.

"How do you feel?" He turned his head so he could see Mylah on the back of the horse.

"The same, but less tired I guess." Mylah's exhaustion had lifted as they'd exited Turrikar. But otherwise, nothing else had changed yet.

"That's good."

"None of us can speak of what happened in there," Farren said, worry lacing his voice. "Otherwise, people all over may attempt to do as you've done. Granted, most wouldn't be able to get in, but the influx of attempts couldn't be good for Turrikar..."

"And they'd have to convince Ailsa to help them," Mylah reminded him.

"That's not the hard part. You know she'd do it for anyone if they let her connect her mind to theirs, as you've done."

"It's going to be hard to hide once my transition happens, if it ever does," Mylah pointed out.

"No one needs to know the details," Farren said.

"I'll do my best," Mylah promised.

Twenty Three

Crane leaned against the wall in Castien's study. Korriane and Ana occupied the chairs beside him while Torin and Killian each perched on the large windowsill at the back of the room. Castien stood in front of the round table at the center of the room holding a letter in his hands.

"Sovereign Keir has summoned us for a meeting," Castien announced.

Crane couldn't help but be nervous since he'd never been to any kind of formal event outside of Adair, let alone a war meeting with another kingdom.

"When do we leave?" Korriane asked.

"Tomorrow. I'm hoping that Elias and Mylah will be able to meet us there as well. I sent Elias a letter as soon as our invitation arrived."

"And we're all attending?" Killian asked.

Castien nodded. "Yes. Everyone in this room... Plus Davina. I don't trust her enough to leave her alone in the castle," Castien smirked but Torin scowled.

Crane sensed there was more to it than that. Davina had been included in much more lately and it seemed as if she may be growing on Castien, too.

"You should send her back to town. There's no reason she needs to be here any longer," Torin said.

"Did you bring us here to discuss anything else, or is the rest of this meeting to be talk about Davina? Because I have better things to do." Crane couldn't help the irritation that rose in him whenever they talked poorly of Davina. He'd befriended her in the past few weeks and couldn't understand why Torin still held a grudge against her.

"You've received another letter as well," Castien said, grabbing a letter off the table and holding it out towards Crane.

His hands shaking, Crane took the letter and read it.

Crane –

There isn't much to report on my end. King Florian is keeping most of the council in the dark on all matters pertaining to the war. I think he suspects a spy. There will be a meeting amongst the royals of the human kingdoms and possibly a councilman from Hyrdian. I believe they will be arriving any day now.

I hope you are all well. I'm sorry I don't have anything more useful to tell you. I can't help but wonder when I will see you again. If things have changed for you, I understand. Don't worry about me.

Love,
Cassia

Crane gripped the parchment so hard it ripped. He crumpled it up and shoved it into his jacket pocket. Castien gave him a sympathetic look.

"I need to get back to Adair," Crane ground out.

"Impossible," Castien said, and Crane whipped his head towards him.

"What does the letter say?" Killian asked, stepping away from the window and approaching the table.

"King Florian is having a meeting with the other royals of the human kingdoms and a representative of Hyrdian," Castien told him, and he nodded.

"Hyrdian? But aren't Elias and Mylah trying to get them on *our* side?" Ana asked.

Crane looked over at her and saw the fear in her eyes. He understood that fear all too well.

"Hyrdian has yet to make a decision," Castien said.

Torin rolled his eyes. "They'll most likely decide not to involve themselves, as always," he grumbled.

Anger welled up inside Crane at that and he couldn't stay in the study any longer. He needed to get outside into the fresh air.

"If I'm no longer needed..." Crane said as he made his way to the door.

"Don't do anything stupid," Castien warned.

Crane clenched his fists and clucked his tongue, unable to find a proper response that wouldn't wind up with himself in the dungeon.

Pacing the halls of the castle, Crane bumped into Davina as she left the library, a sprite at her shoulder.

"I thought you were done with the escort?" Crane joked halfheartedly.

"It was just a little reprieve. Castien doesn't trust me *that* much." She let out a huff and pulled the book she held in closer to her chest. "I guess I'm lucky Castien hasn't thrown me out on my ass yet," she said with a smirk.

"True. I am curious how you ever wound up with Castien in the first place, though," Crane said, figuring they'd been friends long enough now that he could ask that kind of question.

Davina sighed dramatically and began walking towards the garden door, glancing back at Crane, and jerking her head for him to follow.

Once they were outside, Davina finally spoke. "I'm not proud of it, but I was seeing Torin first."

Crane's eyes widened. He'd known, of course, that there was history between them, but he figured it was the proper reaction to her story.

Davina continued, "Torin and I met at a bar in town. He'd returned from the border and needed some comfort I could provide," she said this with a knowing smile.

Crane thought a little pink enter her cheeks. He'd never seen Davina embarrassed.

"One thing led to another, and we wound up together for three years," Davina paused, taking a seat on the bench in front of the rose bushes.

Crane's eyes widened in earnest that time. He hadn't realized how long Davina and Torin had been serious, he'd assumed it had been a fling. Sitting down beside her, he waited for her to continue her story.

"Torin never once brought me to the castle, the entire time we were together. I don't know if he ever saw us as a serious relationship, or if I was only a hand to hold on the darkest of nights. Or at least I *didn't* know. Not until I decided to attend a revel at the castle and met King Castien." Davina placed the book she held in her lap and wrung her hands as she spoke.

Crane reached out and placed his hand over hers and she turned a surprised gaze on him but said nothing about it.

"Castien, of course, had no idea who I was to Torin. That night, he happened to be looking for a new consort, and I offered to fill the role. I was tired of constantly wondering what I was to Torin, and I wanted to make him jealous." Davina dipped her chin to her chest. "I'm a horrible person," she muttered.

"No, you're human," Crane said before he realized the words he'd used.

"Not exactly, but you could argue the human genes in me were shining through that night," Davina said, nudging him playfully. "The look on Torin's face when he saw me with Castien... I hurt him. In that moment, I knew I'd meant something to him. Whether I meant as much to him as he did to me, I never knew, but it doesn't matter now."

"After that night, my parents heard the talk around town that I had been chosen as a consort for the king and they told me if I ever lost that position, they'd throw me out. Because as a consort to the king, our entire family received praise, gifts, and more, and they didn't want to give that up. They honestly thought one day I may become queen, though I knew that was unlikely," Davina's voice softened and faded out.

Crane removed his hand from Davina's, and she flattened hers against the book in her lap. Crane finally looked at it and smiled as he noticed the title, *A Dance with the King*. It was a romance novel, Crane assumed.

"Thought I might be able to gain a few pointers from this," Davina said, noticing Crane's attention on the book.

He flicked his eyes back to hers. "Have you ever apologized to Torin?" he asked.

Davina shook her head lightly, her unbound hair shifting and tickling his shoulder as she did. "I don't know how," she admitted.

"I'm pretty sure you say 'I'm sorry for what I did. I didn't mean to hurt you, I only needed to know you cared,'" Crane said.

Davina huffed, "I guess you're right. I should apologize."

"Let me know how that goes for you, and if you need anything, I'll be around." Crane wasn't sure if he should offer to help Davina with her apology, figuring she might want a third party in case things got ugly, but he knew she could handle herself.

Davina leaned her head against Crane's shoulder, and they sat like that in a blissful silence for what felt like hours.

The following morning, Crane sat beside his mother on that same bench in the garden. He hadn't had the patience to talk with her sooner. She kept her eyes trained on the wall that rose up past the gardens, the wall built to keep out any unwanted visitors. Crane twiddled his thumbs as he tried to figure out what to say to her.

"I have to leave Elowyn," he said, deciding to dive right in. Elena blinked slowly, giving away nothing. "Castien has asked me to go with him to Amaris." A slight incline of Elena's head made Crane think she had nodded. "So, that's it then?"

Disgraced

Crane couldn't help but be frustrated with his mother. She hadn't talked to him in days, always seeming far away or engrossed in a task. The most he'd seen of her since their trek into the Unbounds was at dinner, where she remained silent and then returned to her room.

"I should have known better than to think you'd care." He stood, turning his back to Elena and was about to storm off when her hand gripped his forearm, holding him in place.

"Crane," she said, her voice coming out hoarse from disuse. "I'm sorry."

He sat back beside her, and his shoulders dropped as he took in the complete devastation on her face.

"Mom..." he said but she shook her head.

"I've been a horrible mother these past few weeks. Not just to you, but to your brother," Elena said, burying her head in her hands.

"There's nothing we can do for Greyson right now," Crane reminded her.

"That doesn't mean a mother stops trying. I've been trying to figure out what your f..." she stopped, her voice cracking and tears welling in her eyes. "What your father would have done."

"So have I," Crane admitted. "He always knew the answer, didn't he?"

Elena smiled and Crane pulled her into a hug.

"I'm sorry I haven't been as strong as I should be," her voice broke on a sob.

"No one expected you to bounce back from losing Garrick. We understand you need time. Your children are grown, you don't need to worry about us, Mylah included." Crane pulled her close.

Elena laughed softly, "Yet I still worry, constantly. There's nothing that will ever change that. You've all attracted trouble your whole lives, like your father and Emil." Wiping away her tears, she smiled.

"Well, at least we don't go looking for it like they did," Crane pointed out.

"What will I do while you're gone?" she asked.

"I don't know..." Before their conversation, Crane had assumed she'd continue doing what she'd done the past few weeks, sulking in the gardens. "I guess whatever you'd like."

"I think I'd like to go into town. Maybe stay in town. I don't want to stay here with only the guards for company. It will feel too...hollow." She wrapped her arms around herself and sighed.

"I can talk with Castien. I'm sure that will be fine," Crane said.

"You don't have to continue to baby me, Crane. I'll talk with the king. It's about time *I* become the parent again." Elena patted his hand. "Have some fun while you're in Amaris. When you return, we'll talk about how we'll help your brother."

Instead of saying that there was no way they'd be able to help Greyson, Crane nodded. If anyone could find a way to help his brother, it was their mother.

"Crane?" Davina came around one of the hedges and smiled when her eyes met his. "Good morning, Elena," she greeted her.

"Davina," Elena said. "So nice to see you."

"I'm sorry to interrupt, but the king is ready to depart," Davina said, glancing pointedly at Crane.

"Right. I have to go," he said to Elena who kissed his cheek and motioned for him to follow Davina.

"I'll come with you to speak with the king before you leave." Elena stood with Crane and walked arm in arm with him. Davina strolled at Crane's other side.

"So, Davina, I see you every night at dinner, but I know so little about you," Elena said as they walked.

"And I'm sure what little you know is all bad things," Davina said, and a blush bloomed in her cheeks.

"Not at all," Elena swatted Davina's arm across Crane. "Tell me about yourself. What do you do?"

Davina sighed and fiddled with the hem of her overcoat. "That's a loaded question. I guess if you were to ask anyone else around here, they'd tell you I don't do much of anything."

"Nonsense. The king wouldn't invite you along with his cadre if you weren't useful to him in some way," Elena pointed out and Crane realized she had a point.

"Well, that's kind of you to say. I think it's more of a *'keep your enemies close'* kind of thing. I'm ashamed to say I did some horrible things in the past." She ducked her head in shame and her hair fell in a curtain to cover her face.

"Haven't we all?" Elena said and Crane turned his head to his mother, opening his mouth to question her before she winked at him. He laughed instead, figuring he didn't want to know what kind of trouble his mother used to get in. "What is it that you want to do now?" Davina appeared thoughtful and Crane watched her as a whole host of emotions played across her face. She'd never revealed so much to him before.

"That's a good question. I used to think I wanted to be queen," Davina said, laughing a little, though Elena remained enrapt, waiting for the real answer. "But my family pushed that on me. I never truly wanted it for myself. I do enjoy helping King Castien, though. Trying to find ways to help our people."

"You should see if you can become a permanent fixture here, then," Elena said. "The king can never have too many council members."

"Elowyn doesn't have a council, mother," Crane said, and she waved him off.

"Maybe they should. Davina can be the first council member. You can live among your people in the town and bring their concerns before the king."

"That sounds great, but I doubt Castien would go for it."

"Well. That's something you can discuss with him on your journey. If you need backup, I'll be here when you all return." Elena winked at her, and Crane chuckled.

They continued out of the garden towards the group waiting for them by the front gate. Castien stood beside his horse while everyone else had already mounted theirs. Crane and Davina would be riding together since they still didn't trust Crane to be able to handle riding alone on the enchanted horses for a longer trek.

"King Castien," Elena greeted him and bowed slightly. "I wish you well on your travels, but I have a request before you go." Castien cocked his head to the side but waited for Elena's request. "I'd like to stay in town while you all are gone."

Castien pursed his lips. "Interesting request, but I don't see what harm it would do. So long as you allow one of our guards to stay with you."

Elena dipped her head to him. "That would be fine."

Disgraced

"Very well." Castien snapped his fingers and a handful of guards approached. "Find Lady Elena a place to stay in town. Stella and Petra will stay with her."

Crane turned to see a woman approach, a guard he'd never noticed before.

"Yes, your majesty," she said, bowing to him. "Elena, I'll help you pack."

Elena walked over to Stella and stood beside her. Crane joined Davina at their horse, waiting for her to mount it first.

"Oh no, you're in front," Davina said, smirking. "Can't have you flying off the back." Crane rolled his eyes but didn't protest as he climbed up into the saddle. Davina hopped up behind him and gripped the reins on either side of him. "Cozy."

"Get a hold of yourself," Crane teased her. "I'm spoken for."

Davina scoffed, "As if I'd stoop so low. I have my sights set a little...higher." Crane turned his head in time to see Davina's eyes flick to Torin and he wondered if she'd already apologized to him. If she had, it didn't seem to have changed the tension between them.

Clearing her throat, she dipped her chin to her chest before setting her sights on the gate. "Well, are we going?"

In answer, Castien mounted his horse and led the way out of the gates. Once they were in the open, two guards flanked him while another two went ahead of him. Ten guards in total were accompanying them, surrounding the group.

They began their trek to Amaris.

Twenty Four

Mylah and Elias returned to the inn to find a letter from Castien waiting for them.

"He's requested we meet him in Amaris on our way home," Elias said as he scanned the letter.

They decided they would leave the next day, as long as Mylah was feeling up to it. Since returning to the inn, she still felt no changes.

After dinner, they returned to their room, having got rid of Elias' room, and Mylah hid in the bathroom for a while. She sat in the tub, surrounded by bubbles, and soaked. Her thoughts raced at a mile a minute, thinking about everything. She was about to become a shreeve if Ailsa's spell worked. She was now connected to one of the most powerful witches in the world, and she was about to return to Elowyn where she'd be preparing to fight her home kingdom in a war.

She closed her eyes and tried to imagine her mother, though the image of her had progressively been fading over the years. It became harder every day to remember the exact pitch of her voice, or her precise smell that always made Mylah feel at peace.

"What would you say if you were here?" she murmured to herself, her mouth half submerged in the water. It came out garbled and made her smile as it brought back a memory.

"Mylah, no splashing in the tub please." Her mother hovered by the side of the tub holding the soap.

Five-year-old Mylah giggled and wiggled her fingers on the surface of the water. "Sorry, mumma."

Vita couldn't hide the smile on her face as she leaned forward and began scrubbing the dirt from Mylah's face.

"You and Cassia are going to be the death of me, I know it," she said, laughing. "Why is it that Greyson is the only one of you who returned spotless?"

"Because he didn't want to play," Mylah said. "He climbed a tree while we pretended to be chased by a shreeve."

Vita paused in her scrubbing. "Why were you doing that?" Her voice had changed to one of concern.

"We learned about them today," Mylah told her. Since there wasn't a formal school in Adair, the children were either taught by their parents, or someone else's parents. Cassia's mother, Alessia, happened to be the one who taught them most of the time.

"What is it that you learned?" Vita asked, resuming her scrubbing.

"They attack humans! They are super-fast and strong, and scary!" Mylah's voice rose as she became more excited.

"Is that what Alessia told you?" Vita's eyes widened in surprise.

"Well, not exactly." Mylah shrunk down in the tub, sheepish. "But they seem scary!"

"Not everything is as it seems, Mylah." Vita placed the soap back on the side of the tub and dumped a bucket of water over Mylah's head. "Now, come on. It's dinner time."

Mylah dunked herself under the water and as she resurfaced, a stabbing pain started in her back where her wound had been. She lurched forward, pulling her knees to her chest as she gasped. Clenching her eyes shut and grinding her jaw against the pain, Mylah let out a short cry. She slapped a hand over her mouth as tears began to well in her eyes. The pain only increased, spreading from the point of origin to the rest of her back, and then to her arms and legs. It moved slowly, as if it were burning away the poison in her veins, little by little. It was all Mylah could do not to scream.

She gripped the edges of the tub as she began to thrash and finally a scream ripped out of her. Mylah couldn't believe she didn't pass out, but she figured that had something to do with the transition.

Elias burst into the room, his eyes searching until they found hers. Mylah screamed again and he fell to his knees at her side.

"What can I do?" he asked as his face crumpled.

Mylah wound her arms around him, and he stood pulling her out of the tub and carried her to the bed. Mylah clung to him as he laid beside her and spasms wracked her body, leaving trails of what felt like fire in their wake.

Vicious sobs caused her to cough and sputter as she tried to catch her breath. Elias stroked her hair that was still dripping wet from the tub, as was the rest of her body, but the pain was all consuming and she couldn't bring herself to care about that. Elias pulled the blankets up over them and warmth began to seep into Mylah, easing some of the pain.

"It hurts," she whimpered, abashed by the powerlessness she felt.

"It's only temporary," Elias reminded her, and she focused on that sole statement.

This is temporary. This is temporary. This will pass, she recited over and over in her mind as the pain wreaked havoc through her body.

Every time she thought the pain was beginning to subside, it would sweep over her again, coming and going in waves. A whimper would escape her every now and again, and she continued to shake despite the fever that had begun to set in. Sweat replaced the bath water on her body, and she had to push the blankets off, but she kept Elias close despite his body heat. His presence kept her sane, reminded her that she was still alive and needed to continue to push through the pain.

"I don't know…how much…more…I can…take…" she panted as she forced out the words.

"You can do this," Elias reassured her, his breath hot against the top of her head. "This won't break you."

"Distract me," Mylah gasped out as another wave of pain washed through her.

"How?"

"Tell me a story. Anything. Just… please?" Mylah whimpered.

"Okay. A story, uh, okay. Here's a story." Elias took a deep breath. "Once upon a time, there were two princes,"

"Were their names Elias and Castien?" Mylah said through gritted teeth. A laugh escaped her through her sobs.

"Who's the one telling the story?" Elias asked before he continued. "The two princes were not blood, but they were brothers. One day, they went out into the forest to find an adventure and they came across a herd of kelpies, which is extremely uncommon."

"Kelpies?" Mylah strained against the pain now gripping her head.

"A whole herd of them. Usually they travel alone, but not this day. The princes observed them from the safety of a nearby tree and marveled at the creatures who appeared majestic when they weren't trying to eat anyone. But the wonder didn't last. The younger prince broke a branch as he tried to climb down from the tree and the entire herd instantly became aware of the princes."

"I'm sensing some exaggeration in this story." Mylah tried to laugh again but the pain overrode the sentiment and she winced instead.

"None whatsoever. The older prince offered to stay behind to give the other a chance to get away, but the younger prince refused to leave him. So, together they faced the kelpies. Unbeknownst to the older prince, the younger prince had magic. He had no idea how to use it, but he knew when he was scared, or angry it would burst out of him, and it did then. As the kelpies raced towards them, a ripple of magic flowed out from the prince and knocked the kelpies back with such force, those that rose again ran the other way."

"Together they rode back to the castle and boasted to all their friends that they had bested a whole herd of kelpies. Of course, the king caught wind of the story and called them to the throne room. He questioned them and reprimanded them for being so reckless. But he smiled at the thought that his two sons had come back victorious. It was the first time he'd ever seemed proud of the princes and that carried the younger prince for a long time, even though it never happened again."

"That's depressing," Mylah said, and Elias laughed. "Has Castien ever used his magic in front of you?" she asked, and Elias stiffened against her.

"Castien doesn't have magic," he stated.

"Don't lie to me now," Mylah groaned. "It's pointless, and…" She let out a hiss at the pain that caused her legs to cramp up. "Rude," she finished.

"I've never seen him use magic," Elias modified his statement and Mylah believed him. "As far as I know, he's never used it."

Mylah decided to keep what she had learned from Raelynn to herself. She would talk about it with Castien when she saw him. It didn't make sense to her that Castien would keep his magic to himself when it would be helpful in their war against Adair and Queen Aveda.

"Is it any better?" Elias asked.

"A little," Mylah lied. Pain lit up every nerve in her body. Somehow, she was remaining conscious, and she would credit Elias for that.

"Let me know what else you need me to do," Elias said. His hands stroked Mylah and she caught one in her own.

"Where did your scars come from?" she asked as her fingers traced one of the worst ones that ran across the back of his hand.

"You already know my father was not a kind man…" Elias began, and Mylah stiffened. For some reason she had not thought that the scars may possibly be from Elias' own father. "These were a punishment for some slight indiscretion. I hardly remember what I did to deserve them."

"You *didn't* deserve them," Mylah said, her own pain slightly lessened. Whether that was because of her feeling sorry for Elias, or because it was receding, she couldn't be sure yet.

"Well, he thought I did. He inflicted these himself, too, not wanting anyone else to know about it, I guess. He used a knife, or maybe it was a letter opener... Maybe I blocked it from my mind. Then he wrapped up my hands and had me tell people I'd injured them in training." Elias rubbed his hands over Mylah's back, and she sighed, leaning into him even more.

"Did Castien know?" she asked, not sure why it mattered, but it did.

"No. I never told him. I think he must have figured it out once he finally saw the scars, but by then, it was in the past and nothing could be done." Elias shifted and a flare of pain went through Mylah's arms. She pulled them in close against her chest.

"And your fae blood didn't heal the scars?" she asked, distracting herself once again from her own pain.

"No. He liked to use special potions that would ensure you'd keep your scars, as reminders of what you'd done. Of course, clearly it didn't work since I can't remember anything about that day." Elias chuckled darkly.

"Tell me about the heartbreak that Ailsa made you feel," Mylah said suddenly, changing the subject.

"Why?"

"I want to know everything about you. Even things I may not want to hear, like about your past heartbreaks..." Mylah and Elias had never discussed his previous relationships. From what he'd told her when they first met, he hadn't been in any serious relationships because most people were using him to get to his brother.

"Well, it's not what you're thinking," Elias sighed. "But if you really want to know…" Mylah nodded against his chest. "There was a girl who I fell for… Hard. Except, she wasn't who I thought she was, and then, when I thought I could forgive her, I learned that she'd revealed my darkest secret to my worst enemy. Or so I thought." Elias' words struck home, and Mylah curled in on herself.

"Your heartbreak, I did that," she whispered, worrying that saying it aloud would make him realize that he didn't want to forgive her anymore, that he should leave her again.

"Yes," Elias shuddered.

"Does it make it hurt less if I tell you I'm broken too?" Mylah asked.

"No, because I know *I'm* part of the reason for that," he sighed. "And I want so badly to undo all the hurt and pain I caused you, and to go back in time to tell myself how stupid I was being."

"But you can't. Just like I can't go back and tell myself how stupid *I* was being." Mylah noticed the pain had begun to subside, but she remained curled up against Elias. "I'm sorry, for everything."

"Me too." He kissed the top of her head. Mylah turned her face up towards him. Elias gasped before smiling as he looked into her eyes. "Your eyes." He lifted his hand, stroking his thumb across her cheekbone.

"What color?" she asked.

"Your irises stayed the same, but the whites are light orange, like Castien's. They're beautiful." He ran a hand down her arm and shivers followed his touch. The pain hadn't entirely subsided, leaving behind echoes, but Mylah was able to roll out of bed and walk to the one mirror in the room. Standing before it, she gasped.

Blue and green markings had appeared on her arms, legs, and torso. Her eyes were the hardest thing to adjust to, they seemed foreign to her. Otherwise, not much had changed, except her hair was glossier and tamer, her skin clearer and smoother. She ran a hand over her face, marveling at herself and gasped when she noticed her ears were slightly pointed. It wasn't as noticeable as Castien's ears, but there was no mistaking them for human ears.

Turning away from the mirror, Mylah grabbed her shirt from the chair beside it and pulled it over her head. A chill had settled in since her fever had broken. Her transition may appear complete, but her body was still adjusting to the changes.

"You should get some rest," Elias said, standing from the bed. "You can have my side," he offered. Mylah realized her side was damp from the bath water and her sweat.

"We can both fit," Mylah said, not meeting his gaze. After all they'd revealed to each other, she wasn't sure where that left them, but she knew she wanted him close. Without waiting for his response, she walked to the bed, settling close to the middle, but avoiding the wet spot she'd left. Elias changed out of his wet clothes, pulling on loose fitting pants that hung low on his hips, and leaving his torso bare.

He laid in bed behind Mylah, pulling the blanket up over them again. She nuzzled herself back against his chest and he draped an arm over her. Even though they'd just been in a very similar position, for some reason this felt more *intimate.* Before, Elias had been comforting her and distracting her from her pain.

Though Mylah was tempted to relive the last night they'd spent together in that bed, exhaustion overtook her, and she fell asleep within minutes.

When Mylah woke in the morning, Elias had already packed his bags. They sat by the door while he was nowhere in the room. Mylah climbed out of bed, rubbing the sleep from her eyes, before she headed to the bathroom. After dressing, she packed her bag and left it beside Elias'. Catching sight of herself in the mirror, she jumped, forgetting the markings and the change in her eyes. It would take some getting used to, but overall, she felt stronger – *better.*

As Mylah was about to leave the room, Elias opened the door and blinked in surprise at her. Clearly, he was still getting used to the new Mylah as well.

"Sorry I left, I wanted to bring you breakfast," he said, holding a bowl of porridge out to her. Mylah's heart swooned before Elias added, "It's better if no one who knows you sees you."

Mylah deflated, "Ah, right." A blush heated her cheeks. She hadn't thought of that. She took the porridge and sat in the chair to eat it.

Elias stood waiting by the bags, looking at everything and anything but Mylah.

"Is something wrong?" she asked as she finished her porridge and set the bowl on the floor.

Elias' gaze locked on hers. "No, why?" he responded too quickly.

Mylah sighed and stood, heading for her bag. Elias stepped in front of her forcing her to look at him again.

"It's just..." he paused, crooking a finger under her chin, and tilting her head up. When Mylah didn't pull away, he leaned down and kissed her.

Mylah placed one hand on the back of his neck and the other on his chest, deepening the kiss before Elias pulled back.

"Is that all?" Mylah teased, breathless.

"The stable boy is bringing our horse around, we shouldn't keep him waiting," Elias said, though he lingered, his arms still around her.

"Mmm," Mylah grinned, pulling him back down for one more kiss before murmuring, "Our horse awaits." This time Mylah pulled away and Elias groaned, making her grin.

Mylah put on her cloak, pulling her hood up to conceal herself in hopes that no one would see the changes that had come over her on the way out.

"Sabine and Broderick should be waiting for us at the border, and they will escort us to Amaris," Elias said.

"Where we'll have a whole lot of explaining to do since Castien probably informed Sovereign Keir that I'm human," Mylah said. It was going to be hard to explain her transformation without giving away too many details.

"We'll cross that bridge when we come to it," Elias said, and together, they left their room behind.

Mylah and Elias rode out of town towards the Hyrdian wall. Every sound reached her much louder and clearer than ever before, every smell became more potent, and every color brighter as she became accustomed to her new and improved body. It reminded her of the first time she'd stepped into the Unbounds, and all the colors and sounds seemed amplified. But this was ten times more intense than that. Not only were the colors brighter, but everything was sharper too. It made her think she'd been seeing through a haze her entire life up until now.

She heard titters from the surrounding trees that she attributed to pixies.

"Do you think I have any magic?" Mylah asked Elias, craning her neck to look at him. His scent wafted over her, filling her with a sense of belonging, and she couldn't help but smile.

"I guess we'll find out," he said, and her smile turned to a pout. She'd hoped he'd suggest they try out some magic.

Mylah lifted her hand to stare at it, wiggling her fingers, thinking maybe some sparks would fly out or something. But that had never been how it worked for Elias. He'd had to use intense focus, but that had been more to control his powers, not so much for using them.

As she moved her hand, the sunlight glinted off her ring, reminding her of when it had shone in Turrikar. Even Ailsa had been intrigued by that, and it worried Mylah. She cast the thought aside and turned her mind back to magic.

She focused on a rock in the distance, thinking maybe she could lift it as Elias had done with the objects in Farren's office. As she stared at it, it didn't so much as budge, but she did feel something stir deep inside of her, along with the flicker of a presence in her mind.

That's it, girl, Ailsa's voice was like a whisper at the back of her mind, but it made Mylah jump.

Elias shifted behind her. "Everything all right?" he asked.

"Mmm..." Mylah closed her eyes. *Hello?* She tried, wondering if she could speak directly to Ailsa. The presence had faded, and the witch did not respond. Mylah opened her eyes again, annoyed that Ailsa could come and go as she pleased but wouldn't answer when Mylah wanted to chat.

"You seem tense," Elias noted, and Mylah did her best to try to relax.

"Just nervous about what everyone is going to say when they see me," she lied. Though, that *was* a concern of hers.

"I'll do the explaining so you don't have to deal with that," Elias promised.

"How are you going to explain it without giving away what really happened?" Mylah knew most of their friends wouldn't accept a vague explanation, and they deserved better than that.

"Well, I'll tell Castien the whole truth, and as for everyone else, we'll give them most of the truth. No one else needs to know the full story."

"I don't like lying to everyone again…" Mylah had had enough of secrets and lies for a lifetime.

Elias wrapped one of his arms around her.

"I don't want to lie either. We'll tell them as much of the truth as possible. It will be fine, I promise," he said, his lips close to her ear, making her shiver in anticipation. He chuckled and released his grip on her, taking hold of the reins again.

Sabine and Broderick had kept their word and were waiting for them on the other side of the wall when Mylah and Elias arrived. Mylah made everyone get off their horses so she could embrace them both.

As she pulled away from Sabine, Sabine gasped, and Mylah knew she had realized the change.

"Mylah!" she yelled, making Mylah laugh. "You... How is this possible?" She looked to Elias who shrugged. Broderick observed Mylah carefully, noting her eyes and her markings.

"This can't be real..." he said.

"We can't tell you everything," Elias said, keeping his word to explain. "But this was the only way to save Mylah."

"Don't tell me you tried to get yourself killed again?" Sabine groaned, but the downward tilt to her lips and her pinched features gave away her concern.

"It's not my fault the world is out to get me!" Mylah said. "We should talk and ride though, because we have some news for the king." Sabine and Broderick nodded.

Once they were all back on their horses and riding away from Hyrdian, Elias and Mylah filled them in on all they had learned in the Forsaken Mountains. When they finished talking, they went at full speed towards the Amaris border, knowing that the information they had would be essential in getting Amaris to agree to help Elowyn in the war against Adair.

At the border, they ran into Amarian soldiers, who recognized Elias and let them pass, insisting on escorting them into Amaris. Castien's cadre had arrived a few days prior and were waiting for them at the castle.

Mylah wore her hood to conceal her pointed ears as they were led towards the castle. They passed a few different villages on their way, each smaller than the town in Elowyn.

The castle sat up on a hill surrounded by a moat and a wall similar to the one that protected the Elowyn castle. The bridge that led over the moat was made of white stones and it shone bright in the sun that beat down on them. It was an unseasonably warm day and Mylah loathed the cloak she had to wear as sweat beaded on her forehead and trickled down her back.

Past the bridge, trees lined the road leading to the castle that reminded Mylah of Adair. For the first time in a long time, thinking of Adair didn't bring with it a wave of homesickness. The realization made her smile and she leaned into Elias a bit more. He said nothing but his arm drifted to her waist.

Twenty Five

After Crane and the others spent a couple days settling in, and met with Sovereign Keir and their men, Mylah and Elias finally arrived. They'd been waiting to have a formal meeting until Mylah and Elias arrived in case they had any news from Hyrdian's council that may pertain to the war.

Castien stood somewhere to Crane's left, beside Torin at the end of their welcoming line in the courtyard. Ana and Korriane were directly beside Crane, holding hands, while Killian stood a little behind them. Davina was on Crane's right with her arm looped through his. She'd informed him that she'd tried apologizing to Torin, but he'd given her no indication of whether he forgave her or not, which explained the lingering tension between them. Crane couldn't worry about that now, though.

The anticipation electrified the air around them and none of them spoke as they waited for Mylah and Elias to come through the gates.

Holly Huntress

As the gates creaked open, a few Amarian soldiers emerged first, followed by Elias and Mylah on their horse. The electricity in the air dissipated as each of them let out a breath of relief at seeing their comrades again. Crane couldn't stop the grin that plastered on his face as soon as he saw Mylah. Her hood was up, but most of her features were still visible. Before they dismounted their horse, Crane noted the arm Elias had casually around Mylah's waist, and he wondered if they had managed to patch things up while they were gone.

"Welcome to Amaris," Sovereign Keir said from beside Castien.

Crane had almost forgotten they were there, which seemed impossible. Sovereign Keir was an unforgettable person. Everything about them was regality personified. They stood a whole head taller than Castien, their muscles on par with Torin's. Their brown skin was radiant in the sunlight, along with the gold hair pieces that decorated their long, black, braided hair. The copious braids had to have taken hours to make them look so perfect. The crown that sat atop their head was made up of intricate golden leaves that intertwined and created a circlet that complemented the hair pieces in their braids.

"Thank you," Elias said, taking Crane's attention from the sovereign.

Elias and Mylah dismounted from their horse, who was led away by a stable boy. Elias and Mylah both bowed to Sovereign Keir who grinned, revealing their perfectly straight and white teeth, along with their one gold incisor.

"I'm sure you want to catch up with your king, so I will leave you to it. Once you are settled in, please send word and I'll arrange for our meeting." Sovereign Keir stepped back, inclining their head to them before heading back into the castle. The guards dispersed, besides the two who remained on guard at the door.

Elias approached Castien and whispered something to him, his hand still at Mylah's back.

They definitely patched things up while in Hyrdian, Crane thought, laughing inwardly. Mylah could be stubborn, but he was glad that she and Elias had been able to forgive one another. A pang of loneliness had Crane clutching at his heart for a moment, turning his thoughts to Cassia.

"Hey, we're headed inside," Davina said, placing a hand on Crane's arm and interrupting his train of thought. He jerked his head towards her before following everyone inside. He noticed Mylah hadn't taken off her hood yet which he thought was odd. She had to be overheating in the sun.

A guard led the way to Elias and Mylah's room but left them all there once they were inside. Crane had originally assumed Mylah would be staying with him, but now he guessed, things had changed. He'd looked forward to catching up with her, but he'd find time to do that some other way.

Crane entered the room last, shutting the door behind himself. Sabine and Broderick remained outside the room, on guard. The room was much nicer than his own, which only contained a bed, a small sofa, and a small bathing chamber. This one had a whole sitting room, which they were now standing in, and double doors to the left which opened to the actual bedroom.

"There's been a...complication," Elias said.

Korriane, Ana, Killian, and Davina all dropped onto the couches that faced each other in the center of the room.

Torin perched himself on the windowsill at the back of the room, opening the window a crack to let some air into the stuffy area. Crane remained near the door he'd shut, crossing his arms as he waited for Elias' explanation.

"What kind of complication?" Castien asked, sitting on the arm of one of the couches.

Mylah and Elias shared a quick look before Elias nodded and Mylah lowered her hood. At first, Crane didn't notice anything odd. But as everyone else gasped, he looked closer and realized the glaring change. The orange that now surrounded Mylah's iris glinted in the sunlight from the window. Removing her cloak, she revealed the markings on her arms.

"How is this possible," Castien murmured, rising and striding towards Mylah. He lifted her arm and inspected it, touching one of the blue markings as if it may come off like paint.

"It's not possible..." Killian muttered as he stared at Mylah from across the room.

"No one has been transformed as you have since Ailsa herself created the shreeve," Korriane added.

"We can't tell you the whole story," Elias said, though he gave Castien a pointed look that told Crane he would be telling his brother everything once they were alone.

Crane didn't like the idea of being in the dark about something so important, especially since it pertained to Mylah.

"But if I hadn't been turned into a shreeve, I would be dead," Mylah said, her voice catching on the last word.

"What do you mean?" Crane snapped and everyone turned to him as if remembering he was there. "What happened?"

"I was poisoned somehow while we were investigating what was happening in the Forsaken Mountains," Mylah explained.

"You have a habit of being poisoned, don't you?" Davina commented.

"Apparently, I keep escaping fate..." Mylah said, laughing, but Crane could tell it wasn't funny to her. Her eyes, though different, still gave away her true emotions. He noted fear there that she tried to hide by sweeping her hand over her face, brushing her hair to the side.

While Elias and Mylah filled the room in on everything else that happened in the mountains and Hyrdian, Crane kept his gaze trained on the floor as he considered the implications of this change in Mylah. Before he realized she'd even moved, Mylah stood beside him and took his hand in hers.

"What are you thinking about?" she asked, keeping her voice low so she wouldn't interrupt the others who were discussing Queen Aveda and her plans.

"You," Crane admitted.

Mylah's smile disappeared and her brows drew together. "I'm still me, just, different," she said.

Crane shook his head. "I don't care about the physical changes. You seem happy, and healthy, so that's all that matters." Crane rolled his shoulders. "It's the fact that you endured yet another near-death experience. That takes a toll, Mylah."

"I'm fine, though," she tried to say, but Crane scoffed.

"You're not fine, Mylah," he said a little too loudly. The others in the room turned to look at them, but Castien regained their attention quickly. "You're not fine," Crane whispered.

"I guess I'm a little worried because the witch who helped me said that fate is real and wants me dead, but there's nothing I can do about that, right?" Mylah's voice remained steady, but Crane didn't miss her swallow and her eye twitch.

"Screw fate. Screw destiny, and whatever else is out there trying to take you away from us." Anger bubbled up in Crane and he clenched his fists, cracking his knuckles in the process.

"Exactly," Mylah said, smiling for real. "That's why I love you, Crane. You always know what to say to make me feel better." She laid her head on his shoulder while they watched the others in the room. Crane didn't take in anything they were saying as he thought of all the ways he could keep Mylah safe. No one would take his sister away from him.

Twenty Six

It bothered Mylah that Crane saw through her mask so easily. She was thankful that he had, but it meant that she could never hide anything from him. She assumed that's what came from growing up with someone, but she could never read him as well as he could read her. Maybe *that's* what really bothered her.

After everyone left that night, she and Elias remained in the sitting room for a while, talking over what they would tell Sovereign Keir, and how they would explain her change to all of Elowyn.

"Let's leave that for when we return to Elowyn," Elias said with a yawn. "My brain hurts from thinking too much."

"I agree," Mylah said, standing from where she'd been on the couch. Elias made to stand as well, but Mylah placed her hand on his chest and pushed him back down with a smirk dancing on her lips.

Elias' eyebrows rose and his lips parted as Mylah placed a hand on either side of him and leaned in close, her hair sweeping over her shoulder as she did.

"I think I know how to help," she said, trying her best to sound seductive, but she'd never really done this before. Her past experience was minimal and when they'd been together before, it had been rushed and in the heat of the moment. Now, everything slowed down and his breath brushing past her arm sent shivers down her spine.

Elias placed his hands on her waist as she straddled him and the evidence of his arousal pressed against her core, lighting her up inside. Leaning forward, she touched her lips to the curve of his jaw. He shuddered beneath her.

Elias' hands trailed from her waist to her thighs, squeezing her tightly as her mouth finally found his.

"A message from the sovereign, sir!" someone called through the door as they banged on it loud enough to wake the whole castle.

Groaning in frustration, Elias lifted Mylah off him, surprising her with the ease at which he recollected himself. At the door, he straightened his shirt and ran a hand through his hair before opening it.

"Here you are, sir," a man handed Elias a rolled-up bit of parchment.

"Thank you," Elias said, taking the message and closing the door before unrolling it. "The sovereign wants to meet with us in the morning," he said, tossing the parchment onto the coffee table.

"That's good. We can get that out of the way," Mylah said, running her hands through her hair to try to smooth out the curls.

Disgraced

"Now, where were we?" A devilish gleam lit up his eyes and he leaned down, scooping Mylah from the couch into his arms. A squeal of surprise escaped her followed by a laugh. "Ah, yes, I was about to ravish you." He carried her to the bedroom, not bothering to close the doors to the sitting room behind him.

Mylah woke the next morning feeling more well rested than she had in weeks. The bed that they'd been provided with was like sleeping on a cloud. She wished she could bring it back with her to Elowyn.

Sitting at the vanity, she readied herself for their meeting with the sovereign. Their war general, along with some other higher ups in the kingdom would also be in attendance, but Mylah didn't bother trying to remember all the names that had been listed in the sovereign's note, there were too many.

Mylah tied her hair back before remembering she should keep her ears covered. She stared at her reflection, studying the changes as she had when she had first seen them.

It was strange seeing herself this way. It almost felt as if she were looking at a portrait of someone rather than at herself. The orange that surrounded her irises reminded her of the orange in Castien's eyes, though hers were a lighter shade. They would give her away instantly when the sovereign saw her up close.

"Mylah, are you almost ready?" Elias stood in the doorway, watching her.

"I can't..." she closed her eyes. "I can't hide that I'm not human anymore." Tears pricked her eyes, and a shuddering breath broke free from her chest.

Elias closed the door behind him and strode to her side, crouching down next to her chair. He lifted a hand to her cheek, stroking away a tear with his thumb as he smiled up at her.

"You don't need to hide yourself. I will find a way to explain to the sovereign why you are not human, as we told them you were," he said, trailing a finger over one of the markings on her arm. "Come on." He stood, pressing his lips to her temple and held his hand out to her. Leaving her hair up, Mylah took his hand and let him lead her out of the room.

They were escorted, along with the rest of their group, to the sovereign's meeting chamber which reminded Mylah a little too much of King Florian's council chambers. It made her skin crawl as they were led towards the dais where Sovereign Keir sat with their daughters on either side of them. They were as beautiful as the sovereign. Elias had informed Mylah that the princesses' mother had died a few years ago from an illness.

Each of the princesses wore a tiara atop their black hair that had been box braided like Sovereign Keir's. The princesses' braids had been wound up on their heads, though, and their tiaras rested upon them. Their purple irises were surrounded by a light gray.

"They must be twins," Mylah whispered to Elias who nodded in confirmation. They even wore similar dresses; light pink gowns that swept low across their breasts and clung to their curvy frames. The trains of their gowns were connected to the middle finger on each of their left hands.

"Thank you all for coming," Sovereign Keir said as they all sat. "Whenever you are ready, my council has assembled." They waved their hand to the left where a group of people had already been seated.

Elias stood and stepped up onto the dais. He recounted his excursion with Mylah and all that they'd discovered while in the mountains.

"Queen Aveda is planning to invade not just Elowyn, but more likely all of Olliria. We are only the beginning." Elias finished his speech, and the sovereign clasped their hands before them, giving no indication whether they would choose to join in the fight or not.

"We will take this into consideration as we deliberate," the sovereign said. "In the meantime, we will be hosting a masquerade to keep you entertained while you stay with us." Mylah's jaw dropped at the cavalier mention of a ball when they were supposed to be worrying about a *war*. "Two days from now. If any of your party would like to head into town to find an outfit, feel free to put it on my account and it will be a gift from me to you."

"Thank you but that is unnecessary," Elias said but the sovereign scoffed.

"Nonsense. What kind of host would I be if I didn't outfit my guests in the best finery and throw them a ball worthy of Hosath himself?" Sovereign Keir stood from their throne, their daughters rising beside them. "You can expect an answer from me the morning after the masquerade." With that, they turned and left the room with their daughters and the council on their heels.

Back in the sitting room of Mylah and Elias' room, their own group gathered to deliberate whether the meeting had gone well.

"I mean, they wouldn't have thrown us a party if they were going to say no, right?" Ana said.

"Unless they're trying to soften the blow," Davina pointed out.

"I don't think they'd do that," Korriane said, plopping onto the couch beside Ana. "Sovereign Keir may rule with a firm hand, but they aren't stupid. If they don't help us now, Queen Aveda will come for them next."

Mylah sat in one of the armchairs that flanked the couches. She had her hands pressed together against her lips as she considered all the possible outcomes of this. What would happen if Sovereign Keir refused to help them? What would be the next step if they agreed to help? Who else might assist them against the might of Queen Aveda's army? Sovereign Keir hadn't even mentioned that Mylah was clearly not human. Maybe they didn't remember that she was supposed to be.

A hand landed on her shoulder, distracting her from her thoughts. Turning her face up, her gaze found Elias standing beside her. He sat on the arm of the chair and brushed her ponytail back over her shoulder.

"How are you doing?" he asked, quiet enough so the rest of the group didn't stop their own conversations.

Mylah dropped her hands into her lap and played with the ring on her finger, the ruby catching the light and casting sparks around the room.

"I don't know," Mylah admitted, keeping her gaze on her mother's ring.

"Do you want to take a walk?" Elias suggested.

Mylah sighed, placing her head in her hand. "No, I think I need a minute alone," she said, standing from the chair and heading for the bedroom. She closed the double doors behind her and held her breath for a moment as silence enveloped her. A few muffled voices penetrated the walls, but otherwise, all noise had stopped. Mylah stepped away from the doors, letting out a long breath and stared down at her hands as she'd done on the journey from Hyrdian.

"Magic would be useful," she said aloud, wondering if it would trigger something. "We are going to be fighting against fae and other beings led by Queen Aveda. What use am I if I don't have some kind of magic or skill?" *What use am I?* Maybe she had no use, she realized. Maybe that was why fate had tried to kill her time and again, to get her out of the way.

Dropping to her knees, Mylah cursed herself. "Why didn't I die with my parents if you wanted me gone? Why make me suffer through the years without them?" she pleaded with fate. "There has to be a reason. No one survives the banshee's warning... No one defies fate as I have."

Mylah began rocking on her knees, her head in her hands as tears streamed down her cheeks. She thought she felt a breeze in the room, but she ignored it, her anger and sorrow completely overtaking her. At some point, a scream erupted from within her, and she fell forward, her hands slamming into the floor as energy and heat clashed within her and around her. She thought she felt someone gripping her, but she'd lost all sense of being, caught in a strange vortex of swirling mist and fury.

Calm your mind, Ailsa broke through the haze somehow and Mylah reached out for her.

"Please, help me?" she pleaded with the witch.

No one can help you but yourself.

"I can't do this. Please, *help me*." But she could sense Ailsa's presence had left her again.

Someone was yelling nearby, "Ana, get in here!" The words registered in Mylah, and she realized she was no longer alone in her room. *Her room...* She reeled herself in, trying to feel the floor beneath her again, and regain her sense of self.

The torrent around Mylah calmed and she could feel strong arms wrapped around her, cradling her into a solid chest and body. *Elias,* she thought, knowing that body well.

Opening her eyes, Mylah came face to face with Elias who held her against him as he knelt on the floor.

"You're okay," he said, letting out a breath of relief as her eyes locked onto his. He loosened his grip on her but didn't release her, and she didn't wish him to.

Ana stood before Mylah, her eyes darkening with fear, before she blinked, and they returned to normal. She'd used her gift to calm Mylah down.

Castien came into view, placing a blanket over Mylah since her clothes had been burnt to a crisp. Mylah blushed as Castien helped her to her feet and he practically shoved her aside as soon as she was standing so he could kneel in front of his brother. They sat, knee to knee, as Castien took hold of Elias' wrists, raising his arms to look at them.

Mylah gasped at the burns that marred Elias' arms and hands. Even his shirt and pants had been singed.

"I'm fine," Elias said, pulling his arms back to his sides.

"I'll send for a healer," Castien said, rising from the floor. Elias didn't argue as he left the room, Ana trailing after him.

"Did I...did I do that?" Mylah asked as Elias stood.

"Don't worry about it," he waved her off, and Mylah burst into tears.

"I'm so sorry," she gasped between sobs. Elias' arms came around her and she tried to break free. "Don't touch me! I'll only hurt you again..." But Elias didn't release her.

"Mylah, look at me," he said, using his finger under her chin to lift her gaze to his. "I'm fine. The burns aren't that bad, and a healer should be able to fix me good as new, if my magic doesn't heal them on its own before they get here."

"I never wanted to hurt you again," Mylah said.

"At least we know the answer to your question now." Amusement lit Elias' eyes. "You definitely have some magic." He smiled and Mylah swatted at his arm.

"This isn't funny!" she cried out. "I could have killed you..." The words terrified her.

"Probably," Elias said. "But you didn't." He released her from his embrace and took a step away from her.

"Aren't you afraid of me now?" Mylah couldn't help asking, even though the answer had the power to break her.

"No. Are you afraid?" He brushed his knuckles over her cheek, sweeping away the last of her tears.

"Yes, I'm terrified..." she said, the words coming out quiet and small.

"And that's why I'm not." He sat on the bed and Mylah sat beside him, clasping her hands in her lap. "Remember when I was training with Farren, and you trusted that I wouldn't hurt you?"

"Yes," Mylah murmured. "But that was different."

"No, it wasn't. This is just like that. I trust you not to hurt me."

"But I *did* hurt you," Mylah pointed out, lightly brushing her finger over his burns.

"That's nothing."

Before Mylah could respond, Castien came into the room with the healer. The healer carried a bag of clinking bottles with him that he placed on the floor. He pulled a chair from the vanity over to the bed to sit on and Elias held his arms out towards him.

As the healer considered the burns, Mylah held her breath. As soon as he reached into his bag for something, she released her breath, glad he didn't say the injury was too severe to heal.

A vial of salve was applied to Elias' burns, and they immediately began to look less red and angry. The healer left another vial with Elias to apply the following morning and said the burns should be gone within the next few days.

Mylah couldn't show her face that night, no matter how many reassurances Elias gave her that no one would judge her or be afraid of her. While everyone else ate dinner in the sitting room right outside the door, because they all refused to leave her alone, she sat on the window seat in the bedroom staring up at the moon. Elias had left the doors to their bedroom cracked so she could hear the conversations taking place between the others, but she ignored them. When the door creaked open, followed by soft footsteps, Mylah turned to see Ana coming to sit with her on the window seat.

"You're being dramatic," Ana said, laughing as she sat beside Mylah, pulling her legs up and wrapping her arms around her knees.

"Thanks for your support," Mylah responded, snorting. But she couldn't help smiling.

"I'm not saying you don't have the right to be dramatic, but I thought I'd point it out. I've had my fair share of drama this month." Ana shrugged, smirking.

"How are you doing?" Mylah asked, realizing she had never asked after they'd returned from Adair. She'd been too distracted by her own grief.

"Better," Ana said, tucking her hair behind her pointed ear. "Korriane has been helping me." A light blush dusted Ana's cheeks.

"She's great," Mylah said.

"Yeah, she is. We've actually been hanging out a lot and I like her, but I don't want to make anything weird between *us* if it doesn't work out." She waved her hand between herself and Mylah.

"Don't ever worry about me! I will always be here for you, whether you and Korriane stay together forever, or call it quits after a week. You will always be welcome in our group." Mylah took Ana's hands. "I'm sorry I've been a bad friend. I should have been the one to check up on you when we got back from Adair. I was so wrapped up with my own problems I forgot about everyone else."

"I know." Ana patted Mylah's hand. "Losing a parental figure, like Garrick, is hard. Especially after you've already lost so much."

"I miss him, but I don't like to talk about it in front of the others. In front of Crane. I feel like I don't have a right to miss him." Mylah dropped her head to her chest.

"You know that Crane doesn't think that, right?" Ana asked, placing her hand on Mylah's arm.

"I know. But Garrick was his father, not mine." Tears brimmed Mylah's eyes.

"You'll get over that, some day. I think," Ana smirked, and they both laughed. "I wish I could say I know how you feel, but I don't."

"That's okay, I appreciate the effort."

"Mind if I cut in?" Castien stood in the doorway leaning against the doorframe. Ana stood, winking to Mylah before she left. Castien shut the doors behind Ana and made his way to the window seat, leaning against the wall instead of joining Mylah as Ana had done.

"Are you here to warn me to stay away from your brother?" Mylah said, only half joking.

"Even if I thought that would work, I wouldn't." He rubbed his hands together, playing with the rings that adorned his fingers. He'd put on his best airs for Sovereign Keir.

"Why not?" Mylah asked, nearly pleading with Castien. If she'd gravely injured Elias... She didn't know what she'd do. But she also wasn't sure if she'd stay away from him even if Castien ordered her to.

"Because I've been where you are, and it hurts to see you going through this too."

Mylah furrowed her brows and bit the inside of her cheek.

"You've asked me about my magic before, and I know I'm always cagey and aloof about it. About my past." Castien paused and Mylah nodded for him to go on. "My magic wasn't like Elias'. It was untamable."

"Was?" Mylah murmured.

"Was," Castien repeated. "Elias isn't the only one who accidentally killed someone with their magic. But when it happened to Elias, I knew that we couldn't have two unstable magic users in the castle. I would never make Elias give up his magic, of course, so I made the decision to give up my own."

"How...? Why would you do that?" Mylah scooted closer to him, but he remained fixed against the wall.

"To be king. To ensure everyone would be safe." Castien lifted his chin, his jaw set, and his eyes flickered with certainty. "There is something else, though," Castien's gaze fell to the ring on Mylah's hand.

"What?" she asked, her gaze flicking the ring as well.

"You can't *get rid of* magic. It has to go somewhere," Castien said, and Mylah had an inkling she knew where this was headed. "When I became king, I chose to put my magic into that ring." He pointed to the ring and Mylah lifted her hand to inspect it as if it might have changed in the time since she'd been wearing it.

"Why would you give it to me if it had your magic in it?" Mylah asked, removing the ring from her finger, and holding it out to him. "I shouldn't keep this. What if I lose it?"

Castien stepped towards her, and his hand curled around hers, closing over the ring.

"There was a protection spell placed on the ring to keep my magic safe, but also to ensure whoever wore the ring was also protected," Castien explained. "I gave it to you the night before you went to Adair..."

"Why?" Mylah couldn't help but ask.

"Because if I haven't made it abundantly clear, I care about you. Maybe not in the way my brother does, or the way Crane does, but in my own, warped sense of love kind of way." Castien struggled to get out the last few words as he ran his hands through his hair. "Sascha was my everything, and I could never love someone as I loved her, so it wouldn't be fair to ask someone to love me the same. Which is why I never pursued you, or anyone else for that matter."

"Castien…" Mylah said, his name coming out as a whisper as she tried to grasp everything he was saying to her.

He turned away from her and began pacing beside the bed.

"That's not even what I wanted to tell you. The real reason I'm here is because somehow, when you were transformed into a shreeve," he paused, and stopped pacing to look at Mylah again. "My magic was released from the ring and given to you."

Mylah's heart seemed to stop beating for a moment as time slowed.

"How do you know?" she asked once she'd gathered her wits again.

"I recognized it when you were losing control earlier. All magic feels slightly different, it has a signature almost. And your magic, felt exactly like mine, and the way it was manifesting was as it had when I lost control." He finally sat beside her on the window seat. "You'll need to learn to control it as Elias has, or else…"

Mylah gulped. "I heard about the men you killed when Sascha was executed…" she said and Castien hung his head.

"They were King Haldor's guards," Castien confirmed.

"And nothing was ever done for their families to acknowledge the deaths," Mylah pointed out and Castien winced.

"That was my father's doing. He swept it under the rug and sent me away to join the border patrols so I wouldn't be a problem for him. Of course, that didn't help my control over my magic at all. Did Torin ever tell you how he received his burns?" Castien closed his eyes as he waited for Mylah's response.

"No," she said quietly, knowing what would come next. Her stomach twisted in knots thinking about all Castien had held in and given up for his people.

"Back then he was just another guard on border patrol. He caught me and some other men tormenting pixies and tried to stop us. I lost control of my magic, as you did, and lit the forest on fire. Thankfully there were some shreeve nearby who had the power to douse the flames, but not before Torin suffered his burns. He refused to return to the castle to have them treated, saying he needed to keep an eye on me." Castien sighed and leaned forward with his elbows on his knees.

"That's –" Mylah started.

"Horrible?" Castien finished for her. "Yeah. I was a horrible person for a while. I can't even blame Sascha's death for that. It wasn't the first time I'd hurt someone else for my own entertainment."

"My parents..." Mylah said and Castien shook his head.

"I didn't enjoy their deaths if that's what you're wondering. Torin pulled me back from a horrible place, though he may not take credit for that." Castien smiled as he thought of Torin.

"I do," Torin grunted from the doorway. Mylah and Castien had been so enrapt in their conversation they hadn't noticed him come in. "Stop sulking and come join the party," he said, jerking his head towards the doors before leaving again.

"You heard him," Castien said, his voice much lighter than it had been moments before. "Come on." He held his hand out to Mylah and she took it, letting him pull her to her feet.

"I have one more question," Mylah paused, glancing at her ring once more. "If there's a protection charm on the ring that's supposed to protect me, how was I poisoned?"

"It only protects you from lethal physical wounds," Castien said with a sigh. "Unfortunately, protection charms aren't a catch all and there's a lot of gray area for what they actually protect against. But, if you'd been harmed physically in a way that would have resulted in death or being gravely injured, the ring would either heal you or repel whatever was about to cause the damage."

"Oh." Mylah held the ring out in front of her. "Is the protection charm gone now that your magic has left the ring?"

"There's no way to know without having a witch test it." Castien held his hand out to her once more. "Come on, lets worry about that later." He led her into the sitting room.

Korriane and Killian sat on one couch, and Ana sat on the floor leaning against Korriane. Torin had joined Crane and Davina on the couch opposite the twins. Elias stood leaning against the table that was filled with plates of food. Mylah waited for his eyes to meet hers and she smiled, releasing Castien's hand as she crossed the room to tuck herself into Elias' side, his arm coming around her shoulders. Castien took a seat in one of the armchairs.

"So, what now?" Elias asked the room.

Davina stretched herself out like a cat, laying her head in Torin's lap and crossing her legs over Crane's. Mylah was surprised at the casualness between them all but said nothing. She did note that Torin's features pinched slightly in discomfort, but he didn't move.

"What now?" Davina repeated. "We head into town in the morning and spend some of the sovereign's gold. That's what."

"That sounds fun!" Korriane said as she began to play with Ana's hair.

"It's not fun, Kor, it's politics. They're buying our loyalty," Killian said, but Castien spoke over him.

"We need a little fun in our lives, before we return to Elowyn and fight our war."

"Who wants to be my date for the ball?" Davina asked, waving her hand above her in the air. Castien scoffed and Mylah laughed. "Oh, come on. I won't bite." Davina tilted her head back to look up at Torin. "Unless you ask nicely."

"Real nice, Davina," Ana sputtered as she giggled.

"Crane will be my date, won't you?" Davina fiddled with his shirt sleeve, and he rolled his eyes.

"If no one else will have you, I suppose I could be your escort," Crane said.

Again, Mylah was surprised by their familiarity, but she'd been gone for a month and had no idea what they'd been doing in that time.

"Aww, what a gentleman," Davina said, patting Crane's leg. "Since Ana is Korriane's date, and Mylah is obviously going with Elias, Torin and Killian can join my entourage." Davina winked at Torin. "The more the merrier."

"Pass," Killian said, but Torin remained quiet. Mylah noticed Ana blushing and wondered how Davina had known about her and Korriane, since Ana had only mentioned it to Mylah a few minutes ago.

"Now that that's sorted, who wants to play a game of Jacks?" Castien pulled a deck of cards out of his pocket and placed it on the coffee table between the couches.

For the rest of the night, they took turns losing to Castien in Jacks, which, as it turned out, Mylah was horrible at. She'd played cards a few times with Greyson and Cassia, but never Jacks, and it took her more time to learn the game than it did to play a round of it. Davina kept trying to cheat and slip cards under the table to Korriane, who had no idea what was going on most of the time.

Mylah found herself laughing and smiling more that night than she had in a long time. Her cheeks hurt by the time everyone decided to call it a night. Everyone filed out of the room, muttering curses directed towards Castien who had won every round but one, which Davina had won before they realized she'd been cheating.

Mylah and Elias remained curled up on the couch, Mylah too tired to move as she held onto him tightly. He kissed the top of her head and she shut her eyes, drifting off as he carried her to bed.

Twenty Seven

Two days before the gala, Captain Andreas hung the assignments on the bulletin board in the bunkroom. The guards crowded around it like children crowding around a shiny new toy. Greyson hung back, waiting for a path to clear.

Once everyone dispersed, Greyson approached the board and found his name on the list, *Greyson Callister: Ballroom duty*. Out of curiosity he continued scanning for Julian's name and found it, surprised that there was no last name for him. *Queen Aveda's entourage,* it said beside his name. Greyson hadn't even realized that had been a possibility. In fact, he didn't see that assignment beside anyone else's names.

"At least we'll both be in the ballroom," Julian said, stepping up beside Greyson.

"Why don't you have a last name?"

"I don't know," Julian said, squinting at the list to read it. "Weird."

"And why are you the only one in the queen's entourage?"

"Queen Aveda requested a single guard from King Florian's command, and he chose me."

Greyson shook his head and turned away from the board. Kolt and Acton were walking by, but neither of them even glanced at him.

"Want to follow them?" Julian asked, mischief sparking in his eyes.

Greyson hesitated, but he couldn't help the extreme curiosity burning in him to know more about Kolt and Acton's involvement with the Hosath worshippers.

"Let's go," Greyson said.

Julian grinned, leading the way out of the bunkroom. They stayed far enough back from Kolt and Acton, so they didn't seem suspicious, but if they turned, there was nowhere to hide.

Kolt and Acton made their way to the front of the castle where two horses waited for them.

"I guess this is where we lose them," Greyson huffed.

"No way! We know where they're headed. We'll give them a head start, and then follow."

They hung back in the shadows until Kolt and Acton had left through the gates and were well on their way to the village.

"We have to get permission from the king before we can leave the castle," Greyson groaned as he remembered the inconvenient fact.

Julian laughed. "Wait here a moment." He left the shadow they'd been hiding in and approached the footman near the carriages that were always ready to depart at a moment's notice. He chatted with him for a minute and handed something to him before waving Greyson over.

"This fine gentleman has agreed to give us a ride into town. What better way to travel than in style?" Julian waved his hand to the carriage with a flourish.

"What better way to be noticed!" Greyson said, exasperated. "We can't take this thing!"

"Don't worry so much. No one is even around to see." Julian made a show of turning in each direction and scanning to prove that no one was around.

"Your carriage, sir," the footman said, bowing to Julian before opening the door and waving him inside.

Julian gave Greyson a wink and climbed in. Greyson groaned but followed Julian into the carriage.

"This is madness," he grumbled as he sat on the opposite side of Julian, their knees brushing and causing heat to creep up the back of Greyson's neck.

The door shut and the carriage began rolling. There was no turning back.

As Greyson and Julian rolled along in the carriage, Greyson couldn't help thinking about all the times he'd ridden in his family's carriage. It had only been about two months since he'd last done so, but it seemed like a lifetime ago.

"Don't look so glum, we're going on an adventure," Julian said, breaking Greyson's reverie.

"Right. An adventure that *when* we get caught, because there's no way we aren't getting caught stealing the king's carriage, I'll be dismissed from the royal guard and have a black mark on my name telling no one to ever trust me again."

"Always the cynic," Julian chided. "We'll be fine. Trust me."

Greyson couldn't help but feel his spirits lift as Julian smiled at him. They kept the curtains of the carriage shut, so they had nothing to look at but each other, and Greyson tried his hardest to look anywhere *but* at Julian. When he did, a strange sense of longing came over him and he wasn't sure what to make of that. So, he avoided it, as he'd done with his feelings for Mylah for years.

The carriage came to a stop and the door opened. Greyson and Julian slipped out, Julian giving a two-finger salute to the footman, before they hurried down an alley.

"The Hall of Hosath is this way," Greyson said, leading towards the rundown building.

As they approached it, Greyson realized it wasn't as rundown as it had been only a few months prior. The windows that had been boarded up before had been replaced, and the door had a fresh coat of paint. The rest of the tall, stone building looked the same, though. The ivy still crept up the sides, covering the two statues of Hosath and his love, Myda, that were carved on each side of the front door. The spires that rose into the fog settling over the village that day, still had chunks of stone missing from them. The old musty smell of mildew remained as strong as ever.

"This place is...something," Julian commented as they approached it.

"We should probably go around back, in case Kolt and Acton come out," Greyson said, and Julian nodded.

They headed around the side of the building, keeping low so they wouldn't be seen through the windows. Once they'd reached the back of the building, Greyson peered into one of the windows.

Disgraced

"There's a lot of people inside," Greyson whispered.

Gazing through the window, he saw one large room filled with rows of benches all facing the back of the building where one robed person stood on a pedestal speaking to the room. Kolt and Acton stood on either side of them.

"That must be their leader," Julian said as he peered into the room.

"But why are Kolt and Acton here?" Greyson wished they could hear what was being said, but he could only make out a muffled murmur through the thick glass window.

"I can almost make out what they're saying," Julian said. "Something about Hyrdian, and a..." he paused, straining as he leaned closer to the window. "Voyage? No... Pilgrimage."

"They make one every five years to Hyrdian and the temple there for the day of sacrifice. It must be coming up," Greyson explained. "But what do Kolt and Acton have to do with that?" Greyson couldn't puzzle out why they were there and why the king had brought them into the council chambers.

Julian listened again, his eyes narrowing as if he were trying to read the speaker's lips, and his jaw clenched as he focused.

"Kolt and Acton are going on the pilgrimage. They are bringing something into Hyrdian," Julian said.

Greyson's heart stuttered. *That's where Mylah is*, he couldn't help thinking. "What is it?" he whispered.

"They didn't say. Or I didn't hear." Julian leaned back and sighed. "But let's assume it's something bad."

"Why Hyrdian, though?" Greyson pulled at the sleeves of his jacket, trying not to think that the king would go so far just to get to Mylah. "They're not a part of this war. One of their representatives is coming to the castle tomorrow. Why would the king want to jeopardize losing their support by doing whatever he's planning?"

"I don't know. But they wouldn't be *sneaking* into Hyrdian if they had *good* intentions," Julian pointed out. "And no one will stop the pilgrimage even if we warn them because then they'd have a whole other fight on their hands."

"And we can't warn them," Greyson said. "I'm bound to the king. I can't betray him in any way."

Julian tilted his head to the side and pursed his lips. "Bound, you say? By magic?"

"Yes." Greyson's head dropped to his chest, ashamed that he'd made such a commitment to a man he was quickly realizing didn't deserve his loyalty.

"Interesting. Was it a witch who did the ceremony, or a fae?" Julian asked.

"Why does it matter?" Greyson groaned.

"I guess it doesn't. As you said, you are bound, and nothing can be done about that." Julian shrugged.

"We should go before Kolt and Acton leave." Greyson changed the subject. "Come on."

They made their way back around the building and veered off towards the next street so that if Kolt and Acton came out, they wouldn't see them walking away from the Hall of Hosath.

"How are we getting back to the castle?" Greyson asked, realizing Julian had only said the carriage would be bringing them into the village, not that it would be returning them home.

"It's a perfect day for a walk," Julian said, smirking.

"It's cold and foggy. Not exactly walking weather." Greyson frowned at the thought of walking all the way back to the castle.

"You know, in some places they pray for weather this nice during the winter months." Julian lifted his face to the sky as if basking in the nonexistent sunshine.

"So, walking it is." Greyson trudged onward as they came to the end of the street and began the trek back towards the castle. "Kolt and Acton will pass us on their way back."

"And so what if they do? Are we not allowed to spend our day off strolling through the village?" Julian swung his arms merrily as he walked.

"It's not our day off," Greyson reminded him.

"You're too hard to please," Julian said playfully.

"I feel like you don't take any of this seriously," Greyson said, stopping in his tracks, and turning towards Julian with his fists clenched at his sides. "I don't know how you grew up, or what you've had to deal with, but this is all I know." Julian turned to Greyson, concern wrinkling his forehead for once. "My parents were on the king's council, and then I was, and now I'm a part of the royal guard. There is nothing else I know how to do. There is nowhere else I can go if this falls through."

"You're right. I get it..."

"You don't though. You make a joke of everything, and you think it will all turn out okay. Which leads me to believe that it always has for you. Nothing's ever gone so horribly wrong that you worry about things like stepping out of line or speaking your mind."

"I'm sorry. But you're right. A great deal of my life was like that. I always got everything I wanted and could do anything I wanted. Until I couldn't anymore, and I still haven't changed, though maybe I should." Julian's eyes darkened and guilt dropped into Greyson's gut.

"No..." Greyson said. "You shouldn't change." He turned towards the sun that was trying so hard to break through the fog. "Forget I said anything. I don't know what came over me."

"At the very least, I should be more considerate of other's feelings. I think we can agree on that," Julian said, trying to lighten the mood. "I'll keep an eye out for Kolt and Acton and if I see them coming, we can hide from them."

Greyson couldn't help but laugh at the absurdity of that sentence. He felt like a child, trying to sneak back into the house after a meet up with Mylah and Cassia.

"That seems like a good plan," Greyson composed himself long enough to say.

"You don't laugh very often," Julian pointed out and Greyson stopped. "I like to hear you laugh." Julian's nose crinkled with his smile and then he was turning back to the road and strolling away, leaving Greyson with butterflies again.

Halfway back to the castle, Kolt and Acton came into view. Julian pulled Greyson to the side behind the trees and pressed him up against one of them. Greyson's entire body felt as if it had gone up in flames as Julian's chest pressed against his own and the fresh, woodsy scent of him crashed into Greyson's senses. Julian seemed unfazed and had his head leaning to the side so he could watch as Kolt and Acton passed by. Greyson tried to keep his breathing steady and shut his eyes as he leaned his head back against the tree.

When Julian moved back and Greyson felt the absence of his body, he opened his eyes. Julian smirked at him in a knowing way.

Disgraced

"You okay there?" he asked, and Greyson nodded, worried that if he tried to speak it would give away how *not* okay he was. "Well, they're gone, so we can keep moving."

Greyson held up a finger and took a deep breath before stepping towards Julian, who only raised his eyebrows slightly.

"There's something I need to do, before we go back into the castle and the royals arrive and everything is crazy," Greyson said before he could change his mind.

Julian tapped his chin before saying, "I think I like where this is going, but just in case; please tell me you want me to kiss you."

"Something like that." Greyson laughed and closed the space between them.

Julian's arm hooked around Greyson's back, pulling him in tight against his chest as their lips met and Greyson's hands went to Julian's hair, which he hadn't realized how badly he'd wanted to touch.

As soon as they'd come together, the wheels of a carriage crunching down the road broke them apart. It was the carriage they'd taken into the village returning to the castle.

Greyson gave Julian an accusatory look. "You said we had to walk back," he exclaimed, and Julian lifted a shoulder casually.

"I never said we *had* to walk. But I had a feeling we wouldn't have had time to get to this part if we were in the carriage."

"Well, that would have been a tragedy," Greyson joked.

Julian placed the back of his hand against his forehead in mock horror making them both laugh.

"Indeed. Come on," Julian said, flagging down the footman who stopped the carriage and let them inside.

The next day, a whole fleet of carriages arrived. Greyson was among the guards stationed at the front gate, so he had a front row seat to all the incoming rulers. First came King Aeron of Umbra and his entourage. Greyson noted that he appeared quite a bit younger than King Florian, though his hair was graying. Greyson wondered if that was a hereditary thing, or from the stress of ruling. Standing a whole head shorter than Greyson, King Aeron had a petite physique that contrasted his strong jaw and harsh disposition. He had no queen yet, but Greyson was sure it wouldn't be long before he settled down and began producing heirs.

Queen Calvina of Cambri arrived next, her entourage considerably larger. With her came her husband, who bore no title – Draco. He was a formidable type; big, burly, long beard, and hair, and a permanent grimace. Greyson had the sense to avoid eye contact with him as Queen Calvina descended from her carriage. Her brilliant green eyes and red hair contrasted her husband's black eyes and hair, just as the rest of her was in direct opposition to him. Long, beautiful legs could be seen through her sheer skirt which revealed more than Greyson had seen of any woman. Though in size and presence it seemed as if Draco would garner all the attention, Queen Calvina had an air of superiority about her that kept Greyson enrapt. The way she held herself and the way she moved reminded him of Queen Aveda, but more deliberate.

"What a sight for sore eyes, huh?" the guard beside Greyson murmured.

Disgraced

Greyson didn't respond but continued to watch as another carriage arrived carrying Hyrdian's representative. Greyson had been most interested in seeing this person, since they would be a witch or warlock, and he'd never met anyone from Hyrdian before.

A tall, lanky, poised man exited the carriage. He wore an impeccable black suit of the finest material, as far as Greyson could tell. He didn't know much about clothing, but from what he could see, this man had spent a fortune on his appearance. His dark red eyes threw Greyson off for a moment. He'd never seen anything like them, but otherwise, there was nothing too out of the ordinary about the man.

"Welcome, Councilor Aspertine," King Florian said, stepping forward to greet the man. Greyson blinked in surprise; he hadn't noticed the king come out of the castle.

"Please, call me Eryx," the man bowed slightly, but not as deep as one should for a king.

Greyson noted the irritation on King Florian's face. The king said nothing though and led Eryx inside. The rest of the carriages which had brought guards and guests of each of the royals and the councilor, emptied out and were dealt with, all while Greyson and the other guards stood by and watched.

After the grand arrivals, Greyson had the night off, but he had to pick up his clothes for the gala. Since they weren't guests of the gala, they would be given whatever had already been made closest to their actual size and have to deal with whether it was too big or too small. Thankfully, Greyson was of average size and build, so they had an outfit that fit him almost perfectly. Some of the others were not so lucky.

As he walked back to the bunk room after picking up his clothes, he overheard loud whispers in the hallway around the corner from him. He paused, holding his breath as he snuck closer to the whispers.

"Do you actually think that Queen Aveda is going to play nice once they take Elowyn and leave the rest of our kingdoms alone?" a woman spoke.

"We have no reason to suspect that she will turn on us," a man answered. "You've always been a skeptic, Cal." He chuckled.

Greyson assumed the woman must be Queen Calvina, but he couldn't figure out who the man might be. Perhaps King Aeron.

"And it's kept me alive on more than one occasion," Queen Calvina hissed. "Don't be so naïve to think that Queen Aveda would come all this way to simply take one kingdom and be done. She is ambitious and conniving, like all fae."

Greyson began to back away, realizing that if he were caught listening to them, he could be charged with treason.

"At least hear them out. We can always let them deal with Elowyn first, and then reassess afterwards."

Greyson turned and hurried away before he could be discovered. To think that even some of the royals weren't trusting of Queen Aveda had him even more wary of her intentions. There was nothing he could do about it though, without breaking his vow to the king.

Returning to the bunk room, Greyson scanned the room, hoping to find Julian. He wanted to tell him about what he'd overheard, and he'd hardly seen Julian since they'd returned from the village the day before. They hadn't had a chance to talk about what happened, or to repeat the action, which Greyson resented. But that night at dinner, Julian plopped beside Greyson as he finished eating. Julian let out a long sigh before placing a beaming grin on his face. Greyson could tell it was a mask but didn't want to say anything in front of the other guards.

"Have you eaten?" Greyson asked instead.

"Yes," Julian said even as he swiped Greyson's apple from his plate, taking a large bite. Apple juice dripped down Julian's chin and without thinking, Greyson reached out and wiped it away with his thumb. The stares from the guards around him burned into him as he lowered his hand to his lap and wiped it on his napkin.

Julian swallowed his bite of apple and cleared his throat as he ran his hand over his face. Conversation continued around them, and Greyson couldn't help but smile as he watched the torrent of emotions playing across Julian's face.

Julian steepled his hands in front of his mouth before lowering them. "I should go," he said, and Greyson's face fell.

"I'm sorry, did I do something...?" he trailed off, not wanting to say more in case his public display had been what tripped Julian up.

"No. No. You did nothing. I have something I need to do." Julian's smile was still clearly forced and did nothing to assuage Greyson's fear that he'd already screwed up whatever they had between them. Julian rose from the table and left before Greyson could say anything else.

Twenty Eight

Korriane woke Mylah and Elias the next morning by banging on their bedroom door. Sabine and Broderick had been permanently assigned to their main door and had apparently not seen an issue in letting her in before Elias or Mylah had risen.

"Wakey wakey!" she called through the door. "Everyone is ready to head into town."

Elias rolled over, removing his arm from Mylah's waist, and groaned. "Give us a minute," he yelled back.

Mylah turned onto her side, gazing at Elias as she propped her head up on her hand. "Do you think if we ignore her, she'll go away?" she asked, smirking.

Elias pulled her close, kissing her once before the banging on the door started up again.

"I'm not going away!" Korriane said, and Mylah could hear the laughter in her voice.

It was Mylah's turn to groan as she pushed against Elias' chest, rolling away from him.

Disgraced

Elias finished dressing first and headed into the sitting room to appease the waiting group, who had all gathered there in the short time since Korriane woke them. Mylah followed shortly after, happy to see all her friends even if they had interrupted her sleep.

Mylah flopped down onto the couch beside Torin.

"Hi," she said, not sure exactly how to act around him now. He'd been her rock for a few weeks before leaving for Hyrdian, yet it seemed like everything had changed since then.

"Hi," he said, nudging her with his shoulder. "Glad you made it back in one piece."

Mylah laughed, happy that things hadn't totally changed between them. "Glad to see you found someone new to warm your bed," she joked, and his brows pinched in confusion. "Davina?" Mylah spoke quietly enough so the rest of the group, who chatted animatedly about the plan for the day, wouldn't overhear.

"Oh, no. We're not... She's not... I don't know..." he hesitated.

Mylah realized he was conflicted about how to answer and put her hand on his arm. "You don't need to explain," she said.

Torin nodded his head and relaxed back into the couch.

"Everyone ready to head out?" Korriane asked, her voice rising above all the others.

For their ride into town, they each had their own horse. It was strange for Mylah not to ride with Elias as she had for the past month. She was sure if she had asked to ride with him, no one would have objected, but riding alone brought with it the appeal of freedom, along with it being more comfortable.

The first town they came to was visible from the castle. Beyond it was a forest that hid the next town. They stopped at a stable where they paid to leave their horses for the day while they wandered through town.

The men and women went their separate ways, since Davina insisted on the dresses being a surprise. They agreed to meet up at the only tavern in town after. It had been recommended to them by some of the guards back at the castle.

"This is it," Korriane said as they stopped outside of a dress shop. Three dresses hung in the window, drawing the eyes of every passerby. Each dress had such fine detailing Mylah assumed it must have taken years for them to be created. She stared at the dresses with her jaw dropped.

Davina snickered and pulled on Mylah's arm. "Come on, let's try them on."

"These seem a little flashier than what I like to wear," Ana said as they entered the shop. Inside, dresses lined the walls, leaving a wide-open space in the center of the room where a round platform had been placed with mirrors and couches surrounding it.

"Welcome, welcome!" A woman chirped from behind a desk. Mylah glanced at her, taking in her curvy form that had been nicely packed into a tight, but flattering, dress, and her perfectly coiffed hair. She hustled out from behind the desk and grinned at them. "You must be the sovereign's guests. They told me you'd be coming today! My name is Hilda."

"We'd like to try on the dresses in the window," Davina said, pointing towards where the dresses hung.

Disgraced

Hilda's smile faltered, "Of course," she said, smoothing her hand over her dress though it had no wrinkles. Mylah gave her an apologetic look. There were hundreds of dresses hanging and ready for trying on in the store, and Davina had to choose the ones painstakingly displayed on the mannequins as their first picks.

"Perfect." Davina grinned.

Hilda headed for the window, heaving a long sigh. Mylah almost offered to help her, but Davina took her hand and pulled her down to sit on the couch with her to wait.

"We're going to look at the dresses over here," Korriane said as she and Ana walked towards the wall on the right.

"So, I see you and Elias have finally made it official," Davina said, skipping the pleasantries of, *how are you? How's the magic treating you? Are you still being tormented by the fact that you almost died, yet again, and could still be targeted by fate?*

"Well, we haven't exactly talked about whether it's official or not," Mylah said, rubbing her arms. Though it seemed like everyone else had accepted Davina wholeheartedly into their group, Mylah hadn't had a chance to decide whether she'd truly forgiven her yet. Sitting in the dress shop and talking as if they were friends made her world feel as if it had been flipped upside down yet again.

Hilda returned with one of the dresses from the window, saving Mylah from more conversation with Davina. It was lavender colored with white flowers stitched all over the bell skirt of the gown. The bodice was cinched and covered in what appeared to be actual white flowers that had been preserved in some way.

Magic, Mylah thought, and her body thrummed in response.

"That one looks more your style," Davina said, waving a hand to Mylah.

"The changing room is right over there," Hilda told Mylah, pointing to the back of the shop.

"Thank you." Mylah headed for the dressing room but realized once she was in there that she'd never be able to get into the dress alone. She poked her head out around the curtain and called to Ana.

"Yes?" Ana walked towards her.

"Can you help me?" Mylah asked and Ana laughed before joining her in the dressing room. "This dress is ridiculous. I don't know why Davina insisted on us trying them on."

"Because it's Davina," Ana said. "And because it will look gorgeous on you."

Mylah undressed down to her underwear and waited as Ana held the dress out for her to step into. Mylah shimmied into it and Ana pulled it up, tightening the laces at the back. It was sleeveless, which Mylah liked, but it showed off the new markings on her arms. There was one snaking up each of her arms, from her wrists to her elbows. She caught Ana staring at them.

"I know... It's weird," Mylah said.

"It's not weird, just different," Ana said. "You'll get used to seeing them." Ana pulled off her overcoat and revealed her own arms. The only markings on her arms were on her shoulders. "Most of mine are on my back and legs. It's different for everyone. No one really knows why, though there is some correlation between the amount of magic people have and how many markings they have."

"That makes sense. Elias has way more markings than I do." As Mylah said it, she realized she wasn't sure if that was true. She hadn't had the time to take a good look at herself since transitioning and she definitely hadn't thought to compare her markings to Elias'.

"You two seem happy," Ana commented as she pulled her overcoat back on.

"So do you and Korriane," Mylah said, smirking.

"Yeah. I guess I was the only one who didn't realize everyone knew we had feelings for each other. Other than you, of course, but you had an excuse."

"Are you two coming out anytime soon?" Davina called to them.

Ana rolled her eyes, laughing, before she left the dressing room with Mylah on her heels. Davina stood in the center of the room on the platform in a gorgeous teal colored dress. It fit tight against her curves and belled out at the bottom like a mermaid tail. When she moved, the dress shimmered in the lights, making it seem like it had scales.

"It's perfect for you, Davina," Mylah said, awestruck.

"I know, but that one..." She scrunched her nose at Mylah's dress.

Mylah looked down at herself and knew what Davina meant. It was way too frilly for her.

"Hilda," Davina called out and Hilda reemerged from the front window holding the last dress. It was black, but like Davina's dress, the top half of it shimmered in the light. "Get out of that thing," Davina said, turning back to Mylah.

Mylah sighed before heading back into the dressing room with Ana who helped her out of the dress. Hilda passed them the new dress and Ana helped Mylah into it. This one fit a little tighter, and it had two panels made of shimmering tulle that extended up from her belly button, covering her breasts, stretching up over her shoulders and meeting at her waist in the back. The satiny skirt of the dress fell smoothly over her legs, pooling slightly on the floor. A slit ran up the length of her left leg, stopping only a few inches below her hip.

"This one is much better than the last one," Ana said, whistling. "Come on. Let's get Davina's stamp of approval."

When they exited the dressing room again, Korriane stood on the platform while Davina lounged on a chaise beside it, back in her normal clothes. Korriane wore a two-piece dress, the skirt similar to the one Mylah had taken off, but the top was basic, matching the skirt in its peach color, revealing her midriff. Ana lit up at the sight of her.

"You look amazing!" Mylah said and Korriane and Davina turned towards her.

"Speak for yourself!" Korriane said. "Damn, that dress was made for you."

"I knew it would be perfect," Davina said, smug. "Now it's Ana's turn."

"I already picked out a dress." Ana pointed to a gray dress that had been slung over the counter. "I don't need to try it on."

"Oh, boo," Davina said, pursing her lips. "You two change so we can go."

Disgraced

Twenty Nine

"You've been awfully quiet over there," Torin said, nudging Elias' boot with his own. "Something on your mind?"

Elias sighed. They'd been waiting on the viewing couch, in the *Finery for All* shop, for Castien to decide on an outfit for the last hour. The entire time Elias' mind had been occupied with worrying about Mylah. He knew logically that she was fine, and he needn't worry about her, but it was hard to be away from her.

"Hellooo, Elias?" Torin waved his hand in front of Elias' face.

"Sorry. I'm finding it hard to focus," Elias admitted.

"What, Castien's tenth dress coat he's tried on holds no appeal for you?" Torin smirked and placed his arm on the back of the couch. "Tell me what's on your mind."

Elias scanned the room, lined with racks of pants, coats, fine armor, and other things one might need for a formal event. The lights bobbing above them were too bright, and the room too echoey, so the noise was almost unbearable.

Torin gripped his shoulder, pulling him back again from his daze. "Elias, you're starting to scare me," he said with a half-smile. "Is it what happened with Mylah's magic?"

"Not exactly," Elias said. He leaned his head back before bringing it forward again and letting it fall into his hands. "That's part of it, but it's also this whole thing with becoming a shreeve. What if our people don't accept her? What if something else happens to her, and I can't save her? What if King Florian uses the Book of Creation and we're all —"

"Woah, slow down." Torin interrupted him. "Mylah is strong, and whatever gets thrown her way, she can handle it. She has all of us behind her to support her, and nothing is going to happen to her."

Elias groaned but said nothing.

"As for the rest; we can't control what happens with the Book of Creation, but we can do our best to make sure it never gets used. We *will* win this war, Elias. Forget about the what-ifs and believe in that." Torin squeezed his shoulder once more before removing his arm from the back of the couch. "Let's speed this up so we can get you back to your girl." He winked before standing and striding over to Castien who was rotating in front of a mirror.

"It's perfect," Torin said. "I've never seen you look better."

"I agree, Cas," Killian chimed in. "It fits you perfectly."

"Dear Hosath, please let this torment end," Crane murmured from the other side of Elias on the couch. "Also, I overheard your conversation," he said, turning to Elias. "And Torin's right about Mylah."

"Thanks," Elias muttered, not entirely convinced yet.

"But on another note," Crane's gaze flicked towards the others before he continued. "Hurt her, and King Florian will be the least of your worries."

Elias chuckled, his heart lifting. "I would never dream of it."

Castien wound up picking the first jacket he'd tried on that day, which caused them all to groan, but at least they were done with shopping.

"Time for a drink!" Torin cheered as they left the building they'd spent far too long inside. "I'm sure the ladies finished hours ago." No one argued that. Castien didn't always care about what he wore, but when it was something as important as impressing Sovereign Keir in hopes that they would choose to lend aide in the war, he made sure he was dressed to impress.

"I don't know why you're all complaining. You could be home right now, sitting on your asses doing nothing," Castien said.

"That sounds amazing," Crane joked, making them all laugh.

As they approached the street with the tavern where they were meeting the rest of their group, Elias spotted a jewelry store and had an idea.

"I'm going to stop off in here," he announced. "Don't wait for me. I'll catch up."

"You're not going alone, we'll wait," Castien said as he stopped and turned back to Elias.

"The tavern is right over there, I'll be fine," Elias argued. He didn't need them waiting on him and rushing his decision-making.

Castien curled his lip but jerked his head in a nod. "One of the guards will stay with you," he said, waving to one of the three guards from the castle who had been trailing them all day. The extra protection was a nice gesture, but unnecessary. Though, Elias wasn't entirely sure that the sovereign hadn't sent the guards to keep an eye on them, rather than protect them.

"Fine," Elias agreed and veered towards the jewelry store. He turned back and called to Castien once more, "Don't tell Mylah where I am, I want it to be a surprise."

Castien waved to him to let him know he'd heard, and they went their separate ways.

Thirty

Mylah and the others left their dresses at the shop to be delivered to the castle. Outside, the temperature had dropped quite a bit. The tavern was only about a ten-minute walk from the dress shop, and normally she would have been shivering, but with her change, the cold barely bothered her.

Davina entered the tavern ahead of them, choosing a table while Korriane and Ana got drinks. Mylah requested water and sat with Davina while they waited for the others. It was dimly lit in the tavern, but Mylah could see that everyone at the surrounding tables stared at them. They probably knew they were outsiders because in a small town, everyone knew everyone.

"I hope the guys get here soon," Mylah said, rubbing her hands together, more from nerves than trying to warm up.

"Castien will hold them up. He's probably taking forever picking the right ear cuff to wear to impress the ladies," Davina scoffed.

"Has Aleese been around much since I've been gone?" Mylah asked, curious if Castien had returned to his normal behavior.

"Who?" Davina asked, though Mylah knew Davina knew exactly who she was talking about. They'd been friends, or at least Mylah assumed they'd been friends.

"His consort," Mylah clarified, prodding Davina's side.

Davina snorted, "Consort? I'd hardly call her that." She laughed, but the smile fell from her face. "No. He hasn't had any kind of revel or gala since you and Elias left."

"Is that strange for him?" Mylah couldn't help being worried about him after what he'd admitted to her last night. She wanted him to be happy, but he'd said he would never love anyone as he'd loved Sascha, and Mylah was inclined to believe him.

"Yes," Davina sighed. "He hasn't had a stretch this long without having some sort of gathering as long as he's been king. Though, it could have something to do with the war that's brewing around us."

"You're probably right." Mylah realized she was foolish to think that anything more was wrong than the simple fact that they were preparing for a war.

Ana and Korriane joined them at the table, placing the drinks down in front of them. Davina sipped hers slowly, scanning the room.

"So, are you and Crane friends now?" Mylah asked, her curiosity getting the better of her.

Davina lifted her head and her eyes met Mylah's.

"Yeah, I'd probably consider him to be the best friend I've ever had. Which is sad because he most likely would not say the same about me." She bit her lip and shook her head.

Disgraced

"Oh. Wow," Mylah couldn't help saying. For some reason, knowing that Crane had befriended Davina made Mylah's opinion of her improve slightly. Crane's opinion meant the world to Mylah, and if he had accepted Davina, maybe she could too.

Mylah smiled at her, ready to try out this friendship thing, but before she could say anything else, the door to the tavern opened and Castien strolled through it, followed closely by Torin, Killian, and Crane. Mylah couldn't help the pit that opened in her stomach as she waited for Elias, but he didn't enter.

"Ladies," Torin said, dropping into the seat beside Davina.

Killian pulled over two chairs for himself and Crane, while Castien ordered their drinks at the bar. Mylah couldn't help but think it odd that the *King* was ordering the drinks, and not one of his entourage, but she didn't question it. Torin's visible eye never left Castien, though, and she knew he was watching for any sign of danger.

Crane nudged Mylah's elbow with his own. "Don't look so glum. He'll be here soon," he said.

"Huh?" Mylah met his gaze.

"Elias. He stopped next door to grab something, and he'll be here soon," Crane clarified.

"Castien didn't want to wait for him? He wouldn't let Elias go out alone in their own town." Mylah's heart raced at the thought of all the trouble Elias could get into alone in a strange town.

"He has a guard with him, and there are two more stationed outside the tavern."

Mylah relaxed, but only slightly. *Elias can handle himself*, she thought.

Castien sat down beside Torin, pulling Mylah out of her own head. "They'll bring the drinks over in a minute," he said. "How did your dress hunting go?"

"Well," Korriane answered for them all. "I'm sure the sovereign will be impressed by the amount we spent." She eyed Davina who ignored her in favor of watching a game of knife throwing on the opposite end of the tavern. A quick succession of thuds reached Mylah and she turned to watch as well. The three daggers that had been thrown all had hit the target, but none struck close to the bullseye.

"I could do better," Davina said, standing and striding over to the two men who were playing.

The men turned to Davina, who, even in her heels, was dwarfed by them. Their muscles rivaled Torin's and their beards disguised half of their faces. With all their similarities, Mylah wouldn't have been surprised if they were brothers.

They took in the sight of Davina, in her blue-grey gown, with the neckline that dipped to her sternum and their eyes lit up.

"She may need backup," Mylah said, more interested in being front row for Davina's knife throwing than anything else. As Mylah approached them, she overheard Davina.

"Do you mind showing me how to throw one of those?" Davina's voice was high and breathy.

Mylah laughed to herself as she walked over and gripped the wooden pillar that marked the edge of the throwing area.

"You brought a friend?" One of the men asked and Davina turned to see Mylah. "Does she want to have a go as well?" He angled his head and gave Mylah a smile.

Disgraced

"Mylah, this is Luca and his brother Marc. They were telling me how they are champion dagger throwers here in Amaris!" Davina said and Mylah nodded, trying to appear impressed.

"And Davina wanted to learn how to throw," Luca reminded her, and Davina bobbed her head. He led her to the line where they stood to throw and handed her a dagger. He stood behind her, guiding her into the correct position and helped her throw the first dagger, which missed the target completely, clattering to the ground.

Davina giggled and Mylah rolled her eyes.

"Let me try myself," Davina said, taking another dagger straight from Luca's belt. She turned back to the target and threw the dagger, missing the target again, but only by inches.

"Not bad," Luca said.

"We should make a wager," Davina said, walking her fingers down Luca's chest.

"I hardly think that would be fair," Luca replied, grinning at her, but Marc stepped forward.

"Now, brother, what kind of gentlemen would we be if we turned down a lady's request?" Marc said as he slapped his brother on the back.

"Yay!" Davina clapped her hands together and waved Mylah over. "Mylah and I against you two!"

"If you insist," Luca shrugged. "Marc, you first. Show them what they're really up against."

Marc wore a cocky grin as he stepped up to the line and let three daggers fly in quick succession, each narrowly missing the bullseye in the center.

"I'll go easy on you this time," he said as he backed away, leaving the path clear for Mylah to step up. She cleared her throat as she took the daggers Luca held out to her. They didn't feel quite right in her hand as Garrick's dagger had. Closing her eyes, she pushing that thought aside and recentered herself.

"Thank you," she said before aligning herself with the target. She didn't feel the need to show off as Marc had, so she took her time. Her first throw landed directly below one of Marc's daggers, knocking his loose and it clattered to the floor. Her second throw landed a hair closer than Marc's daggers to the bullseye and she heard his intake of breath behind her. With the last dagger, she hit the edge of the bullseye. She cursed herself silently. It had been too long since she'd practiced.

"I guess we should have had *you* show us your skill level before agreeing to the wager," Luca joked, but his smile was strained. "I'll go next." Luca took Mylah's place at the line and as Marc had done, he let his three daggers go in quick succession. He knocked two of Mylah's daggers from the target and hit the bullseye dead center with his last dagger.

"Yikes," Davina said, sweeping her hair over her shoulder. "I guess it's my turn." She stepped up to the line, taking three daggers from Luca. After taking a deep breath, she took aim and, one after another, landed all three of her daggers in the center of the bullseye, knocking Luca's from the board.

"You let the lady hustle you," Marc grumbled.

Davina turned back to them all with a wide grin on her face as she held out her hand to Luca.

"I should know better by now than to trust a beautiful woman." Instead of handing over any money, though, he took Davina's hand in his and kissed the back of it. "I'd like a rematch." Davina let her head fall back as she laughed.

"Of course you would, and I'd be happy to show you up yet again." Davina grinned and her eyes twinkled with mischief.

"I look forward to that." Luca leaned in close, and Davina turned her head slightly, feigning shyness.

Mylah glanced over at their table and noticed both Crane and Torin watching Davina intently. Elias still hadn't arrived yet.

"Rematch it is," Mylah said, figuring that it would help distract her from worrying about Elias.

"What is it, exactly, we're wagering?" Marc asked as he stepped closer to the group with the daggers he'd retrieved in a basket.

"Well, for round one, you can buy me a drink," Davina said. "But I'd like something a little...flashier when I win round two."

"*When* you win?" Marc asked. "As I said, I was going easy on you round one. Now that I know I don't need to hold back, things will be different."

"Mmhmm, I'm sure," Davina mocked. "We'll give you the advantage this time, and we'll go first."

Mylah threw first this time, and managed to hit the bullseye each time, though they were only the edges again. She made a mental note to start practicing again as soon as they returned to Elowyn.

When she finished her turn, she returned to the wooden pillar, leaning against it as she watched the door. As she did, the door opened and her heart leapt, but two women entered, and she sighed in disappointment. Chewing her lip, Mylah began running through all the possibilities for what may be holding Elias up. *What if fate decided to take him because it couldn't have me?* Was the most pressing, and terrifying thought she kept coming back to.

"Mylah." Davina had come up beside her. "You okay?" she asked, her eyes searching for something on Mylah's face to explain her behavior.

"No. Is it okay if I bow out?" Mylah decided to be honest. She couldn't keep playing games while her brain created worse and worse scenarios for Elias' absence.

Davina smirked. "You think I can't handle these two on my own?" She threw a look over her shoulder to the target where her daggers had once again held firm in the bullseye.

"Thanks." Mylah tried to smile back but it didn't last more than a second before she hurried back to the table, stopping beside Crane. "Keep Davina out of trouble," she said to him before continuing towards the door.

"Where are you going?" Castien called after her. The scrape of his chair against the wooden floor told her he followed her. Pausing at the door she waited for him.

"I'm going to find Elias," she told him once he'd reached her.

"He'll be here any minute," Castien tried to reassure her.

"Tell that to the million scenarios in my mind where he winds up hurt, or worse," Mylah's voice came out strangled.

"And I thought I was paranoid," Castien said, laughing, but Mylah didn't join in.

"I need to see him. I need to know he's okay," Mylah said. It was irrational, but after everyone she'd lost, and now knowing that fate might be real, she shuddered to think what was waiting for them all.

"Just, wait five more minutes, and if he's not here, I'll go with you to find him," Castien promised.

"I can't wait. There's something we didn't tell you." Castien's eyes narrowed. "You're going to think it's ridiculous and I know that Elias doesn't put any stock in it, but the witch, Ailsa, said I'm escaping fate. And she's not the only one. Nala from the council in Hyrdian mentioned fate to me as well. They seem to think it's a real thing. And, what if because fate couldn't take me, it decided to take the person I care about most?" Tears had welled up in Mylah's eyes and her hands began shaking.

"It's not ridiculous," Castien said, quietly, to Mylah's surprise. "I don't know how much power fate truly has over us all, but I do believe in it somewhat."

"Then please let me go make sure Elias is okay. I won't be able to think straight until I do," Mylah said, gripping Castien's arm.

"Fine," he consented with a groan. "But I'm coming with you."

Mylah turned on her heel towards the door and pushed it open. The guards outside appeared surprised when they saw her, but they only waited as she and Castien left the bar before one of the guards followed them down the street.

"We left him in that store, there," Castien pointed to a jewelry store across the way and Mylah veered towards it.

They could see in through the large oval window that revealed the entire store and Mylah almost cried out in relief as she saw Elias standing at the counter, laughing with the man handing him a package.

"I told you he was fine," Castien said. He nodded to the guard who stood outside the store. "Now can we go back to the tavern before he realizes I failed in keeping you distracted while he was gone?"

"I suppose..." Mylah wanted to walk into the store and wrap herself in Elias' arms, but it was irrational. He was fine, fate had not taken out it's wrath on him. *Yet*, her mind said, unbiddenly.

Before they could leave the store behind, Elias turned and saw them through the window. The smile fell from his face and a concerned frown replaced it. He waved to the man behind the counter before hurrying out of the store, tucking the package he'd received into his jacket pocket.

"Is everything alright?" he asked as he met them on the street, his eyes searching Mylah and Castien both.

"I –" Mylah started, about to admit to her fear when Castien spoke up.

"Just needed some air and Mylah was kind enough to join me. She spotted you through the window and was curious what you were up to," Castien lied effortlessly with a smile. "Should we head back to the tavern?"

Elias put his arm around Mylah's waist, kissing her temple and putting her mind at ease. Tension seeped from her body, leaving her tired, yet restless.

Back in the tavern, Luca and Marc had joined the others at the table and everyone was laughing at something. It lifted Mylah's spirits to see them all so happy and carefree.

"Welcome back," Torin said, standing so Castien could have his seat. "We ordered another round."

A weight dropped in Mylah's stomach. As much as she enjoyed spending this time with her friends, all she wanted was to curl up in bed and sleep.

"I think we're going to head back to the castle," Elias said, as if he'd read Mylah's thoughts. Turning her face up to look at him, she smiled and gave his hand a squeeze. "We'll see you all in the morning."

Castien opened his mouth as if he was going to argue, but instead, he nodded curtly. "Take a guard with you," he said, and Elias nodded in agreement. "See you in the morning."

Elias and Mylah walked hand in hand back to where they'd left the horses. Their guard trailed behind them.

"How did you know I wanted to leave?" Mylah asked, nudging Elias with her elbow.

He chuckled and kissed her temple. "You stiffened when Torin mentioned another round of drinks. It was a lucky guess."

When they made it back to their room in the castle, Mylah readied for bed in record time. If she had to guess, her body was still growing accustomed to the changes she'd gone through, and it left her feeling overexerted and exhausted.

Elias climbed into bed and turned to face Mylah, kissing her softly before pulling back and lifting his hand to brush her hair out of her face. Smirking, Mylah took his hand and kissed it.

"Why didn't you want to share a room with me in Hyrdian?" she asked.

"Because I was stupid," Elias said, rolling his eyes.

"Tell me," Mylah said, poking his chest and he laughed.

"It feels like a lifetime ago now," he sighed. "I had no idea how you felt about me. Whether you hated me or what. I couldn't blame you if you *did* hate me. I was horrible..."

"Don't go down that road," Mylah warned, her eyes softening as she put a finger to his lips.

"Every night I laid beside you in that bed and wasn't able to touch you, was torture. I could barely sleep thinking about you mere inches away," he groaned and Mylah smirked.

"If it makes you feel any better, it was just as hard for me," Mylah admitted.

Elias wrapped his arms around her and pulled her close, making her laugh. A yawn escaped her, and her eyes drifted closed as her exhaustion won out.

"I love you..." Elias murmured.

Mylah wasn't entirely sure if she was dreaming or not, and she didn't respond as sleep overwhelmed her.

Thirty One

The castle was aflutter with activity preparing for the gala. Greyson had been tasked with helping carry in tables for the food. He never saw Julian the entire day, and when he went to get dressed for the night, Julian seemed to be the only guard missing from the bunkroom.

"I should have known," Kolt said as he stalked towards Greyson. "I mean, the way Julian carried you out of the bathroom the day we beat the shit out of you."

"Is there a reason you're talking to me right now?" Greyson asked as he shrugged his jacket on and turned to Kolt.

Kolt scoffed. "You'll get what's coming to you," he sneered.

"What is it that makes you hate me so much?" Greyson dared to ask. He'd had enough of Kolt's pestering.

Kolt rolled his eyes. "You're so wrapped up in your own world you really don't know, do you?" Kolt asked and Greyson shook his head slightly. "Of course not. One of the guards who was killed by the people *you* let escape that night in the tower; he was someone I cared about more than anyone else."

Greyson flinched. Not once had he thought about the guards who had died that night. He'd known none of them, and after the funeral, they weren't brought up often in conversation. Guilt flooded him.

"I'm sorry, I didn't know," Greyson's voice came out thick and low.

"Save it. I don't want your apologies. I want justice." Kolt kept walking, knocking his shoulder against Greyson's.

Greyson watched him go for the first time with understanding rather than hate. Greyson grabbed Mylah's necklace from beneath his pillow and shoved it into his pocket. It brought him some comfort to have something that reminded him of his old life, even if she was the reason his old life had been ripped from him.

"Time to move out," Captain Andreas called out to the remaining guards in the bunkroom.

Greyson strapped his sword around his waist and followed the other guards out of the room.

In the ballroom, Greyson couldn't help but be reminded of Mylah's birthday gala. The blue dahlias had been used for ornamentation again, along with the large vases. A pink hue colored the room from some special lights that had been magically enhanced by either a witch or possibly one of Queen Aveda's entourage.

Greyson kept to the edges of the room, remaining partially concealed in the shadows of the pillars. He could pick out the guards among the guests easily because he knew them, but they did blend in fairly well. Everyone was already in the ballroom except for King Florian, Queen

Aurelia, and Queen Aveda. Greyson assumed they had a grand entrance planned.

    King Aeron and Queen Calvina stood side by side surrounded by their own people, not quite meshed with the rest of the crowd. King Aeron wore a smile, but Queen Calvina scowled and wasn't even attempting to appear pleased at the revelry around her.

    Greyson stepped closer to them to try to overhear what they may be talking about.

    "...closer to the mountains," Queen Calvina finished whatever she was saying. "I sent a patrol out there a couple weeks ago, and I haven't heard back from them."

    "Could be the Unbound creatures. I heard the trolls and orcs have been venturing further from the mountains," King Aeron reasoned but the queen rolled her eyes.

    "Don't play that game with me, Aeron. The trolls are easily tricked, and the orcs only come out at night. My men know how to avoid them. This has something to do with Queen Aveda, I know it," she hissed, but stopped talking as a trumpet sounded.

    Greyson turned as the crowd parted, clearing a path to the double doors that swung open revealing King Florian and Queen Aurelia. He ignored them, searching the room for Cassia. He saw her parents, but she wasn't near them.

    Someone grabbed Greyson's elbow and he jumped. He turned and found Cassia laughing at him.

    "You're jumpy tonight," she said.

    "I was looking for you!" He hugged her quickly. "While everyone's distracted." He took her arm and led her away from the crowd.

    "How are you?" Cassia asked.

"I'm okay." He thought about telling her about Julian but then decided against it. After last night, he wasn't even sure there was anything to tell. "But you asked me whether I knew any of the king's plans... And I can't betray the king, so I won't. But there's no harm in telling you what I know."

Cassia's eyes widened but she said nothing.

"He plans on using the followers of Hosath for something. I'm not sure what, but two of our guards will be joining their pilgrimage into Hyrdian."

"That's only a week away," Cassia said, and Greyson nodded. "Thank you."

"And..." Greyson took a deep breath. "If you can, let Crane know I'm okay and let Mylah know I'm sorry."

Cassia's eyes softened and she stretched up to kiss his cheek. "You'll get to tell them yourself," she said. "Oh, here comes Queen Aveda. She's beautiful, isn't she?" Cassia turned towards the doors and Greyson followed her gaze to find Queen Aveda arm in arm with another fae. His dark brown hair and eyes matched hers.

"That must be a relative," Greyson said. "I haven't seen him around the castle."

The man smiled at the queen, and they began moving forward again, into the room. He was taller than her, and probably taller than Greyson. His tight and defined muscles were visible beneath his shirt, which had rolled up sleeves, revealing, not shreeve markings, but ink tattoos on his forearms.

"He's just as beautiful as her," Cassia commented, and Greyson nodded in agreement. "Come on." Cassia took Greyson's arm again and led him closer to the path that the royals were taking to the back of the room.

Disgraced

"I shouldn't..." Greyson halfheartedly tried to protest but didn't fight Cassia.

"Now we can see them better," she said, keeping her arm looped through his.

"Queen Aveda and her long-lost brother, Prince Lachlan," someone announced.

"Interesting," Cassia murmured.

The queen and prince approached where Cassia and Greyson stood, and Greyson found himself holding his breath. The prince scanned the room, a smile pasted on his face. There was something familiar about him that Greyson couldn't place until the prince's gaze found his and his fake smile changed to a real grin. Realization dawned on Greyson, and he gasped, causing several heads to turn his way. Fumbling backward, he tripped over someone else. Cassia thankfully still had a grip on him and held him upright.

"What's wrong?" she asked, following him back through the crowd to the shadows.

Greyson shook his head, unable to muddle through his thoughts and make sense of it all. It was Julian, it had to be, but... It wasn't. Then Greyson remembered the fae who had escaped the dungeon and had been unaccounted for. He'd been told fae could glamour themselves to look like anyone.

"I need air," Greyson said, his hand pressed to his chest as he struggled to calm his racing heart.

"Yeah, okay." Cassia led the way out of the ballroom through a side door.

Greyson didn't even care anymore whether the king saw him shirking his duties. Maybe if the king decided to discharge him from the royal guard the binding would be broken, and Greyson could be free.

"What was that about?" Cassia asked once they were in the gardens.

Greyson didn't speak for a moment as he fought to form a coherent sentence. "I think I know that fae – Prince Lachlan."

"You've seen him around?" Cassia asked.

"No, I know him. He's a guard too... I kissed him." Greyson rubbed the back of his neck.

"What?! You didn't tell me?" Cassia laughed and squeezed Greyson's arm.

"This is the first time I've seen you," Greyson pointed out.

"I know. I'm glad you're here tonight." Her gaze softened.

"But I should be getting back," Greyson said. Now that his common sense was returning, he realized how careless he'd been to abandon his post.

"You can't drop that you kissed a fae prince on me and then leave!" Cassia blurted.

"Sorry, Cass. We'll have to catch up another time." Greyson laughed at the annoyance on her face, but she didn't argue.

They returned inside and stopped in their tracks as they reentered the ballroom and almost ran right into Prince Lachlan. His eyes widened in surprise for a moment, but he quickly schooled his expression.

"Greyson," he said. "If I could have a moment with you."

Greyson's mind whirled. He sounded like Julian, but his hair was longer, his ears pointed, and his face more angular.

"This is Cassia," Greyson said instead, and the prince seemed to notice her for the first time.

"Yes. Very nice to meet you, Cassia," he said, giving her a half-hearted smile before returning his attention to Greyson.

"The pleasure is all mine, Prince Lachlan." Cassia curtsied and dipped her head to him.

Greyson realized he probably should have bowed or something too, but it felt all wrong.

"A moment," the prince repeated, and Cassia released Greyson's arm to walk away, but Greyson gripped her hand tightly, refusing to let her go.

"Don't leave." He turned pleading eyes on her, and she stopped, giving him a small smile before returning to his side. Greyson kept her hand in his and turned back to the prince. "I'm on duty, and Cassia has requested my presence at her side tonight." He wasn't sure if that was something that could happen, but it seemed like a good enough excuse not to be left alone with the prince.

"Of course." Prince Lachlan pursed his lips and folded his hands behind his back. "Though, I've already told King Florian that you will be at *my* side tonight, so if I may pull my rank here?"

Greyson's nostrils flared and he gritted his teeth, squeezing Cassia's hand so tight she let out a yelp and smacked his arm.

"Sorry," he muttered, releasing her hand.

"It's okay." Cassia patted his arm. "I'll leave you two. But I will say, this is a bad first impression, *Prince* Lachlan," she said, using his title as an insult.

"I do apologize. I hate to give Greyson's best friend a bad impression, but I cannot change what has already been done." He lifted his hands in an apologetic shrug.

"You could, but you choose not to," Cassia corrected him. "If you do anything to hurt Greyson, I promise I will return the favor ten times over." Her eyes narrowed and she leveled her finger at his chest.

His lips quirked and he bowed his head to her. "I promise to do no such thing," he said.

"Good," Cassia snapped before turning on her heel and striding away toward the food table.

Greyson's pulse beat erratically as he considered being alone with Prince Lachlan. Rage mixed with curiosity and longing all warred within him.

"I assume you've guessed who I am," Prince Lachlan said as he clasped his hands behind his back and leaned forward slightly.

"You're Prince Lachlan. I think your announcer made that clear," Greyson ground out.

"Call me Lachlan." His eyes softened but his jaw twitched. "Greyson," he said in a huff.

"Lachlan, Prince, *Julian*..." he hissed. "What does it matter what I call you?"

"It doesn't. Call me whatever you like. Just talk to me, please?" His head dipped down, but his eyes stayed locked on Greyson's.

"You're her *brother*. You asked me to get information on her and you knew all along. Were you trying to set me up?" Greyson lowered his voice, trying not to be overheard by the people surrounding them. Thankfully the music and chatter drowned out most of the conversations.

"No." Lachlan reared back. "Of course not. I genuinely had no idea what her plans were." His eyes rounded and he reached out to put a hand on Greyson's arm, but Greyson stepped out of reach.

"But you know now," Greyson stated. "And you've decided to join her."

"Not exactly." Lachlan rolled his head to the side. "Can we get out of here?"

"I'm on duty," Greyson said more harshly than he'd meant to.

"As I said, I've already told the king you'll be my guard for the night. It would be weird if you *didn't* leave with me." Lachlan gave him a crooked smile and Greyson caved.

"Fine," Greyson said through gritted teeth. He followed Lachlan through the same door he'd used with Cassia. Greyson's hands were fisted at his sides as he tried to keep control over his composure.

"That's better," Lachlan said as soon as the door closed behind them. He shook his shoulders as if shaking off a facade.

"So, this is the real you then," Greyson said. They walked through the hall, side by side. Electricity seemed to fill the air around them.

"Yes, though I was technically always the real me, just with a different face," he joked, trying to lighten the mood. "Everything I told you, everything we had, it was all real."

"Everything... Like you realizing it was all a mistake? Leaving me at dinner last night..." Greyson's face heated.

"No, that was me trying to save you from getting hurt," Lachlan said, wincing.

"Oh. Well, job poorly done." Greyson folded his arms over his chest as if he could hide the hurt he was pretty sure was written across his face.

"I know. I didn't want to kiss you with that glamour. I wanted you to really know *me* before it got that far. But I got caught up in the moment and forgot myself." He winked, but his smile appeared forced.

"And that day, when you convinced the footman to take us into town, did you use your magic on him?" Greyson asked.

"Yes and no. I removed my glamour for him because Queen Aveda had made a few select people in the castle aware of my presence in case I needed assistance. Though, even the king is still unaware of who I really am," he explained.

Greyson shook his head. He should have realized something was off then.

"Is it wrong to say that I prefer this version of you to the other one?" Greyson admitted. He wasn't sure why, but something about Lachlan fit better than Julian. Whether it was the name or something deeper, Greyson couldn't be sure.

Lachlan chuckled. "I'm actually happy to hear you say that. It would be a little awkward if you preferred Julian, considering the fact that he's not real."

"Don't think this means I've forgiven you." Greyson's hardened his features once more.

"You know, it's interesting. Your friend Mylah did something very similar to what I've done, but in Elowyn. There's a reason I chose to stay here, you know."

Disgraced

"Because you wanted to find out more about her?" Greyson guessed. He clutched Mylah's necklace in his pocket, letting it dig into his skin to distract him from the sting of Lachlan's betrayal.

"Yes and no. I was curious to find out more about the man who let her go." Lachlan played with a lock of his hair that curled up behind his ear and Greyson couldn't stop staring.

He cleared his throat as he forced himself to look away. "Ah. So that's what kept you around," Greyson tried to sound amused. "Trying to sniff out the traitors?"

"You should know, I've told no one of anything we did. The Hall of Hosath, or our conversations. You can trust me, as you trusted Julian." The earnestness in Lachlan's eyes had Greyson faltering, but he wouldn't trust him so easily.

"To be fair, I never fully trusted Julian. He was a bit sketchy," Greyson said, surprising himself that he was able to joke.

"Fair enough. But you still fell for him." Lachlan brushed his shoulder against Greyson's and this time, Greyson didn't move away.

"I still fell for him," Greyson admitted, defeated. "And now..."

"Now, here we are." Lachlan stopped walking as they approached a large window with a window seat overlooking the gardens. Lachlan sat first, and Greyson followed his lead reluctantly. "There is something else I have to tell you."

"What's stopping you?" Greyson stared out the window at the gardens.

"I can get you out of your deal with the king."

Greyson's head whipped back toward Lachlan, and he gave him an incredulous look. "How? I'm magically bound to him."

"I also have magic," Lachlan reminded him as he rotated his wrist and splayed his fingers, letting a trail of purple mist dance between them. "Nothing is permanent when it comes to magic."

"But what will I do then?" Greyson was hit with the realization that he had no one and nothing in Adair outside of the castle, besides Cassia. But she had her family to worry about.

"Become my personal guard."

"Guard you? From what exactly? I think you're more capable of protecting yourself than I am." Greyson never felt more powerless than in that moment. Lachlan was fae and had no use for a human to protect him.

"Do you want out of your deal with the king, or not?" Lachlan asked, exasperated.

"Yes, I want out," Greyson admitted.

"Okay." Lachlan grinned. "Is it okay if..." before he could finish, Greyson closed the gap between them and kissed him swiftly, but deeply.

"Sorry, I've been wanting to do that since we left the ballroom," Greyson said, breathless.

Lachlan laughed. "I thought you were still upset with me," he said.

"I was... I mean, I am. This changes nothing. I wanted to make sure you were worth sticking around for before committing to anything long term," Greyson joked. "Julian was a good kisser, but Lachlan I wasn't sure about."

Disgraced

"And what is the verdict?" Greyson was about to answer when Lachlan held up his hand. "Wait, let me give you more material to base that comparison on."

They kissed until footsteps echoed down the hall towards them and they broke apart. There were many sets of footsteps approaching briskly, which startled Greyson.

Lachlan bit his lip as he turned back to Greyson and took his hands.

"I'm so sorry," he said, giving Greyson one more quick kiss. "I'm going to need you to trust me again."

"Who said I ever trusted you? What's going on?" Greyson asked, but Lachlan stood and clasped his hands behind his back as a group of guards accompanied by the king rounded the corner.

"Greyson Callister," the king's voice boomed in the small space of the hallway. "You've been accused of treason and conspiring against the throne."

"What?" Greyson whipped his head from side to side, flicking his gaze between the king and Lachlan. "No, I didn't..." But he had, he realized. He'd told Cassia about the Hosath worshippers, and he'd told Lachlan he wanted to break his deal with the king. *I'm going to need you to trust me...* Lachlan's words echoed in his mind. Against every instinct, he decided his only choice was to do just that.

Greyson lowered his head and waited as two guards took his arms, pulling him to his feet.

"Thank you for the tip, Prince Lachlan," King Florian said, sneering down at Greyson.

A tug in Greyson's chest at the idea that Lachlan had betrayed him to the king had him doubting his decision to trust Lachlan.

"Just doing my duties, your majesty," Lachlan's voice was cold and hard, and Greyson turned his face up to him.

Greyson's eyes shuttered as he mouthed the word 'Why?' and Lachlan flicked his emotionless gaze away. No matter how hard Greyson tried to convince himself that it was all an act, he still wanted to claw his own heart out.

"Take him to the dungeons," the king ordered the guards, who Greyson recognized but he didn't know their names. "Why don't you rejoin the gala with me, Prince Lachlan?"

"I'd enjoy nothing more." Lachlan strode away at the side of the king and Greyson couldn't help thinking how natural he looked beside royalty.

Greyson rolled his head to the side and back to the front, trying to shake the sensation of freefalling.

"It was only a matter of time," Kolt's voice jerked Greyson's head up. "We all knew you were a traitor; it was just about finding the evidence."

"I guess you'll finally get your justice," Greyson's voice came out hoarse and cracked, reflecting what was happening to him inside.

"Hardly. I still have a debt to repay," Kolt snarled. "I'll be sure the king keeps you alive to see it."

Greyson was hauled past Kolt and down to the dungeons, which were mostly empty. A few faces peered at him from their cells as they passed, but Greyson tried not to think too much about why they were down there and whether they deserved to be, or if they'd been framed like himself.

The guards pushed Greyson into a cell and slammed the barred door shut behind him.

Disgraced

Greyson spent the night in the dungeon, unable to sleep as he wondered when he'd be summoned for a trial, or if he'd even get a trial. It was possible he'd be exiled or executed. The thought didn't scare him as much as it should have.

For a moment, he had something more. He had something to look forward to, someone to share his world with. For a moment, he had hope. And it had all been ripped away sooner than he could catch his breath.

"Do you think anything happens for a reason?" Greyson asked anyone who may be listening. For a few minutes, no one answered, until a scratchy and unused voice drifted down to him.

"Not anything, but *everything*," the voice said, and Greyson stiffened. "That's the saying, you got it wrong. And no. Fate is a sham."

"Oh," Greyson huffed.

"Life is what you make it."

"I'd agree with that," a familiar voice reached Greyson before Lachlan glamoured as Julian came into view.

Greyson jumped up and raced to the bars, gripping them tightly.

"What are you doing?" he hissed.

"Shift change. I'm on duty." Lachlan winked, and did a shimmy, making Greyson smirk.

"Doesn't the king know..." Greyson started but Lachlan cut him off.

"No." He gave Greyson a warning glare and flicked his eyes to the surrounding cells. They couldn't trust anyone.

"Right. Well," Greyson wasn't sure what else was safe to say.

"Your trial has been set for two days from now. Captain Mardoc will be accompanying you."

"Why him?"

"Because Captain Andreas is advocating for you." Greyson felt a swell of pride at that. "Along with some council members. It promises to be a very interesting and *spellbinding* trial." Lachlan wiggled his eyebrows and Greyson shook his head and held in a laugh. *Spellbinding*... Lachlan was trying to tell him that he'd have to stick it out to the trial before he could break the magical bond between Greyson and the king.

"I'll do my best to keep things entertaining for everyone," Greyson joked.

"That would be much appreciated. No one expects you to go down easy."

"I'll go down fighting if I have to," Greyson said.

Lachlan laughed. "Alright, traitor, keep talking big," he said, and Greyson realized someone else was entering the dungeon. Lachlan continued down the walk through the dungeon and Greyson returned to the floor, trying to appear miserable.

Greyson didn't see Lachlan again before the trial. Kolt and Acton were the guards sent to fetch him from the dungeons while Captain Mardoc watched with a sneer plastered on his face. Greyson earned a few bruises from Kolt *accidentally* stepping on him and elbowing him a few times. Greyson knew better than to complain to the captain.

They brought him to the council chambers through the back door, as they'd done with the prisoners from Elowyn only two months prior. *I'm no better than them...* Greyson kept his head down, refusing to look into the crowd and see all the disapproving stares from those who had once been his peers.

"Thank you, Captain Mardoc," King Florian said, as if the captain had done anything other than cast a few scathing glares Greyson's way.

Without lifting his eyes, Greyson could see the king standing to his left while Queen Aveda sat in one of the thrones. Queen Aurelia was absent. There were a few others standing on the edge of the dais, but Greyson didn't turn to see who stood there.

Hands pushed down on Greyson's shoulders from behind, forcing him to his knees. The impact of hitting the stone slab had Greyson's teeth clenching as he inhaled sharply.

"I bring forth, Greyson Callister," the king's words rang through the chambers and a few murmurs reached Greyson from the crowd. "Caught conspiring against Adair and your king."

"No surprise there," someone close to the dais whispered, though Greyson heard it loud and clear.

His head snapped up and his eyes met with Atticus Calhoun's, and the man scowled at Greyson. His sons sat on either side of him wearing similar expressions. Greyson bared his teeth at them.

"As we all know, Greyson's family was exiled for treason, and though I suspected Greyson may follow in their footsteps, I decided to give him the benefit of the doubt. I showed him mercy, allowing him to stay on as a member of my guard as he attempted to prove himself loyal." The king paused and Greyson sensed the air thickening around him as he awaited what would come next.

"As this is a more... critical time, since we are on the brink of war, Greyson's sentence has already been determined and there shall be no trial," King Florian said, and remarks of protest came from the council. "For his acts of treason, he shall be put to death."

Greyson's heart dropped into his stomach, and he pitched forward at the waist, his forehead touching the floor as the weight of his fate pressed upon him. A ringing in his ears drowned out the words from the council, whether they were in favor or against his sentencing, it didn't matter.

Then he remembered what Lachlan had said to him in the dungeons. *No one expects you to go down easy.* Taking a deep breath, Greyson straightened and turned his face so he could look the king in the eye. To his credit, King Florian seemed unfazed.

"So, you'll murder me then, as your men did my father?" Greyson spoke loud and clear so that everyone in the room would hear him.

A collective gasp echoed through the chamber and whispers broke out along with a few shouts.

"Your father was a traitor to this kingdom!" the king's voice rose above all the rest. "There were many casualties that occurred the night of the shreeves' escape, including your father. You cannot blame me for his choice to turn his back on his people." His voice came out like venom, piercing straight through Greyson's heart. The words were true enough, but that did not expunge the king of any guilt in Greyson's eyes.

"My father was a good man! He believed in you and trusted you until you decided you wanted to take on an entire race because of your own prejudices!"

Disgraced

Kolt's fist cracked against Greyson's face, sending him sprawling across the stage, his hands still tied at his back and unable to brace himself. The entire room erupted in shouts and movement. Greyson's eyes were blurred from the strike, and he couldn't clearly make out what was happening.

"Enough!" The king barked out. "Everyone, return to your seats."

The room quieted, but there were still a few disgruntled voices.

"This will not be tolerated," King Florian began, but he stopped abruptly, along with all the other voices in the room. Greyson turned his face to the side, still resting his head on the floor, and saw him... Lachlan.

"If I may step in." Lachlan's words rang with authority and even the Queen sat at attention, though Greyson could see curiosity in her gaze more than anything. "My dearest sister." Lachlan waved his hand towards her as if there was any question that they were related.

"Yes," she said, drawing out the word.

"If you'd be so kind as to repay your debt to me and free Greyson from his bond to the king." Lachlan bowed to her, and she threw her head back as she laughed.

"You'd use that debt now, here, for him? A *human*?" The disdain was clear in her voice, but Lachlan didn't waver, only raised a brow, and kept his gaze pinned on her. "Oh fine. What do I care?" She waved a hand and Greyson felt a weight lift from him. "Take him."

There was a collective gasp that echoed through the room. Lachlan approached Greyson and bent down, placing his hand on Greyson's arm.

"Come on." Lachlan helped Greyson to his feet as King Florian realized what was happening.

"No! He is a traitor to my kingdom and shall be punished as such!" the king nearly shrieked, and Greyson couldn't help the smile that pulled at his lips.

"This is greater than you or your kingdom," Queen Aveda said flippantly, shrugging off the king as he continued to argue with her.

Greyson let Lachlan lead him down the steps of the dais, past the council, and out the double doors. None of the guards stopped them. Everyone whipped their heads between the king of Adair and the queen of Cyprian, confused about who to listen to. A few of the council members fumbled into the aisle, thinking to catch them, but Greyson and Lachlan were too quick and left them all behind.

It wasn't until they left the confines of the castle and were seated in a carriage that Greyson was able to speak.

"Wha- How?" he managed to get out and Lachlan took his hand, squeezing it tightly in his own. They sat across from one another in the carriage, their knees brushing against each other's as the carriage bumped and swayed.

"I promised you I'd get you out of there," Lachlan reminded him, raising his hand to Greyson's cheek which smarted under his touch thanks to the punch Kolt had delivered on the stage. Greyson inhaled sharply. "Sorry," Lachlan murmured as he removed his hand.

"But what about my oath to the king?" Greyson asked.

"My sister ended that. It was weak magic, easily broken," Lachlan said matter-of-factly.

"But why was she in debt to you? Why did she help me?" Greyson couldn't help but feel guilty that Lachlan had used whatever sway he'd had with his sister to help him.

Disgraced

"The only reason I was in the dungeons all these years was to spy on King Florian for my sister. But, while he kept me there, he also had some control over her. I could have left at any time, but neither of them knows that." Lachlan smirked. "My sister underestimates my power."

Greyson gaped at him. "You mean you stayed in the dungeon all those years, willingly?" Greyson shook his head. "That's ridiculous."

"Yet I learned enough to help my sister get a foothold here, and I earned a favor from her which saved your life. So, you should be thanking me." Lachlan raised his nose in the air, but he couldn't keep in his laughter.

"You're right," Greyson said. "Thank you. So, what now?"

"I guess that's up to you. I have an idea of where I'd like to go, but if it's alright, I'd like to stay with you."

Greyson thought about that. Where did he want to go? Cassia was his only friend, and she was back in the council chambers, most likely watching the king have a fit. He'd have to ask her about that later if he saw her again. He smirked at that thought.

"I guess the only logical place for me to go would be Elowyn, to find my mother and brother," Greyson said before he could think better of it. He was most likely considered a traitor there, too, but he needed to atone for the wrongs he'd committed.

"If that's where you'd like to go, then I'll take you there."

"And you'll stay with me?" Greyson said, the words coming out much softer and quieter than he'd intended. The response he waited for meant more to him than he'd realized.

"As long as you want me around," Lachlan said, leaning forward to brush a lock of hair out of Greyson's face. His hand lingered beside Greyson's ear, brushing his cheek softly.

"I'll always want you around, I think," Greyson said.

"Good." Lachlan bridged the distance between them, and his lips met Greyson's softly at first, and then more fiercely as Greyson leaned into the kiss.

Thirty Two

Mylah donned her mask, which made her new eyes stand out even more. It was black to match her dress, and lace like in appearance, but soft on the inside against her skin.

Ana had helped her with her hair, sweeping it into an updo with a few loose curls, before leaving to put on her own dress. Her black heels had to be tied all the way up to her knees.

Stepping out into the sitting room, Mylah joined Davina who lounged on the couch popping grapes into her mouth. The dress she wore was not the mermaid style she'd been wearing in the shop. It was a simple, deep red, silk gown with a slit up either side and a scoop neck that amplified her cleavage.

"What happened to the other dress?" Mylah asked.

"I didn't want to outshine you," Davina said, winking. "And, as it turns out, it was already claimed by one of the sovereign's daughters."

Before Mylah could respond, the door on the opposite side of the room opened and Ana stepped out. She wore a silver-gray dress that was open at the waist, revealing fitted pants that hugged Ana's slight figure perfectly.

"And I thought you'd chosen something boring," Davina commented, smirking at Ana.

Korriane stepped up behind Ana, winding her arms around Ana's waist and resting her head on her shoulder.

"Not to brag, but I have the prettiest date tonight," Korriane said, and Ana blushed.

"True. Crane is pretty, but he can't compare to Ana or Mylah tonight," Davina joked.

A knock on the door told them that the time had come for them to head to the ballroom. The others all put their masks on, Davina's only covering half of her face.

Ana opened the door, revealing Torin and Castien. Crane, Elias, and Killian stood behind them, waiting.

"You all look quite handsome," Ana said. "Maybe we should do this more often back home!"

"Once we win this war," Castien said, breezing past her into the room. "Is everyone ready?"

The others followed him in, and Elias met Mylah's gaze. She couldn't help the heat that swelled inside of her. Striding over to her, he took her hand, bowing as he brought it to his lips.

"What was that for?" she couldn't help asking, unable to stop smiling.

"Do I need a reason to treat you like the goddess you are?"

"I-I don't know, er," Mylah stumbled over her words. "You look nice tonight," she said, realizing how far that was from the truth. He looked *amazing* tonight. He looked like a king, not just a prince.

Elias smirked. "And you look absolutely stunning. I dare say I'll have to be fighting for your attention all night."

"Hardly..." Mylah murmured.

"Alright, lovebirds, it's time to go," Castien's voice broke through their bubble.

"Give us a moment. We'll catch up," Elias said over his shoulder, and everyone else filed out of the room.

Mylah watched Elias curiously as he shifted and couldn't seem to stop fidgeting as he waited for the room to clear. Once everyone else had left, Elias pulled a box from his jacket pocket and held it out toward her. Mylah's eyes widened and she took the box from him but didn't open it.

"This is why I was in that jewelry store yesterday," Elias said, before urging her to open the box.

When she did, she gasped and nearly dropped it as she took in the exact replica of her necklace she had lost in Adair while escaping.

"It's..." she started, but she couldn't find the words to say.

"I know how much your other one meant to you, and I know this isn't the same because it didn't come from your mother, but... Here, let me help you put it on." He stepped around her and lifted the necklace from the box.

Mylah flashed back to the moment when he had helped her put on her old necklace when they'd first met and her face heated.

"Thank you, Elias. I don't think you realize how much this means to me," Mylah finally was able to say.

His fingers brushed the back of her neck and the crystal heart pendant rested against her collarbone. It almost felt as if a piece of her had been restored.

"I'm glad you like it," he said, remaining behind her and Mylah leaned back slightly, touching her back to his chest. His breath rustled her hair and a light kiss landed just below her ear making her entire body electrify with desire. "We should catch up with the others," Elias whispered in her ear and Mylah nodded, breathless.

Elias offered Mylah his arm and she looped hers through it.

They caught up with the others outside the ballroom, where guards and servants were stationed at the door. Two servants opened the massive double doors which revealed a grand staircase leading down to a marble floor where people were gathered, either dancing, eating, or chatting on the outskirts.

"His majesty, King Castien, the crowned prince, Elias, and their guests," a man announced from somewhere to Mylah's right.

Everyone down below them glanced up to where their group descended the stairs. Mylah clung tightly to Elias' arm for fear of tripping over her dress and tumbling down the stairs. Thankfully, they made it to the bottom of the stairs without incident.

"What do we do now?" Mylah asked as Castien made his way through the crowd towards the sovereign who sat atop their throne at the back of the room, as Castien used to do during his revels.

"I think we enjoy ourselves," Elias said, amusement in his tone. "May I have this dance?" He placed one arm behind his back as he bowed and held out his other hand to

Disgraced

her. It was as she'd seen her father do for her mother when they would dance around the kitchen before they died.

One of Mylah's hands fluttered to her mouth before she could stop herself, while she placed the other hand in Elias'. He spun her out onto the dance floor, keeping her hand in his while his other hand found its place on the small of her back. Whispers began around them, and Mylah could feel eyes upon her. She assumed they were wondering who the random woman with the crowned prince of Elowyn was.

It had never crossed Mylah's mind before how impossible her relationship with Elias was. If he were ever to take the throne from Castien, he would need a queen and she wasn't sure if she was up for that job. Besides, most of Elowyn probably still wanted her dead. They'd never accept her even if Elias *did* choose her to remain by his side.

"I've never heard of her, must be a consort," a whisper reached Mylah's ears and struck her worse than any dagger could.

It wasn't that she thought badly of consorts, but that these people thought there was no way Elias would choose her alone as his partner and possible future queen.

"If he's smart, he'll pair up with one of the princesses," another person said.

Mylah couldn't help but see the logic in that. It would bind Elowyn and Amaris. Her hand tightened in Elias' as he moved her around the floor. He didn't seem to hear the whispers, or else he wasn't affected by them.

As the song came to an end and another picked up, Mylah requested a break.

"I need a drink or something," she said, her mind racing and her pulse quickening.

"I'll grab us some," Elias said, kissing her temple before leaving her on the outskirts of the dance floor.

Mylah turned in place, trying to determine where to go now that she was alone. Someone bumped into her, knocking her into another person, who cursed and scowled at her.

"Sorry," she muttered.

"Mylah."

She turned at the sound of her name and her jaw dropped as she noted Sovereign Keir approaching her. She quickly closed her mouth and regained her composure. Sovereign Keir wore a similar dress to Ana's, with a long, billowing train that flowed behind them and pants underneath. The sovereign's gown though was a brilliant gold that reflected the light in a way that made it appear liquid. It matched their eyes, which Mylah had yet to notice, since she was always trying to avoid their gaze for fear of them noticing her change. The gold was surrounded by the same light gray as the princesses' eyes.

"Sovereign," Mylah said as she dipped her head to them respectfully.

"If I might steal you for a moment," they said.

"Of course," Mylah almost sputtered.

Sovereign Keir waved their hand in front of them, and Mylah led the way towards a door, she looked back once and the sovereign nodded at her, indicating that she should go through the door. It led to an indoor garden, with a large, domed, glass roof that revealed the moonlight shining down on them. There were flowers of every color imaginable and fruit trees lining the edges of the room.

"This is my pride and joy," the sovereign said. "Besides my daughters, of course," they added.

Disgraced

"Of course," Mylah repeated, grinning at the room.

"I asked you here so I could talk to you away from the crowd," they explained. "When King Castien wrote to me before, he mentioned that you were human, and much to my surprise, here you stand, very much *not* human." They continued walking at a steady pace, and Sovereign Keir's tone didn't change in the slightest, but Mylah began to sweat.

"Why are you asking me about this now?" Mylah asked, her voice wavering and giving away her nerves.

"King Castien and Prince Elias are always with you, and they've become very adept at weaving tales for everyone. I wanted to hear directly from you the explanation for this unprecedented change," Sovereign Keir said. Their gaze pierced into Mylah as if trying to reveal all her secrets.

"I see." Mylah's gaze swept the garden, trying to find anything to help her get out of this moment. She gulped past the lump forming in her throat. "It's an interesting story, for sure," she said.

"Please do not patronize me, Mylah." Their eyes narrowed and Mylah ducked her head, ashamed.

"Right. I apologize." Mylah's breaths came short and fast. "I nearly died, you see," she said, deciding to tell as much of the truth as possible. "Poisoned by one of Queen Aveda's generals in the mountains. The only way to save my life was to become a shreeve."

"And how was that possible? No one has been able to do what you've done since the creation of shreeve."

"Mm." Mylah bit her lip, praying someone would intervene, but no one did.

"You can trust me with your truth," Sovereign Keir said and for some reason, Mylah believed them. Letting out a long breath, she resigned herself to revealing what she'd promised to keep secret.

"The witch, Ailsa, helped me. We had to visit her at Turrikar, and she was able to use Elias' blood to recreate her spell that originally created the shreeve."

"I see. I will keep your secret, Mylah. Thank you for your honesty." Sovereign Keir turned them back towards the door to the ballroom. "We should return to the festivities. We don't want to concern the prince."

"If you don't mind me saying, there is something you should know concerning your decision to help Elowyn in the war."

"And what might that be?" Curiosity sparked in the sovereign's eyes and a smile played at their mouth.

"I don't know much about Queen Aveda or her intentions, but I do know King Florian. He harbors a deep hatred of shreeve for some reason, and though he is targeting Elowyn now, I don't believe he will stop there," Mylah admitted. It was a bold claim, but she knew that the men and women in the mountains certainly thought the queen would be pushing for more territory.

"I understand and thank you for your concern. I will take that under consideration." Sovereign Keir led the way back into the ballroom and nodded to Mylah before leaving her in the crowd. She went in search of Elias and found him by the buffet table.

"There you are," Elias said as Mylah approached him. "You had me worried."

She offered him a smile. "Sovereign Keir wanted to speak with me," she explained, and Elias' brow furrowed.

"About what?" he asked.

"My change. I told them everything."

Elias' eyes widened. "What do you mean?"

"We can talk about it later," Mylah said.

Elias clamped his mouth shut, his jaw straining as he was clearly unnerved by Mylah's revelation.

"I thought we'd agreed..." he started but Mylah put her hand up to stop him.

"I didn't have much of a choice," she hissed. "Neither you nor Castien was there to help me or deflect their questioning, and they planned it that way. I trust them for now. It will be fine."

"We'll talk about it later," Elias said.

Mylah rolled her eyes. "As I said," she reminded him. Someone bumped into Mylah, spilling their drink on her, and muttered a halfhearted apology. Gasping as the drink dripped down her arm, Mylah scowled and whipped around to find that the perpetrator was already gone.

Elias turned her back towards him. "Come on, we'll get a towel or something..." he said, leading her away from the table.

Mylah's blood boiled and her mood had been thoroughly soured.

"I'm going to go back to the room," she snapped, trying to pull her arm out of Elias' grip.

"We are guests. We can't leave without being dismissed first," Elias reasoned but the reasoning side of Mylah's brain had seemed to shut down.

"I want to go back to the room," she repeated, her jaw tightening as her anger surged and her skin heated. She'd been judged, cornered, and now was sticky from some sugary drink.

Elias released her, his eyes darkening in concern. "Mylah, you need to calm down," he warned and as soon as the words left his mouth, Mylah felt something in her snap. The world faded away as the flames took over. Screams erupted around Mylah, but they sounded as if they were underwater.

"Mylah!" someone yelled her name, and she vaguely remembered a crushing weight knocking her to the ground and holding her there as someone doused her in water, as everything faded to black.

Thirty Three

Crane watched in horror as Torin pinned Mylah to the ground and Elias used his own magic to send a torrent of water crashing over Mylah and the surrounding area. Ana ran to them, and as she drew closer, using her power to calm Mylah, the flames began to recede, before disappearing entirely.

Crane pushed his way through the crowd, fighting to get to her as screams echoed through the ballroom and people fled.

"Mylah!" he cried out as her eyes fluttered closed and the flames ceased. "Get off her, it's over," Crane growled, shoving Torin, though he barely budged.

Torin stood of his own accord and Crane wrapped his jacket around Mylah since her dress was in cinders. As Crane lifted her into his arms, Castien appeared, his face white as a sheet as he observed the scene before him.

"Take her back to her room. She'll be out for a while," Castien ordered Crane. Without hesitating, Crane turned from the rest of them and fled with Mylah. It would do none of them any good for her to remain in the ballroom. There would be too many questions and accusations being thrown around and he didn't want to hear any of it.

Ana met Crane in Mylah's room and helped him get her into her nightgown before tucking her into bed.

"That was scary," Ana commented as she sat on the window seat. Crane remained on the edge of the bed, unable to move far from Mylah. He hadn't been there to help her. Maybe if he had, this would have never happened.

"I don't know how to help her," Crane said, his voice cracking as he held back tears.

A knock on the door had Crane wiping his tears and clearing his throat. "Come in," he called out.

Davina slipped into the room and eased the door shut behind her. "How is she?" she asked in a near whisper.

"She seems okay," Crane said, turning back to Mylah who was sound asleep. "What happened after we left?" He didn't want to know, but he needed to know.

"Sovereign Keir was able to calm everyone down and sent them all home. Castien is talking with them now about what happened. Torin is with Elias..." Her eyes darted to Mylah before returning to Crane. "They were both burned badly, but Elias got the worst of it since he was right next to Mylah when she lost control. I don't know the extent of his injuries."

"But he seemed okay when I saw him..." As Crane thought about it, he realized he didn't actually *see* Elias. He knew Elias was the one dousing Mylah in water, but Crane's focus had been on Mylah.

"The adrenaline of the moment kept him going until everything settled and he collapsed. Torin took him straight to the healer. I'm sure he'll be fine," Davina said, though she bit her lip with worry. Davina joined Ana on the window seat, and they all sat in silence for a while.

Crane dozed off at some point, and when he woke Ana and Davina were gone. He decided to move to the couch in the sitting room and finished out the night there. In the morning, Castien woke Crane.

"We're leaving today," Castien announced.

Crane stretched his arms above his head and yawned. "Okay," he said. "How is Mylah? Is she awake yet?"

"Not yet," Castien said, grimacing.

"Why don't we stay another day?" Crane couldn't imagine that it would be good for either Mylah or Elias to travel in their conditions.

"Sovereign Keir wants us out as soon as possible. They accept that what happened was an accident, but they don't want Mylah here if she could explode like that again at any moment, and I don't blame them." Despite Castien's words, Crane could see the frustration in the set of his jaw and how his fists were clenched at his sides. "Her magic should be depleted after last night and she won't be able to have another outburst, but I don't know the full extent of her power. I never explored it myself."

Crane sat up as a loud thud sounded from Mylah's room. Castien shot to the door and threw it open with Crane on his heels. Mylah was struggling to stand from the floor where she'd fallen.

"I'm fine," she said through gritted teeth. Castien crouched down to help her, but she pushed him away. "I said I'm fine. Don't touch me."

"I've got this," Crane said, standing beside Castien and nodding to the door. Castien raised a brow but didn't argue as he left the room, shutting the door behind him.

Crane sat on the bed and waited as he watched Mylah struggle.

"Had enough yet?" he asked, trying to keep his voice calm though it pained him to see her so distressed. She'd stopped trying to stand after Castien left. Sitting on the floor, she wrapped her arms around her legs and pulled them into her chest.

"What happened last night?" she asked.

"You tell me," Crane said, crossing his arms over his chest.

Mylah sighed and tucked her hair behind her ear. "I lost control of my magic... Again," she said, her face turning red. "What happened after that?"

"You burst into flames and Torin had to pin you down while Elias doused you in water," Crane said.

Mylah buried her head in her arms, groaning. "Is Elias mad at me?" she asked, her voice muffled against her arm.

"Not exactly..." Crane started, unsure how to tell her that she'd nearly killed him, or if he even should. Her head lifted and her gaze found his and he knew he had to tell her the truth. "He's with the healer, recovering. He got burned pretty bad."

"No," Mylah gasped as despair filled her eyes and she tried rising from the floor once more. This time she was able to get to her feet, though she remained shaky. "I want to see him."

"You're still recovering, too, Myles. You depleted your magic last night and it's taken a toll on you physically too. Castien said we're leaving today, so you need to get as much rest as you can before we go." Crane tried to convince her, but she ignored him and started walking towards the door. He caught her arm and she paused to look back at him.

"I won't be able to get any rest until I see him," she said and the utter dejection in her voice and eyes made him let her go.

"At least put on a robe or something," he said, smirking.

Mylah glanced down at her nightgown and laughed halfheartedly. "Right, we're not at home." She shuffled to her wardrobe and pulled out a robe to cover herself.

Crane wondered if she realized she'd referred to Elowyn as *home*.

Castien waited in the sitting room and stood as Crane and Mylah entered.

"Will you take us to see Elias?" Crane asked him and he narrowed his eyes.

"Elias needs to rest, as do you, Mylah," Castien said, a warning in his tone.

Crane stepped forward, keeping a hand at Mylah's back to support her. She held herself up fine, though, her new shreeve form bouncing back much faster than her human self would have.

"Take us to Elias," Crane repeated more firmly. "Please," he added.

Castien tilted his head and pursed his lips as he considered Crane's request.

"Elias isn't here," Castien finally admitted. "His injuries were too severe, and I had him transported back to Elowyn where Madame Edris could attend to him." Castien ground his jaw and Crane could tell it was causing him pain to be away from his brother.

Mylah covered her mouth with her hand as tears filled her eyes and Crane pulled her into a hug. Sobbing against his chest, Mylah tried to speak.

"I'm s-s-so s-orry," she gasped out.

"Torin is with him, he's keeping me updated," Castien added.

"So, Torin is fine then? Davina mentioned he was burned as well," Crane asked and Castien jerked his head in a quick nod.

"The healer was able to help him. By the time he got to Mylah, the worst of the flames had been doused." Castien cleared his throat and Crane wondered if he was fighting back tears as well. "Elias was right next to Mylah when her magic exploded, and he got the worst of it."

Mylah shook even harder against Crane, and he hugged her tighter.

"Can we be transported back to Elowyn?" Crane asked.

Castien shook his head. "Sovereign Keir has a warlock in their employ who offered to transport Elias for us, but he is staying with Elias in case he needs to be sent for help. Besides, he only has the power to transport one person at a time and after transporting Elias and Torin over such a long distance, his magic is most likely already depleted."

Crane nodded in understanding, though he wished he could help Mylah get to Elias faster. He knew she would be suffering until she saw him again.

"So, when can we leave?" Mylah asked, wiping her tears as she put on a brave face.

"As soon as the horses are ready," Castien said as someone knocked on the door.

Disgraced

"Time to go," Korriane yelled through the door. Mylah hurried back into her bedroom, Crane following behind her, and together they packed up the belongings of her and Elias.

Ana came in to check on them after a few minutes and sat on the bed while they finished packing. "Don't worry about Elias," she said. "Madame Edris is one of the best healers I've ever known. She'll take good care of him."

"It's not just that," Mylah said, pausing as she shoved a pair of pants into her bag. "I could have seriously hurt other people too. People who didn't even want me here to begin with."

"What are you talking about?" Crane asked, placing his fully packed bag of Elias' things on the bed.

"They think Elias should be with one of the princesses, not some common...whatever I am," Mylah gave up on trying to close her pack. Somehow, even though everything had fit in it fine on their way there, it was overflowing now. Crane shook his head as he moved to help her.

"Forget about that. It's not up to them," Ana moved from her spot on the bed to Mylah's side, putting her arm around her.

"And what about Castien? I'm sure *he* gets a say. I know he's upset with me and probably doesn't want me anywhere near Elias ever again." Mylah leaned into Ana's side and Crane stepped up on her other side to lend his comfort as well.

"Castien isn't mad at you," Ana sighed. "My gift allows me to sense heightened emotions, so I'll know when to ease people's minds. He's not upset, he's afraid. And from the way he looks at you, he's not afraid *of* you, he's afraid *for* you."

"What–" Mylah started, but she was cut off by a guard appearing in the doorway.

"I guess that's our cue," Crane said, picking up Mylah's bag and forcing it closed. He slung it over his shoulder before grabbing the pack he'd set on the bed and followed Ana and Mylah out of the room.

At the front gates, Sovereign Keir saw them off. They apologized for having to unceremoniously send them away but promised to send word as soon as a decision had been made about whether Amaris would join in the fight against Adair and Queen Aveda.

Crane rode with Davina again, while Mylah rode with Castien. Her eyes were glazed as she leaned against Castien, and Crane could tell her thoughts were far away. *If I could take your place, I would*, Crane thought, sighing as he looked back to see the castle fading into the distance.

Epilogue

Florian stormed into his study to find Aurelia there, reading a book and sipping her tea. As she turned to face him, she placed her book on the table beside her.

"What is it now?" she asked. The past few weeks every time he talked with her it was to rant or complain. Taking a deep breath, he sat down in the chair opposite her and grabbed himself a cup of tea.

"Queen Aveda has taken it upon herself to release Greyson Callister after I condemned him to death. Why do I feel she is undermining me on purpose?" His hands shook and some tea slopped onto his pants making him curse.

Aurelia reached out and took the cup from him, placing it back on the table. Her hands clasped around his and she held them steady.

"You are the power in charge here. Ensure she remembers that," Aurelia said, her eyes flashing with anger. "If you must cut ties with her…"

"I can't do that," Florian spat, wrenching his hands from Aurelia's. "We've started a war with Elowyn. Without Queen Aveda, we will never win."

"And why are we even at war with Elowyn?" Aurelia sat back in her chair, clasping her hands in her lap. "Queen Aveda is the one who wanted that book to begin with, and now it has caused us nothing but trouble."

"You know as well as I do that it's not all about the book. Ever since King Castien expanded his territory into the Unbounds, we lost our access to the trade isle. Without Queen Aveda and Cyprian, our people would suffer... All the human kingdoms would suffer."

Aurelia sighed in resignation. "I know," she said.

"If Garrick hadn't released Prince Lachlan from the dungeons, Queen Aveda would have never stayed here. It was supposed to be a quick visit to check in. Her brother in my dungeon was the only thing keeping her at bay, now... Now I have no sway over her." Florian hated to curse the dead, but Garrick had caused him far more trouble than he'd probably realized at the time.

"Then find new leverage," Aurelia suggested. "There is always something else; a lover, a friend, a child." Her eyes darkened with the last word. "Whatever it takes to keep our kingdom safe."

"Whatever it takes," Florian repeated.

A squeal erupted in the hallway as Ari and Mina bounded into the room. Florian scowled at the interruption and left the children for Aurelia to deal with, making his way back towards his chambers.

Find new leverage. He considered Aurelia's words. As Florian passed one of his guards he paused.

Disgraced

"I have a task for you," he said. "I need you to join Queen Aveda's guard. Inform me of *everything* you hear, no matter how insignificant it may seem."

The guard didn't react other than a swift nod before he set off on his new task.

New leverage it is.

Holly Huntress

Disgraced

About the Author

Holly Huntress is a self-published author and content creator. She graduated from the University of New England in 2015 with a bachelor's degree in English, but she has been writing stories since grade school. She is driven by the desire to share her writing with the world and to encourage others to do the same. All her books are currently available on Amazon. If you want to connect with Holly on social media, find her at the handles below!

TikTok: @livingthroughwriting

Instagram: @hollyhuntressauthor

Printed in Great Britain
by Amazon